LEOPARD

Also by Richard La Plante

MANTIS

LEOPARD

Richard La Plante

LITTLE, BROWN AND COMPANY

A *Little, Brown* Book

First published in Great Britain
by Little, Brown and Company in 1993

Copyright © Richard La Plante 1993

The moral right of the author has been asserted.

A CIP catalogue record for this book is
available from the British Library.

ISBN 0 316 90410 4

Typeset by Solidus (Bristol) Ltd
Printed and bound in Great Britain by
Clays Ltd, St Ives plc

Little, Brown and Company (UK) Limited
165 Great Dover Street
London SE1 4YA

Special thanks to Officer Michael Cullin of the Lower Merion Township Crime Prevention Unit.

To Lieutenant Martin Taylor of the Philadelphia Police Department.

To Terry O'Neill and Fighting Arts International.

To Dave Hazard.

To Ian of Reading.

To Yoshi Ohta and Mariko Watanabe.

To Dave Lowry and Dr Simon C. Holmes.

And to my father, Roy.

A man who is fully tattooed is stable, unchanging. He has solidified his own skin and become a solid object ... indelibly dyed, his skin supports him. Specifically, it defines him.

Donald Ritchie and Ian Burma, *The Japanese Tattoo*

By firelight, we talk about the snow leopard. Not only rare, but wary and elusive to a magical degree. So well camouflaged that one can stare straight at it from yards away and fail to see it.

Peter Mathiessen, *The Snow Leopard*

Prologue

The Shinjuku district of Tokyo is well known. Businessmen, gamblers, college boys looking for some action; all find their way to this maze of nightclubs and gaming houses and the street hustlers who promise everything from Western women to 'awakening powder', a euphemism for Japan's preferred leisure drug, crystal methamphetamine.

The entire Shinjuku district is governed by a compatible mixture of the Korean and Japanese Yakuza. The Yakuza, similar to the Mafia, is organized and run like a family, governed by father figures known as *oyabun*.

The financial aim of each *oyabun*, like the head of any commercial organization, is to ensure that his branch of the main 'firm' generates a profit. Businesses are ruthlessly scrutinized. They must earn.

There are a few exceptions, artisans with their small shops and traditional crafts. Reminders of a bygone era, when modern Tokyo was known as Edo, and when groups of young townsmen – known as the 'honorable outlaws', the forerunners of the modern Yakuza – defended their territories against marauding bands of masterless Samurai.

These premises are 'protected' by the *oyabuns*, shrines to their heritage.

Yukio Yamada was the proprietor of a 'protected' property, a small, plain-fronted, single-story building in the heart of Shinjuku.

He was a tattoo artist; one of a dying breed in a country that viewed tattoos as the mark of the rebel, the criminal class. A country of one hundred and twenty million people, out of which fewer than two thousand were tattooed.

It wasn't always this way; one hundred years ago, the beautification of the skin by the injection of colored pigment was a mark of pride and strength. Tattooing was an honorable craft, an art form.

Yukio's ancestor, Sokaku Yamada, in compliance with tradition, had changed his professional name to Horimada, affixing the prefix '*horu*', meaning 'to dig'; in this case, beneath the skin.

Three generations later, Yukio, working under the name of Horimada III, continued the family craft.

He worked in the 'old method', with the *hari* – bundles of small, ink-covered needles, inserted into a wooden handle – held at an angle to the client's body, tapped with the heel of the hand, injecting color beneath the epidermis.

Despite sporadic business, Horimada III was very selective with new customers. Understandable when considering that the completion of a design often required one hundred hours.

By their very proximity, the relationship between client and master was an intimate one.

He had refused sailors and laborers; men who desired only a *katabe-bori*, or a single arm tattoo.

In the bathhouse *katabe-bori* were regarded as incomplete, unfinished. Often the product of 'modern' tattooists, using the electric needle; some who laced their ink with cocaine to kill the pain of their efforts.

Like his predecessors, Horimada III created full bodysuits: complete tattoos, extending from neck to mid-thigh, covering the entire back and buttocks and most of the chest, except for an open space between the breasts, down to the stomach and loins.

And, like his predecessors, Horimada III did not work in 'originals'. He based his patterns on the *Suikoden*, or *The*

Water Margin – a book of fourteenth-century woodblock prints, depicting fierce, heroic men bound together in revolt against a corrupt society. Men of honor.

To translate such a print into a full-body tattoo required time, endurance, and money. Usually a man could stand only an hour or so of work in a session, particularly if cadmium – an intense yellow pigment affecting the color of deep red when introduced beneath the epidermis – was used.

The human body can not tolerate much cadmium. Fever, even death can result.

Had Horimada III been using cadmium on his most recent client he would have purposely overfilled his needles.

He hated the man. Could not bear the sight or smell of him. Since the day the tint-windowed limousine had drawn up outside his premises and the stranger had knocked on his door.

Tall and lean, his hands and wrists articulated with ligament, sinew and vein; he had presented Horimada with a letter of introduction, written in the longhand of Tak Ofudo.

Ofudo was the most powerful *oyabun* in Shinjuku. Not a man to cross.

The letter introduced its bearer as 'a personal friend' and requested that the tattooist perform any work that the man might require.

Minutes later Horimada's new client had stripped to a loincloth and was kneeling on the cloth-covered tatami, throwing back cups of sake from a bottle that he had concealed in his overcoat.

Horimada III was not easily intimidated. Heavy set and very strong, he had trained at the Kodokan during his youth, learning the throws and strangles of sport judo. At fifty-six years old he was still a formidable man. In the past, he had evicted several 'would be' clients from his premises; he did not work on drunks.

The ganglord's friend, however, was not a 'drunk'.

Although, during the course of a session, he consumed at least half a bottle of sake he never lost the hard concentration in his black eyes. He rarely spoke. And when he did, to give instruction or pass comment on a completed design, his soft, somehow effeminate voice carried the edge of a blade beneath its surface.

There was another problem, revealed when the purpose of the alcohol became apparent, flushing his capillaries and reddening his skin. The man was already tattooed. Completely. And the design was most certainly an 'original'.

Front and back, even upon the skin of his face, he was decorated with yellowed patterns, like pale rosettes against the crimson flesh.

Like the markings of a cat, a leopard, camouflaged for the mountains and the snow, Horimada thought, estimating from the paled pigment that the work was fifteen to twenty years old.

'The design is faded; I wish to have it renewed.' More a demand than a request.

Horimada examined the piece.

Fine and intricate; it remained unsigned. Perhaps the reason that the artist had not, as was the custom, incised the characters of his professional name into the design was that he, like Horimada III, had been coerced into complying with his client's requests.

Requests which included going over particular details of the pattern several times in order to give the work a certain patina, or layering. That, in itself, was not unusual. What was unusual was the type of ink required, a rare, white pigment, invisible until the skin was flushed, and the fact that the man insisted on two-, even three-hour sessions.

The continual shading of partially healed work was very painful and within the first few visits Horimada understood that his client enjoyed this pain.

He had never been so ill at ease with a customer.

The man had a smell to him, a pungent animal odor. A sickly sweet aroma that lingered in Horimada's place of business for hours after he had gone. Like a cat marking its territory.

Something to do with the disturbance of his pores, Horimada reasoned. *Tattooing always affects the sweat glands*. He reassured himself, fighting off a fantasy that he was actually working on some sort of malignant creature, disguised in the shape of a human being. A creature who was trying to return to its original form. Through ink and through pain.

The days in his appointment book designated as 'Leopard' caused Horimada sleepless nights; he had begun to tremble at the purr of the limousine's engine, as the car pulled to the curb outside his front door. He wanted to finish. To put the man out of his life, bury him in his memory.

Sometimes it was all he could do to hold the *hari* steady, reminding himself to be patient, not to rush the design. The Leopard was fastidious in his examination, any work less than perfect was done again, immediately.

The threat of castration came on the twentieth visit. It was then that Horimada III refused to tattoo the Leopard's genitalia.

'That type of work is never done on these premises. I would prefer you to leave,' he stated, laying down his *hari* and motioning toward the curtained door. 'No need to pay, just go.'

The Leopard smiled, a thin, sadistic smile. He was wearing his white loincloth, kneeling on the tatami and blood was trickling from the recently tattooed skin surrounding the nipple of his left breast.

As Horimada tried to rise, the Leopard gripped the soft sac below the woolen waistband of his trousers. His fingers dug in like cruel steel.

'They tear easily. Then you bleed to death. Very simple,' he whispered, tightening his grip on the tattooist's testicles, while with his free hand he untied the knot at the side of his own loincloth.

The cloth fell away, revealing his penis; erect and quivering with anticipation.

Horimada barely withheld his tears: born of indignation and swamped by fear.

Then, carefully, he reached forward and cupped the Leopard's shaved testicles, allowing the man's erect penis to press along the underside of his forearm. Sickened by the heat of him.

The tattooing took two hours and twenty minutes, measured in the ticking seconds of the wall clock and the constant mopping of blood from the wounding. At times Horimada was certain that his client was near orgasm, but that, like everything else, remained within the creature's control.

Before the bandaging, the Leopard examined himself slowly in the mirror.

Satisfied, he dressed, handed Horimada III an envelope containing five thousand US dollars and walked to his waiting limousine.

I Tradition

Execution

Tokyo, August 1992

The night had been a hot one, a *nettai-ya*, humid with temperatures in the mid-nineties.

And now, at eleven a.m. the sun was perched just above the Tokyo Tower, Japan's highest building and the thermometer was nudging one hundred degrees.

Five miles west of Tokyo proper, in the wealthy suburb of Den-en-Chofu, a maze of landscaped gardens and two-story houses, hidden behind high stone walls, sat in affluent contradiction to the noise and sweltering congestion of the city.

Hironori Tanaka was a resident of Den-en-Chofu. In his early forties and handsome in the tradition of his Samurai ancestry, he had black, medium-length hair combed straight back. His skin, pale by peasant standards, was flawless and the high, refined cheekbones of his oval face were highlighted by clear brown eyes, set wide behind a slightly aquiline nose.

He smiled often and his teeth were strong and white.

Today he sat in front of the open window of an especially modified bedroom, overlooking a landscaped acre of rock, lawn and flowers. The room was one of three on the upper floor of his father's seven-room, two-story house.

Hironori enjoyed the view, particularly as it allowed him to see above and beyond the six-foot wall that separated the garden from the street, giving him a sense of freedom.

A still, consuming heat touched his face, wafting inward from between the parted shutters of the window, warming the conditioned air of the room.

Hironori was concentrating on the mirrored surface of the garden's meditation pond. Breathing inward, exhaling slowly, tuning his thoughts to the shimmering blue-green water, as gradually, rising from the well of his subconscious, an image formed. The image of a bird, white and graceful, plumed wings and slender neck, long, black beak and piercing eyes. A crane, a white crane, the bird of life, long life.

Hironori closed his eyes, inhaled and experienced the 'feeling' of the great bird: solitary and strong, self-contained, dignified.

He held the 'feeling' in his mind, opened his eyes and lowered his head, gripping a long, bamboo-handled brush between his teeth, dipping its soft, rabbit hair bristles into a jar of water before feathering them against a small block of black ink, a 'cake' made of carbon, derived from pine soot, mixed with glue and then heated.

Shifting his head position again he began work on a sheet of thick porous paper, endeavoring to capture not so much the image of the white crane as the creature's 'essence'.

A single drop of perspiration fell from his brow onto the paper.

He raised his head, the brush still between his teeth, drawing back in a practiced movement, allowing the sweat to drip down his cheeks, trickling into the thick hairs of his beard. A few drops ran through, tickling as they rolled onto the skin of his neck. He closed his eyes as the droplets touched the area between the muscles of his neck and his windpipe.

After that the liquid caress ceased.

Hironori could feel nothing below his Adam's apple,

parallel to his third cervical vertebra. The vertebra which had lacerated his spinal cord, dislodged by his brother Josef's misdirected roundhouse kick in the All Japan Karate finals.

It all stopped there. All physical sensation. Real sensation, that is. Sometimes there were phantom perceptions – a tingle in his fingers, pins and needles in his toes.

Once, in the beginning, he celebrated these feelings as proof that he would recover. Only to learn, sadly, that his experience was common with most quadriplegics and amputees. 'Residual activity of the cerebral cortex', 'latent muscle memory', a host of explanations to the fact that he would never stand, walk, or crawl again.

Hironori Tanaka had occupied a wheelchair for fifteen years, enough time to become adept at *suibokyga* – traditional Zen painting with water, ink, and brush.

His work demanded a high level of concentration. The same concentration with which he once repeated the linear movements of the fighting forms, or *katas*, now went into the flowing curves of his mouth-held brush against paper.

'How does it feel, having been one of our country's finest athletes, to face life as a prisoner inside your own body?' That was the question that the interviewer from *Royalty* magazine had asked him three years ago. The interview was supposed to be about his third one-man exhibition at the prestigious Gyuama Gallery in downtown Tokyo. What did being a 'prisoner inside your own body' have to do with it?

'Does the imposed solitude aid your art?' the insensitive young woman added when Hironori lowered his eyes, unwilling to grant her admission to his private torment. When he raised them he had regained mental control; he prayed he wasn't crying. Sometimes it was hard to tell.

'My condition adds to the intensity of my experience,' he answered, then sat stoic and silent until the embarrassed woman turned off her tape recorder and left his room.

No more interviews after that. He decided to allow his work to speak for him. People could read into it what they wanted, or what they needed.

Today's work, however, was not for sale or exhibition; it was in honor of Josef's wedding announcement.

Have you forgiven yourself for what happened? Hiro wondered, thinking of Josef, as he consciously relaxed the muscles of his neck, remoistening the bristles of his brush.

Hiro and Josef were actually half-brothers, Hiro being the single child of Mikio Tanaka's first marriage. His real mother, a Buddhist, was deceased; her death caused by an inoperable brain tumor, two years after Mikio Tanaka had divorced her to marry an American socialite.

Fortunately, Hironori had been too young to hate his father or resent the new woman in his life. And by the time he was old enough to understand what had taken place, he looked upon Grace Tanaka as his own flesh and blood.

It was this, along with his belief in Zen's precept that all experience is education for the soul, that got him through after the 'accident'.

'I have accepted my life, Josef, but have you accepted yours?' he asked as he applied the first fine layers of ink, moving his head slightly, drawing the brush along the paper in the gentle downward curve of the bird's sloping neck, until, gradually the 'feeling' of the white crane returned, superseding his thoughts. Disrupted only by the thin line of perspiration beading again on his brow.

He raised his head, replaced the brush in his chest-mounted holder and turned toward his voice-activated speaker, intending to summon the house servant; she would mop his brow properly. Stand by, if necessary, to keep him dry while he worked. He was always reluctant to call her; he considered it a negation of his independence, like the catheter which collected his urine and the rubber diapers that were changed twice a day.

'Noriko.' He was about to speak her name when he noticed a black Mercedes slow down and park directly across from the entrance gate, in line with his window.

The car was a new model: elongated wheel base and tinted windows. Hiro assumed it to be a recent addition to his father's business fleet. He studied the car, postponing his call.

The rear passenger door opened. A huge man slipped gracefully from the seat, leaned forward, spoke quickly to the driver, then closed the door.

The man stood still a moment, staring straight at Hironori's window.

Hiro's face flushed with embarrassment. He hated being seen from the street; it made him feel vulnerable, strangely paranoid. Some sort of fugitive from the outside world.

He lowered his head and made contact with the chin-level control level, activating the electric motor of his chair, pressing down against the contoured bar. The chair reversed with a quiet hum, stopping in the shadow of the room, permitting Hiro to see without being seen.

His eyes remained riveted on the visitor. Hiro had never seen a man of his size dressed in the gray suit of a business executive.

He must be six and a half feet tall, a real giant, he thought as the man walked forward, up the stone path and toward the front door of the house. It was the way he moved that captured Hiro's interest. Inside the impeccably tailored clothes, Hiro recognized an athlete's grace, quick and light, his footsteps silent against the paved walkway.

Rikishi, Hiro told himself, using the preferred term for sumotori. In the West they called these giants 'sumo wrestlers', a misinformed nomenclature for the thrusts, trips and throws of the devastating art.

This one was probably from a Tokyo stable. *But why*

would a rikishi be visiting my father's home? Then Hiro remembered a recent business deal his father had mentioned, something to do with a cable television network. A sports channel?

It was equally as likely that his father had put money into a new stable for the *rikishi*. Tokyo land prices were the highest in the world and Mikio Tanaka, Japan's first national karate champion, often pledged money to the traditional martial arts.

The man strolled quietly through the arched trellis, completely filling the frame with his massive body. His jet black hair was oiled and swept back from his forehead.

Hiro tried to place the round, flat face.

Not a famous player, he decided. At least no one he had seen in the recently televised tournament, or *basho*.

As the man turned sideways, continuing toward the front door, Hiro noted that he did not have a topknot. That meant he was no longer competing.

Perhaps he is an oyakata, a coach, Hiro speculated.

Either way his visit was an honor. Once she had informed him that neither Mikio nor Grace Tanaka was at home, surely Noriko would present the *rikishi* to their elder son.

Hironori depressed the lever again, turning his head to the right, guiding the wheelchair to his dressing table. He studied his reflection in the mirror then maneuvered the chair into the divided center of the walnut vanity unit.

Two hair brushes had been mounted on chrome stalks, one on either leaf of the unit.

Grooming was a slow and laborious process. Almost an aesthetic discipline, yet it bolstered Hironori's sense of independence.

It required several runs of the wheelchair and much raising and lowering of his head to get his thick hair to settle down along the sides of his head.

By the time he had finished he was aware of being

observed. Not that he could see anyone within the reflection of the mirror; it was a feeling.

'Noriko?' he asked. Perhaps she had come into the room to announce their guest. No reply.

'Noriko!' Louder. Still no answer.

His senses heightened.

It was a male presence. Always heavier than female, the difference between mist and clouds.

'Who's there?' he asked. Still silence.

There was danger within the presence.

Danger. A sensation that Hiro had not had since his days of competition. The anticipation of an attack.

Fear began to surface; he tried for self-control but his battle instincts were rusty. His jaw was trembling as he leaned forward, pushing against the control lever.

The chair turned and he caught a glimpse of a man behind him. The big man from the garden, the man he supposed was a *rikishi*.

'Who are you?' Hiro asked.

The man stared at him.

'What do you want?' A note of authority.

Hiro was facing him now. Looking up into eyes so deep and heavily lidded that they constituted only a darkness beneath the overhanging frontal bone of the man's forehead. *Something wrong here, very wrong*, his instinct warned.

'Leave this room, at once!' he commanded, feeling his throat constrict as the words left his mouth. He had not used his vocal cords in this manner for so long that the effort was exhausting.

'A cripple? He did not say you were a cripple.' The man whispered to himself as he took a step towards the wheel-chair. There was aggression in his movement.

Got to do something. Attack. Attack, Hiro told himself, lowering his head, pushing down hard on the lever.

The chair lifted slightly on its back wheels then jolted

forward. The battery-operated engine was capable of propelling it at five miles per hour on a straight floor. It was doing four by the time it connected with the big man's legs.

The giant stopped it dead. Then reached forward, gripping Hiro's arms, on top of the arms of the chair, lifting, turning both chair and occupant within his grip, maneuvering with such control that not even a drop of water spilled from the jar. Placing him down in front of the mirror.

'Noriko! Noriko!' Hironori shouted.

The man was directly behind him now; Hiro could see him in the mirror.

'Noriko!' Hiro screamed the house servant's name, his mouth already dry and the flow of rising air like broken glass against his windpipe.

'Shut up,' the man hissed. A moment later he leaned forward and thrust his open palm into Hironori's jaw. The jaw splintered as if made of brittle wood, hanging loose and numb.

His attacker stepped back, studying Hiro with a clinical detachment. Then, as if in preparation for a more formal ceremony, the giant carefully removed the semicircular unit which contained Hiro's brushes, water, paper, and ink.

When their eyes finally met, Hiro saw no hate or anger.

In the years that he had been confined to a wheelchair Hiro had seen eyes like these many times. Doctors' eyes. *No. There was a difference*, he realized. In the doctors' eyes, behind the veil of impartiality, there was always compassion. There was detachment here, but no compassion.

The big man stood in front of him as if he had all the time in the world. The tightness of his thin lips and the furrow of his brow suggested indecision.

Hiro was confused.

'Why?' He tried to shape the word but his mouth did not respond.

His attacker smiled. A smile which indicated that he had

made up his mind about some important issue.

He stepped behind the wheelchair. Rolled it forward just enough so that he and its occupant were fully visible in the mirror.

Hironori's view was now restricted to a reflection. He watched as the man removed a cigarette-pack-sized camera from the inside pocket of his gray jacket, adjusting the shutter speed before positioning the camera on the adjacent lip of the vanity unit. Stepping back to make sure the lens was aimed perfectly, taking in both captor and captive.

Then the man moved closer, wrapping both arms around Hironori's head. Locking his wrists, he began to squeeze. Slowly.

Hiro kept his eyes open. Studying his situation rather than reacting to it. His capacity to express fear completely intellectualized, his muscular system unable to respond to the secretions of his adrenal glands.

The grip intensified as the camera clicked another frame. One frame every three seconds.

The true pain began on the third contraction, like a steel band tightening around his cranium. Biting inwards.

Hiro lowered his eyes, choking a howl which began low down in his throat. Pictures flooded his mind. Visions of him defending himself against this outrage. Punching and kicking, locking and breaking.

Another click of the camera. Hiro looked up, into his reflection. There was blood running from his nose, ears and mouth.

The big man was breathing deeper, squeezing harder with each exhalation and Hironori's skull was moving with the motion of the executioner's enormous arms. He could actually feel his skull depress, then expand. Feel and see it, understanding that the man was timing his movements to the click of the camera.

By the sixth contraction, Hiro was suffering acutely, his

tear ducts had opened and his face was streaming with salt water, and blood. He was making sounds, attempting to say 'please', over and over again. Begging for the pain to stop. Until the crunching began. Like stone grinding against stone.

Hiro was looking down. Through his tears. He could see that the bag had come loose from his catheter, leaving the lap of his white gown soaked with urine. The stench of it assailed his nostrils, as the crunching of bone grew louder inside his head.

He tried to look up. Was unable. Mercifully not realizing that his eyeballs had dropped from their sockets but remained connected by their optic nerve.

The sound of the man working above him was like a locomotive engine, breaths chugging in then out, reliable in their rhythm.

He closed his eyelids. The movement did nothing to block out his vision of the stained gown. *Maybe he hadn't shut his eyes*; he was no longer sure.

Hironori was dying. That was the single certainty in what had become a wash of blood, noise, and pain. Dying helplessly and pitifully. Without knowledge of who his executioner was or why he was being executed. A shameful death. A death which mocked the triumph of his spirit, his life, and his art.

Our Father, who art in heaven ... The voice began from far away. Hiro recognized the words. He had heard them before. Once. Fifteen years ago. In the Budokan, inside the fighting square.

Hallowed be Thy name ... It was Josef's voice. Josef the Christian. Guilty for maiming his older brother. He was trying to revive him, to resurrect him with his prayer.

Go away, Josef. Don't look at me.

Another memory. Being carried into his father's house, on his back, strapped to the portable hospital bed. Humiliated.

Josef staring at him. Hiro turned his head away.

Thy Kingdom come . . . He could see Josef. Look right into his eyes. There was love and compassion in his eyes. And guilt, terrible guilt. Like a scar across their watery surface.

Don't look at me, Josef. Don't look. I can bear my pain but your guilt is too heavy . . . Don't look at me . . .

'Don't look at me!' The words were clear as he thought them. Garbled as they fell from his broken mouth.

Babbling. The victim is babbling, the executioner observed. It often happened in the latter phases of an assignment.

Squeeze inward . . . Yes . . . That's right. The coronal suture was giving way, disconnecting the two frontal bones from the recessed bones of Hironori Tanaka's temples, the tips of which, known as the 'great wings', were pointing inward toward his cerebrum. Like deadly white blades.

Click. The shutter blinked. Three seconds till the next frame.

The executioner relaxed. He was sweating profusely; he was also fully aroused. He told himself that it was because of the friction between his groin and the back of the wheelchair. He knew differently. It had happened during his last two assignments. Just as the Leopard said it would.

Hironori was barely conscious. Time had been compressed in his damaged brain. Josef kept saying things to him. Apologizing for what was taking place. Promising revenge.

'Two seconds.'

The executioner inhaled, deep and low, drawing air through his nose, concentrating, getting his timing right. He could smell the odor of pomade coming from the victim's hair. Like fresh apples.

'One second.'

Thy will be done . . . Josef was with him now. Tall and strong. Josef would not permit this cruelty to continue—

'*Yi-ia*!' The executioner shouted, a combination of war cry and the ecstacy of orgasm. His fierce eyes and twisted face frozen in the camera's eye. Like some medieval gargoyle, gripping Hironori's imploding skull in his stone arms.

Then everything was still, just the controlled sound of breathing as the big man's pulse subsided. And the 'pitter-pat' of Hironori's internal fluids, falling from the remains of his cranium to the arms of his wheelchair and down onto the wooden floor.

Finally the executioner stepped free of the viscous liquid. Wiping his long, thick fingers against the line of his lapels, leaving a rust-colored trail. Lifting the camera from the vanity unit, glancing once in the mirror, concerned that his suit was stained beyond repair.

Then he walked quickly from Hiro's room, snapping a picture of the servant's body before exiting the house.

Settsuku (Connection)

Eight thousand five hundred miles west of Tokyo, in a single-bedroomed apartment on the east side of Rittenhouse Square, smack in the center of Philadelphia, Josef Tanaka was sweating. Lying in his bed, sweating. Rachel Saunders was asleep beside him, on her side, her warm hips pushing outward in a near fetal position. The same position she had been in when they had drifted off, five hours ago. Her side of the bed was relatively undisturbed, hardly a ruffle beneath the duvet. Josef's was a mess, pillows bunched and thrown to the floor, sheets twisted and pulled from the underside of the mattress.

It was four thirty in the morning, a Sunday, and Philadelphia was quiet.

Josef had been praying. Again. The Lord's Prayer. The only prayer he had ever committed to memory, years ago, in Tokyo, before his confirmation as an Episcopalian. Now he used the prayer to calm his mind, centering himself on its meaning.

Thy kingdom come, Thy will be done, on earth as it is in heaven.

Josef had been praying a lot lately, for himself, for Rachel. He glanced over at her; she was breathing quietly, almost inaudibly, like a peaceful child. Her blonde hair, once long enough to touch her hips, was cut short now, almost like a man's, gelled back at the front and parted at the side. She hadn't asked him, she'd just gone and done it. He had loved her hair long, but he understood why she wanted change. At least he thought he understood. It certainly hadn't made her less attractive to him. Physically it made her ice-blue eyes appear even larger, and her mouth ... God he loved Rachel Saunders' mouth. Full and soft and sweet.

He shifted to his side, reached out and laid his hand gently on the rise of her hip. He felt her shiver, a quick involuntary tension beneath her skin.

'Josef?' It was a sleeping voice, soft and husky. Its sexuality tainted by a trace of fear.

He moved closer, touching her gently with his own nakedness. Half aroused, controlling his desire to press inward, toward the warmth between the silken hairs on the underside of her hips. He thought briefly of sex, how good it had been. Then he turned his mind away. Cuddled her, a gesture of reassurance. Her tension evaporated.

''S'all right, Rachel. Still early ...'

They had made love only once in the past nine months. Since Rachel's abduction, since she had watched Josef beat her abductor to death, nearly losing his own life in the process. Succeeding only because the man had wanted to die, had chosen Tanaka to kill him.

Willard Ng. Tanaka would never forget his name, as long as he lived. The tabloid press had christened Ng 'the Mantis', after the insect that he worshipped, emulated. Tanaka could remember every detail of his domed head and diamond-shaped face, from his sharpened, pointed teeth to his pitted eyes. No lashes, no eyebrows, no emotion.

Rachel remembered nothing. Not at first.

'Post traumatic stress disorder.' That's what Stan Leibowitz, the police psychiatrist, had called it.

Leibowitz had seen a lot of PTSD; he was a Vietnam vet and now, when he wasn't compiling criminal psychiatric profiles or working with combat-stressed police officers, he ran a group for vets suffering from PTSD.

*

'The hidden wound,' he'd said. 'One day you just freeze up; you can't speak; you can't move.'

Doctor Rachel Saunders' 'freeze' happened in the middle of surgery. She had been performing a skin graft, rebuilding the left breast on a patient who had been disfigured by a partial mastectomy. Relocating the nipple, stretching the skin across the rib cage. And suddenly she couldn't move. She'd stood, hovering above the woman on the operating table, anxiety turning to panic around her.

In her mind, as if running on some preprogrammed loop, like a video cassette, was the image of the Mantis. His chest puffed up and looming, nipples removed and white waxen flesh pulled taut across the striations of his pectoralis muscles. Not a memory; he was there, in the room.

Her assistant had taken over, completing the surgical procedure. Rachel Saunders was led away, her career saved only by the compassion and discretion of her peers.

Then came Stan Leibowitz and the 'Israeli' procedure. PTSD was nothing new in Israel; soldiers had been suffering from it for years.

When the nervous system is subjected to a continual overload of life-threatening signals, and is unable to respond with the usual 'fight or flight' reaction, such as in the bombing of men in trenches over a long duration, the system survives by 'shutting down'. The brain, however, stores the precise details of the trauma, filing total episodes that may be triggered into replay at some later date.

The Israelis had combined the use of hypnotherapy, Sodium Pentothal, and a 'safe' environment, in which the trauma could be re-enacted. It was a cathartic type of therapy, one that gave relief and a long-lasting, but rarely permanent, cure.

Rachel underwent the treatment within twenty-four hours of her 'freeze'.

Because he was a doctor, because he was assigned to the police forensics department and because Rachel Saunders felt 'safe' with him, Josef Tanaka had remained in Stan Leibowitz's Trauma Care Center, a twenty by twenty padded room, during Rachel's therapy.

It had torn his heart out to see her writhing in agony across the matted floor, her legs bent and twisted into a shape resembling the yogic lotus posture, identical to the position her captor had forced upon her. Then it started, like the sound of someone struggling for breath, wheezing inward, sucking air, building, building into screams of pure terror, uncontrolled and unrestrained. Continuing for thirty minutes, until Rachel lay dry and exhausted.

Finally she had looked up, found his eyes and whispered. 'He didn't rape me, Josef. I wouldn't let him rape me.' Then she slept, right there on the mat, for twelve hours. Her first peaceful sleep in one hundred nights.

Things were better now, Rachel was seeing Leibowitz once every five weeks, and the psychiatrist was pleased with progress.

Tanaka settled back in the bed, relaxing, letting his thoughts drift to Tokyo. It would be hot there now, hot and sticky. But in the fall, after the rains, the weather would be crisp and dry.

He and Rachel had decided to marry in Tokyo. In St Peter's Church, on the outskirts of the city. The church where Josef had been baptized. It was a choice made more from consideration of Josef's family than sentiment.

His brother, Hiro, could never make the trip to Philadelphia. Not without three nurses and a wheelchair. And Josef wanted Hiro to be there, beside him. Rachel had no objections. She was an only child and her mother and father, both doctors, had died within a year of each other, one cancer, one heart attack.

Besides, he and Rachel needed a break. The 'Mantis' case had made front page news, been blasted all over the television. At first, Rachel's business had fallen off. As if, by being victim to the freak, she was in some way guilty. People had to forget in order to trust again.

It wasn't so bad for Josef; he was, after all, connected to the police department. That had legitimized his involvement. And then there was Lieutenant Bill Fogarty. He was the tabloid star.

POLICE DETECTIVE STALKS MANTIS TO LAIR,
ENDS CITY'S PLAGUE OF TERROR

That's how it read, crediting Fogarty with the 'kill'. Fact was that the lieutenant had blown an already dead man's head clean from his shoulders. A wise act. Saved an investigation and two careers. Tanaka's as a forensics doctor, acting without authority on a murder hunt, and Fogarty's as a policeman, a policeman who had crossed a state line and searched a guilty man's home without a warrant. And had very nearly blown the case.

They made an unlikely team, Fogarty and Tanaka, the Irish-Catholic cop and the Japanese doctor, but they were close now, best friends. In fact, Tanaka intended to give Fogarty a ticket to Tokyo. Bill Fogarty was 'family'. And when things got as tough as they had been in the past year, 'family' was the only thing that mattered.

Tanaka was still thinking about 'family', who was and who wasn't, when the telephone rang. He saw Rachel stir beside him, her slender arm reaching out for the night table and the ringing phone.

'Let it go. The service'll pick it up,' he whispered. He hated for Rachel to be disturbed, wanted to protect her, even from the demands of her own patients. Knowing, at the same time, that normality was essential to cure.

'Doctor Saunders speaking.'

Tanaka smiled. Her eyes were barely open yet her voice sounded as if she were seated behind the walnut desk of her office.

'Please speak up, I can barely hear you,' Rachel continued, propping herself up on an elbow. She pulled the phone back slightly from her ear, squinting as she concentrated on the receiver.

'Hold on a moment please,' she said. Then, turning to Josef, 'Somebody speaking Japanese, I think it's an operator. There's a terrible echo on the line . . .'

Tanaka moved closer, took the phone.

'*Moshi. Moshi. Tanaka-desuga.*'

Rachel studied the features of her fiancé's face as he communicated with what sounded, to her, like staccato bursts of verbal gunfire. His entire demeanor changed when he spoke in his native language. He actually became, in Rachel's perspective, a 'foreigner', his mouth drawn tight and his eyes intense, while his hand gestures appeared to cut and poke the air around him. It had always been the strange thing about their relationship; Rachel Saunders felt that Tanaka knew her completely, while she knew only half of him.

Maybe the trip to Japan will fill in the missing pieces. Maybe it's all in my imagination. Maybe I should learn to speak Japanese, I owe it to him.

Tanaka removed his hand from Rachel's shoulder as he sat up rigid in the bed. He was listening more than talking, and when he did speak his voice was inquisitive but somber. Rachel slid from the duvet and stood. Walked to her wardrobe, removed a toweling dressing gown from the hook and slipped it on. Whatever feeling had entered the room, brought on by the phone call, she wanted protection from it. Nakedness was vulnerability.

She walked back and sat on the side of the bed. Waiting. Beginning to understand, intuitively, what the call was about.

She had been in medical school, in the middle of final exams, sleeping late after an all night cramming session when her call had come. From her aunt Elizabeth in Florida, a woman she had met only three times.

'Rachel, your father's had a heart attack. They don't think he's going to pull through.' Her aunt's voice had created a vacuum, a hollow inside her. An emptiness that filled the room.

That same emptiness surrounded her now, Josef had already been swallowed by it. His face was pale when he lowered the phone.

'Hiro's dead . . .' His voice was a monotone.

She moved closer to him, taking his hand softly in her own.

'His lungs seized. He suffocated in his sleep.'

Rachel was crying, shaking her head, silent tears rolling down her cheeks.

Pain was everywhere in the room, there was no escape. *Hold still. It will pass. Everything will pass*, she told herself.

'My brother. My big brother,' Josef continued. It was his voice that touched her, low and masculine, but with the sentiment of childhood. 'My big brother – won't be at our wedding.' He looked up, found Rachel's eyes, focused. 'You won't get to meet him. My brother Hiro. You'll never meet him.'

At last Josef reached out and pulled her to him, burying his head against her shoulder. His body was still and his breathing quiet, but she could feel the wetness of tears, penetrating her robe, touching her skin.

He remained that way only a few moments, then he pulled away, meeting her eyes as his expression changed.

Suddenly there was a strange, almost defiant quality to his face, as if he blamed her for permitting him the shameful act of self-pity.

He stood abruptly, still staring down at her. His eyes had

narrowed, exaggerating their darkness, giving the illusion that they were slanted above his high cheekbones. Then he turned and walked from the room.

Lieutenant Bill Fogarty had taken up golf. He tried to play every Sunday morning. At the Cobb's Creek Golf Course, a public green. Not exactly the Merion Golf Club, but then again, there was no waiting list to join.

Today he'd gone only nine holes and felt tired all the way. The feeling persisted, even as he wheeled his old Le Mans north along City Line Avenue toward his condominium in the Presidential Apartments.

The lieutenant had begun to feel old in the past year, almost to the point of obsession. It wasn't so much a matter of vanity, most of that had been shredded along with half his face, ground into the asphalt of New Jersey's Highway 71 in a traffic accident that left two people dead: his wife Sarah, and Ann, his only child. It was more a weariness, a fatigue that felt centered behind his eyes, deep and unforgiving. Nothing a good night's sleep or even two weeks away could touch. The type of tiredness that made him want to avoid people's eyes when he spoke to them. As if he would be revealed as 'spent', or 'used up'.

The Mantis case had nearly finished him, both as a man and as a policeman. His physical wounds, a reconstructed trachea and a right knee full of carbon fiber ligament, paled beside the damage to his mind. *Mind, no that wasn't correct; it was more a darkening of the soul.*

Yet there had been a bright side to the past year. There was Diane Genero, divorced, sophisticated, and living in Santa Fe, mother of the killer's third victim. Hardly a likely companion for Bill Fogarty, yet they had become friends, remained in contact, a few letters and two visits, both by Diane Genero to Philadelphia. Fogarty could never quite make the trip out west. He told himself he didn't have the time. Untrue. It was the guilt of commitment. After his wife and daughter, Bill Fogarty made sure he was never too happy.

Rachel Saunders and Josef Tanaka had become his surrogate family. Close enough that Rachel had offered to upgrade the reconstructive work on the scarred side of the lieutenant's face. He was tempted; he trusted Doctor Saunders, her long, sure fingers and steady eyes. It was, once again, a question of guilt that held him back. His scars were a reminder that he had been drunk and out of control when he wrecked the car, destroyed his family. He didn't want to look any better than he allowed himself to feel ...

Rachel and Josef, he got a good, warm feeling when he thought of them, his 'family'. *I could take'm out tonight. Dinner at Bookbinders ... they like Bookbinders ... Call'm as soon as I get home ...*

Rachel Saunders picked up the receiver on the third ring. Relieved that it was Bill Fogarty and not another long-distance operator, speaking broken English.

'You all right, honey?' Fogarty asked, tuned to the tension in her voice.

'Josef's brother died ...' Rachel answered.

'How?' It was a policeman's question.

'Suffocation ... Paralysis of his respiratory tract ... It happens with quads,' Doctor Saunders replied.

'How long ago?'

'Josef got the call this morning. Early. He's already booked a flight—' Rachel hesitated, about to say 'home', '... to Tokyo.'

'How's he taking it?' Fogarty enquired.

'You know how he felt about his brother, Bill. To him, this is just an extension of what happened fifteen years ago.' Her voice was starting to break.

Fogarty thought of the upcoming wedding, Rachel and

Josef's, and their trip to Tokyo, the three of them. He had
been looking forward to it. Now it seemed a long way off.

'Where is he, Rachel? Can I speak to him?'

'He's gone to the lab. Wanted to finish off some
paperwork that he and . . .'

'Couldn't that wait?'

'You know how he is, Bill.'

'Yes,' Fogarty said.

There was a silence on the line.

When Rachel spoke again her voice was controlled but
strained, 'I'm not being selfish, Bill, believe me, but after he
found out about his brother, he changed; he cut me off, as if
whatever he was going through had nothing to do with me
. . . You know what I'm talking about, I know you do. You've
seen it, the Japanese side . . . The Josef I don't really know
. . . I'm not part of that side, that life . . . And I'm afraid if he
goes over there alone—' she hesitated, 'I'm afraid I'll lose
him.'

Fogarty knew exactly what Rachel meant; he'd seen it
himself, the Japanese side, the stoic discipline, the guilt and
buried emotions. He wanted to have an answer for her but
there was no answer for something that he'd never fully
understood. Still he was determined to help, to be there for
them. They were as close as he'd been to love since his
tragedy; and now he wasn't going to stand back and watch
Josef blow it.

'I'm going to drive down to the lab, Rachel. I'll talk to
him,' he promised.

'Thanks, Bill,' Rachel whispered, and the phone went
dead.

The Philadelphia Police Department's pathology lab is a
relatively new, two-story, red-brick building. Located at 321
University Avenue, in the west part of the city, it is adjacent
to the campus of the University of Pennsylvania.

On a Sunday, without the usual commuter traffic, it is an easy ride from the Presidential Apartment building. A right turn out of the main gates, right again onto the Schuylkill Expressway, then follow the river. Five, maybe six miles.

It had been gray and overcast all morning. The humidity was high, but now, at noon, the sun had broken through and the river bank was alive with people, picnic baskets, and frisbees. An army of joggers and crews of rowing shells, out for post-season practice.

This part of town – the river, its boat houses, and the art museum, built on its east bank – was as beautiful as any place in the world. Any place that Fogarty had ever been. Paris, London, Madrid ... Philadelphia, on a sunny Sunday morning, was right up there.

Fogarty took the 30th Street exit then headed west onto the Penn campus. He was sad for Josef, but his sorrow was muted by a feeling that an early death was inevitable for Hironori. He and Josef had discussed it many times.

'Forty, sometimes fifty, that's about as long as a quadri-plegic has. Too many medical complications,' Josef had told him.

Hiro must have been close to forty, Fogarty calculated, sliding the Le Mans alongside the curb in front of the medical building. *This is a blessing in disguise.*

Josef's brother had been a black cloud above the doctor's head. He had never forgiven himself for the accident. As if he had purposely aimed his instep at his brother's neck.

Christ, Fogarty thought, remembering the East Coast Karate Tournament that he and Josef had attended. *Those guys are movin' so fast it's a miracle nobody gets killed.*

He stepped out of the car and walked to the side of the building. Saw Tanaka's Harley Davidson, cleaned and polished, leaning against its kickstand, basking in the afternoon sun.

'Maybe now the kid can get some peace of mind,' he

mumbled to himself. There were times when the lieutenant had hated Hironori Tanaka. Not that he had ever met him, or had anything against him personally, it was simply a friend protecting a friend. He had seen Josef through some black moods. And vice versa.

Burying Sarah and Ann didn't help you much, Fogarty reminded himself. 'That's different. You were drunk,' he said out loud. Then he pushed inwards against the narrow metal-framed door. It was locked. He rang the buzzer below the entry phone.

'Who is it?' Tanaka's voice crackled back.

'Joey, it's me. Bill. I was in the neighborhood . . .'

Thirty seconds later Josef Tanaka opened the door. He was wearing a plain white T-shirt, blue jeans and his beat-up black engineer boots. Alongside the Harley Softail, he could have looked like a rich urban poser. Another look at his sinewy arms, broad shoulders and dark, intense eyes would dispel any notion of a put-on. Tanaka was real enough, just impossible to pigeonhole.

'You've been talking to Rachel. You know, don't you?' Tanaka said. There was a hard set to his full mouth.

Fogarty nodded and walked into the corridor, turning to place a hand on his friend's shoulder.

'You all right?'

Tanaka nodded.

'This was going to happen. You said so yourself.'

'Yeah.' Tanaka answered, short and sharp.

'No reason to be in here today. Nothing that Bob Moyer can't put together. Why don't we lock this place up, go somewhere, sit down, have a coffee?' Fogarty suggested.

He could feel the tension begin to drain from Tanaka's shoulder.

'Five minutes. Five minutes and I'll be through . . .' His voice was easing.

Fogarty followed the doctor into the files room, sat down,

and waited while Tanaka made notes and rearranged his papers.

The university coffee shop was a three-minute walk from the lab; it was nearly deserted. Fogarty and Tanaka took a booth in the far corner. Neither man had spoken, other than to order.

The waitress was a college girl, dark hair, black denim jeans, and a light blue, sleeveless blouse. She was plain-faced until she smiled, then she sparkled.

'Here you are, Doctor,' she said, placing the steaming cup in front of Tanaka. 'Not used to seeing you in here on a Sunday ... Anything else?' Tanaka looked at Fogarty and the lieutenant shook his head.

'That'll do it, Susie,' Tanaka replied. His voice was dry and pleasant, no indication of grief. Fogarty noticed things like that. With most people the voice was a good barometer of the emotions. He knew Tanaka well enough to know it didn't mean a thing.

'I'm on a United Airlines flight from Kennedy at eleven tomorrow morning, the funeral's on Saturday,' Josef said.

Fogarty knew what he wanted to say. He just needed to find a way in – a way past Tanaka's guard. The last thing the lieutenant wanted was to come on like he and Rachel had been talking behind Josef's back.

'Things gonna be okay with your father?' he asked. Knowing he was touching a nerve.

Tanaka bristled. Things had never been 'okay' between Mikio Tanaka and Josef. Not since that moment in the fighting square, fifteen years ago. When Josef had crippled Mikio Tanaka's first-born son, his Samurai son.

'No, not really,' Tanaka answered, 'I don't think he wants me there. It was my cousin Ken who made the phone call. He's more a son to my father now than I am.' He hesitated, 'But I'm going to be there. It's something I have to do. For my mother, for Hiro, for myself, even for my father.'

'What about Rachel?' Fogarty asked.

Tanaka looked at him. 'This isn't a wedding ... It's a funeral,' he answered.

Fogarty nodded his head, as if to say he understood.

'I killed my brother,' Josef continued, 'now I've got to go bury him ... It's family business.' There was no self-pity in either his voice or the expression on his face.

'Rachel is family,' Fogarty answered.

Tanaka looked deeper into the policeman's eyes. There was something so old in those eyes. Old and tired and wise ... He felt a twinge of anger, then the anger faded. 'What are you suggesting?' Tanaka's voice was edgy but soft.

Fogarty held his gaze. 'You may need a friend over there, Josef, and Rachel is the best friend you've got.'

Josef Tanaka thought about 'the best friend you've got' all the way back to Rittenhouse Square. By the time he'd shut off the bike, locked it up and thrown the heavy tarpaulin over it, he knew Fogarty was right.

He did pull away from Rachel whenever the subject of Japan or his family came up. As if by denying her access, that part of him would go away. Yet there was no resolve in his denial. It only divided them. And now he was doing it again, pulling away, denying.

Rachel was in the kitchen when he entered, polishing a large Edwardian serving tray, a family heirloom, left in her father's will. She often polished the silver tray when she was angry or upset.

'Are you all right?' she asked.

Josef could see her eyes were red from crying. 'I'd be a lot better if you would come with me,' he answered, 'to Japan.'

She put the tray down and raised the polishing cloth to her face; she was going to cry.

Josef intercepted her hand, pulling her close to him.

'I love you, Rachel,' he whispered.

They postponed their departure for a day, giving Doctor Saunders time to adjust her appointments. Because of her wedding plans she had already instructed her secretary and assistant to schedule no surgery till late fall, so a two-week break now was not a problem.

She got in a call to Bill Fogarty, told him what had happened and thanked him for whatever he had said to Josef.

'Joey and I owe you so much, Bill, we really do,' she said at the end of their call.

The words made Fogarty blush, his voice even cracked as he told her to have a safe trip.

Japan

Japan Airlines flight 005 touched the Tarmac of Narita Airport on Wednesday, twelve noon, Tokyo time. Tanaka looked at his watch. Ten p.m. in Philadelphia. Then he looked across at Rachel; she was rubbing her eyes, just waking up.

They were seated in the middle section of the aircraft, in 'coach'. Rachel had the aisle seat and Josef was crammed next to a man who must have weighed three hundred pounds, spread mainly sideways; every time the man moved, his elbow had dug into Josef's side. For the first two hours Tanaka had contemplated several forms of counterattack. The situation hit crisis point during dinner, after Rachel had dropped her small white tab of Halcyon, a surefire sleeper, and fallen into a controlled coma. Leaving Josef to do battle with the fat man.

Tanaka had ended up using only his fork, as anything attempted with the right side of his body, like cutting with his knife, resulted in a jarring collision with the man's left arm. When Tanaka had finally had enough and turned to say something, his dining partner extended his hand and introduced himself. 'Jake, a shoe salesman from Dolyestown.'

It was Jake's first trip East and he thought he'd struck lucky, seated next to a real Oriental. Tanaka forced himself to be polite. Answered all his questions. 'Yes, sumo is Japan's national sport ... Yes, Japan has two professional baseball leagues, the Central and the Pacific ... No, kabuki theater does not have any female performers. Men take on

39

the roles of women . . . No, I am not a Buddhist . . .' Until he got tired. Then he closed his eyes and tried to sleep. Tried . . . He envied Rachel her pills; he'd never been able to take a 'sleeper' on an airplane. He needed to be conscious. As if, somehow, in an emergency, he would be able to take over on the flight deck or hold the wings on with the strength of his arms. Samurai phobia.

Tanaka, one of the few passengers to have a Japanese passport, cleared customs quickly, then waited for Rachel in the baggage area of the terminal. He had a single piece of luggage, a Vuitton suitcase; she had three. He loaded them onto a trolley and they marched through the 'nothing to declare' lane and up the arrival ramp. Scanning the line of faces on the other side of the guard rail. Dark and foreign. Japanese. He'd been away a long time.

A few of the children, standing with their parents, pointed at Rachel and giggled. Tanaka could see their lips forming the word '*gaijin*', meaning 'outsider or foreigner'; he hoped Rachel didn't notice.

'I've never seen so many people in one place,' she said, moving closer to him.

No one was there to meet them. He hadn't expected family, maybe a car. *Look for a placard with TANAKA printed on it*, he told himself. Another scan of the small dark people. Nothing. *The unwanted son returns. The killer returning to the scene of the crime.* Above the exit door a sign read TAXIS. He guided Rachel toward it.

'Josef-san! Josef-san! *Kochiradesu!*'

The voice calling his name and shouting 'Over here!' came from behind him. He knew who it was before he turned. The strange, somehow endearing quality. A trifle high, almost adolescent, like a voice that was just about to break but never would. When they were kids, thirteen or fourteen, Hiro and he had joked about Ken Sato's voice.

'He's a castrati ... A male soprano. His testicles never dropped.' Never to Ken Sato's face. Not even Hiro wanted to test Cousin Ken's legendary temper.

They turned as he approached.

Wearing a beige linen jacket, loose pleated slacks and expensive slip-on shoes, Ken Sato walked with a graceful confidence, smiling beneath a pair of square, black-framed sunglasses. He looked 'quick'; it was a unique quality, a certain awareness. As if he were on constant alert, ready to react. And imposing, at least a head above the people he passed.

Cousin Ken had always been tall for his age and notoriously fast with his fists. Military school had curbed his temper. That and an obsession with kenjutsu, the art of the sword. Not kendo, which used the wooden *shinai*, or practice swords, but with iaido, the study of drawing the proper Samurai sword from its scabbard and striking the enemy in a single fluid movement.

There were rumors about Ken Sato. The most notable was that he had been an *uchi-deshi* or private student, of Yukio Mishima, Japan's legendary novelist and right-wing activist. That Ken had actually participated in the siege at the headquarters of the Japan Defense Forces, an accomplice in Mishima's attempt to reinstate the values of 'old Japan'. That he had witnessed his master's ritual suicide as the coup failed. Watched, as an older student attempted to end the agony of Mishima's disembowelment, hacking crudely at his master's neck, trying to behead him. Until a general in the Defense Forces took the sword and completed the job.

That Ken Sato had avenged Mishima's shame by cutting off both of the fumbling student's hands.

The fact that most of Mishima's 'Red Brigade' had been rounded up and incarcerated led Tanaka to discredit the story. Still, it gave Cousin Ken a certain mystique.

'Josef-san, Josef-san,' Sato repeated as he stood in front of Josef and bowed.

Tanaka whiffed just the hint of fragrance, more a perfume than a cologne, delicate and sweet. He drew back, searching for the eyes beneath the dark lenses of the glasses.

'These are sad times,' Ken whispered.

'Ken-san,' Tanaka said. 'Thank you for coming.'

Ken Sato bowed again.

Rachel stood there, by Josef's side, looking straight at Ken Sato. The features of his face were refined, aristocratic; cheekbones set so high they seemed on the verge of bursting though his smooth, amber skin, a narrow, straight nose which sat symmetrically above wide, thin lips and a pointed jaw. And hair so slick and black that it seemed painted on top of his head.

At first she smiled at him, until the smile, unreturned, grew stale on her face. He seemed to stare right through her.

Maybe he doesn't realize we're together, she thought, *no one could be that rude*.

Finally Josef turned toward her. Rachel sensed embarrassment.

'Ken-san, I want you to meet my fiancée, Rachel Saunders.'

She detected the hint of apology in Josef's voice. *He's sorry he brought me*, she thought.

She tried on the smile again, held out her hand and stood there as Ken Sato stepped back, away from her.

Sato said something in Japanese then bowed. Rachel withdrew her hand. At any other time she would have been insulted and angry, but here, in this airport, teeming with little jibbering people, she felt only confusion.

Josef spoke in Japanese, answering whatever it was his cousin had said, then turned to Rachel. 'Ken-san has invited us to stay with him,' he explained.

Now Rachel was totally mixed up. Cousin Ken obviously found her repulsive, yet he was inviting them to live in his home. On top of this she couldn't ask Josef for an explanation, not in front of Ken; he seemed to speak English as well as she did.

'My apartment is large. You will be comfortable. It is my honor to have Josef share my home.' Ken addressed them in English. Leaving no doubt that it was 'Josef' who was to be his 'guest'; she was little more than additional baggage.

Rachel wanted to refuse the invitation, felt encouraged when Josef hesitated to answer. They had planned on a hotel. *Please turn him down*, she willed.

Then Cousin Ken removed his dark glasses. 'Josef, I understand what you have been through. I know what it means for you to come here. I want you to stay with me,' he turned to Rachel, it was as if he were forcing himself to look at her, 'both you and your fiancée . . . Sincerely.'

There were tears rimming Ken Sato's dark eyes.

'Thank you, Ken-san, thank you, we would be honored,' Tanaka answered.

Ken whistled for a porter and the three of them followed the luggage to the car park.

Ken drove a black Honda NSX, a two-seater sports car with just enough luggage room for Tanaka's Vuitton.

'Rachel, you ride with Ken, I'll get a cab and follow you,' Josef suggested.

Rachel looked at Sato; he was grimacing.

Right, she thought, her temper finally on the rise, *you really think I want to be stuck inside that black capsule with you?*

'No, no, no . . .' she answered, forcing a hard smile, 'I'll follow in the cab; you and your cousin Kenson,' she pronounced it awkwardly on purpose, 'will have a chance to get reacquainted.'

Josef Tanaka and Ken Sato had grown up together; they had attended the same elementary school, Ken being between Hiro and Josef in age.

Ken was the son of Mikio Tanaka's only sister. A product of an arranged marriage to a retired school teacher, Omi Sato. He was already seventy years old when Ken was born and died of a heart attack three months afterwards.

Mikio Tanaka had acted out of both love and moral obligation, taking over the bills, paying for Ken's education then insisting on military college when discipline became a problem. And Ken had repaid him with hard work and respect.

Ken Sato had been there, in 1976, at the Budokan Hall; he had seen Josef maim his older brother. Later he provided an emotional bridge over which Josef and his father could meet. Beyond that there was little anyone could do.

After Josef's departure, he and Ken began to lose touch. At first there was the occasional letter. Reports that Mikio had invited Ken Sato to join the legal department of Tanaka Industries, to negotiate contracts between labor and management, aiding in the control of overseas shipping. To settle labor disputes on the docks. A tough job, particularly for a young man torn between the academic life of a philosopher/writer and the practicality of a career in corporate law.

In Ken's case, practicality prevailed. The family business was expanding and Mikio Tanaka needed advisors he could trust. So Ken became a lawyer and negotiator. That was the way it was in Japan, family first. Always.

It was an eighty-minute ride from Narita airport to downtown Tokyo. Sato drove fast, navigating the tight corners and badly marked one-way streets, almost as if he wanted to lose the small Nissan taxi cab which followed them. Josef kept turning around, trying to catch a glimpse of Rachel through the NSX's tinted rear window. He knew she was angry and he understood why. He would explain it to her later, the inherent chauvinism of Japan. For now, she was learning first hand.

Sato's NSX received stares at all the stoplights, particularly from the young men mounted on their Kawasaki superbikes, with their hair slicked back Western style and their fringed leather jackets. Ken Sato viewed them with scorn.

'They all want to be from New York ... No more values. Whatever happened to tradition?'

A quarter of an hour later they were passing the Tokyo Tower, en route to Gotanda.

Josef remained quiet, overwhelmed by the traffic and congestion. As if the roads had narrowed by half and the population doubled in the ten years that he had been away. They had slowed now, and the cab was directly behind them.

'Tired?' Ken asked, pulling onto the down ramp of an underground parking facility to an expensive-looking apartment building.

'I didn't remember so many people,' Tanaka answered. His voice sounded weary.

'Twelve million in Tokyo. Seven thousand people for every square mile ...' Ken said, steering the NSX into a slip designated with his name printed on the wall above the space.

The taxi rattled to a halt on their right.

Josef climbed from the NSX and helped Rachel from the back of the cab, paid the bill and collected her bags.

He could feel her bristle as she walked beside him, stone silent toward the elevator.

They stopped at level three, the door opening directly into Ken Sato's apartment. The first thing that struck Josef was the purity of the large reception room. The floor, beyond the entrance mat, was dark red wood, polished like a mirror. Lacquered pillars stood in each of the four corners, in front of the shoji cloth partitions which separated the main room from the rest of the apartment.

Directly in front of them, twenty feet away, a circular mirror, framed by intricately carved wood, sat on top of an altar, two lion-like statues of the guardian, Koma-inu, positioned to either side. Jars of rice and sake were on the first shelf.

'Shinto, the old religion . . . The mirror reflects the unseen gods,' Ken said as Josef removed his shoes. 'Welcome home.'

Josef smiled, experiencing a rush of emotion. *Home. Home.* The word played in his mind.

All the way from Narita, through the squalor of the housing estates that lined the narrow roads, bathed in the stink of gasoline and bad air from the refineries, all the while he had felt alien, a man on a mission, a stranger. Yet now, he had arrived at an oasis, a timeless monument to what Japan had been, would always be, and he was 'home'.

He was hardly aware of Rachel beside him, removing her flat shoes, mirroring his moves, her anger dissipated, replaced by a strange awkwardness.

'Come, Josef-san, I will show you to your room.'

They followed Ken Sato through a sliding door and along a narrow corridor. 'You want to lie down, sleep awhile before we go to the house of your father?' Ken asked.

'No, Ken-san, thank you. I couldn't sleep. Not without seeing . . . my parents,' Josef answered. Finally turning to Rachel, 'Are you all right?'

'I could do with a wash,' she said softly.

Josef nodded and turned to Ken. 'Maybe a bath and a change of clothes.'

'Please, bathe, relax,' Sato offered, sliding the door open to a bathroom.

A wood-slatted *furo* stood on cast-iron mounts in the far corner of the room, behind a large, tiled washing area. The *furo* or tub, had a piece of sheet metal for its base; beneath it a sealed gas-fired heater warmed the water.

In Japan no one would consider bathing in the same water they had 'washed' in. And, in some of the older sections of town, with water scarce, it was not unusual for an entire family to use the same bath, one right after the other, making a separate 'washing' area a requirement in the bathroom.

'There are sponges, water jugs and fresh towels in the closet,' Ken said. 'In the corner there is a shower.'

Tanaka turned. Met his cousin's eyes, understanding that the information about the shower was for Rachel. Knew how hard Ken was trying in order to please them.

'Your home is beautiful, Ken-san. And I thank you for making us welcome,' he said.

Ken Sato smiled, lowering his head, self-conscious. Then he looked up, at Rachel.

'You sleep at the end of the hall, it is not a large room and, for that, I apologize.'

I don't get to sleep with my fiancé? she thought, but kept quiet, following Ken to the closet-sized room with the single-width futon.

Josef insisted that Rachel use the bathroom first.

She locked the door, then checked the bolt lock again before removing her clothes. Her revulsion to Ken Sato was as much physical as psychological; he was just too precise, too immaculate. Sterile, like antiseptic.

In the shower room she was claustrophobic, disliking its white-tiled walls and floor and the narrow glass door. She turned on the water from the outside, adjusting the temperature and flow, then stepped in and pulled the door closed. It snapped shut like a vault. She pushed against it once, just to make sure it would re-open then closed it again.

Must be some way to get to a hotel, she thought, as the thick beads of water pounded her head. She adjusted the temperature again until the water was hot then turned around, letting it beat against the small of her back, bending forward to touch her toes, stretching. Beginning to unwind, relax.

She understood that Josef would go alone on this first visit with his family; it was going to be tough enough without having the added burden of his American fiancée. *Burden*, she was already thinking of herself as a burden. She straightened up, turned and breathed in the steam, gulping a mouthful of water in the process. Coughing, she tried to shut off the tap, twisting it the wrong way and scalding her shoulder. She backed toward the door, pushing against it. Nothing; it wouldn't budge. She gasped, sucking another lungful of hot, humid air.

The air, the thickness of it, the heat, it touched something inside her, deeper than her lungs, deeper than anything physical; it touched the 'memory'. It was the same air, the same texture, the same clinging claustrophobia. The same as that place the Mantis had taken her, to that room at the zoo, down the stairs, behind the old boilers, in back of the discarded cages. And suddenly it hit. The panic.

'He' was there, in the tiny cubicle, inside the heat and humidity, rising from the vapor, reaching for her with his callused fingers and dead eyes, his penis inflamed and probing, pushing up against her anus, trying to dig inside her body, making her so frightened that she had no will to resist. 'He' owned her. The Mantis owned her.

She screamed, silent and hollow, then flailed with her arms. Her elbow smashed against the shower room door and it flew open. She was out and free. *Deep breaths, take deep breaths, control it, control your breath, your breath controls your flow of thought. Memory is only thought. Control it, Rachel, control it*. She could hear Stan Leibowitz's voice, calm and centered. She sat down on the floor and breathed. And as she breathed, the domed head with its shining eyes and broken beak-like nose became small in perspective.

Then slipped back into memory. Then disappeared.

She spent another few minutes in the bathroom, cleaning up, drying the floor, drying her body. 'Mustn't let Josef know. No problem. I can handle it, no problem. Just breathe, keep breathing.' She was all right by the time she unlocked the door.

Josef greeted her in the hallway. Smiling apologetically, he kissed her lightly on the neck.

'You'll get used to Ken,' he promised, 'he's just a little threatened.'

'Threatened?' Rachel repeated.

'My mother has told him that you're a very high-powered doctor in America.'

'So what?' Rachel asked.

'Ken's a traditionalist; it's hard for him to accept a woman as his equal, let alone a foreign woman . . . but he'll get over it,' Josef whispered, smiling as he walked past Rachel and into the bathroom.

Josef shaved, scrubbed himself, rinsed and lay in the bathtub. Splashing his face, rubbing beneath his eyes, feeling his pores tighten, allowing the cool water to refresh him. He had forgotten what it was like to bathe properly, to feel truly clean.

He dressed in a beige linen suit, white cotton shirt and olive green silk tie. The type of clothes he would wear to the office, appropriate dress for the *otsuya*, the gathering of family to pay respect to the deceased.

The funeral, of course, would be different, formal, black suit and black tie.

Weddings and funerals, same suit, different color tie. White for a wedding, black for a funeral, women wore black kimonos or black dresses. Even the *noshibukuro*, a formal envelope containing between ten and fifty thousand yen, depending upon the giver's relationship with the family, was distinguished only by the color of ribbon. White and red for a wedding, white and black for a funeral ... Weddings and funerals ... He looked in the mirror, studied his reflection. Wondered if he'd ever wear the white tie ...

'Ready, Josef-san?' Ken Sato's voice caught him from a million miles away. He turned to see his cousin standing in the doorway.

'You feeling okay?' Ken asked.

Tanaka didn't answer at once.

'I spoke to your father. He is expecting us,' Ken added.

'Better go then,' Tanaka replied. He sounded abrupt. Didn't mean to, but his grief was now masked by nerves.

He walked down the hall, stopping outside the shoji partition to Rachel's room.

'Rachel, we're on our way, see you in a couple of hours,' he called through the cloth.

Rachel slid the panel open; she was wearing a cotton bathrobe. She wanted to kiss him but Sato's presence inhibited her. Instead she whispered, 'Good luck,' then watched as Josef followed Ken down the hallway and out through the front room.

Ken Sato drove, without conversation, to Den-en-Chofu; he parked along the curb, in front of the family house, shut off the V-6 engine, and turned to Josef.

'Everything okay, Josef-san, everything okay,' he whispered. Not a question, a reassurance.

'I knew this day would come, Ken,' Tanaka said. Then he slid from the car and walked resolutely toward the brown, wood-framed house.

He was still thirty feet from the entrance when the front door opened.

Grace Tanaka stood in the shadow beneath the overhead trellis. She was still a handsome woman, tall and broad-shouldered. Her green eyes flashed below a cascade of curling auburn hair. She was smiling, lifting her arms in preparation for an embrace, her cheeks wet with tears.

As Tanaka walked closer everything felt surreal, motion slowed, as if he were being sucked through the vortex of his past life. Memories of traveling up this same path, home from school, Hironori by his side, laughing, running. To be met by his mother. He'd always thought his mother was the most beautiful woman in the world. Like the models in the Western magazines; he was so proud on 'parents day' at school. 'That's my mother! That's my mother!'

'Josef ... Josef!' Her voice had the familiar ring, still young and full.

'Grace. Grace Tanaka ...' She had saved him. Helped him go to America. To break with Japan ...

He was closer now, a few feet away. He could see she'd aged. The same face, the same smile, just older, tainted by sadness, lined by the passing years.

'Mother,' he said softly, hugging her. He was barely keeping his tears back, withholding them only because he could sense his father, close by.

Ken eased his way past them, bowing slightly in respect to Grace Tanaka, then walked through the door.

'Let me look at you, Josef ...' Grace Tanaka said, holding her son at arm's length. 'You've put on weight ... You look like an American.' Her own New England accent broke through on the 'American'.

Josef looked deeper into her green eyes. Found their loneliness. As familiar to him as the eyes themselves. The loneliness had always been there, since he could remember. In the past, he had never been certain as to why.

Now he knew.

For him, it came in the autumn, in Philadelphia. When the leaves fell and he thought of Japan, of his family, his home.

Sometimes he contemplated his own death, wondering if he would die in America, be buried there. If his spirit would rise from his body and travel, lost and searching for its true home, the place of his birth. He experienced it then; a deep, melancholic loneliness, a longing for his roots.

Finally, he understood the sadness in Grace Tanaka's pale Western eyes.

'I've missed you,' he said, studying her face.

In the background, in the reception room of the big house, he could hear men talking. He could distinguish two voices among them; Ken Sato's and Mikio Tanaka's. They were speaking low, respectfully. Even so, there was an unmistakable timbre to his father's voice. The kind of voice that could either soothe or maim, a velvet weapon.

Grace Tanaka smiled. 'Let's go inside,' she whispered.

Tanaka breathed inward, calming himself as he crossed the threshold of the family home. There were six or seven people there, uncles, aunts, and nephews. Conversation stopped as he entered.

He was so nervous he nearly walked onto the main floor without slipping off his shoes. It was only his mother, holding him by the arm, that gave him a presence of mind. He had met each of these people in the past. At family gatherings, times of celebration, he knew each by name.

He bowed to the group.

'Josef-san ... Josef-san.' Voices in unison as the group returned his courtesy. With the exception of Mikio Tanaka. He stood still, an ambiguous expression on his face.

Doesn't want me here. Doesn't want me. The thought repeated as he walked forward, drawn, like a magnet, to the dark, brooding man. He was an arm's length from his father when he stopped, the room hushed around him. So dominated by the brown, hooded eyes and full lips, held tight by the clenched muscles of Mikio Tanaka's square jaw that he had very little awareness of his own posture or expression. Then he noticed his father's hair, what should have been a fleeting, random detail in this barrage to his senses. But one that registered, a catalyst.

Mikio Tanaka's hair was dyed. Jet black, the color it had been when Josef had last seen him, but now, more than a decade later, the blue-black color was artificial.

Mikio Tanaka, the Samurai, the icon, had become human. Age and vanity had made him mortal. Josef felt something stir within his own frozen senses. A wave of pity.

'Father, I am sorry for your loss and for the loss to our family . . . I loved my brother.' The words fell naturally from his mouth. He bowed. When he looked up Mikio Tanaka's face had tightened. Not out of anger but from his effort to control his own emotion.

'It is good to have you home, Josef. We need all of our strength in this time of mourning. Thank you for being here,' his father replied.

A half-hour later, after exchanging greetings and condolences with his relatives, Josef slipped away from the gathering and walked along the corridor to the winding staircase. There was still something left undone. He mounted the stairs, walked to the landing then down the upper hallway.

He stopped at the last closed partition.

Beyond, inside the room, his older brother had lived his life, lived and died. While Josef had travelled, moved to America, studied medicine, fallen in love, experienced people and emotions; all this time, Hironori had lived in this single room. In a wheelchair, surrounded by walls and memories.

Josef turned, unable to slide the partition and face the reality. Entering the room seemed a final violation of his brother's privacy. As if he were robbing a grave. Yet, at the same time, he was compelled.

The partition opened easily, the tongue and groove a perfect fit along the base of the wood frame.

Sunlight flooded the large room, blanketing the '*hinoki*' floor, made with slats of cypress, in a warm gold. Hironori's artwork hung everywhere, flowers and trees, snow-capped mountains, waterfalls and streams, rocks below the surface, reflections of sunlight against the still water. Fine portraits: Hoetei, the big-bellied laughing monk; Muso, Teacher to the Nation; Zen monks and warriors, all depicted in delicate tones on heavy white paper. Josef slid the door closed behind him.

A single chair sat against the far wall, a visitor's chair. Josef sat down. Allowed his eyes to settle. Envisioned his brother, positioned in his wheelchair, in front of the wide, south-facing window, painting. Painting his beautiful pictures.

A sense of quiet and peace pervaded the room; it had required an inner tranquility to create the beauty that adorned its walls, an acceptance and a deep wisdom.

Josef looked from the window to the bed, then at the vanity unit, with its twin mounted brushes and wide mirror. Noticed the wooden floor, in front of the mirror; the *hinoki* had been worn from the wheels of the chair, rolling back and forth, back and forth. Worn and discolored . . . *Discolored*?

Josef walked to the mirror, squatted down, touched the wood with his fingertips. *Stained,* it had definitely been stained. Stained, then bleached in an effort to remove the stains. Something had spilled, creating a broken pattern which formed a perimeter surrounding the shallow imprints from the wheels of the chair.

Ink, probably ink, he told himself, trying to imagine Hironori upending his work-tray while brushing his hair. *Possible, in fact probable*. Still, there was something out of context in the stained wood, something which defied the harmony of the room.

Paranoia, fatigue, a doctor's instinct? He questioned himself as he looked up, staring at his own reflection in the mirror. Saw his brother staring back, just for a second, the image fading as he focused on the darkness shadowing his own eyes. *Thirty hours without sleep, give yourself a break ... Go back to Ken's. Go to bed, get yourself together.* But the peace of the room, its tranquility had deserted him. He felt bone-tired and mentally unsettled. As he stood, Ken Sato slid back the partition, entering behind him.

'Josef-san. You okay? Your mother is asking for you.'

'All right, Ken-san ... All right, just tired. Very tired. Time for me to go. Get some sleep. I'm not thinking too clearly.'

Ken Sato nodded his head, smiled, his eyes gentle as he scanned the room.

'I think you accomplish much today, Josef-san. Now is the time for rest. Come, we will say good-bye to the family and I will take you home.'

Rachel was still awake when Josef and Ken Sato returned; she had tossed and turned, lapsing into sleep before jolting herself awake in quick defensive spasms.

Finally she had walked from her sleeping area and down the corridor of the apartment. Entering the main room with its polished floor and Shinto shrine, then into a small white-tiled kitchen.

Cleaner than most hospitals, she observed. There was not a fleck of dust anywhere, from the wooden floor to the glazed work tops surrounding the stainless steel sink.

She wanted a glass of water but was reluctant to touch anything, as if her fingerprints would defile the sanctity of the room and reveal her intrusion. At last she opened a cupboard above the sink, hoping to find a drinking glass; it contained a fine porcelain pot, several cups, and a whisk for stirring. She was about to lift down one of the cups but her intuition stopped her again; she knew the cups were not for drinking water. Instead, she bent over the sink, turned on the tap and drank from the long bending spout.

After that she slipped back to her futon and lay down.

It seemed like hours before she heard their voices in the hall, muffled, as if not to disturb her. They spoke in Japanese but it was easy to separate Josef's low tones from the higher-pitched voice of his cousin.

She listened as her fiancé entered his room and closed the partition. Then she slept. With Josef close by to protect her.

Tanaka was out as soon as his head hit the hard pillow. His sleep black and without dreams. When he woke up, he turned against the mattress, reaching out for Rachel before staring at the shoji wall, disoriented and uncertain as to where he was. He rolled over and switched on the bedside lamp. Picked his wristwatch up from the low table. 3.05 a.m. He had been asleep since seven. *Eight hours, I've been asleep for eight hours.*

His mind cleared and he began to feel better. Memory of yesterday's visit to the family home seemed to exist in a separate time frame. As if he had awakened from a general anesthetic to find that some particularly difficult surgery had been performed and that the operation had gone well. It was over and he wouldn't have to face it again. The ice had been broken.

He thought of the room, Hironori's room. The paintings, the peace. And the stain on the floor. Why did he react to the stain on the floor? Allow it to ruin his 'communion' with Hiro's spirit. Fatigue? He had been so tired. Too tired to think straight. But it wasn't a thought; it was pure feeling.

Then there was Rachel; he wondered if she was still sleeping. He lay back and listened, not a sound. He contemplated getting up and walking to her room, lying down beside her on the futon. He couldn't do that, not in Ken's home; it would be in poor taste. But as soon as the burial was over they'd get a proper hotel room, enjoy what they could of Japan, discuss their wedding.

*

Josef spent the next two hours reading *Confessions of a Mask*, Yukio Mishima's bleak novel about a boy obsessed with a sado-masochistic fantasy. It was one of three hardbound books which lay on the table beside his bed. All had been written by Mishima. Tanaka had read each of them as a college student but the quality of the prose, poetic in its rhythm, remained captivating. Quiet footsteps from the hallway caused him to look up. At first he thought they were Rachel's, but there was a different quality to them, light but more precise.

'Josef-san?' Ken's voice whispered from behind the partition.

'I'm awake, Ken-san, please come in.'

Ken Sato slid the door open. He looked fresh and rested, his face newly shaved. He carried a leather gym bag in his right hand, a long, cloth sword bag in his left.

'You sleep well?' Ken asked.

'Yes ... Very deep,' Josef replied, standing up from the bed. He was wearing white cotton, boxer-style undershorts. He felt Ken's eyes on him.

'You are in good condition, Josef-san. Body is lean. Have you continued karate-do ... In the United States?'

Tanaka turned. There was something childlike, innocent, in the way that Ken was looking at him. Curious, without inhibition. He relaxed.

'With Azato-sensei. In Philadelphia. A very good dojo,' he explained.

'I would like you to come to my dojo, Josef-san ... Come this morning. A great honor for me.'

Josef met Ken's eyes and nodded, all the time thinking of Rachel; it was going to be tough having her with him, here, in Japan. Tough splitting his loyalties, between family obligations and his committment to her.

He walked to the closet and took a silk dressing gown from his rack of clothes. Slipped it on.

'Ken-san, I must see if my fiancée is awake – tell her where we are going.'

'Of course, Josef-san, explain that you will be back by eight o'clock.' Sato's tone indicated that he believed Josef to have full authority over his woman, no possibility of her objecting to being left alone, again.

Rachel was lying on her side, facing away from him, when Josef looked into her room.

'*Okiteru?*' he whispered.

Rachel turned at the sound of his voice.

'Are you awake?' he asked again, this time in English.

'Just,' she replied, looking up, 'I heard you come in last night, after that I was a goner ... How did it go with your family?' Her voice was tentative.

'As well as it could,' he answered. 'We'll talk about it later, it's still early.'

He hesitated a moment, lowering his voice, making sure that Ken could not overhear him. Knowing that his cousin would interpret his courtesy as weakness.

'Would you mind if I went with Ken to his dojo? I'll be back here by eight.'

Rachel understood that Josef's immediate family would come first for a while, that they would require his attention, his love. It was natural.

'Not at all; it'll give me time to use the bathroom, get dressed.'

'Thank you, Rachel,' Josef whispered, bending down to kiss her.

Kenshi (A Master Swordsman)

Iaido is an elite Japanese martial art. It developed from the sword combat techniques of iaijutsu, dating back to the eighth century, its purpose being to draw the *tachi* or *katana*, the fighting sword, and kill the enemy in a single, fluid motion.

It took until the twentieth century for iaido to take its place alongside the other accepted forms of Japanese *budo*, or Ways of the Warrior. And only then because its few surviving masters set forth that iaido was more than a 'killing art'; it was a discipline for man's character, a road to enlightenment.

A unique characteristic of iaido is that it is not a 'two-man' combat art. Each technique consists of four separate actions: *nukitsuke*, drawing the sword from its scabbard; *kiritsuke*, cutting with the sword; *chiburi*, shaking the enemy's blood from the blade; and *noto*, sheathing the sword, and is performed alone.

The Asano Shinto Ryu was the oldest school of iaido in Japan, located in an immaculately kept two-story building on the outskirts of the Akasaka section of Tokyo, near the Akasaka Guest House, famous for the housing of foreign dignitaries.

Members of the Asano Shinto Ryu signed an undertaking to follow the teachings and rules of the school. Signed with their own blood.

*

At six o'clock in the morning there were five men on the polished dojo floor. Each was using a 'live' or sharp sword and each was careful to maintain a correct distance between himself and his fellow practitioners.

Ken Sato stood in the center of the group. He was attired in a training costume, a simple black *hakama*, the cotton split-skirt; and the *uwagi*, a heavy cotton jacket, its sleeves reaching just below his elbows.

He was executing a series of single-handed cuts, rising each time from a kneeling position, drawing his sword, slicing through a vital organ or joint of his imagined opponent before shaking the blood from the blade and resheathing the weapon, sliding its razor-sharp blade between the thumb and index finger of his left hand, careful not to allow skin contact with the steel as he returned it to its scabbard. All in a single motion, within the blink of an eye.

There were rarely spectators at a practice session and there was certainly no accommodation for them. Josef knelt in *seiza*, knees folded, hips touching heels, and watched from the edge of the floor.

Ken Sato's shoulders were wide, developed from years of practice with the three-foot long *katana*. His balance was superb. Even as he walked from the *kata* practice area to the back of the dojo to begin 'cutting' against the fixed, tightly packed cylinders of straw, Tanaka recognized the deep-rootedness of his cousin's footsteps; it appeared as if each of his toes individually gripped the pine floor.

Over and over Ken Sato repeated the two-handed draw and horizontal cut against the straw cylinder. So relaxed and fluid that he neither sweated nor broke the regular pattern of his breathing.

At one time, the Samurai tested their swords and techniques on the bodies of condemned criminals, sometimes forcing two or three men to stand back to front, or lie face-up one on top of the other. Endeavoring, with a single cut, to slice cleanly through the mound of human flesh. Restacking the remains and continuing until there was not a piece of flesh left larger than an ear.

The rules of practice had changed, but Tanaka clearly saw the intent in Ken Sato's eyes. Reminding himself that to kill was the purpose of many of the karate techniques that he himself practiced.

His cousin concluded his hour-long drill with a difficult technique: a rising, single-handed strike, delivered backhand. Repeatedly cutting at a slight upward angle, along the length of the shaft. Reducing it in six-inch sections until the straw target was a ragged stub. Then he performed the *chiburi*, resheathed his *katana*, bowed, and walked from the dojo. Straight by Josef without so much as a nod of acknowledgement.

Half an hour later, in the restaurant, while eating his raw eggs on rice, Ken Sato looked up and met his cousin's eyes.

'I love iaido.' His voice was reverent, 'For me it is traditional Japan. Ordered and precise. Every action, every object has its place. Everything in harmony. Working for the perfection of the whole.' Then Ken Sato grinned, his teeth white against his skin.

Josef Tanaka smiled back, using his smile to disguise his discomfort. Inside, he felt like a traitor, to Japan, to tradition.

Yesterday, he had been surrounded by his own people, speaking his native language. This morning, in Rachel's bedroom it had taken him a few moments to click back into English; the first time in years he had been aware that it was not his first language. That he, like Japan, had been assimilated by the West.

A second look at Japan

When Josef and Ken walked from the small, corner restaurant, adjacent to the dojo, there was a silver, chauffeur-driven Mercedes waiting.

'For you and your fiancée, Josef, while you are in my home,' Sato explained, pointing to the car. 'My work requires all my days and sometimes half the night so I want you to be comfortable.' Then he handed Tanaka a set of keys. 'For my apartment,' he added.

That afternoon, after phoning his family's home and speaking to his mother, Josef got into the back of the silver Mercedes with Rachel and instructed the driver to take them to Den-en-Chofu.

Rachel was wearing a gray and black pin-striped Armani suit, a white silk shirt, black silk tie and matching ankle boots. She was nervous and Josef's silence only added to it. Twice she opened her handbag, using her mirror to check her makeup, taking a quick spray of breath freshener. She had looked forward to this day so many times in the last year, never thinking it would take place under such circumstances. If she was uneasy in Ken Sato's presence, she dreaded to think of how it would be facing Mikio Tanaka. Yet it was inevitable. Everything was inevitable, from the death of Josef's brother to whatever lay in front of her today. And whatever it took to see it through, she was equal to it. That's what her own father used to say to her, whenever things at medical school got tough, 'You're equal to it, Rachel, you're equal to it.' He was a good father; she had come from a good family, and she was 'equal to it'.

The driver slowed as he rounded the corner of a narrow tree-lined street. Rachel could see only the roof tops of the homes which were concealed behind a line of walled gardens. A quarter of the way up the street the driver pulled the car to the curb. He stopped, got out and opened the door for them.

'Are you ready?' Josef asked, the first time he had spoken during the entire ride.

Rachel nodded, took his hand and climbed out of the car.

The wood-framed house which lay behind the stone wall looked surprisingly American, upper middle class. She had expected something more grand, like one of the five storied pagodas she recalled from her geography books in high school. This was almost colonial in design, with the exception of the large garden, that had been created with a more definite purpose, an artistry.

She could feel the sweat on Josef's palm as they walked up the stone path to the front door.

A house servant admitted them and again Rachel was taken aback by the 'Western' quality of the entrance hall, the paneled reception room and its furnishings. She followed Josef as he removed his shoes, bending to unzip her boots. When she looked up, a tall, handsome Western woman was walking toward them from an adjoining room.

'Rachel ... Welcome to Japan.'

Perhaps it was Grace Tanaka's accent, perhaps her tone of voice, or maybe the fact that she seemed to radiate a warmth in the midst of uncertainty, but Rachel accepted Grace Tanaka's embrace as if the two women had known each other for a lifetime.

'Is Ken looking after you?' Grace Tanaka asked.

'We're doing fine, thank you,' Rachel answered.

Grace looked into Rachel's eyes. *Nothing hidden in those*

eyes, she thought, refreshed to see an American face, hear an American voice, intuitively understanding her.

'Ken has a real way with women,' she added, a hint of sarcasm in her tone, just enough to make Rachel smile. 'Anything you need, you ask me,' then she turned to Josef.

'Your father is in the reception room; he's taken the day off from work, waiting for you.' A formality suddenly touched Grace Tanaka's voice.

Then the nerves came back, transmitted from Josef to Rachel.

The three of them walked toward the high arched doors that separated the two rooms.

Mikio Tanaka was seated in a high-backed chair, facing the large bay window on the southern side of the thirty-five-foot long drawing room. He stood as he heard them approach.

Rachel's first impression of Mikio Tanaka was one of dignity; he was dressed in a dark tailored suit, soft blue shirt and striped tie. As he walked toward her she was aware of the same animal grace that had first attracted her to Josef. A quality that defied age.

'Father, I would like you to meet my fiancée, Rachel Saunders,' Josef said.

Mikio Tanaka smiled and extended his hand.

'My great pleasure, Rachel.' His voice was silken smooth and his demeanor was nothing like her preconception; Mikio Tanaka appeared neither hard nor unforgiving.

'Please, we will have tea,' he continued, guiding Rachel to one of the leather-covered chairs that formed a semicircle around a low Georgian table. 'I am sorry your first visit to Japan has had to coincide with our family tragedy,' Mikio Tanaka said as they sat down.

Rachel saw Josef straighten but she detected no barb to Mikio Tanaka's words. Instead, as their conversation continued, she sensed that he was somehow beaten. Looking for consolation, even forgiveness. It was just something that flickered in his eyes, in the way that he glanced at Josef.

It was there, buried beneath his formality. As if there were something he wanted to tell Josef, something which was clinging to his heart, devouring him from the inside. Rachel felt a peculiar sympathy for Mikio Tanaka.

She noted that Grace Tanaka, during the course of her husband's conversation, remained quiet, seeming to treat him with deference, yet, at the same time, Josef's mother lost none of her own stature. Her behavior was more a form of etiquette than subservience.

'When all this is over, when my elder son has been laid to rest, I wish for you and Josef to spend many hours in my home; I want you to feel that you are part of my family, Rachel,' Mikio Tanaka said as she and Josef were getting ready to leave.

Rachel shook his hand again at the door.

Grace Tanaka walked with them to the waiting Mercedes. She held Rachel's arm, stealing a quiet word with her as Josef spoke to the driver.

'You understand the word "*gaijin*"?'

Rachel looked at Grace Tanaka and nodded. Josef had explained the meaning of *gaijin* to her. Warned her that, being tall and blonde, she would be stared at in the streets, that the Japanese would not feel comfortable with her; she had already had a taste of Ken Sato's reserve.

'Outsider,' she answered.

'That's right,' Grace said, smiling, 'but you'll be fine here, I can always tell . . . You're equal to it.'

You're equal to it. Grace Tanaka had actually said it. Like déjà vu.

'Thank you—' she was about to say 'Mrs Tanaka'; it didn't feel right.

'Grace,' Grace Tanaka filled in.

'Thank you, Grace.' Then Rachel reached over and embraced her again.

'I'll phone you after Saturday; we'll sit down and talk,' the older woman whispered.

During the next few days Josef showed Rachel the city. Each day choosing a different location. From the downtown Asakusa district in the north-east, with its famous Buddhist temple, to the Ginza, Tokyo's busiest shopping area, in the south.

Occasionally, people stared at Rachel; they even stared at Josef. Mostly it was the very young children or the very old that stared; the adolescents and their middle-aged parents rarely batted an eye as Josef and Rachel passed them on the crowded sidewalks. They were familiar with Westerners, everyone from Arnold Schwarzenegger to Michael Jackson had appeared at one time or another on the TV screens, plugging everything from Japanese beer to Pepsi-Cola.

'It has all changed so much,' Josef kept telling her, 'look at it: McDonald's, Kentucky Fried Chicken, The Gap ... Even the people, the way they act, it's all so Western.'

Rachel nodded and walked on, unable to comment. To her Tokyo seemed like any other huge cosmopolitan city – New York or Paris. The people were just smaller, talked faster, and there were more of them.

The further they walked and the more Josef saw, the more he thought of Ken Sato, of his Samurai sword and his Shinto shrine, standing alone against the dissolution of his culture. He understood his cousin, or at least his cousin's desire for tradition.

Japan, what is becoming of Japan? ... And how can I, with my Western mother and my Western fiancée, stand in judgement? Josef Tanaka wondered.

We smile, even at death

It rained on Saturday, the day of the viewing. A warm, soft rain, falling from a sky that was nearly silver.

Tanaka had not slept well. Had tried his Christian prayer, but that had not stopped his imagination from conjuring up scenarios of the day ahead.

He steeled himself for what was to come.

No tears, simply a heart-felt silence, an acceptance of the beloved's passing. That was the requirement. A show of compassionate strength.

Yet he was full of doubt and trepidation. He had faced his brother's room but he had not yet faced his brother. His dead brother.

No tears. Important to maintain his composure, for himself, for the welfare of his family. He was the surviving son. Mikio Tanaka's last son.

He shaved meticulously, then sat a long time in the bath, until the water became cold. Dried himself with a rough cotton towel.

Awareness, that was the necessary discipline. Awareness of his emotions, the ability to sense them before they surfaced; to internalize and to control them.

He stopped at Rachel's room after his bath; she was sitting on the edge of the futon, expecting his visit. She could see the doubt in his eyes.

'Things are going to be all right, Josef, they'll be all right,' she whispered, stroking his back as he sat beside her. 'I'll be waiting right here. Waiting for you.'

69

Rachel understood perfectly why she had not been asked to attend the ceremony; Grace Tanaka had put it in one word, *gaijin*; she and Josef were not yet husband and wife, so there was no necessity to risk the harmony of the ritual.

Josef kissed her softly and quickly on the mouth, then got up and walked from her room.

Ken Sato was waiting for him in the sitting area of the apartment, a three-tatami space to the side of the Shinto shrine.

This time, he and Josef were dressed identically, black suit and black tie. The same as every other man who would attend the ceremony.

Women would be wearing black kimonos or simple black dresses. And each family would carry a *noshibukuro*, the money envelope, marked by the characters *goreizen*, meaning, 'before the spirit of the dead'.

Ken Sato was seated on a tatami, his legs folded and his *noshibukuro* held loosely in his right hand. He stood as Josef entered the room. His eyes searched Josef's.

'Are you ready, Josef-san?'

Tanaka nodded.

Ken Sato took another step toward him. His eyes were gentle and his lips pursed as though prepared to speak. He hesitated, reached out and touched Josef's arm, his fingers barely gripping the biceps. Finally he whispered,

> 'We smile
> even at death
> this happy morning.'

Haiku, Japanese poetry in three lines. So popular in Japan that there are over fifty magazines devoted to it. Beyond poetry, beyond literature, a good haiku uses words in a way that results in the enhanced perception of the reader or listener, producing intuition or insight.

> *We smile*
> *even at death*
> *this happy morning.*

The words played over and over in Josef's mind, merging with the sound of the NSX's engine, the hum of the tires against the road, and the wash of faces from the street as Ken Sato drove to the family home.

It was nine o'clock when they arrived, parking the Honda in line with a dozen other cars parked along the curb.

Ken took his arm as they walked along the stone path toward the open front door. His hand felt warm and reassuring.

'We smile, even at death—' The muffled sound of voices reached out from the front room. The rain had let up and a sliver of sunshine penetrated the thin layer of cloud . . . 'this happy morning.'

He was going to be all right, everything was going to be all right. His mind was clearing.

Inside, the immediate family, relatives and close friends, gathered in small groups. There were twenty to thirty people, most of whom Josef recognized. His entrance was subtly noted as a line began to form, leading into the reception room, toward the cedar coffin which contained Hironori Tanaka's embalmed body.

Ken Sato left Josef's side only long enough to place his *noshibukuro* alongside the others on the low lacquered table. Then he was with him again, his presence giving Josef strength. *I will not forget you for this, cousin Ken. Never*, Josef thought as he joined the line, behind his mother and father. Ken Sato walked ahead, leaving Mikio, Josef and Grace in their proper place. For it was the immediate family that, by rite, would be the last to view the body.

Beside the coffin, on an ornately carved table, an incense burner glowed, wafting its scented smoke through the room. Each person, following the viewing, was required to take a stick of incense from the tray beside the burner and place it into the fire, offering a silent prayer for the spirit of the departed. Once *shoko*, the burning of the incense, was complete, the immediate family would lower the lid of the coffin and seal it with three nails.

Ken Sato was last in line before the immediate family. He hovered a moment above the opened coffin, bowed his head, then walked to the incense table.

Grace Tanaka cried as she approached her dead stepson, her sobs barely audible as she raised a black silk scarf to wipe the tears from her cheeks. Mikio Tanaka stood at her side. His face appeared stern, but there was a mask-like brittleness to its severity. He looked down, into the coffin, only once. Then he turned and found Josef's eyes, willing him to step forward and complete the ceremony.

It was a single step that separated Josef from his mother, father, and brother. A single step and a single glance downward. Then the lid could be closed and the final nails driven in.

Josef held Mikio Tanaka's eyes, nodding slightly, as if to assure him of his support. He felt more for his father at this moment than he had permitted himself in nearly half his lifetime. And although his lips were closed, Josef's mouth was formed into a half smile. A smile that reflected both love and acceptance.

> *We smile*
> *even at death*
> *this happy morning.*

Ken Sato's haiku played like a song in his mind. He understood. Death was part of the natural order. Death was the final lesson, the cessation of attachment. Accepting death was accepting life.

The aroma of incense grew stronger as his senses heightened. His mother's sobs added an equilibrium to the room. Tears of sorrow, tears of joy. Sweet, blessed release. He stepped forward, taking his eyes from his father. Slowly looking down into the dark wooden box. His knees buckled.

Not my brother! That is not my brother! Not Hironori Tanaka! The revelation was so sudden, so intense, that Josef fell forward, gripping the side of the coffin. Gasping for air, as the entire room seemed to fold inward around him. He turned, caught in the sea of faces, eyes staring. *Conspirators. All of them. Teamed against me. To punish me?* Then Ken Sato was by his side, arm around him, holding him.

'Be strong, Josef. Be strong,' his cousin whispered before stepping away. Leaving Josef to stand alone.

This time he could see that the body was Hironori Tanaka; he recognized the features of his brother's face. It was the shape of the head and the painted-on hair that disturbed him. The thick makeup that covered the jaw and the cheeks, concealing the bruised skin and lining the left eye socket . . . The entire skull was a reconstruction. The kind of work he had watched Bob Moyer perform. Hironori Tanaka had been mangled. Severely.

Doctor Josef Tanaka noticed all these things, took them in with a single intake of breath. At the same time remembering the stained wooden floor of Hironori's room. *Blood, my brother's blood.*

Having recovered his composure, he bent down and lightly touched the sides of Hiro's head. Using just enough pressure to verify that papier-mâché had replaced bone in the rebuilding of the skull. Disguising the intent of his movement with a single kiss upon his brother's cold lips.

Vowing, with that kiss, to find out the truth.

Then he stood and lowered the lid of the coffin. Taking his

nail from the table, he hammered it into place.

Two hours later the procession of mourners' cars was winding its way through the busy streets of Tokyo, under police escort, toward the *yakiba*, the 'place of burning'.

Mikio Tanaka sat next to his wife in the back seat of the black Mercedes. Josef and Ken Sato sat facing them. They traveled silently.

Every now and then, when the limousine stopped at a red light or slowed to allow the following cars to maintain their positions in line, Josef would cast a furtive glance at his father. Catch his eyes, linking with them for a second, trying to read behind their disciplined passivity. As if to free the secret he was certain they held. Willing it to their dark, shining surface. And each time, when it seemed they would yield, give up their burden, Mikio Tanaka turned away. Looked at his wife or out of the window, staring at the crowded streets and shops. Returning his gaze to Josef only when he had reestablished control.

The *yakiba* was a flat-roofed single-story building on the southern corner of the Shinjuku National Garden. Its most distinguishing external feature was a tall, white concrete chimney.

It was a sunny day, the humidity mercifully low, and the awning above the *yakiba*'s large stone patio was wound back, allowing the sun to shine upon its visitors. The gray paving stones were bordered by lush private gardens. These connected directly to the National Gardens, giving the area a vast space. The combined scent of a thousand wild flowers gave a sweetness to the air.

Against the side of the crematorium, adjoining the patio, two archways were cut into the concrete wall, a conveyor belt running through them, leading to and from the furnace.

The coffin containing Hironori's body was positioned on

the conveyor belt, midway between the two openings. A stone altar stood beside the coffin, directly in front of the belt. Long, wooden *hashi* – specially designed chopsticks – lay on the flat top of the altar, beside a porcelain urn.

Ando Akio, the operator of the crematorium, was a diminutive man; his face stretched thin by years of narrowing his eyes and tightening his lips as he greeted the bereaved. Recently he had been troubled by dandruff and the shoulders of his black gabardine suit had a slight shine, a result of his furious brushing an hour before.

He bowed solemnly as the family walked onto the patio. Noted the particularly tall man, half-caste, assuming him to be Mikio Tanaka's younger son.

Josef . . . That must be Josef. Akio always made a point of learning the names of the close family. Besides, this was a particularly interesting job. He could still remember the scandal when the elder Tanaka had divorced his Buddhist wife and married the American. It made all the Tokyo papers. This tall half-caste would be the product of that marriage.

Akio watched as the small group walked toward the coffin, lowering their heads in final prayer. Within seconds their fellow mourners had filled the patio behind them.

Ando Akio was meticulous, orchestrating his services with the same skill that his partner, Mas Kadama, employed on the embalming and preparation of the deceased's body. The two men had been in partnership for twenty years, employed by the finest families of Tokyo.

And now, as he steadied his gaze on Hironori Tanaka's coffin Akio recalled his partner's words. 'Terrible injuries. Absolutely terrible. Worst I've seen in all my years. And the way the body was delivered. Disgraceful. Carried from the back seat of a company limousine, wrapped in a shawl, hooded—'

His thoughts were interrupted by silence; the mourners had settled down. It was time. He pressed the start button on the wall-mounted control panel. Detected just the hint of noise, like a dull click, as the motor engaged. Making a mental note to have the service engineers lubricate the ball bearings, he watched Hironori's coffin travel through the low archway.

Josef Tanaka lifted his head in time to see the tail end of the wooden box disappear through the opening.

Hiro, my brother. My dear brother. How I learned from you, admired your courage, your wisdom, your ability to accept this life. I thank you for the many times you stood by me, protected me. I thank you for forgiving me. I love you my brother, I love you. When his thoughts stopped, his feelings took hold. Strong and warm, beginning in his stomach, churning upwards, flushing his face. He didn't fight them, or the tears that followed.

Mikio Tanaka wrapped his arm around his wife, drawing her close to him. Both were staring at the empty archway. The coffin had vanished beyond the opening, and the conveyor belt had stopped.

Josef turned. Saw that Ken Sato was also crying. Josef touched his cousin lightly on the arm and together they walked into the garden. To wait.

Inside the furnace, the temperature was eight hundred and seventy degrees centigrade. Fuelled by gas, a constant even heat.

The coffin burned almost instantly, the cedar combusting, rising in flames of yellow-gold.

The human body is a different matter. The hair incinerates virtually at once while the outer flesh – because it consists primarily of water – dries, then becomes crisp before breaking away from the skeleton and dissolving.

The bones, however, particularly the base of the spine and thick femur bone of the thigh, require time.

In Western countries, the process of cremation is generally allotted sixty to ninety minutes. In that time the entire body turns to ash. Another forty-five minutes to cool sufficiently and then the remains are scooped up and placed into a container.

In Japan, the procedure is not the same. Not as much time is given in the furnace. In order to facilitate the use of the *hashi*.

Amid the singing of birds and the occasional rustle of leaves, there had been only muffled sobs, and quiet whispered prayers. No conversation.

An hour passed before the conveyor belt returned to life. A soft purring sound.

Josef was seated on a stone bench, in contemplation, looking over the manmade lake of the National Garden.

He knew what the sound meant. He stood and walked behind his father and mother to the *yakiba*.

Ken Sato remained a step behind. Knowing that he was not part of this final ritual.

Ando Akio studied the small pile of ash as it appeared from the far archway.

Excellent. He congratulated himself on his timing. He had already removed the skull, extracting the three gold fillings from the deceased's teeth, and Hironori Tanaka's remaining bones were just the right size. Incinerated enough to fit perfectly into the porcelain urn, cool enough to be handled. He pressed the stop button, halting the conveyor belt directly in front of Mikio Tanaka.

Akio watched as the father of the deceased hesitated, staring down at the remains of his elder son.

The cremator felt a wave of sadness for the handsome, expensively suited man. His first son. His Japanese son. Gone forever. It was a tragic loss. He admired Mikio Tanaka's composure. He had seen so many break down at this point, barely able to continue the ceremony. But this man was different. He was Samurai.

The *hashi* felt cold and hard in Mikio Tanaka's hand. One stick made of bamboo, the other of polished wood; they were longer and heavier than the sticks used for dining.

He held the bamboo stick between his index and middle finger and the polished stick between his thumb and ring finger, keeping it stationary. He leaned forward and gripped the largest piece of bone; it was grey, perhaps three inches long and no thicker than the upper end of the *hashi*. Surprisingly light.

'That is the upper arm of your departed son,' Akio whispered. It was part of his profession to know and identify each fragment of bone as it was placed into the urn.

Mikio Tanaka choked back a sob as he lifted Hironori's remains. Five times he returned to the ash.

Ando Akio named the bones as Mikio Tanaka placed them, one after the other, inside the urn. Then he turned and offered the sticks to his wife.

Grace Tanaka accepted them, her hands shaking. There was a terrible moment when, hovering above the ash, she nearly lost her hold on the bottom stick. She breathed inward, tears causing her mascara to run in dark rivulets down her cheeks, gained control, and fulfilled her task. There were two pieces of bone remaining when Josef removed the sticks from his mother's hand.

He could feel the eyes of everyone present, concentrating upon him, holding him steady. Like a player on a stage.

Josef Tanaka performed well. Even Ando Akio admired the dexterity with which the tall half-caste handled the last and smallest pieces of bone. Concluding his part of the ritual by capping the urn, lifting it and handing it gently to his father.

Mikio Tanaka placed the urn in a specially prepared box, covered in fine white silk.

Then, carrying the box in his arms, carefully, as if it were the living body of his deceased son, he led the mourners away from the *yakiba*.

Ando Akio bowed as the procession passed. Noticed, from the corner of his eye, that Josef Tanaka had remained behind, lingered on the perimeter of the patio. *Why?* the cremator wondered. *Has something displeased him?*

Car doors were closing and the driver of the Tanaka family limousine was standing outside the car, his face anxious, looking toward Josef, who was walking resolutely in the direction of Ando Akio.

The cremator stood, face flushed, awaiting him. He ran through the ceremony in his mind. Surely everything had gone properly. The bones had been the right size, not too few, not too many. The silk which covered the resting box had been of first quality, the urn was fine porcelain. All etiquette had been observed.

He lowered his head as Josef approached. His heart beat loud, pulsing against his ear drums.

'Akio-san.' There was an unexpected kindness to Tanaka's tone.

The cremator looked up, submissively.

'The ceremony was perfect. Conducted with great dignity. Thank you, Akio-san,'

The cremator bowed, his heartbeat receding.

'Thank you, Tanaka-san, thank you. It was, for me, a magnificent honor to serve you and your family. Thank you, Tanaka-san.' Akio bowed three times as he spoke, once on each 'thank you'.

Tanaka returned the last bow.

'And the body, Akio-san. Prepared beautifully. After such terrible injuries. Who may I thank for such art?'

Ando Akio looked again into Josef Tanaka's eyes. Strange eyes. Straight, like Western eyes. Yet with an Oriental soul. Far away, impenetrable, demanding.

Akio had been cautioned. 'Say nothing about the body. Discuss it with no one.' And now he was trapped.

But this man knows already. Knows about the injuries. And this man is Mikio Tanaka's son, the brother of the deceased. He reasoned with himself.

Josef Tanaka stood, waiting for Akio's answer. Behind him, the limousines had filled, the mourners ready to begin their convoy back to the Tanaka home. To witness Mikio Tanaka place his son's ashes on a shrine in the center of his reception room, where they would stay for the forty-nine days until the burial.

They could not begin their journey until Josef joined the immediate family in the lead car. And Josef was not moving.

Ando Akio cleared his throat. When he spoke, his voice was just above a whisper. 'Mas Kadama, Tanaka-san. My partner, Mas Kadama, prepared your brother's body.'

'Where?' Tanaka asked.

'We have offices in Ikebukuro.'

'Thank you, Akio-san,' Tanaka answered, bowing before he turned and walked briskly to the black limousine.

He held himself together during the drive back to the family home, then nearly exploded during the ritual placement of the urn containing the ashes. Suddenly it was all a sham, an orchestrated charade and Josef could not decipher the difference between the players and the audience.

He excused himself following the service, said he needed time alone and asked one of the family chauffeurs to take him back to Gotanda.

From there Josef hailed a cab, instructing the driver to go north to Ikebukuro.

The best shabu in Tokyo

They drove past the Tokyo Dome, a glass-topped, astro-turfed arena and home of the baseball team, the Yomiuri Giants, and into the 'new town' of Ikebukuro. An entire district overlooked by a single building, the NHK skyscraper which houses the Japanese Broadcasting Corporation, and stands surrounded by a small concentration of office blocks.

Josef asked to be dropped off on the sidewalk at the base of the building.

Akio, Kadama, Inc was easy to find. A large black and white sign hung above the glass-fronted office. A receptionist looked up from her phone call as Josef entered.

'Please. I have come to see Mas Kadama-san.'

The secretary smiled, nodded, and finished her business on the telephone. She had begun to leaf through her appointment book when Tanaka said, 'My name is Tanaka. Josef Tanaka. I have no appointment.'

'I am sorry, sir, but—'

'Mr Akio has just cremated my older brother; I have come to pay my family's respects to Mr Kadama,' Josef continued.

The small, dark woman looked puzzled.

'For the fine work that Kadama-san performed on my brother.'

'I understand, sir,' she answered, picking up the phone.

Within seconds of hearing the name Tanaka, Mas Kadama walked from his office.

He was a short man, even by Japanese standards, and

heavy set, perhaps ten years older than Akio, his partner. He bowed ceremoniously.

'Tanaka-san, it is with great honor that we receive your visit.'

Tanaka returned Kadama's bow.

'Perhaps you would extend the honor to joining me in my office,' Kadama continued, stepping aside to allow Josef access to the open door.

Josef stepped into a Western-style office, complete with wrap-round walnut-veneered desk, leather-upholstered sofa and twin guest chairs. The only thing Japanese in the twenty-foot square room was the set of mortician's certificates which adorned the beige-papered wall.

Josef remained standing as Kadama shut the heavy wooden door.

'Please, Tanaka-san, sit down. Enjoy my new furniture; it arrived only last week. From Harrods department store, London, England.'

Tanaka sat on the sofa. The smell of new leather permeated the room.

Mas Kadama sat imperiously in the swivel chair behind his new desk. Tanaka could not see if his feet actually reached the ground.

Josef began politely. 'Kadama-san, you and I are in a similar business. I also work with the bodies of the deceased. Occasionally, my profession involves reconstructive procedures, following violent death.'

He noticed Kadama's small deep-set eyes narrow as his right hand tightened on a silver Mont Blanc pen.

'I am a medical doctor with the American department of health. We are affiliated with the police department.'

Kadama laid the pen down and held his hands together, as if in prayer. He began nodding, his mouth tightening.

'I would like to ask you a few questions regarding the work you performed on my brother.'

Kadama stopped nodding.

'What exactly was the extent of his injuries?'

Mas Kadama remained silent. He had known that Josef Tanaka would be coming. Ando Akio had warned him. Still, he was unprepared for the manner of the man, so direct, so American.

The mortician braced himself and began to lie. 'Nothing much out of the ordinary, Tanaka-san, a few minor abrasions below the left eye . . . from falling forward—'

'Falling forward?'

'Yes, Tanaka-san, in his wheelchair.'

'I was told my brother died in his sleep.'

Kadama held Josef's eyes, searching for a way out. There was no avenue of escape, but he tried anyway. 'Perhaps he was asleep when he fell, Tanaka-san.'

Tanaka nodded. 'I see. A fall from a chair. Perhaps three feet to the floor. Pitching forward.'

'*Hai*, Tanaka-san, *hai*,' Kadama confirmed.

'And that accounts for your need to have reconstructed his entire skull?'

Kadama sat mute.

'To have rebuilt his face?' Tanaka was not going to let go.

Kadama tried again. 'Because of his condition, Tanaka-san, he would not have been able to raise his arms to soften his impact.'

Tanaka listened patiently, leaning forward. Now it was his turn to lie.

'Naturally, we have affiliations with the Japanese National Police. We are considering an international investigation into my brother's death. The investigation could begin here, with your business. That could be long, detailed, and very embarrassing. I am trying to help you save face, Kadama-san.'

Kadama inhaled long and deep, thinking of the million yen he had concealed in last year's tax, the mistress he was keeping in the Ginza district, the ten vials of liquidized 'awakening powder' stashed in his office safe. He spoke on the out breath.

'I did as I was told, Tanaka-san. It was not my position to ask questions. I worked as well as I was able, under the circumstances.'

'What were those circumstances?'

Now Mas Kadama thought of the two men who had carried the corpse into his office, their instructions, 'ask nothing about what you are about to see. Make him look good . . . No questions.'

Then the third man, the man who had come this morning, the giant. Kadama stuttered and stalled.

Josef Tanaka was on his feet, leaning across the desk top, towering above the mortician. Kadama had not even seen him stand up. He was just there, his eyes spitting fire.

'Talk to me, Kadama-san.'

'Your brother's head was no more than pulp when his body arrived in my office,' Kadama began.

Tanaka stared at him, his eyes continued to threaten.

'The reconstruction was the best I could do. Please forgive my clumsiness, please forgive me, Tanaka-san,' Kadama groveled.

Tanaka backed off, remained standing. 'What happened to my brother?'

Mas Kadama had begun to sweat. He could feel the dampness right through his cashmere socks, probably staining the insides of his new Gucci loafers.

'I do not know, Tanaka-san. That I swear to you. His injuries were severe. Very severe. His head crushed completely.'

'Had he been beaten?' Tanaka pushed.

Silence.

Tanaka moved closer. 'Had my brother been beaten?'

Kadama's stomach had begun to feel upset and he needed to urinate. His resistance was gone.

'I thought so at first. His jaw was broken and his left cheekbone crushed. But there was very little impact bruising to the skin of his face. No wounding to his body. It was his skull, it was—' Kadama hesitated, his features pinched as he remembered. Certain moments in his professional career would remain with him forever, imprinted on his memory. The image of Hironori Tanaka, as the hood was lifted from the remains of his head, was one of them.

'His skull was—' he suddenly thought of the first thing that had come to his mind when he saw the head of the corpse, *like a piece of rotten fruit, a melon or gourd, crushed and dripping* – hardly a medical analogy.

He cleared his throat, then completed his sentence, 'Compressed. Caved inwards ... not the work of fists or a bludgeon.'

'And not the type of injury consistent with a fall?' Tanaka asked.

Kadama shook his head. 'No fall could have caused such trauma.' Then he raised both his hands, resting his fingertips on the shiny surface of his greased black hair, a palm's width above his ears. He pushed inward.

'His coronal suture had given way evenly, collapsed. As if his cranium had been gripped in a vice. A very powerful vice.'

'And still you certified that my brother's death was caused by a fall from a wheelchair? Why?'

'Tanaka-san. I did as I was told.'

'Told ... Told by whom?' Josef let the fury creep back into his voice, forcing Mas Kadama to cross the final line.

'By Mikio Tanaka. Your father ...'

Mas Kadama watched as Josef walked from his office, out into the humid afternoon. The sweat was already cooling on the mortician's brow when he returned to his office, locked his door and dialed the combination to his wall safe.

He removed a plastic-wrapped syringe and one glass vial of the *shabu*, the liquid methamphetamine. Unwrapped the syringe and popped the needle through the rubber cap of the vial.

He was an old hand at the *shabu* and needle. A habit he'd acquired while driving a cab to pay his way through university.

Kadama sat down at his desk and removed his right shoe and sock. He preferred injecting between his big and second toe; it was discreet, no marks on his arms.

He drove the half-inch needle inward.

'Best *shabu* in Tokyo. Made from white diamonds.' That's how the giant had described it when he laid the ten pharmaceutical containers on Kadama's desk.

He depressed the plunger slowly.

'When the half-caste comes, asking questions, you say nothing about the others, understand?' The giant had demanded.

Kadama felt the hot, precious liquid enter his blood stream.

'After he leaves I will have another "gift" delivered to you.'

The tube of the syringe was three quarters empty when the mortician's stomach tightened, an involuntary reaction.

'Best *shabu* in Tokyo.' He repeated the promise to himself; it coincided with the next small convulsion. 'It must be strong. Very strong.'

He began to feel the flood of confidence as his nerve endings came alive.

Of course Hironori Tanaka had been murdered. Tortured and murdered. In the same way that the Taoka boy had been murdered, and the Yamamoto heir before him. Sons of Japanese industrialists; Mas Kadama had worked on them too. Received 'gifts' for his silence. He was privy to something big here. Something important. He could feel it.

Something worth far more than ten or twenty grams of *shabu*.

He was contemplating just how much more, when he squeezed the last drop into his body.

A second later the strychnine-laced methedrine reached his heart, causing it to freeze in mid-beat before it caught and restarted.

Mas Kadama reared back against his chair.

'Oh sweet Buddha, they have poisoned me. I am dying.'

He managed to pull the syringe free before the second attack. This time his heart exploded. His face had just begun to turn blue when he pitched forward, breaking his nose against the polished veneer of his new desk.

II   Behind the Mask

Faded sun

Josef arrived in Den-en-Chofu at ten o'clock, instructed the driver to wait, and walked to the front door of his family's home. The house servant answered and informed him that his father and mother had retired for the evening.

Josef walked past the man and into the house. The white porcelain urn containing Hironori's ashes sat on a long wooden table in the far corner of the main room.

'Please tell my father that I am here and that I insist upon seeing him,' Josef said.

'But, Tanaka-san, your father gave strict orders that he and Mrs Tanaka should not be disturbed. No visitors, no phone calls. The past week has exhausted them and—'

'Shall I go to their room myself?' Josef threatened. He began to walk toward the staircase.

'No, sir, please.' The house servant insisted.

'It is all right, Tameo-san . . .' Mikio Tanaka's voice came from the top of the stairs. 'Please,' the elder Tanaka continued, walking down from the landing, 'my son and I will require privacy.'

The house servant was gone before Mikio Tanaka arrived in the main room.

Josef's father wore a heavy black cotton kimono, tied tight at the waist with a black sash. The family insignia, a Samurai crest which dated back to the sixteenth century, was embroidered in red and gold silk thread on the left breast of the robe, just above Mikio Tanaka's heart. It was the profile of a cat's head, a wild mountain cat, silhouetted in gold against the faded red of the rising sun.

He stood barefoot in the dim yellow light of a single lamp, his shoulders squared and broad and his hair shining black. His demeanor suggested a warrior ready for battle; the signs of age, which his son had perceived as vulnerability, had vanished.

For a moment, all the insecurities of youth revisited Josef; he was a child again, quaking in his father's presence.

'I am sorry to disturb you—' he hated the weakness of his own voice, 'but it is time we talked.'

'Yes, Josef-san, yes,' Mikio Tanaka answered, walking forward. 'I have been expecting your visit.'

Josef was caught by surprise. 'Expecting my visit?'

'Many things to discuss, Josef-san, concerning our family business. You are my only son, Josef, my only child. While you are here, in Japan, we must arrange meetings with our company lawyers, accountants. It is my duty to make you aware of the extent of our holdings and enterprises. You are soon to marry and—'

'Father, I am here to talk about Hironori, my brother.'

Mikio Tanaka seemed to deflate. His face fell and he slumped forward. Finding the armrest of the high-backed Regency chair, he sat down.

'It is still too early for me to discuss such matters. The wounding is too fresh in my heart,' he said.

'Why has the truth been withheld from me, Father?' Josef continued. He felt as though he were attacking a fallen man, an uncomfortable feeling.

Mikio looked up, a question in his eyes.

'My brother did not die in his sleep. I know that, Father.'

'Leave it alone, Josef,' Mikio warned.

'Leave what alone, Father?'

'Your brother died of natural causes. That is all you need to know . . .' Mikio was firming up.

'Father. That is a lie.'

'A lie! A lie!' Mikio boomed, standing up to face his son. 'You accuse me of deceit?'

Josef remained calm. 'My brother's head was crushed, the bones of his face broken—'

'A fall. Hironori fell from his wheelchair.' Mikio insisted, but there was desperation in his tone.

'Why, Father? Why are you doing this?'

Mikio Tanaka hesitated, his eyes locked onto the eyes of his son. Finally he answered.

'For the safety of my family. For you and for your mother.'

'What happened, Father? Talk to me. I can help.'

'You want to help?' Mikio asked.

'Of course I do.'

'Then take the next flight to the United States of America.'

'That is not the answer I am waiting for, Father.'

Mikio Tanaka reached out, touched Josef lightly on the cheek.

'Fifteen years ago, I blamed you for taking my elder son from me. Hated you. Cursed the day you were born.' His voice was trembling.

'That seems like another lifetime,' Mikio continued, 'I was a fool, locked inside my own ego, my own vanities. The passing time has stripped me of such notions. Laid me bare ... Do you know how often I have thought of you in these past years? Secretly begged your forgiveness?'

Josef stood silent, shaking his head.

'With your brother it was different. There was no question of looking back, of blaming or forgiving.' Mikio continued, 'Many times I would enter his room as he worked, just to sit quietly, listening to the bristles of his brush touch against the paper, inhaling the faint aroma of the ink. And Hironori knew, yet he never turned or spoke. As if he knew why I had come. Searching for something that was there, in that room . . . Hironori had found peace.'

'What happened to him, Father?' Josef asked again, this time softly.

'They took him from us, Josef,' Mikio answered. His hand had fallen from Josef's cheek and rested gently on his shoulder. He had begun to cry.

It was a sight that Josef could never have imagined, yet there was no weakness in his father's tears; they seemed, instead, to give him strength.

'I am pleading with you, for myself and for your mother . . . Go back to America. Allow me to resolve this matter. You can do nothing here. You are in danger, Josef.'

'From whom?'

'I do not know,' Mikio answered. 'Believe me, I do not know.'

'Are you being blackmailed?'

Mikio dropped his hand from Josef's shoulder. His face hardened. 'I am unable to speak about my situation.'

'But it involves me, Father. It is my right—'

'It is my duty to protect my family,' Mikio answered.

'You have informed the police. Surely . . .' Josef said.

Mikio nodded, yes, his lips sealed tight.

'Is this some kind of extortion, your business, your holdings? Yakuza?'

'Josef, I have asked you. Please return to America.'

'Father, thirteen years ago I honored that request, even though, then, you did not voice it. I fled to America because I could not face my life in Japan. Because I could not face my brother, or you. Because I could not bear the weight of my own guilt. I was under the misconception that I could leave it here; the bitterness and the memories. But it followed me, dogged every part of my life.'

'This is not the same, Josef. Believe me,' Mikio promised.

'For me it would be the same. Running away.'

'I am begging you,' Mikio pleaded.

'And I am begging you to share this with me.'

They stood, eye to eye, father and son, both reminded of the wall that had separated them, yet neither willing to rescind his stance.

Finally, Josef turned and walked from the room, leaving the door of the house open as he headed towards the waiting cab.

Rachel Saunders had been alone the entire day. She had gone out in the afternoon, held a piece of paper with 'GINZA' written on it in front of the chauffeur's face and sat back in the Mercedes as the man navigated a sea of automobiles to deposit her into a sea of people.

She didn't last long in the Ginza. Alone, without Josef, she felt incredibly vulnerable. People did stare and she was painfully aware that she was the only lone female, let alone *gaijin* female, on the street.

She ended up in Matsuzakaya, a large Westernized department store, rifling through a rack of Chanel scarves with no particular focus as to what she wanted or what she was actually doing there. The only thing that struck her was the price, a scarf that she could buy in Philadelphia for two hundred and fifty dollars was marked at seventy-five thousand yen. Divided by a hundred, that made the scarf seven hundred and fifty dollars. An impossible figure. *How do these people afford to live like this?* she wondered, turning to meet the stares of a circle of older women who had gathered at the lingerie counter.

Rachel Saunders was a fighter and she was determined not to be intimidated. When the sales woman finally approached her, Rachel turned with such ferocity that the tiny woman froze in her tracks. Rachel felt a total fool, apologizing in English as she backed out of the ladies department.

There was nothing she wanted anyway, nothing she

actually needed, except Josef. And that realization angered her more than any of the others, as if she couldn't cope in this strange place without a guide and interpreter.

On her way back to the car she made a point of meeting the stares of the men and women who seemed so obsessed with studying her. Without exception, each of them lowered their eyes, and averted their faces. Rachel was winning but it was an uncomfortable victory, and one she did not really understand.

She arrived back at Ken Sato's apartment at three o'clock in the afternoon, starving hungry. Ken had showed her his kitchen, instructed her in the use of the stove and cooker and pointed out the switch that operated the ventilator fan; he had even given her a quick course in the boiling, chilling and dipping of the cold noodle, a mainstay in the Japanese diet. Followed by a demonstration of 'slurping' the entire bowl of *soba* in under a minute.

So Rachel dined on cold noodles and soy sauce-flavored soup. It gave her a degree of satisfaction to prepare the food and feed herself, at least she could do that much independently. And when it came to slurping, in the privacy of Ken Sato's kitchen, Rachel Saunders could slurp with the best of them.

Then she bathed, avoiding the shower cubicle in favor of the bath tub. Cleaning everything thoroughly when she had finished, much more precisely than she would have done in her own home; there was something about the sterility and order of Ken Sato's apartment that forced a type of respect, competitive in nature, as if she were defying Josef's cousin to find fault in her physical habits.

By eight o'clock she began to wonder where Josef was, grateful that after today she would again be part of his life; she had felt very much the outsider recently, and she could accept that only because her condition was temporary.

*

It was past eleven when the door to the apartment opened; she knew Josef's footsteps, markedly heavier than cousin Ken's. She listened as he walked the corridor toward her room, surprised when he stopped at his own and went inside. She waited, thinking perhaps he was removing his clothes, replacing them with a silk robe before he came to visit her. Twenty minutes later and nothing but silence emanated from the walls of Ken Sato's apartment.

Rachel got up and slipped into her robe.

The partition to his room was open and Josef was sitting on the side of the futon, holding his head in his hands; Rachel thought he might be crying and was about to turn and go when he looked up.

'You've got to go back to Philadelphia,' Josef said. His eyes were dry and his voice was cold and dead.

Rachel stood shaking her head. 'I don't understand,' she said.

'I want you to go home,' he ordered.

She almost snapped, right there and then. It was only the realization of the strain that Josef was under that held her back.

'Talk to me, Josef, please talk to me,' she whispered, walking towards him.

He wanted to, he really did. At least that's what he told himself. But he was protecting her, the same way that his father was trying to protect him. Another voice said that this was family business and Rachel Saunders was not 'family'. He looked up, at her halo of blonde hair, into her blue eyes.

'You don't belong here, Rachel.'

His words hurt her, in a deep and private place, like a betrayal of some inviolable trust.

She stared down. Wasn't this the Josef who had seen her at her most vulnerable, naked and twisted and at the mercy of a psychotic animal, a freak? Then, again, reliving her memory, writhing in agony on the padded floor of a cell in the psychiatric unit of a hospital? It didn't get any more intimate or honest than that, or more raw. And now this same man was denying her access to his grief. As if it were his private territory. Dismissing her with the words, 'you don't belong here'.

'And where do you belong, Josef? Where do you belong?' she asked, the color of anger beneath the softness of her voice.

'With my family, Rachel,' he answered.

She felt like hitting him, reaching out and smacking his face. She could feel her body tense, her stomach tighten; she wanted to hurt him, like he was hurting her. Instead she turned and ran from the room. Out of the door and into Ken Sato, dressed in a silk robe, coming from his bathroom, steam drifting from the open door.

They took each other by surprise, nearly colliding. Their eyes met and locked.

It happened then; the monster swam upward from the deepest waters of her soul. Exploding to the surface. Piercing eyes, yellowed skin.

Rachel stumbled.

Ken Sato reached out to prevent her fall.

Mantis hands coming forward, stubbed fingers and clawed nails; she could smell his breath, the sweet sweat of his body.

Rachel screamed and struck out with her hands.

Ken easily side-stepped and wrapped her with one arm, holding her—

Like the grip of a vice, he was going to force her to her knees, roll her forward, twist her body, expose her private parts, pry them open—

'No! No!' she screamed.

'Let me have her, Ken, let me have her!' It was Josef's voice, excited, shouting. Then it was Josef's hands upon her.

She knew Josef's hands. Picking her up, carrying her.

'Breathe, Rachel, breathe deep, count the beat of the breaths, concentrate on the breath. That's right ... One, two, three, exhale. I'm here. I'm here. Josef's here.'

Until she was in bed and Josef was with her, kissing her forehead, holding her to him. It was Josef, the Josef she knew, trusted. The only barrier between Rachel Saunders and the creature ... She had seen him again, smelled him, sensed him ... Twice now since she had been here ... twice ... Two attacks in one week ... More than she had had in the past seven months ... more severe ... more 'real'...

She fell asleep with Josef holding her; awakening only once, two hours later. She could hear voices, purposely soft, speaking Japanese. Josef's voice, and Ken Sato's. Talking. Very serious tones, very serious ... Then she drifted off again.

She woke up, seven hours later, remarkably refreshed, relieved. It was always that way, following an attack. Like a poison had been purged from her system, leaving her pure.

Josef was dressed and seated beside her on the futon. He had a cup of green tea in his hands. He offered her the cup.

The tea tasted slightly bitter but not unpleasant and the caffeine hit her instantly.

'How are you feeling?' Josef asked. His voice was soft, concerned.

'Embarrassed ... How would you feel?'

Josef exhaled and smiled.

'I totally freaked out in front of your cousin, didn't I? ... What did you say to him?'

'Not much,' Josef answered, knowing that wasn't enough. 'I said you hadn't been feeling well,' he added. He knew that still wasn't enough.

'Listen, Rachel, Ken Sato is part of my family. I've known him since we were boys. I don't have to explain anything to my cousin Ken and he's not going to ask. So relax, forget it.'

'At least he won't be "threatened" by me anymore,' she said, sitting up to hand Josef the empty tea cup.

He smiled again. 'Don't be too sure of that, I think you caught him with a nice finger-jab in the eye.'

And suddenly it was the old Josef, relaxed and self-assured. Seeing him that way brought back a flash of memory, of being together, making love.

Rachel reached up and took hold of his free hand, guiding it down, beneath the heavy quilt, placing it between her legs.

'I've missed you,' she whispered.

She hadn't shaved the top of her thighs in months, as if by ignoring it she could deny her sexuality, her femininity. Block out the part of her that had been violated.

Her pubic hair, long, fine, and blond, was silken soft to his touch. And wet, she was very wet.

He allowed his hand to linger, lightly and without motion. Felt his own excitement, closed his eyes, allowing the sensation to linger.

Then he trembled slightly, as if he were awakening. His fingers tightened and he withdrew his hand.

Rachel remained quiet, waiting for him to speak. When he did his voice had changed again, the tension she had perceived through his fingers had reentered his tone.

'My mother called for you this morning. She wants to take you to lunch.'

Rachel met his eyes.

'Afterwards, we'll talk about getting you back to Phila-delphia,' he said.

She was about to protest when he shook his head sharply. 'There is a reason, Rachel, believe me there is a reason.'

'What is the reason?'

'Later, we'll talk later.'

Then Josef got up from the futon and walked from the room.

Rachel listened to his footsteps as he walked down the hallway and towards the front door. And, at that moment, she felt betrayed by him. Abandoned. She hated him.

They took him from us. The words repeated in his mind as Josef left the apartment. The image of his father, tears streaming down his face, filled him. In spite of his strength, Mikio Tanaka had appeared helpless. Helpless and alone. *They took him from us . . .*

'They', his father had said. 'They'. Who were 'they'?

Dominance

The bath house was small, private. A white-pillared room with a high arched ceiling. Quiet and peaceful. Just the lazy sound of water dripping from a soapy sponge onto the tiled floor.

The lights were dim and there were two people in the washing area, both men and both naked. There was a marked physical contrast between the two men; one was hard and angular while the other, taller and darker in skin tone, was heavy, almost fat. Thickly muscled, the pectoralis region of his chest so developed and bulky that his breasts hung like a woman's tits.

The larger man, the man with the tits, held a sponge which he dipped into an open container of soapy water before applying it to the back and shoulders of the light-skinned man. He moved the sponge in a circular motion, working downward along the line of his partner's spine and into the small of his back, before squatting on his elephantine haunches, a position which enabled him to guide his sponge between the cheeks of the lighter man's buttocks, then up beneath his scrotum. Lingering only a moment before traveling the length of his hard, lean thighs, over his well-developed calves and onto the tops of his feet.

Then, the larger man squeezed the sponge, dipped it again into the soapy water and repeated the process, this time concentrating more on the area between his partner's thighs. A caress this time, obvious in its intent to promote sexual arousal.

There was no coyness or embarrassment between the two men, simply a sureness of an act they had performed many times.

Then the recipient of the sponge spread his legs, bending slightly at the knees, permitting greater access to his tight scrotum and erect penis. No groaning or heavy breathing, nothing that would ordinarily have been associated with a sexual act; this was something else, an act of dominance.

By the time the sponge had been squeezed and placed again in the porcelain bowl, the tall man had walked to the *furo*, a submerged tub of clear, steaming water.

His penis remained erect as he settled into the steam, sitting so low in the large bath that only his head was visible above the water line.

The heavy man began to apply the sponge to his own body, particularly to the area of his rectum; he worked the suds into a thick lather, completely covering the short, coiled black hairs that grew from his buttocks and inner thighs. Keeping an eye on the man in the bath, waiting for what, to him, still seemed a miracle.

The first time he had witnessed the 'transformation' was eleven years ago, in this same bath house. He had been seventeen years old and a virgin, fresh from the country prefecture of Aomori, on the far northern coast of Japan.

And now, after all this time, he was still in awe of the creature that rose from the steaming water. Awed and frightened; it was his fear of the unknown. For in the passage of years he had been permitted access to the man, never the creature.

Walking slowly toward him, up the three steps, the Leopard was breathing low and deep, his sure, muscular toes gripping the coarse tiles surrounding the *furo*. His nostrils were flared, his mouth a thin line and his jaw thrust forward. His eyes appeared yellow in the dim overhead light; they did not blink. His skin was flushed red. His face and body, including his scrotum and the length of his penis, were covered with an intricate pattern of markings; pale rosettes of various sizes and shapes, some six-pointed like stars, others rectangular, while others were smaller and circular, joined together to form what appeared to be figure eights against his skin.

The heavy man stared as the Leopard approached, his movement rhythmic, feline. He had the feeling – more like the knowledge of an absolute truth – that this creature could tear the flesh from his body and devour his heart.

It was the creature's will that he felt, entering him. Overpowering and undeniable. It had been this way since their first encounter.

He submitted now as he learned to submit then, with no thought of choice.

Dropping to his knees, bending forward so that his forehead rested in the palms of his hands, breathing deeply to relax the muscles of his sphincter.

He experienced no sexual arousal when the Leopard's sharp incisors bit into the skin at the base of his neck, an instant before the creature's phallus penetrated his posterior, sinewed arms wrapping like steel bands around his waist.

His mind switched off and everything became feeling.

It was a strange experience to give way to another animal, to submit so totally and inextricably to an outside power. Perhaps it was like dying.

The heavy man had felt the same submission in most of his own victims, when their bodies relaxed and their wills dissolved.

In all but one, the cripple. The cripple never gave way, not completely. His will resisted until his dying breath.

The Leopard was moving faster now, biting deeper, tearing, with his fingernails, into the sensitive flesh of his partner's nipples. Rising up on the balls of his feet, adding power and depth to his thrusts. The big man exhaling loudly at the end of each movement, the air forced from his lungs. Controlled by steel arms and sharp teeth, totally dominated.

Even in this base and primitive act, the Leopard was the master.

What homicide?

The Japanese are rightly proud of their superb peace-keeping system. The streets of Tokyo, compared to the streets of major cities in other countries, are safe at all hours of the day and night.

Koban, or small, one-roomed police offices, exist on most street corners throughout all Japanese cities and towns, and the officers who man them are, at all times, available to the public.

The Central Station of the Tokyo Municipal Police is headquarters to both the City and the National Police. It is a large, concrete building, eighteen stories high, located in front of the Imperial Palace, in the center of Tokyo.

Josef arrived at the main desk of the central station at ten-thirty in the morning. He gave his name and requested to speak to Mr Norikazu Ohtsuka, Head of Criminal Investigations. When there seemed a hesitancy on the part of the desk officer in charge, Josef mentioned the name Gichin Yamashito.

Yamashito had been Tokyo's Chief of Police for twenty years, until his retirement in 1990. He was also a personal friend of Ken Sato.

That morning, when Josef told Ken Sato that he had some police business to resolve while in Tokyo, his cousin had not asked any questions, simply suggested that Yamashito might be of help. He was.

Josef was sitting in Ohtsuka's office within five minutes.

107

The chief inspector had broad shoulders and a thick neck. His hair had gone at the forehead and crown, leaving only the sides which had been shaved smooth.

Josef estimated Ohtsuka to be in his mid-forties, although with his bald head it was difficult to tell; he could have been younger, closer to Josef's age.

The inspector asked Josef how he had come to know Gichin Yamashito, then nodded as Josef explained that his contact came through Ken Sato, his cousin.

Yes, Ohtsuka knew of Ken Sato, through the dojo. And although his own preference was judo, their training halls were next door to each other.

'One of our finest with the *katana*. I have seen him give two demonstrations. Fast, and his technique is near perfection ... Although I have never had the pleasure of meeting him,' Ohtsuka enthused.

'A fine swordsman,' Josef agreed.

'With many friends on the police force,' Ohtsuka acknowledged.

These pleasantries extended, the inspector got down to business.

'And how may I be of service to you, Tanaka-san?'

Josef came right to the point.

'I have come to discuss a homicide investigation.'

Ohtsuka looked puzzled.

'My older brother, Hironori Tanaka. Murdered on the sixteenth of August.'

'Your brother, a homicide?'

Tanaka sat still. The chief inspector appeared genuinely shocked.

'That is impossible,' Ohtsuka stammered.

Tanaka waited for the man to continue.

'I am familiar with your family, Tanaka-san. Your father is, of course, one of our country's leading industrialists. I know that his older son was recently cremated. I know this because I read the papers. But a homicide? Certainly there was no homicide.'

'My older brother was murdered, Ohtsuka-san,' Josef insisted.

Ohtsuka picked up his phone and pressed one of the seven amber buttons.

Josef listened as the inspector asked for a Mr Miyuki Hashimoto, waited for the man to come to the phone, then questioned him respectfully with regard to any existing files on the subject of a homicide in the Tanaka family. Their conversation was brief and Josef had the uneasy impression that Ohtsuka was covering at his end for whatever was being said.

'I am sorry, Tanaka-san,' the inspector said as he put down the phone, 'there is no record of any crime involving your family. No file, no case.'

Josef looked at the policeman. Perceived the hardening in his eyes. Wondered what exactly had been said during the brief phone call.

'Is there anything else I can do for you?' Ohtsuka asked. His tone remained cordial but the same hardness that Josef saw in the inspector's eyes now underlined his words. Ohtsuka rose behind his desk.

Josef understood that their meeting was over.

You could tell me what the hell is going on, he thought. Perhaps, in America, he would have demanded the answer, pushed until he got it. But this was Japan, the land of two faces; one public, one private. Secrecy and discretion were an art form here. He would get no further with Ohtsuka. Nothing he could do would penetrate the inspector's veneer.

'Ohtsuka-san, you have been very courteous. I thank you for your time,' Tanaka said, bowed and left Ohtsuka's office.

He took the elevator to the ground floor of the building, stopping in the main entrance hall to check the alphabetical list of names beneath the heading 'Tokyo Police Department'. Miyuki Hashimoto's name was not listed.

Josef went to the reception desk. The duty officer remembered him, no doubt for his connection with the former chief of police. The man seemed anxious to please.

'Would you please tell me in which section Mr Hashimoto is employed?'

There was no hesitation in the man's answer. 'Hashimoto-san is the superintendent general of our National Police, sir.'

'And would Mr Hashimoto be involved in a local murder investigation?'

'Never, sir. Unless the incident had relevance to national security. Inspector Ohtsuka-san is in charge of all criminal investigations in Tokyo.'

Tanaka thanked the man and walked from the building.

It was quarter past eleven and already the pavement was crowded with office workers. In another half-hour there would be two hundred thousand people milling in this four-mile square area. Standing in line to buy their *bento*, or boxed lunches. 'Buy in the morning, peace of mind at lunch' was a popular slogan for the *bento* shops. Most of them bought at lunch anyway, pickles and chicken, sushi and salad.

The streets were as congested as the sidewalks and the ride to Ken Sato's apartment took nearly ninety minutes.

The peaceful and austere Shinto shrine greeted Josef as he removed his shoes. His cousin's place really was a sanctuary.

He walked to Rachel's bedroom, expecting to find her, then remembered his mother's invitation for lunch. He sat down on the futon. Breathing in, he could smell Rachel's perfume in the air.

You may need a friend over there, Josef, and Rachel is the best friend you've got. He remembered Bill Fogarty's words.

Rachel Saunders and Grace Tanaka sat at a side table in the dimly lit dining room of the Chagne Restaurant, surrounded by silver tureens, long-stemmed glasses filled with champagne, and Samurai in Western suits.

'It's all male, male, male, on the surface, but if you look around this room, at all these macho executives eating their two-hundred-dollar lunches, I guarantee there is not one of them who doesn't give his wife his entire pay check at the end of every week and isn't paying for his *coq au vin* on his allowance ...' Grace Tanaka hesitated, allowing Rachel to sneak a discreet glance at the adjoining table of Japanese Calvin Kleins, 'the allowance the little lady gives him. And the little lady can be pretty tight, so eating at a place like this is a very special occasion. Either that, or they're entertaining clients on the company account.'

'Even Joseph's father?' Rachel asked.

Grace Tanaka laughed. A loud, uninhibited laugh, the kind that caused people to turn and look. She didn't care; she was having a good time. Talking American.

'Oh, he's on a very tight leash ... Old Mikio was a bit of a lady's man in his day. I'm testimony to that, swept me right off my feet, the great Samurai and all. I didn't even know he was married, till it was too late.'

'You met him here, in Japan?'

Grace shook her head. 'Back home in Boston. He was the guest of honor at a banker's dinner. My father owned the bank. Then Mikio stayed on for a month, doing business, or so he said. It turned out I was the business. When he left Boston, I felt like the bottom had dropped out of my life ... All the men I'd been dating seemed so—' she hesitated, looking for the word.

'Undisciplined?' Rachel filled in.

'I forgot. You've been there,' Grace answered. 'When he came back here, he got the fastest divorce in Japanese history and gave away his only son doing it,' she continued, her eyes misting over.

'I don't understand,' Rachel said.

'Divorce is fairly uncommon in Japan, but, when it does happen, it's almost certainly the man who gets custody of the children. Mikio gave Hironori to his ex-wife. He felt that bad about what he was doing.'

'But he did it anyway?'

'Yes, he did it all right, and I did it too.'

It had been over thirty years and Rachel could still see the tinge of guilt in the older woman's eyes.

'I always feel that things like that come back on you,' Grace said, finishing the last of her champagne. 'And they did,' she continued, 'first with Hiro's mother's death and then with the accident . . . and now this.'

Rachel remained silent. Grace looked on the verge of tears.

'We've just got to be equal to it,' Grace concluded, her eyes clearing as they met Rachel's.

Rachel nodded in sympathy. 'My dad used to use that expression; you're the first person I've heard say it since him,' she said softly.

Grace smiled, a stoic smile.

'You seem like a very strong woman, Rachel, it makes me feel good having you here.' Then she reached across and gripped Rachel's hand.

'So why does Josef want me on the next flight to the United States?'

She hadn't meant to say it like that, hadn't meant to say it at all; it just came out.

'What?' Grace Tanaka appeared shocked.

It was just past midnight in Philadelphia, hot and humid.

There was a distinct rattle in the air conditioning unit that was driving Fogarty crazy. He had reported it to the Presidential's maintenance crew a week ago and still no one had been around to repair it.

Can't sleep with that racket. Better to open the window and sweat, he concluded. He was half-way out of bed when the telephone rang.

'Joey? Where you calling from? I can hardly hear you ... Hold on a second.'

Fogarty picked up a shoe from beside his bed and hurled it at the old gray air conditioner. The Floursheim brogue hit the unit in the grille, a good solid shot, causing a thirty-eight caliber bullet to roll off the top and fall to the floor. The rattling stopped and the machine was immediately quiet.

'Just a little mechanical problem,' the lieutenant explained. 'Go ahead, the line's clear.'

He listened as Tanaka went over the events of the past week. If Fogarty hadn't known the doctor he would have written off Tanaka's ramblings as acute paranoia.

'Your brother was *murdered*?'

'Murdered ... And the police are giving me nothing; I think they're covering up. My father's too frightened to talk. All he wants is for me to get the hell out of here.'

'Your father's right,' Fogarty said.

'What?'

'If the police aren't cooperating, you've got nowhere to go,' Fogarty reasoned.

'It is my duty to protect my family,' Josef answered, realizing afterwards that they had been the exact words his father had used when trying to convince him to leave Japan.

Fogarty had been through this before, this Japanese business of duty and honor. It had taken them both to the brink of their friendship. Still, there was someone else to consider.

'I agree with you, Joey, but you've got Rachel over there with you and—' he began.

'That's why I called ... I'm getting Rachel out of here,'
Tanaka answered, 'I'd do it for her safety anyway, but she's
not been too well.'

'What do you mean?'

'The stress disorder. She had an attack last night, pretty
severe ... It scared me, Bill ... I'd like you to keep an eye
on her. Make sure she gets to Stan.'

'Of course I will, Joey, you know that ... But how about
you? Are you sure you know what you're doing?'

'I've got three weeks coming to me. Two of them were
going to be our honeymoon.'

That means the marriage is off, Fogarty thought, saddened. He said nothing.

'And if I can't find the bastard who murdered my brother,
in three weeks, I'll stay longer ... I'll stay as long as it
takes,' Tanaka answered. There was passion in his voice.
Dangerous passion.

'Joey, you're not making sense.'

'I'm making as much sense as I can right now.'

'Joey—'

'I'm not coming back until this is finished. Do you
understand me, Bill? They murdered my brother, crushed his
skull. He was crippled, couldn't defend himself. Do you hear
what I'm saying?'

Fogarty heard all right, and he didn't like any of it. 'Give
me your phone number, the address of where you're staying.
Come on, Josef, I need to know how to reach you.' Fogarty's
voice cut through Tanaka's emotions.

'The phone number, Joey, give me the phone number.'

Tanaka stopped talking, looked down at the phone, read
the numerals to Fogarty then gave him Ken Sato's address.
'It's my cousin's place. He's a friend.'

'How much does Rachel know?'

'Nothing,' Tanaka answered.

'How much are you going to tell her?' Fogarty asked.

'Just enough to get her to leave.'

Then there was a silence. Fogarty wondered if the connection had gone dead.

'Joey? Joey? You still there?'

Tanaka cleared his throat. 'Yes, I'm here, Bill, I'm here.'

'Don't you worry about Rachel, I'll talk to her when she gets back. Call me again when you've got her flight number, and the number of the connecting flight to Philadelphia – I'll need that. I'll meet her at the airport.'

'I don't want her scared, Bill; she's been scared enough.'

'Leave it to me, I'm a master at personal relationships.'

Tanaka laughed. He hadn't laughed in a long time; it was a strange feeling. Then the feeling turned inwards and became a dark, lonely hollow.

'You've been a good friend to me, Bill.'

'We're family, Joey. Don't you forget that,' the lieutenant said.

'I wish you were here,' Josef answered. His voice bounced back on itself, leaving an echo on the line, reminding him of the distance between them. Then he put down the phone and sat quietly, reflecting on the call. He hadn't realized how close he had been to breaking point. How badly he needed an ally. He was vulnerable and wide open.

'Josef-san?' Ken Sato's voice caught him from the doorway.

Josef looked up. At first he wondered how much of the conversation Ken had heard. Then he looked into his cousin's eyes and it no longer mattered.

When the time was right, Ken would help him. Josef knew that; it was understood.

Josef received the telephone call from his mother before Rachel had even arrived back at Ken's apartment.

'What do you mean, you're going to send Rachel home? Why?'

His mother's tone of voice showed her obvious affection for his fiancée and told Josef that Grace Tanaka knew nothing of Hironori's murder; she, like Rachel, was an innocent.

'Josef, this sadness will pass. Believe me it will pass ... I know how you feel now, I've always known how you felt, but your brother was at peace with himself. He knew this had to come. He loved you, Joey, and he wanted you to be happy. More than anything in this world, he wanted you to be happy.'

No time to hit her with his true concerns, no time to panic her, only time to lie, or half lie.

'This has nothing to do with my feelings, Mother, it's about Rachel. I'm worried about her. She's not been well, emotionally. Not since what happened in Philadelphia. I don't think it was a good idea to bring her here.'

'She seems fine to me,' Grace answered.

'It's not like that, Mom, it's not something that she carries on the surface. She's completely functional till she has an attack, then she needs help.' He felt like a traitor as he spoke, but it was the only hook he had.

'Rachel is one of the strongest-willed women I've ever met—'

'You haven't seen her when it happens,' Josef said, cutting her off. 'Now you're just going to have to trust me on this.'

'Josef, the girl came over here to see Japan, to get married, and she has ended up spending a week alone, inside Ken Sato's temple to purity. And now you're talking about shipping her home. That's not a very good way to begin a life-long relationship,' Grace Tanaka said, then held her tongue; she knew she'd pushed it, but she had her own instincts and they all told her that Josef was over-reacting. Projecting his personal guilt and grief onto Rachel Saunders' state of mind. But Rachel was her son's fiancée. And that was that. She swallowed hard before she spoke again.

'I'm very fond of Rachel, Josef . . . I just want what's best for both of you.' Her words were a retreat.

'I know you do, Mother.'

'I love you, son.'

'I love you too.'

The lone ranger

As soon as the JAL 747 got into the air, and the seat belt sign was turned off, Rachel Saunders walked down the aisle to the lavatory.

She went inside, locked the door, and filled the tiny metal sink with hot water. Then she washed her hands, scrubbing them as if she were going into surgery. It was the third time she had washed her hands since arriving at the airport.

She still couldn't get the feel of 'him' off her. That leathery callused texture of his skin, cool and slightly moist, like hard slippery rubber. She told herself it was from the hours that Ken Sato had spent practicing with the sword, the calluses, the roughness.

Maybe she did need to see Stan Leibowitz again. She needed something. It had nearly happened right there at Ken Sato's front door, right there on the mirrored floor in view of his shrine. Another attack. She had felt it coming, the instant their hands locked. This time she controlled it, breathed into the fear and darkness. Allowed the illusion of the Mantis to dissolve into the reality that it was only Josef's cousin who was wishing her goodbye, condescending to a 'Western' handshake in respect of her departure.

Josef hadn't explained anything. In fact he had been downright abrupt, stating that it was a particularly trying time for his family, that he needed to devote his time to them, and that it would be unfair, both to themselves and to his mother and father if he forced the situation. He couldn't consider marriage, not now and certainly not in Japan; he left no room for question or compromise. The only thing for certain was that Rachel was on the next flight to New York. And, by the end of Josef Tanaka's monologue, that was fine with Rachel Saunders.

She washed her hands five more times before the plane touched down in New York. She cleared customs, collected her bags and grabbed the two o'clock shuttle to Philadelphia.

Bill Fogarty looked like the Lone Ranger, standing nervously in the arrival area, arms at his sides like he was about to draw and fire.

Rachel spotted him before he saw her. She was truly touched; Josef had said he would be there but seeing him was reassurance on a grand scale.

'Well, that was the worst fucking experience of my life,' she said as their eyes met.

They both laughed, a spontaneous release of nerves.

They didn't really talk until they were inside Fogarty's Le Mans and wrapping round the circuitry of interconnecting roads leading from the airport to Interstate 95.

'When was the last time you spoke to Josef?' Rachel asked.

'Yesterday, after he took you to the airport, he called me from his cousin's place.'

'And?'

'He sounded a lot better for getting you out of there.'

'Why?'

'He was worried about you, Rachel,' the lieutenant answered.

'Did he tell you that I freaked out in front of his charming cousin?' she asked, turning her head away from Fogarty and staring out the window at the cold, gray Delaware River. She could feel her anger building.

'No, he didn't say anything about that . . .'

Rachel picked up the lieutenant's lie from the quickness of his response.

'Why then, Bill? Was I embarrassing him? In front of his tight-assed cousin Ken and the rest of the Samurai clan ... Did he banish me 'cause I was an embarrassment?'

'It's got nothing to do with that, Rachel.'

'Oh really, well that's not what it felt like ... It felt like he was keeping me locked up inside his cousin's apartment, hiding me. You know, Bill, they really are convinced that they're the master race.'

Rachel kept thinking of Ken Sato as she spoke.

'I don't know who Josef is kidding,' she continued, 'he's not even one of them. Jesus, his mother's more American than I am. And his cousin, now there's one for Stan Leibowitz; the guy's so macho he carries a cock substitute around in a canvas bag ... calls it a sword. Do you know something, Bill. At this particular moment I don't give a shit if I ever see Josef Tanaka or—'

'His brother was murdered.'

Fogarty's statement tore a hole in her anger.

'That's what Joey thinks,' Fogarty continued, 'and that's why he wanted you to come home ... He didn't want you to go through it again.'

The lieutenant's words hit her like a fast, sobering slap to the face.

'What?' she asked, suddenly weak.

'Joey's in a real mess over there; he didn't want you in it with him.'

'Oh, Bill ... Why didn't he say something?'

'What would you have done if he did?' Fogarty asked. It was a variation of the same question that he had been asking himself for two days. If his friend was in a jam, what was he going to do to help?

'I'd have tried to stay with him, given him some support,' Rachel answered, sealing Fogarty's fate.

*

If Rachel Saunders had passed Stan Leibowitz on a center city sidewalk she would probably have mistaken him for a high school English teacher who also coached the state championship wrestling team. He was a mixture of intellect and athlete; he usually wore a cashmere pullover beneath one of half a dozen corduroy jackets, varying in color from navy blue to bottle green, with a pair of Levi 501s and docksiders. He had a full head of steel gray hair and a face without a line, until he smiled, then there were twin spiders' webs under his green eyes. These, and the color of his hair, were the only indication of his fifty years.

He ran twenty miles a week, along the east bank of the Schuylkill, practiced aikido, and lifted weights on Thursday and Sunday mornings at seven sharp. He was obsessive – compulsive by his own diagnosis and believed totally in the harmony of mind and body.

Stan Leibowitz, muscular guru, was a very reassuring man.

'There's not much wrong – I can take one look at you and tell you that. Your eyes are clear, your skin is fresh, your hair is shining,' he said, standing at the door of his Pine Street office, watching Rachel Saunders walk the last ten yards to his front steps.

'Hi, Stan, it's good to see you,' Rachel answered, accepting a friendly hug.

Inside his office, the psychiatrist was more serious.

'I'm listening to you, Rachel, and what I'm hearing is not consistent with your past episodes.'

Rachel sat in the soft highbacked chair in front of Leibowitz's desk. He was the best listener she had ever encountered; he practiced a non-directive therapy, using a technique in which he paraphrased his patients' statements before requesting them to clarify his paraphrased words.

Often, hearing their own statements rephrased led to insight.

'So you are telling me that Josef's cousin, Ken Sato, invited you and Josef to stay in his apartment, then insisted that you had separate bedrooms? Separate?'

'Yes, he put me in a small room at the end of the hall, separating me from Josef,' Rachel replied.

'Cutting you off?'

'Yes.'

'After he had already refused your hand at the airport then separated you from Josef in the car on the way to his apartment?'

Rachel nodded.

'And when you entered Ken Sato's bathroom, you made sure the door was locked because you felt insecure in his apartment. You were not afraid of Josef entering the bathroom but were concerned that Ken Sato might enter?'

'Yes, I didn't want him anywhere near me.'

'You didn't want him touching you with his eyes, his hands—'

'He's repulsive.'

'Describe him to me.'

'Tall for an Oriental, smooth-skin, light-colored skin, almost like a yellowed wax, and clean ... Too clean, like antiseptic clean ...'

'And his hands, you mentioned he grabbed hold of you.'

'He's strong ... As strong as Josef, maybe stronger.'

'And the texture of his skin – you have touched his skin.'

'Tough skin, like hard rubber – ugh!' Rachel winced.

'Who are you describing?' The question was quick, in like a scalpel.

Rachel Saunders sat back in the chair and exhaled.

'Ken Sato,' she answered.

'Strange, sounded very much like Willard Ng to me,' Leibowitz said, using the Mantis's real name.

'You think I've done some sort of transference don't you,

Stan? Laid it all on Josef's cousin.'

'I think you experienced an intense culture shock, became very vulnerable, and understandably paranoid. I also think that by virtue of coming to terms with two of these attacks on your own, particularly under the circumstance of being cut off from Joseph you have made a hell of a lot of progress.'

Rachel stood up. 'Will you do me a favor, Stan?'

Leibowitz cocked his head back, waiting.

'Give Bill Fogarty a call, tell him that I've seen you and that you think I'm all right. No, better than all right ... tell him I'm in great shape. I think Josef has got him convinced he's my legal guardian.'

'My pleasure,' Stan Leibowitz said, standing to offer Rachel his hand, 'and I want to see you again in one week.'

The psychiatrist's hand was warm and dry and there was a quality to his face that she had never really noticed before – an openness. There was nothing concealed behind his eyes. And, for a moment, Rachel thought of Japan; nothing open there, everything was beneath the surface, and she thought of Josef, alone, in a land of masks.

A social blunder

The Park Royal Hotel is located in the Eastern section of Tokyo, next to the Tokyo City Air Terminal. It is a relatively new hotel, high and modern in design. Being on the outskirts of the city, the Park Royal is a convenient, if expensive, stop for international travelers with a one-night stop over, en route to other destinations.

Bill Fogarty was rarely impetuous. At fifty-three and as a lieutenant in the homicide division of a very active police force, being impetuous was synonymous with being dead. There had been a few exceptions. And now, sitting on the swallow-covered quilt of the bed in his thirty-four thousand yen per night hotel room, following a bumpy sixteen and a quarter hours in the air, and a seemingly endless cab ride, during which the Lieutenant's chief concern had been trying to convert the astounding figures that kept mounting on the meter into dollars and cents, and hoping like hell that he had converted enough dollars into yen to pay for it, he wondered if this was one of them.

It had all made such perfect sense two nights ago, or was it three nights ago? He hadn't yet got the time change together. He had been sitting across from Rachel in Bookbinders, discussing Japan, and Josef, and the trouble Josef was in.

Bill Fogarty felt a moral obligation to his friend.

That was the way it was then, over coffee. And that was the way it was the next morning when he stood in front of Captain Tom Trollet, and asked for his three-week holiday to be moved forward.

'Make it an emergency leave, compassionate grounds, if you need to, Tom. I just need the time now. I got nothing on, my caseload is as light as it's been for the last six months. I need the time. Now.'

The trip was going to cost Fogarty about five thousand dollars: thirty-seven hundred for the flight and hotel, and another thousand or so for food and drink. Enough to cause a big dent in his savings account.

Still, he earned forty-nine thousand dollars a year and his overheads were rock bottom; he had to go.

And here he was, in Tokyo.

It felt like the dark side of the moon. More people than he had ever seen in one place in all his life. From the minute he cleared customs and entered the arrival hall at Narita Airport, there were thousands of them, all talking at once and with such speed that he couldn't decipher the separation of words; it sounded as if they simply breathed in and continued speaking until they ran out of breath. Most were very small and they all seemed to eye him inquisitively. Maybe it was the scars on his face, or maybe it was the way they looked at all foreigners. Very innocent but still disconcerting.

He had brought the bare minimum of clothing and a shaving kit. He had forgotten his toothbrush. Walking briskly towards the door with the word TAXIS above it, he had been plagued by the thought that he had forgotten something else as well. Reaching unconsciously inside his tweed jacket he remembered that his five-shot .38 special, his 'snubby', the short-barreled, stainless steel, police issue revolver was left purposely behind, in his gun safe. No wonder he had been self-conscious, he was naked.

Bill Fogarty had not chosen the Park Royal; it was simply that the hotel was part of his two-week excursion package. Along with a Toyota.

He checked his watch, set to Tokyo time an hour before the plane landed. One o'clock in the afternoon. Pushed the button marked 'operator' and asked the English-speaking girl to connect him with 502–2491.

The phone was picked up on the second ring.

'*Hai*.' Crisp and sharp.

Fogarty thought that he may have been connected to the wrong number. Or maybe this was Ken, Josef's cousin, speaking.

'May I have Josef Tanaka please. This is Bill Fogarty.' He almost said, 'from the United States'.

'Bill?' The same voice, but softer and slower.

'Joey?'

'Bill, you sound like you're right next doors. Is everything all right, Rachel all right?'

And suddenly Fogarty was embarrassed. Acutely. What the fuck was he doing here, in Tokyo? Prying into his friend's life? For a second, he considered hanging up and grabbing a plane home.

'Rachel's fine. Absolutely fine ... She's just worried about you.'

Silence.

'Listen, Joey, I'm in the Park Royal Hotel, in Tokyo.'

'What?' No anger, just sheer disbelief.

'I took my vacation early,' Fogarty answered.

There was a hesitation on the line; it sounded as though Tanaka was about to say something and changed his mind.

'When can I see you?' Fogarty asked.

'I'll be there in a couple of hours,' Tanaka answered.

'I'll be waiting,' Fogarty replied, put the phone down and lay back on the hard mattress. The air conditioning was nothing more than a purr and outside, ten floors down, and beyond the Royal's orange brick walls, he could hear the far-away drone of car engines and muted horns. The noise reminded him of something. He closed his eyes. The memory floated to the surface of his mind.

It was Paris. 1971. He and his wife Sarah. They'd stayed at a small hotel on Rue Cambon, the Castille. The elevator had looked like a birdcage and Sarah had been frightened to get inside. Their room was tiny, like a closet. They'd laughed when the porter placed their suitcases on the floor and then had to press himself against the wall to allow them to enter. They had stayed a week, and they grew to love that room; like a womb, a place to escape the bustle of the sidewalks. A place to make love, on the narrow bed with its hard mattress. Just the two of them, listening to the sound of the city through the old plaster walls. Cars and horns. People laughing. Far away. No telephone, nothing to disturb them, as if they existed on an oasis of time. No telephone . . . No telephone.

Then what was that ringing?

Fogarty opened his eyes, rolled onto his side. A call button was blinking and, for a moment, he didn't know where he was. He picked up the receiver.

'Mr Fogarty-san, you have a guest in the lobby. A Mr Josef Tanaka-san.' The male receptionist spoke with a distinct, clipped English.

Fogarty shot a look at his watch. *Two forty-five. Christ, I must have been flat out.*

'Send him up please,' he answered.

An hour, and a quart of coffee later, and Fogarty was sitting across from Tanaka, elbows resting on the top of the teak table, supporting his jaw in the palms of his hands. They had been through the viewing, the funeral and Josef's visit to the undertakers. They were still talking about Mikio Tanaka.

'You're telling me that your father is worth eight hundred million dollars?'

'I don't know what he's worth personally, Bill, but that's the approximate value of Tanaka Industries. I spent yesterday with his accountants. My father is into everything from entertainment to electronics to sports complexes. Right now, they're negotiating a deal to buy two film studios and a cable TV network in the United States. That alone will commit them to a quarter of their net worth, and all of it in America.'

'Why the hell is your father making you privy to all of this?' Fogarty asked.

'Because I am his sole heir. If anything happens to Mikio Tanaka I control seventy percent of Tanaka Industries.'

'And your mother?'

'Taken care of privately, from his personal estate,' Tanaka replied, then added, 'she knows nothing, Bill. As far as my mother is concerned, Hiro died from suffocation, in his sleep.' Josef looked hard at Fogarty, recognizing the doubts and suspicions which crossed the detective's face like shadows.

'I don't want her involved.'

'And who comes after you?'

Tanaka's eyes narrowed, as if he didn't understand the question.

'In Tanaka Industries,' Fogarty said.

'A board of shareholders. Sixteen of them. My cousin, Ken Sato, is the chairman.'

'Ken Sato?'

'I've known him all my life. He's a friend, Bill. Completely trustworthy. Believe me.'

'Ken Sato.' Fogarty repeated the name. Wasn't he the guy who Rachel described as carrying his cock in a canvas bag? The swordsman?

'I'm staying at his apartment. You'll meet him tonight. We're having dinner at the family house, I've told them you're coming.'

The lieutenant nodded slowly, reached for the phone, pressed for room service and ordered another pot of coffee.

'Okay, Joey, let's go over the whole thing one more time.'

Bill Fogarty had expected to see a castle. Eight hundred

million dollars was an inconceivable figure.

What he saw was a large, very substantial home set on an acre of land.

Like something from Merion or Bryn Mawr, one of those rich, middle-class suburban homes along Philadelphia's main line. Not exactly Donald Trump, he thought as Tanaka pulled the Toyota alongside the curb.

What the lieutenant did not understand was the value of property in Japan. A two-room apartment in Den-en-Chofu could cost two million dollars. The Tanaka residence was worth ten times that amount.

His next surprise was Josef's mother. Rachel had described her, but words never match reality. Fogarty knew she was American, from Boston, but being greeted by a beautiful woman who could easily have stepped from the society pages of the *Philadelphia Enquirer* was something else again.

Grace Kelly, she looks like Grace Kelly, he thought as he shook her manicured hand.

'How do you do, Bill?' Grace Tanaka said, welcoming the lieutenant into her living room.

And the furniture. It was Western: fine old, mahogany pieces.

His wife Sarah had been into antiques, dragging him from the expensive shops on Pine Street to the outdoor markets of New Hope. Fogarty knew good English furniture when he saw it, and this was good. Regency, Georgian, the real thing.

'Bill, I'd like you to meet my cousin, Ken Sato.'

Fogarty looked up to see a tall, dark-haired man coming towards him, lean and elegant, shoulders drawn back arrogantly. No canvas bag, at least he wasn't armed.

Ken Sato stopped a body's length in front of the lieutenant and bowed.

Fogarty was reminded of Josef Tanaka in the days before he got to know him. Or like him. Something threatening in the man's bearing, stiff and formal.

Fogarty returned the bow, feeling the hairs on the back of his neck stand on end as he met Ken Sato's eyes. They were the coldest, deadest eyes that Bill Fogarty had ever seen. No wonder Rachel had reacted the way she had to him.

'Ah, Fogarty-san, we finally meet. Welcome to my home. And welcome to Japan,' Mikio Tanaka's voice boomed from the entrance of his study. He walked toward the lieutenant.

For a moment Fogarty was uncertain, to bow or not to bow.

The elder Tanaka extended his hand.

'How do you do, sir?' Fogarty said, accepting the strong grip.

'Your visit is unexpected,' Mikio Tanaka added. There was a certain chill to his tone. Nothing deep, just a veneer to the words.

'I thought the only way we'd ever convince Josef to come home was if I came and got him,' Fogarty answered, smiling.

'Yes. Very true, Fogarty-san. We are pleased to see you.'

The lieutenant had always wondered what Josef's father would be like. And now, in his presence, he understood both Josef's fear and respect for the man.

Mikio Tanaka seemed to glow; his skin was a golden bronze and his hair shining black. Perhaps too black, but then that was all a part of Mikio Tanaka.

The detective had an immediate sense of the man's vanity; he was like an ageing movie star. Exuding charm and charisma. Yet there was more, something solid beneath the gloss. *Samurai.* Josef had always stressed that his father was pure Samurai. A warrior.

'What may I offer you?' The velvet voice bore no trace of accent, neither Japanese nor American, just a fine, schooled English.

Fogarty met Mikio Tanaka's eyes. No defeat in those

eyes. Hardly a man who was bearing the weight of his older son's murder. And for the first time Bill Fogarty questioned Josef's judgement, the validity of his suppositions.

'Josef said you were a whiskey drinker,' Grace Tanaka added. 'How about some Jim Beam, on the rocks?'

'You already know my weakness,' Fogarty answered, smiling. It was a light, throw-away remark but it seemed to grab Ken Sato's attention, causing him to straighten up, square his shoulders.

The lieutenant hooked onto the cold eyes, held them a moment and tried a half-smile. Ken Sato stared straight through him.

Dinner was another surprise. Roast beef and Yorkshire pudding, served with string beans and baked potatoes, eaten with knives and forks.

Bill Fogarty would have been right at home had it not been for cousin Ken.

Sato had been positioned at the far end of the long dining table, directly opposite the lieutenant. He was being catered for separately.

'Western food does not agree with Ken-san,' Grace Tanaka explained as the first dish was placed before the thin man with the veiny hands.

Fogarty viewed its contents from the corner of his eye. Some kind of chicken noodle soup, he surmised, with a couple of shrimps on top.

Then Ken picked up his chopsticks and it began. The noise. Christ, it was the loudest, rudest noise that Fogarty had ever heard at a dinner table. A sloshing, sucking, slurping noise that seemed to intensify whenever the lieutenant tried to make conversation.

Twice he looked across at Ken Sato. The lieutenant couldn't help it, like some perverse fascination. He had never seen food consumed so rapidly, chopsticks moving at a blur as Sato sucked the thick white noodles into his mouth.

It was the only time that Ken Sato smiled at him, between slurps, when his chopsticks were digging through the soya-soaked noodles to locate a morsel of chicken, or fish.

More a leer than a smile, Fogarty diagnosed.

Dinner ended with brandy. Ken Sato refraining.

After the brandy Fogarty was tired.

No, he was beyond tired; he was exhausted. As if his body had secretly, without him noticing, reached the verge of collapse. Suddenly he was feverish, his hands shaking, vision strained, and ears barely able to tune in on the conversation. Ken's slurping had been the final straw in a delayed culture shock. He glanced discreetly at his watch. Twelve fifteen.

He wanted to go back to the Park Royal, lock his door, listen to the far away traffic, and drift away. He nodded once to Josef.

'I've been wondering how long you'd last, Bill. You've been awake three days,' Josef acknowledged.

'God yes, you must be dead,' Grace Tanaka added. 'That trip finishes me for at least a week.'

Josef pushed away from the dining table. 'Will you excuse us? I'm going to get my friend back to his hotel.'

Mikio Tanaka's hand shot out, caught Josef by the sleeve of his jacket. 'No need, Josef, I have a car waiting for Fogarty-san.'

A car, a skateboard, an ambulance. Just let me get to bed, Fogarty thought as he stood up from the table.

Josef walked close to the lieutenant, guiding him toward the front door of the house. Grace, Mikio Tanaka and Ken Sato walked behind. The house servant had already opened the door in preparation for their guest's exit when the detective noticed the finely glazed white porcelain vase sitting by itself on a wooden table in the far corner of the living room. The piece caught Fogarty's eye. Maybe because it was sitting conspicuously on its own upon the table, or maybe because he hadn't noticed it on his way in.

Fogarty was searching for a pleasantry with which to end the evening. Anything to convey to his hosts that he had appreciated their hospitality. A compliment regarding their home and taste. And he knew a bit about porcelain. Sarah had collected it.

He diverted his course and headed for the vase. He was only an arm's reach from it when some instinct kept him from picking it up and holding it, running his fingers along its smooth surface, forcing a compliment about the quality of porcelain, an enquiry about its age and origin.

So tired I'd probably drop it, he told himself. Standing mute, staring at the white vase, many flattering phrases floated through his head but nothing came to his lips.

'My elder son, Mr Fogarty,' Mikio Tanaka said.

Fogarty continued to stare at the vase, confused by his host's statement. Still searching for an appropriate line.

'His ashes,' the elder Tanaka added.

Fogarty's eyes refocused on the white porcelain. He noticed the two pages of Japanese script, positioned on either side of it. Like prayers on an altar.

Jesus Christ, I'm staring at Hiro Tanaka's funeral urn. The revelation caused Fogarty to flush. He stood still a moment, then, barely recovered, he cleared his throat and turned toward Mikio Tanaka.

'I am very sorry, sir. Truly. Very sorry.' His voice sounded distant.

No one spoke. Grace Tanaka paled and Mikio Tanaka appeared suspended in mid-step.

'Thank you, Fogarty-san, it is with honor that we have you in our home,' Mikio Tanaka said finally.

Josef accompanied him to the waiting limousine, had a quick word with the driver to confirm the lieutenant's destination and asked Fogarty to call in the morning, whenever he woke up.

The streets were not signposted and the ride seemed endless. Fogarty wasn't even sure of what type of car he was in, Japanese, German, whatever; the suspension was like rolling waves.

Another few miles and he had drifted off.

Awakened by the screeching of brakes and the shouting of men's voices, he looked up to see the uniformed driver being dragged from the front of the car, thrown to the street and kicked.

He reached for the door handle on the side opposite the action. Locked, he was locked inside. He had begun to scramble over the passenger seat when a man entered the car through the driver's door. He straight-armed Fogarty, sending him backwards. Another man jumped in through the passenger door; the limo spun a circle in the road and took off.

The man on the passenger side turned to face Fogarty. He was almost 'pretty': large eyes, wide cheekbones and a full mouth, sensual, like a woman's mouth, his features embellished by a thick head of black curly hair.

He was on his knees, his right fist raised. Holding something in his hand, a small stick of wood, or bar of metal, dark and polished. He swung the object in a long curving arc. So fast and fluid that Fogarty barely lifted his left arm in defense.

The first blow connected with the tip of his elbow, transmitting pain, like a bolt of electricity, paralyzing the arm.

The second caught him on the side of his throat, digging into the flesh above his caratid artery. Stopping the flow of blood to his brain.

Time stopped.

Until he heard the voices, calm, subdued. Speaking Japanese.

'*Mō ichido.* (Once more.) *Mō ichido soshite kare wa kodomo ga dekinaidaro.* (Once more and he will never have children.)'

He was being moved, dragged, face down in the gutter, legs spread open.

A hand gripping his face, twisting his neck, forcing him to his back. Above him, the moon, half-full against a black sky. A face descending. Hovering above him. The pretty one.

'You leave Japan, yes?' The voice a low growl, fingers tightening on his mouth.

'Yes?' Again the growl.

Fogarty tried to answer but the fingers held firm.

'Yes?'

He tasted blood as his teeth were forced through the inside of his cheeks.

'You go home?'

'Yes.' His answer slurred but unmistakable.

A final kick to his ribs, beneath his heart; he lay still, never wanting to move again, the sound of the departing limousine like a lullaby.

Can't sleep here, he thought, crawling to his hands and knees, heaving a couple of deep breaths. Struggling to his feet.

The more he walked the better he felt, if better was an appropriate word. At least nothing was broken. All his fingers moved and he could raise his arm above his head. His neck was swollen but flexible.

Leave Japan? Yes, no problem! ... Just show me the way to the airport. A moment later he saw two headlights, winding toward him, along the tree-lined highway. *They're coming back*! A moment of panic before he saw the illuminated 'Taxi' sign on the roof of the car.

He got to the center of the highway and waved like a shipwrecked sailor.

The cabbie stopped, rolled down his window. 'You want to go Disneyland, mister?'

Fogarty stared back at the man. 'Disneyland?' No less sincere, simply fainter.

Fogarty reached for the rear door handle, gripped and squeezed. Locked.

The cab began to pull away.

'No!' Fogarty shouted, running behind it.

The cab slowed down. The driver's window lowered.

'Disneyland. Straight ahead. Closed at night,' the confused man explained.

'Hotel Park Royal. I want to go to the Park Royal, please.'

'Okay. Okay.'

The automatic lock disengaged and the rear door opened. Fogarty slid in, the cab did a tight U-turn and headed back toward town.

The Promised Land

His hotel room felt like the Promised Land. He shed his clothes and fell into bed; he was tired beyond thought.

When he woke up he was uncertain if the beating had actually taken place or if he had dredged it from his nightmare file. His inability to move confirmed the truth. His entire body was sore, the way it had been after the district boxing championship in '72. But that was twenty years ago and he had managed then, at least, to throw a couple of shots of his own. Last night had been one-way fire.

He took a hot shower to ease his muscles, then turned the water to cold to jump-start his mind.

Ken Sato or Mikio Tanaka, one or both had been responsible for his trip to Disneyland. He'd put his money on cousin Ken but that was just intuition, or maybe it was the way the arrogant bastard slurped his noodles.

The telephone was ringing when he walked from the bathroom. It was Josef.

'Bill? Did you get back to the hotel all right?'

Fogarty held back. Surely Mikio Tanaka's driver would have reported the incident, if not to the police, then at least, to his employer. And if Josef was not aware of it, then Mikio Tanaka was playing games.

'Out like a light,' he replied, then, 'I'd like to call your father, thank him for his hospitality, maybe have a talk with him.'

Josef considered. 'Bill, he's going to know exactly why

139

you're here. Going to think that we're working together on him. He won't cooperate.'

Fogarty ran his fingers along the side of his throat; it was still swollen. 'Your father was very gracious. Laying on the limousine and all. I want to thank him personally. Now how about the address of his office?' No give in his voice.

'Should I come with you?'

'No,' the lieutenant answered.

Silence.

'He's going to say things to me that he wouldn't say in front of you,' Fogarty reasoned.

'My father is a hard man to see.'

'That's my problem, Joey.'

'If you're going to see him, Bill, it will have to be today. He goes to Seoul tomorrow, on business. Won't be back for a week.'

The main office of Tanaka Industries was a fourteen-floor building of glass, granite and steel, located in the center of the Marunouchi, Tokyo's main business district.

Fogarty arrived at ten thirty in the morning. He walked through the two sets of high glass doors and into a white marbled lobby. Straight for one of the six elevators which waited at the far end of the room.

He was intercepted midway by two men in plain clothes. The taller of the men spoke English.

'Very sorry, sir, but you must register at the front desk.'

'I am a friend of Mikio Tanaka; he was expecting me at ten o'clock,' Fogarty answered.

The shorter of the two moved a step in front of the lieutenant while the taller remained at his side, flanking him. There was a sureness to their movement, no nerves, simply a polite firmness.

'In that case there will be a record of your appointment at the front desk.'

Fogarty turned in time to see Mikio Tanaka walk through the door. Accompanied by two other men and deep in conversation.

The detective grabbed his chance, changed direction abruptly and headed straight for Josef's father. The men followed his movement, tightening their position. Fogarty could feel them closing in.

'Stop, sir, please stop,' the English-speaking man said, gripping Fogarty's right wrist. Not a firm grip, actually gentle, but as the lieutenant pulled his arm away, the grip changed. A short hard thumb pushed inward against the soft tissue on the outer side of his hand, turning it inward toward his forearm; the pressure causing his entire body to bend forward, away from the pain. Stopping him dead in his tracks.

'Fogarty-san!' Mikio Tanaka's voice boomed, then snapped a few quick, clipped words in Japanese and the lieutenant was free, the two men bowing and apologizing in both languages as they backed off.

A few minutes later Bill Fogarty was inside Mikio Tanaka's vast office.

'You are very lucky, Fogarty-san,' Tanaka said, motioning to four large flowering plants which adorned the space between his desk and the window behind. 'Chinese roses,' he explained. 'You are seeing them at the peak of their beauty.'

Fogarty looked at the red bell-like flowers. A long pollen-bearing spike protruded from each bell.

'In two days time the flowers will roll backwards, form a spiral and drop off.'

Fogarty nodded.

'I have had these plants for six years and each season, as they flower and die, I am reminded of the impermanence of all existence. Great teachers, do you not think, Fogarty-san?'

'I'm not sure,' the lieutenant replied.

'For instance, Fogarty-san, last night you were at my home for dinner. I enjoyed your conversation, your company, the opportunity to meet the man whom my son so admires ... Today you are in my office and I am pleased to see you once again, to have another chance to speak, to practice my English. Then, tomorrow, you and Josef are on a plane bound for the United States. Gone, and I am left with the fond memory of your visit ... Perhaps, next year, you will come again?'

Fogarty heard the edge beneath the smooth voice. Knew he was being told to leave Japan. Again.

'Please sit down, Fogarty-san. You still appear to be suffering from jet lag,' Tanaka continued, motioning to a leather upholstered sofa.

Fogarty didn't move.

'Are you not feeling well, Lieutenant?'

Did he detect a hint of sarcasm in Tanaka's tone? Or was it his own anger, catching up with him? As if it had been left behind, along with his job, in Philadelphia. Rejoining him now, like a tight fist, in the pit of his stomach.

Fogarty held Mikio Tanaka's eyes, took in the fine, proud features of his face. Flashed on Josef's recollections of his father's reign as the first All-Japan karate champion. Trained so hard he urinated blood. Most of the other students wouldn't attend practice if they knew he was there. Punched the straw-padded striking board one thousand times a day. Each hand. Fists like iron hammers.

There was definitely steel behind the smooth façade, but was there a man who could have his own son murdered? And why?

Mikio Tanaka broke the tension.

'I am not responsible for what happened to you last night, Fogarty-san ... nor do I wish for you to undergo any further blows to your honor.'

Fogarty smiled.

Now it was Mikio Tanaka's turn to be confused.

'You find such treatment amusing?'

'No. But until now, I hadn't considered it a blow to my honor. It just hurt like a son of a bitch.' Forgarty relaxed as he answered.

'These people can be much more severe. I assure you,' Tanaka stated.

'Who are "these people"?'

Tanaka's mouth tightened.

'I came to Japan as Josef's friend. To help,' Fogarty said.

'Please, Lieutenant, do not be naïve.'

Fogarty stood his ground, silent.

'I am asking you to go home,' Tanaka insisted.

'Asking me or ordering me?'

Tanaka's eyes hardened. His entire body seemed to surge beneath the fabric of his suit. 'I cannot be responsible for what may happen if you stay.'

'That sounds like a threat,' the policeman answered.

Tanaka took a step forward, staring up and into Fogarty's eyes. 'Call it what you will, Lieutenant,' he said, motioning toward the door of his office. 'Now please leave.'

'No.' The word fell like a gauntlet between them.

Mikio Tanaka's eyes bored into him. So intense that, for a moment, Fogarty felt as though a weight were pressing against his heart; he had an image of himself, lying unconscious on the office floor. Creative visualization. *A bad way to start a fight*, he thought, holding on to Tanaka's glare.

The moment came and went. Instinct flashed like revelation. There would be no fight and Mikio Tanaka was certainly no murderer.

'I came here to help your son,' Fogarty repeated softly.

'Then, for his sake, take him and return to Philadelphia,' Tanaka replied.

'He won't come.'

'You must convince him.' There was the beginning of desperation in Tanaka's tone.

'Convince me,' Fogarty replied.

Mikio Tanaka stood silent for a moment. Indecision replaced the threat in his eyes.

Finally he eased past the lieutenant and to his office door. Pushed the button that locked it. He was trembling as he walked to the far end of the room. Bending down at the base of the floor-to-ceiling bookshelves, he pressed a hidden button. The bottom shelves moved out and away from the wall, revealing a safe.

Tanaka hit the digits on the computerized console and the pneumatic locks opened. He reached in and brought out an envelope, withdrawing two ten-by-eight sheets of paper. At least that's what Fogarty presumed them to be until Mikio Tanaka stood up.

As he walked closer the policeman could see that Tanaka was holding a pair of color photographs. He extended the first, withholding the other.

It was a photograph of Josef, standing, surrounded by a group of somberly dressed men and women. All the men, including Josef, were attired in black suits and black ties. Josef's face was more sad than Fogarty had ever seen it, his eyes pained. In the background of the picture, sitting on a table, in front of a white brick wall, Fogarty recognized the white porcelain vase; the same vase that he had seen in Mikio Tanaka's home. Containing the ashes of Hironori Tanaka.

'Taken at the cremation,' Mikio Tanaka said quietly. Then he handed the lieutenant the other picture.

It took the policeman's eyes a moment to focus.

'Jesus Christ,' he whispered, staring at the nightmare in his hands.

'Now, Lieutenant, do you understand?'

Bill Fogarty had seen a lot of death, bodies so decomposed that only dental records provided hope of identification. He had discovered human organs in jars of formaldehyde and arms and legs in refrigerators. He thought he was hardened to death.

'That is my son. My elder son,' Mikio Tanaka repeated, his arms hanging to his sides, his hands shaking. 'They did that to my son.'

Fogarty continued to stare at the photograph, lost for words.

It was a picture of Hironori Tanaka's execution, taken at the exact time his skull had imploded; his eyeballs hung from gushing sockets and fluid spurted from his ears. His jaw was hanging loose, his lips without expression and his few visible teeth were dark with blood. Half his cranium had collapsed.

Hironori Tanaka's executioner stood above him, arms wrapped like a clamp around his victim's head.

The man was so broad and so packed into his blood-spattered suit that he appeared more a caricature than flesh and blood.

In an effort to conceal his identity a black strip had been drawn across the eyes and nose area of the photograph. His mouth, however, was visible, drawn into a tight grimace which revealed both the extent of his exertion and the pleasure he had derived.

'Sent to me on the same day, Mr Fogarty. The day after Hironori's cremation.'

Fogarty placed the photo of Josef over the death picture and held them both at his side, away from Mikio Tanaka's line of vision.

'Why?' the detective asked.

'My punishment,' Tanaka answered. A twitch had begun in his upper lip.

'Your punishment?'

'That is what I was told.'

'Who else has seen these pictures?'

Tanaka's eyes darted quickly toward his office door, then back to the detective. 'No one.'

Mikio Tanaka was breaking down, Fogarty recognized the signs: hands, mouth and eyes. Now was the time to take control, to gain information.

'Tanaka-san,' Fogarty said reassuringly. 'Please, trust me. This is my business, my profession.' He hesitated. 'Your son once saved my life, my career. I'm not leaving here until we know the truth. It is a matter of duty, and honor.'

Tanaka looked at the policeman.

'Talk to me,' Fogarty said.

Dreams

She was walking down that same sidewalk in the Ginza, beside the big department store, the one with the Chanel scarves. There were streams of people, walking beside her, past her, coming in the opposite direction. Yet, amidst all these people, she was solitary. Unconnected. She wanted to go home, get in her chauffeured car and go home, but she wasn't sure where her car was. And the more she walked, the more disoriented she became. Until she was lost, being carried along in the flow of people.

Then she saw him. Moving through the crowd, coming toward her; she recognized his walk, his height. She felt better already, less isolated; it was Josef. He stood out from the nondescript people around him, people that looked as though they had been moulded from yellowed wax, then clothed in the same drab costumes, like shawls covering their tiny bodies. Some were veiled, others stared blankly ahead. And their faces, everyone had the same face. Deep slanted eyes, small noses, thin lips, no expression . . . But not Josef; he was distinct, clear, a head taller than the rest. And he was coming towards her. She was lost and he was going to take her home. Closer.

'Josef!' She called out to him.

He turned, stared. Wrong direction, he didn't see her.

'Josef!'

He was close now, only a few feet away.

147

'Josef, it's me . . . Here. I'm here!'

He turned, looked and she realized that it was not Josef at all. How had she mistaken this man for her Josef? This man looked nothing at all like Josef. There was no kindness in this man's face. Cruelty, no compassion.

She looked down, averting her eyes, walking forward, trying to lose herself in the throngs of little people. But she could not. They were all the same and she was different; she stood out. And he was walking toward her. He had heard her call.

He? She knew him. One more look and she would be certain. She had seen him before; he had been close to her before, touched her.

She felt him behind her now, his presence, dark and quick.

She was too frightened to look back; she knew who he was, what he would do.

She tried to run, but she could not run. Too many little people to run, melting like wax all around her, causing her feet to stick to the sidewalk.

She was falling . . . Falling . . .

'Josef!'

Sinking down, into the melting people. Going under.

Rachel Saunders gasped for air. Oxygen. Gulping it.

Then she was awake; she knew she was awake. She could feel the wet sheets, bunched in her right hand, the pillow pulled tight to her body like a soft shield. But she could still see him, like a shadow beside her bed. Motionless. Hovering like a fine mist.

She inhaled again, counting the seconds, timing her breath, exhaling. Again. And again. Until, finally, the mist cleared.

She sat up, slowly. Felt the beat of her heart decelerate. Checked the time. Seven o'clock.

She was all right. All right. She kept telling herself that as she got out of bed, looking around the room, throwing on her heavy cotton robe, walking to the main room of the apartment, making sure the door was locked, chained and bolted. Trying to shake the feeling that someone had been in there, right beside her in the night.

She went to the bathroom. Leaving the door open. She ran a bath. She generally showered but today she ran a bath. She didn't want to be in the confines of the shower. No small spaces, no closed doors.

After she was dressed, she made breakfast; Quaker oats, raisins and apples, some dry brown toast, herbal tea. Everything clean; she needed to think clearly.

At nine o'clock she called Stan Leibowitz.

'Stan, I think I'm in trouble.' Like an admittance of guilt.

She ran through it with him on the phone, the 'dream', the feeling in the room.

'All right, all right ... Now let's get real practical.' The psychiatrist asked, 'What have you got on workwise in the next two weeks?'

'Not much, no surgery, no confirmed appointments ... Stan, I was going to be on my honeymoon.' Even the word sounded ridiculous.

'Okay, Rachel, now hear me out. I think you're getting better; I truly believe that. It may be hard for you to hear, particularly since this is happening to you, not me, but I've got my reasons. The main one is there is no "freeze up". You are remaining functional. On top of that you're bringing yourself out of it. Now I want you to do a couple of things for me.'

'Yes?' Rachel waited.

'I want you back at your office. See some patients, get back to a normal pattern as quickly as you can. Don't schedule any surgery, just consultations.' Leibowitz paused. 'Your favorite exercise, is swimming, right?'

'I love to swim,' she answered.

'What's your longest?'

'A mile and a half, in the university pool . . . Twice.'

'Right. Today, at, say, three thirty, I'd like you to meet me at the pool . . . We're going to do some swimming.'

Rikishi

The drive back to the Park Royal was a test of faith. Fogarty knew that the hotel was east of the Marunouchi business district, but he could only hazard a guess as to which direction was east.

He drove out of the underground parking lot, turned left at the first main boulevard and continued straight, trying to retrace his route from the morning, but in the opposite direction.

The streets were an obstacle course of cars, cabs, trucks, motorcycles and pedal bikes; all moving faster than he wanted to drive, pushing him from behind, from the side, from every way he turned as he tried to catch a glimpse of a sign post. Nothing. But everyone else seemed to know exactly where they were going. He went with the flow, glancing down only once at the manila envelope that lay beside him on the front seat.

'If you want Josef out of Japan, you'll give me the pictures.'

At first Mikio Tanaka had been adamant, refusing absolutely to surrender the photographs.

It took the detective some hard persuasion to get them. Whether or not they would convince Josef to abandon his hunt was another matter. The important thing was that the 'death shot' showed the killer.

There couldn't be that many men of that size, not in a country whose average thirty-year-old male was five feet six inches tall and weighed one hundred and forty pounds.

The traffic slowed, finally grinding to a halt. Fogarty picked the envelope up and removed the bottom picture. Lifted the photograph and studied it, taking a moment to get beyond the morbidity of the distorted face.

Christ, that's Josef's brother, the detective told himself, recalling the many times that Josef had spoken of Hironori.

'Handsome, Bill. Much better looking than I am. Samurai, pure Samurai.' Josef had been so proud of his brother. And so guilty.

I can't show this to Josef. Can't do it, he decided, then began to concentrate on the man behind the exploding face. The executioner.

'What is it about the guy's posture?' Fogarty was talking to himself, letting his mind roll, trying to climb inside the ten-by-eight photograph. 'He comes up from behind, grabs his victim's head. Hunches over, locks his arms, right hand over left forearm, left fist clenched. Squeezes. Hard enough to crush his victim's skull.'

Two thousand pounds pressure per square inch. Wasn't that the figure that Bob Moyer had mentioned once, during an autopsy, as the amount of pressure required to break the forehead's frontal bone? In that particular instance the victim had been struck by an iron bar. Fast and clean, death had been instantaneous.

Hironori Tanaka's death was anything but clean, and anything but fast. As he sat helpless in front of a mirror; his body dead from the neck down, yet the nerves in the area under attack alive and sensitive. Sat there while someone photographed his torture. Or, perhaps the camera had been pre-set, triggered by an automatic timer and the killer had coordinated his movements to the shutter speed.

And the house servant? Lying face down beside the front door? Or what should have been face down but in this instance was chest down, face up; her head twisted in a one hundred and eighty degree rotation, front to back, breaking every bone and tearing every bit of muscle and sinew in her neck. Her corpse providing a grotesque preview of what awaited Mikio Tanaka in his son's room.

Fogarty looked closer at the suited man in the photograph. Imagined the great bull rampaging through the house, flattening everything in his path. *But it didn't happen that way*, he reminded himself. *It was not a frenzied attack; it was planned, slow and methodical.*

His eyes honed on the man's hands. Fat, but not fleshy fat, more a muscular fatness. Trained hands, like a chiropractor or masseur, experienced hands. One balled into a fist while the other, the gripping hand, locked onto the wrist of the arm that was drawn like a crowbar across Hironori's forehead. The fingers of the executioner's exposed hand were thick, unusually thick and the middle knuckle appeared to be missing.

A horn, blaring behind him, broke Fogarty's concentration. He looked up to see the tail end of a truck moving away from him and the puffy face of a cab driver in his rear view mirror. He placed the photograph face down against the passenger seat and accelerated.

The lobby of the Park Royal was a hive of activity. Businessmen and women, package tours, people speaking different languages.

Josef Tanaka was sitting in a square-cushioned chair at the far end of the long room, sipping a cup of tea. He stood up as Bill Fogarty walked through the entrance doors.

Tanaka reached out and touched the wound to the side of Fogarty's neck. 'When did this happen?'

Fogarty knew better than to lie. Doctor Tanaka was far too competent to fall for a lie.

'Looks like ten or twelve hours ago,' the doctor continued, pushing his fingertips into the mastoid muscle which extended from behind Fogarty's ear.

'That's about right,' Fogarty answered.

'Any dizziness? Double vision?'

'No,' the detective replied. 'But it still hurts like hell, particularly when you press it.'

Tanaka withdrew his hand. 'Where did it happen?'

Fogarty looked around, suddenly aware of two men watching them. Dark-suited men with expressionless faces. One holding a newspaper, the other attempting to look casual, reclining against the back of a mock leather sofa. It was the kind of act that, after thirty years on the police force, Fogarty clocked instantly.

'Hold on a second, Joey,' Fogarty said.

He walked to the front desk and demanded a different room.

The lieutenant placed the manila envelope on the end of his new bed. If the Tokyo Police were monitoring his conversations or tapping his phone it would take them a few hours to rerig their set-up. Tomorrow he'd change hotels.

They sat at the coffee table, away from the door and close to an open window.

'On the way back from dinner, I dozed off in the car. We slowed down, I think it was at a traffic light. Two guys pulled the driver out and gave him a good kicking. Then they got in, one of 'em drove while the other worked on me. The underlying theme of the exercise was that I should get the fuck out of Japan.' Fogarty rubbed his neck. It wasn't quite as painful as the joint of his left arm, where the stick had connected with his funny bone. He remembered Doctor Tanaka's probing fingers and decided not to mention the arm.

'Who?' Josef asked, as much to himself as to Fogarty.

'Got to be someone close to your family.'

Josef raised his head.

'Someone who knows exactly where we are and what

we're doing. Somebody with access to your life.'

Josef's eyes hardened.

'A person who knew that your mother was away at the time of your brother's death, knew that your father would be returning alone to the house. Timed it so that they could get to him, by phone, before he reported what had happened.' Fogarty hesitated, 'Joey, somebody's controlling this thing right down to the fine details.'

'What do they want?' Tanaka asked.

'I don't know,' Fogarty replied, shaking his head.

'What did my father say to you?'

'He asked me to go home and to take you with me.'

'That's not what I'm asking you, Bill.'

'Your father doesn't know what they're after.'

'I don't follow you.'

'Mikio Tanaka is a very frightened man.'

'I've never seen my father give in to anything, particularly fear,' Tanaka replied.

'He isn't frightened for himself, Joey. He's frightened for you and your mother.'

'Bill, you're not telling me everything.'

'He said he's being punished,' the lieutenant continued.

'Punished?'

'That the pressure will continue until he understands.'

'Understands what?'

'Joey, he doesn't know. Believe me. So far there have been no demands, no extortion, no ransom. A few telephone calls. "Through pain comes enlightenment", that type of thing.'

'He told me he'd been to the police,' Tanaka said.

'He has. It's being handled very high up, very discreetly. They've got a guard on him. And, in case you haven't noticed, they've got one on you too.'

Tanaka glanced at the bed. 'What's in the envelope?'

'A warning. Delivered to your father the day after the cremation,' Fogarty replied.

Tanaka began to stand and the lieutenant reached across the table and held his forearm.

'Joey, I want you to think about going back to Philadelphia.'

Tanaka hesitated. 'I can't,' he said.

'Listen, son, I know what you're feeling. I understand your loyalty to your family. I remember when you told me the meaning of *giri* – that's the obligation for pay-back, right?'

'Yes,' Josef answered.

'And then there's human feeling and emotion? What's the word for that?'

'*Ninjo*,' Tanaka replied.

'Well, if there was ever a case of *giri* this is it. I know that, I understand it,' the lieutenant said.

'I owe my family, Bill. I owe my brother. I can't just walk out.'

'But how about the *ninjo* – compassion for your father and mother? Your mother is innocent. She knows nothing about any of this. It's all on your father, the pain, the burden.' Fogarty hesitated. 'You're just adding to that burden, Josef.'

Tanaka clenched his fist and turned his head away, toward the bed and the envelope.

'What are you trying to do, Bill?'

'I'm trying to get you back to Philadelphia.'

Tanaka said nothing. He walked to the bed, picked up the envelope. Fogarty watched as Tanaka opened it.

'The police haven't even seen those. Your father's kept them locked up; he doesn't trust anybody, doesn't know where to turn.' Fogarty's voice sounded lame. He needed Josef to see the pictures, wanted his opinion. His medical doctor's opinion. But he didn't want his friend to have to endure the pain inside the envelope.

'So he's turned to me, Josef. Trusted me. Let me have those on the condition that I take you home.'

'I am home, Bill.' There was a bite to Tanaka's voice. He began to withdraw the photographs.

Fogarty stood up, walked quickly to Josef's side. Looked down at the first picture.

It was the shot of Josef.

'This was taken at the crematorium. Anybody could have done it. A good lens, thirty, even forty feet away,' Josef said.

He laid the photograph on the bed and stared at the one beneath.

Fogarty waited for the shock to grab hold. Surprised at how steady Josef's hands remained and the stillness of his eyes when he finally looked up.

Then it came.

From deep down inside Tanaka's belly, like the wail of a wounded animal. Somewhere between a scream and a battle cry, a sound that contained grief, anguish and sheer fury.

Fogarty placed his hand on his friend's shoulder. Felt the tension in his muscles.

'They can't do this. Not to Hironori, not to my brother. I won't let them do this.' Tanaka's voice was taut, almost metallic, as if a tape were playing behind the mask of his face. A face that was suddenly drained of color.

'That's why your father made me promise to get you out of Japan,' Fogarty said softly.

Tanaka did not appear to hear him.

'A *rikishi*,' he muttered. 'The man looks like a *rikishi*.' As if the thought defied belief.

'*Rikishi*?' Fogarty repeated the word.

'A *sumotori*, a wrestler,' Josef continued. 'It would take that kind of strength to crush a human skull.'

Fogarty looked at the photograph. A sumo wrestler, an athlete. It made sense. He had heard of these giants, never seen one in the flesh.

'Do these *rikishi* ever work as assassins?' the policeman asked.

'I've never heard of it.'

'Yet you think this guy's one of them?'

Tanaka looked again at the picture, this time with a clinical detachment, judging the man's size in relation to Hironori and the wheelchair.

'He's got to be six foot three or four, and over three hundred pounds. There aren't many men that size in Japan; I'm talking about height, weight and bone structure. I don't know of any outside the sumotori stables. Look at his wrists, his fingers,' Tanaka said, pointing to the photograph. 'Looks like he's been pounding the *teppo*.'

Fogarty appeared puzzled.

'That's a thick wooden pole. It's the sumo's equivalent to a punching bag,' Tanaka explained. 'I'd bet this guy broke his hand on it, his second metacarpal is completely dislocated. Looks like a bad break. Didn't heal properly.'

Tanaka's voice turned bitter. 'This bastard's been trained, developed. Check the muscle tone in his neck, his jaw. Not the kind of muscle you develop in a bodybuilding gym. This kind of muscle gets built lifting people, not weights.' He looked at Fogarty. 'My father would have seen all this. Didn't he say anything?'

'He isn't thinking like that, Joey, not right now,' Fogarty answered, studying the photograph. 'Who else in your family would have any connection to these guys?'

Tanaka thought for a moment.

'Somebody close to your family?'

'What are you getting at, Bill?'

'I'm trying to find a way in,' Fogarty answered.

'And then what?'

'Joey, I'll go as far with you as I can, but you've got to trust me on this. If it starts to get crazy, real crazy, we're out of here. Not just me, Josef, you and me. Back to Philadelphia, to Rachel and your job ... I gave your father my word and I'm already stretching it.'

'Bill, you don't need to be doing this. There's no reason.'

'To me, Josef, you're family. That's enough reason ... *giri*, right? Least that's the way I understand it,' the lieutenant answered. 'Plus the fact that I'd like to put my foot into the little fuck who stiffened my neck.'

Tanaka looked at the big Irish policeman, his worn tweed jacket and size twelve brogues, a face that looked as if half of it had been dipped in wax and drip-dried. Hazel-green eyes, eyes he could trust. With his life.

'My cousin can help us,' Tanaka said.

'Ken Sato?' Fogarty asked.

'Yes, my cousin Ken.'

Misogi (Spirit Cleansing)

Everywhere in Tokyo that Bill Fogarty had been; hotels, restaurants, even Mikio Tanaka's family house, had possessed a kind of half-Japanese, half-Western atmosphere. Ken Sato's home was different.

The policeman's initial reaction to the austere apartment was of discomfort. The bare floor, sparse furnishings and obvious religious connotation of the altar brought back memories of the Catholic chapel he had been forced to attend while a student at Sacred Heart High School in North Philadelphia. Something about the chapel had seemed in direct opposition to his character. Instigated by the fact that the school priest had once sexually propositioned him during confession. Afterwards, the black suit and starched collar seemed a façade for something repressed or hidden.

Following high school Fogarty had returned to church twice. Once to get married and once again to bury his family after the car accident.

Bill Fogarty did not believe in God.

Maybe that explained his aversion to Ken Sato. The guy reminded him of a priest. With his white, high-buttoned shirt, slim dark suit and holier-than-thou manner. Presiding over his private chapel. Slurping his noodles. Rachel had been right. Ken Sato was a creep.

The lieutenant hoped that Josef Tanaka wouldn't give away too much while enlisting his cousin's help. As far as the policeman was concerned, Ken Sato, chairman of the board at Tanaka Industries, was suspect number one. Then again, Fogarty reminded himself, he hadn't met enough of the periphery of the Tanaka family even to have a suspect number two.

Fogarty and Tanaka sat on two raised cushions on the far side of the mirrored altar. Beside them, sitting on a low laquered table, was what looked to the lieutenant like a brass hand-grenade. His eyes kept settling on it as they waited for Ken Sato to return from the adjoining room.

'What the hell is that thing?' he finally whispered.

Tanaka followed the lieutenant's gaze to the closed brass cylinder.

'It's called a *suzu*. See the stick coming out of the far side? You hold that in your hand and shake it. There are two metal balls inside the cylinder.'

'A bell?'

'Yes. Used specifically for *misogi*, a breathing exercise. You ring the bell in time with your breathing; it's part of the old religion, Shinto. It's an exercise in purification, cleansing the spirit; a way to return to the natural respiration of a baby.'

'A religious exercise. Christ, I thought it was a grenade,' Fogarty commented.

Tanaka smiled. 'It was also an exercise of the warrior class. A lot of Samurai practiced *misogi* in freezing rivers and underneath waterfalls. They understood that if you controlled the breath, control of the sword would follow.'

Fogarty thought for a moment. *Like shooting a gun. Coordinate the exhalation with squeezing the trigger. Fire as the last of the breath leaves your body. Think of the weapon as an extension of your arm.* Somewhere along the line it all linked up. He nodded his head, imagining Ken Sato, alone in his 'chapel', methodically shaking his chiming grenade.

A moment later Sato walked into the room. He carried a tray.

Fogarty noticed that Josef's posture changed as his cousin

approached; he straightened his back and tucked his legs beneath his hips. It was the same posture that the lieutenant had seen when Josef had taken him to the Philadelphia dojo to watch a karate class. Tanaka had called it *seiza*, or correct sitting.

Sato placed the tray down in front of his guests. It contained an iron kettle, one earthenware bowl, a tea container, a bamboo whisk, a bamboo tea scoop and two small cloths. Then, quietly he left the room again. This time he returned with a larger empty bowl and a ladle.

He knelt in front of Tanaka and Fogarty, working meticulously, his long, sinewy fingers wiping the tea container and scoop with one of the cloths, before rinsing the whisk in the bowl and measuring the tea.

There was no hurry in Sato's movement; it was as if he were creating a vacuum in time, a space in which his exacting physical motions contained a deep significance.

When he finished his preparation he placed the bowl in front of Josef, the 'principal guest'.

Fogarty watched as Josef bent forward and lifted it, holding the clay vessel in the palm of his left hand, breathing in the aroma before taking it to his lips. He sipped the tea, smiled and bowed to Ken Sato, then continued to drink, slowly, until he had finished the entire bowl.

Finally, with one of the small cloths, Josef wiped the areas of the bowl that his lips had touched and placed it back down, in front of his cousin.

Fogarty looked on. When the invitation had come for tea he hadn't expected the holy communion.

Cousin Ken's precision was making him nervous. He tried to remember the way that Josef had handled the bowl, hoping that his own inevitable clumsiness would not offend his 'perfect' host.

Finally Sato offered him the tea.

Fogarty accepted, catching a glimpse of Josef from the

corner of his eye. Sitting there, watching him. Then the strong aroma, vaguely bitter but not unpleasant, drew his attention to the frothy green beverage.

He sipped. Surprised that it was not boiling, in fact almost cool. Refreshing. He felt eyes upon him and was suddenly self-conscious. Looked up to see Ken Sato.

Last night's impression of Sato as hard and dangerous was contradicted now by the softness of his expression. As if he desired nothing more than to please his guests. Fogarty suddenly felt warmth toward the man. The inconsistency in his own feelings reminded him of the way it had been with Josef, two years ago. He hadn't understood him either, not at first.

Fogarty nodded and half smiled. Ken returned the smile with a slight bow of his head then looked past Fogarty and out the window behind. Fogarty began to relax.

A bird was singing, somewhere beyond the walls of Ken Sato's apartment. In the middle of this crowded nightmare of a city, a bird was singing. Fogarty could hear it; the song filled him. All his concentration became centered on the rise and fall of the warbled notes. Blue notes, they were blue.

Following tea, conversation was easy. The lieutenant's fears of Josef exposing more of their business than was necessary were unfounded. Ken did not pry or push; he simply listened, with the same attentiveness that he had applied to the tea ceremony.

'*Rikishi*? Yes, I know many *rikishi*,' he answered when Josef brought up the subject of sumo.

'Would it be an imposition, Ken-san, for you to arrange an introduction for Fogarty-san and myself to visit one of their stables?' Josef asked.

Ken considered briefly. 'Any *beya* in particular?'

'One in which the main coach would have knowledge of the players from other stables ... we are looking for a specific man,' Tanaka answered.

Fogarty waited. He was, for the moment, comfortable with Ken Sato, but his experience told him not to confuse comfort with trust. Josef's request had given his cousin a perfect and reasonable opportunity to ask questions, to try and ascertain the reason they would be searching for a particular man.

'This man, he is a *rikishi*?' Sato asked.

'Perhaps,' Tanaka answered.

Sato considered, looking first at the lieutenant then at his cousin.

'I think the *Chiba-beya* would be the place to begin. The head *oyakata* is a close friend of mine, and now, before the September *bashos* they will be holding several practice sessions with other stables.'

'Thank you, Ken-san,' Tanaka said.

Bill Fogarty was impressed by Sato's restraint and discretion. 'Ken is a good man, an ally,' Tanaka had promised the policeman. Maybe he was right.

'Usually, visitors are welcome to watch the *rikishi* practice,' Sato explained, turning to Fogarty, 'but now, with the fall tournaments coming up, the stables have closed their doors. My friend's name is Morio Sugino; he was, at one time, an *ozeki*. The word, in English, stands for "great barrier", in terms of sumo it means "champion". Now he is one of our finest *oyakata*. A coach. I will telephone him.'

Lady Remington

Philadelphia, USA

Rachel Saunders waited at the end of the pool nearer the steam cabinets. There was only a handful of swimmers in the water, and still three vacant lanes.

She was wearing a black Speedo swimming suit, the model with the high-cut thighs, making her long legs look even longer; she rubbed her hand across the top of her right thigh. As smooth as silk, thanks to an early morning session with her Lady Remington.

She'd forgotten all about her hairy thighs on her first meeting with Stan Leibowitz. Then, suddenly noticing his eyes on the forest, she'd jumped into the water like an escaping Godzilla.

'You ready? This is the big one-point-five!' Stan's voice caught her from behind.

She turned to see him throw his towel on a bench and continue in her direction. Stan Leibowitz had a terrific body. Not just for a middle-aged guy but for any guy. He was well proportioned with a hard but not overtly muscular torso, long sinewy arms, tight waist and strong, graceful thighs, with well-developed calves and good solid feet. Plus a silver mat of hair which formed a perfect triangle in the center of his chest. And he walked like a lion, alert and sure against the slippery floor. Centered. Rachel allowed herself to notice all these things because Stan Leibowitz was married with three children. He was safe.

Still she noticed.

Maybe the psychiatrist was correct. Maybe she was getting better. Something inside of her was awakening.

The university pool was twenty-five yards long. Seventy lengths to the mile. One hundred and five for a mile and a half.

The first time they had come, eight days ago, they had done thirty lengths and Rachel had quit, out of breath, arms and legs like lead.

'Here's where we go through the tunnel,' Stan had told her, gripping her shoulder when she made a try for the ladder and the locker room.

'Now is the time for you to control your breathing and overcome your fatigue ... We're going to do another ten lengths. Think of it like you're going through a tunnel, if you stop, you'll never get to the other side. Simple as that. Lost in the dark forever. Victim of whatever is inside that tunnel. It's a head game, but you're going to play it with your body. You're going to use your body to change your mind ... Understand?'

Before she could answer he'd said 'let's go' and they were off.

Ten laps. Ten fast laps.

Rachel swam one mile on her fourth day, each day adding ten more lengths. It was a head game.

Now it was day number eight.

'How do you feel?' Leibowitz asked, standing less than a foot in front of her. She could feel electricity from him, a good warm energy.

'Like a mile and a half,' she replied.

The last thirty laps were hard, through the tunnel. Inside the tunnel was her nightmare, darker now, less defined, like the mist beside her bed. She kept on going, powering through it, to the light on the other side.

Afterwards they steamed, showered, dried, and changed into their street clothes. Then met again in the lobby and walked to a nearby coffee shop. Sitting at a small round table, savoring the bite of caffeine from two frothy cups of café au lait. Rachel felt good, better than she had felt in a long time. Like she was accompishing something positive, getting well.

She had heard from Josef, twice in the last week. The last time he had put Bill on the line. Bill hated Japan; she could tell by his tone of voice, the things he didn't say. They both sounded very distant to her. They were all right, safe. Other than that they gave away nothing. Hardly spoke about the 'case'. They were policemen, on business, and she was not part of that business.

Her job was right here, to get well, strong, to work on herself. And her ally was sitting right beside her.

'I want to do a little more regression therapy with you, Rachel, with the Sodium Pentothal,' Leibowitz said softly.

His words hit her sense of well-being like a sledge hammer.

'I don't understand.' She barely controlled the fear in her voice, 'I thought we agreed I was getting better.'

'You are. You're much stronger, inside and out . . . That's why I want to do it. One last purge. See if he is still in there,' Leibowitz said, touching his fingertips to the center of her forehead, 'and if he is, let's get rid of him. Forever.'

She met his eyes.

'Don't worry champ, I'll be right there with you,' he said, smiling.

Hands the size of a fielder's mit

Sumo is as old as Japan. In its early days it tended to be violent; death was not an uncommon end to a match. Its techniques included the thrusts, locks and breaks that would later develop into jujitsu, an art practiced exclusively for self-defense.

It was in the mid-eighteenth century that the sport of sumo took hold in Edo, now known as Tokyo, and the first permanent stables were established.

The *Chiba-beya* is one of the originals. Housed in a gray stone, two-story building in the Ryogoku area of the city, near the Kokugikan Stadium, a national sumo hall.

At six feet four inches tall and four hundred and eighty pounds, Morio Sugino had been one of the largest men in Sumo. Now, at forty-nine, thirteen years had elapsed since his *danpatsushika*, the public ceremony in which the retiring *rikishi*'s topknot is severed. In that time he had trimmed his body-weight to a shade above three hundred pounds.

Two things attracted Bill Fogarty's attention as Sugino ushered the lieutenant, Tanaka, and Ken Sato into the front office of the *Chiba-beya*. The first was the sheer grace with which the enormous man moved; he seemed to glide rather than walk, and second was the size of the hands that hung beneath the cuffs of his tailored gray suit. Huge, leathery

171

hands, *like fielder's gloves*, Fogarty thought. The same type of hands that had squeezed the life from Hironori Tanaka.

But as he turned toward them, his wide moon-like face creased in a welcoming smile, there was nothing malevolent about the *oyakata*; Morio Sugino seemed, instead, to possess a childlike innocence.

'Sato-san. It has been many, many months since I have seen you,' Sugino said, 'nearly a year since you brought me the Watanabe boy.'

Sato smiled.

'Come, please, he is practicing now. You must see for yourself.'

Sugino led his guests into the *keikoba*, a large practice area with a dirt floor and two *dohyos*, or rings, each with a diameter of fifteen feet.

Fogarty noticed the similarity between the altar that was mounted on the far wall of the *keikoba* and the altar in Ken Sato's apartment; it was a Shinto altar, the native religion of Japan. He sneaked a look at Ken Sato. The guy still reminded him of a priest, stiff and clean. Too clean.

They walked to a raised tatami, overlooking the *keikoba*. Fogarty followed Tanaka's lead and sat cross-legged while Sato and Sugino walked down and amongst the twenty giants on the floor.

Fogarty eyed the herd, then noticed the unfamiliar smell of the place. Not like a boxing gym, with its mix of sweat and leather, this had a sweetness.

'Some kind of perfume?' he asked.

'It's the *bintsuke*. The pomade that the hairdressers use to hold the *rikishis'* topknots in place,' Tanaka explained.

'That guy they're watching over there,' Tanaka continued, 'the one using the *teppo*, is Ken's discovery. He's only sixteen. Comes from up north, a country boy. He was a high school swimming champion.'

Fogarty looked toward the outside of the ring. He saw a

tall, skinny kid sliding his feet back and forth, slamming his open hands into the thick pole.

'What do you mean, "Ken's discovery"?' Fogarty asked.

'Ken often travels for my father's company, meeting heads of management, talking to unions. He has spent a lot of time in the northern country, in Hokkaido and Aomori. Since he is a friend of Sugino-san, he always keeps an eye out for potential talent, you know, like a baseball scout. It's common over here, friends, supporters, relatives of the coach. They all like to spot a future champion. Ken's found a couple who have made it to *jonidan*, second division.'

'C'mon, Joey, no way that kid's ever going to grow into one of those,' Fogarty said, looking away from the skin and bones pounding the *teppo* and toward a huge, topknotted *sumotori* who was seated, legs spread, on the floor. As he watched, the *rikishi* opened his legs wider and touched his entire upper torso to the dirt.

Tanaka smiled. 'He's a fully fledged *seketori*, a professional, gets a salary, an apprentice, a silk *mawashi*, that's the layered cloth wrapped around his groin. The Watanabe boy is just an apprentice. He'll be in the bath house, washing that *seketori*'s feet after practice.'

'You telling me that kid is going to end up looking like that?' Fogarty asked.

'You try eating a hundred and fifty pieces of fish, twenty-five plates of beef plus half a dozen bowls of rice for lunch,' Tanaka replied.

'You got to be kidding me.' Fogarty gasped, looking back at the skinny apprentice.

Then something caught his attention. It was just a glance, a look from the corner of the boy's eye. Directed at Ken Sato. The type of glance that a child might give a particularly disliked teacher, when the teacher's back is turned. The same look that Fogarty had given his high school priest. Fear mixed with loathing.

The lieutenant's thoughts were still forming when Ken Sato stepped toward the apprentice. He caressed the youth's sweating back with the palm of his hand before bending down and stroking the developing muscle on the anterior portion of the boy's thigh. Much in the same way that a groom might stroke a race horse. Or it could have been seen that way. Fogarty saw it differently.

Cousin Ken takes advantage of young boys. The thought linked like a piece of a puzzle.

Ken stroked again, said something to the coach, then stood up and walked back to Fogarty and Tanaka.

'I have explained to Sugino-san that you wish to speak privately to him,' he said, mounting the mats.

'Afternoon practice will be over in half an hour,' he added, hesitating, 'I must be going to my business, so I leave this to you.'

The lieutenant wasn't ready for the last phase of afternoon training, *butsukari-geiko*.

Collision training, that's what Tanaka called it, when a *seketori* took the center of the ring and the apprentices lined up against him. Waiting their turn. To charge full speed at the senior man, shoulder forward, smacking at full throttle into his chest, attempting to push him out of the ring.

The *oyakata* urged them on as one after the other was tossed to the ground.

'Teaching them how to fall,' Tanaka whispered as one young hopeful smacked into the dirt head first.

Finally it was Watanabe, Ken Sato's discovery, who took the floor. Eight times he charged the big *seketori*, and eight times the senior man threw the apprentice to the ground. Following the last fall Watanabe crawled to his hands and knees and stared up into the *seketori*'s face.

The big sumo took a step to the side and waited for the novice to regain his feet.

'The guy's completely exhausted,' Fogarty whispered.

'It's called *kawaigari*,' Tanaka answered.

'*Kawaigari*?' Fogarty repeated, in time with Whatanobe's last assault.

'Tender loving care,' Tanaka translated.

Now the *seketori* was giving ground to the novice, allowing him to move him backwards, utilizing the final reserves of the young man's strength.

'Spirit building,' Tanaka elaborated, 'learning beyond the point of exhaustion.'

Another few seconds and the exercise ended; the novice bowed and thanked his senior for the lesson. Then it was leg splits in unison followed by sumo-stomping, each man standing, legs apart, raising one leg high, knee even with his upper rib cage before lowering the foot hard to the ground, exhaling on impact.

'Five hundred times a day, each leg, for strength,' Tanaka said.

Fogarty noted the barbells, dumbbells and exercise bikes that lay on the perimeter of the *dohyo*. Strength, that was an understatement. These men were like prime fighting bulls.

To Fogarty, the communication, following training, between Tanaka and the *oyakata* resembled a pantomime. Hands waving and a great deal of mutual bowing, punctuated by staccato bursts of conversation and the occasional scowl. Completed by an embrace for Tanaka and a handshake for the lieutenant that was as close as his right hand had ever come to being pulverized.

'What the hell went on in there?' he asked as they walked from the *Chiba-beya*.

'I didn't want to offend the *oyakata*,' Tanaka answered.

'Which means?'

'I couldn't suggest he had a rougue sumo,' Tanaka replied. 'That would not only imply shame to the *oyakata*

but would bring bad luck to his *beya*. I had to compliment
him on his stable and on the discipline of his players.'

'I don't understand how that gets us any closer to the guy
in the picture,' Fogarty said.

'It was a way of getting to the fact that my father donates
money to the *Chiba-beya*.'

Fogarty was still puzzled.

'*Giri*, Bill, it's another form of *giri*. Ken scouts a few new
boys, my father contributes cash. The *oyakata* owes my
family.'

'I see,' the lieutenant said.

'Ken already told him why we were coming, that we
wanted information about a particular man,' Tanaka continued. 'I needed to make it clear that the man would no
longer be a member of the *Chiba-beya* or any of the
affiliated stables . . . I forced him to talk without causing him
to lose face.'

They kept walking as they spoke, through the crowded
street and toward the car park. Fogarty listened, frustrated by
his friend's roundabout method of getting a straight answer.
Everybody talked in circles here, even Josef. Fogarty was
beginning to get angry.

He stopped, intending to face Tanaka. As he turned, he
collided head-on with a diminutive woman in a white face-
mask – the type generally worn to prevent flu germs from
spreading. The woman bowed, backing away as she apologized for what was obviously Fogarty's fault. The lieutenant
stared after her.

'Everybody's so fucking polite here!' he blurted.

Tanaka placed a hand on his shoulder, nudging him
forward. Fogarty wouldn't budge.

'Joey, I'm with you on this. One hundred percent. You
know that. But it's starting to drive me nuts. I got to know
what's going on; I don't even know where we're going. I
need some answers.'

'I'm sorry, Bill. Sometimes I just assume you understand the way things are done here, particularly with anything traditional. It's all about honor, "face", saving it or losing it. If I had started to hint that I thought one of the finest coaches in our national sport had rubbed shoulders with a common criminal I may as well spit in his face. I've got to let him come to me, volunteer his information. And, because of *giri*, he's got to do it.'

'And did he?' Fogarty asked.

'He gave me the names of a few gymnasiums, places where the Western-style wrestlers train. A couple of his *maezumos*, men who never made it to the official ranking sheets, dropped out and turned professional. There's fast money in it, same as in the States. The fact that these men were once sumotori gives them instant novelty value.'

Fogarty nodded. At least he was back in the picture. As abstract as it seemed.

The Imperial Gymnasium was the third stop on their tour. It was located on the outskirts of the Ginza.

The Ginza reminded the lieutenant of New York City, somewhere between Fifth Avenue and Forty-second Street. Expensive shops, fine department stores, throngs of well-dressed people and then, as they traveled further south, a strip of gambling houses and what appeared to be brothels.

Another block and they were at the door of the Imperial gymnasium. Decorated by a grubby placard depicting a muscular torso with a disproportionately small head; the poster looked more like a warning than an invitation.

'Do you figure that happens to everybody who trains here?' the lieutenant asked.

Once inside they were assailed by the combined odor of sweat and mildew.

'Not exactly the pomade of the *dohyo*,' Fogarty quipped.

'No damned ventilation,' Tanaka remarked as they walked

a gauntlet of miniature muscle men, deeper into a jungle of steel exercise machines and gradiented dumbbells.

'There they are,' the lieutenant whispered, catching sight of two well-pumped wrestlers practicing inside a raised ring at the back of the gymnasium. Working in counter-time to Tina Turner's 'Simply the Best', which belted out of the wall-mounted speakers.

Another yard forward and they were intercepted by a man with no neck, wall to wall tattoos and two gold rings adorning the pierced nipples of his bare chest.

'What you want, mister?' the human barrier asked, planting himself firmly in front of Josef.

Tanaka answered in Japanese and, after a fitful start, the lieutenant was treated to another machine gun conversation. Until Tanaka turned and began an animated series of hand gestures in his direction. Following which the man studied the detective and grunted.

Whatever Tanaka was saying appeared to be working. The barrier was loosening up, showing teeth, mostly gold, in an expression somewhere between a smile and a grimace. He was also nodding his head. Then he turned and bellowed to the men in the ring. They disentangled themselves, climbed through the ropes and walked towards Tanaka and Fogarty.

The wrestlers were big, well fed and muscular, but they neither looked like nor moved with the class of the *sumotori*.

Fogarty was certain that somewhere within Tanaka's dialogue he heard the name 'Hulk Hogan' and something that sounded like the 'Ultimate Warrior'. After which, both the barrier and the two sides of beef turned and cast appraising glances in his direction.

'What the hell's going on, Joey?' he asked finally.

Tanaka barely broke rhythm as he changed from Japanese to English.

'The guy with the tattoos operates this gym, looks after

these guys and a few others. Trains them, makes their matches. I'm explaining to him how you discovered our two most popular American wrestlers. How you guided their careers and how well respected you are in American wrestling circles ... That you're looking for some new talent.'

So that's it, I'm a wrestling scout, Fogarty realized. He looked the two wrestlers over and smiled.

The wrestler closer to the lieutenant nodded his approval and twitched his pectoralis muscles. Tanaka slipped back into Japanese and the conversation continued. Now the lieutenant, who was suddenly a featured player, recognized the words '*rikishi*' and '*sumotori*'.

Then everything went ice cold.

The barrier ordered both his men to return to the ring.

His next words, directed at the lieutenant resembled the bark of a dog.

'What you want, mister?'

Fogarty opened his arms expansively and said, '*Rikishi, sumotori*!'

And Tanaka and the manager were off on another verbal exchange.

When it lulled Tanaka turned and explained to the lieutenant that there were no *sumotori* currently training at the Imperial. That, at one time, there had been several and, maybe, if they were prepared to return in a few days, the manager could be more helpful.

Following which Josef reached into his pocket, withdrew a pile of yen and handed it to the man. The money was accepted without thanks. A single bow and the meeting was over.

Tanaka turned and looked back just before he and Fogarty reached the steps.

He could just make out the figure of the manager, lit by a bare overhead bulb, standing in his cubicle of an office, behind the ring. He had a telephone receiver in his right hand, dialing with his left. One way or another he wasn't wasting any time.

The worst-dressed guys in the place

It was after nine o'clock when they arrived at the Park Royal. Fogarty had intended to change hotels, to throw off the surveillance team that seemed to live in the Park Royal's lobby. Now all he could think of was a steak, french fries and and getting his head down on a soft pillow.

'Do you feel like dinner?' Josef asked, pushing open the glass-fronted doors.

'Is the Pope Catholic?' the lieutenant replied, then nodded to the two detectives who were attempting to look inconspicuous in the center of the lobby. 'Why are they always the worst-dressed guys in the place?'

Tanaka glanced in the direction of the two men. Polyester suits and cheap ties. 'I'll phone Ken, he'll want to know how we got on at the *Chiba-beya* . . . Maybe he'll join us.'

'Does he have to?' Fogarty asked. There was more negativity in his voice than he had intended.

'Have you got a problem with my cousin?' Tanaka sounded irritated.

'I don't particularly trust him, if that's what you mean,' Fogarty answered.

'What gives you reason to say that?' Josef's voice was louder now and the two undercover policeman were tuned in.

Fogarty knew what was happening. He and Josef were

exhausted, their tempers frayed. He wanted to shut up but couldn't quite manage it. 'There's something wrong with the guy, I just feel it,' he snapped.

'Right—' Josef said, stopping and meeting Fogarty eye to eye, 'like there was something wrong with me ... Do you ever consider that you may be out of your depth?'

'Yeah, maybe. And maybe not,' Fogarty shot back, then turned toward the elevator, 'see you in the morning.'

Josef stared after him.

'Bill!' He called the lieutenant's name one time, just as the elevator door closed.

Fogarty dragged off his clothes, sat down on the side of the bed and picked up the phone for room service. He began to dial and aborted the call. He was afraid he'd be asleep by the time the hamburger arrived.

He lay back on the hard mattress.

What the fuck am I doing here? he wondered.

His self-hate was mixed with self-pity and the acute embarrassment of being a big ugly foreigner in a country of delicacy and manners. On top of that, he was uninvited. Tanaka had not asked for his assistance.

He had taken it upon himself to play The Lone Ranger. *Another attempt to purge my soul.* As if Sarah and his daughter Ann were looking down from heaven, tallying points on his stumbling existence. Trying to decide whether he could join them at the end of his run. And here he was, using everyone in his path, in an awkward attempt to score.

Do you ever consider that you may be out of your depth? Tanaka's question took on universal significance.

'Yes.' The lieutenant answered to the white ceiling of the room. Then he heard a noise, like the grunt of a pig. Every muscle in his body twitched in unison. He jolted upright. 'You're snoring, Bill,' Sarah's voice whispered from some-where in his memory. 'Roll over.' He rolled over and slept.

*

Ken Sato wasn't home and Josef stood a moment in front of the shrine. Staring at the dim reflection of his own face in the mirror. *What an ungrateful asshole.*

He owed Bill Fogarty. The guy was way out on a limb, again. Christ, he owed him so much and all he could manage was an insult.

He walked the corridor to his room, checked his watch. Ten o'clock, that made it eight a.m. in Philadelphia.

He missed Rachel, right down to the empty hollow of his stomach. It was a strange feeling, one that he'd had for several days. A longing for her without the anticipation of seeing her again. As if Rachel had been permanently removed from his life.

He reminded himself that she had been gone only two weeks, that they had spoken four times by telephone; that there was a limit on the time he would be away.

He was going to marry Rachel, spend the rest of his life with her. Yet, the hollow remained.

Tanaka sat on the edge of the futon. He felt tears welling, as if they were conspiring to fill the emptiness that was swallowing him.

He lifted the phone beside his bed. Dialed his own number in Philadelphia, Rachel's number. He needed her to be there. Needed to hear her voice. That soft husky voice would reconnect him, pull him back from the edge.

Six rings and the telephone was picked up.

'Hello, this is Doctor Saunders' answering service.'

He muffled an urge to shout down the phone, to curse the woman at the end of the line, to demand to be put through to Rachel. He slammed the receiver down.

Shouldn't get on to Rachel like this anyway. She's worried enough without me sounding like I've lost it. I'm exhausted. Completely exhausted. Sleep, I need to sleep . . . I'll call her in the morning.

He got out of his clothes, washed and returned to the futon. He drifted off in starts, slipping in and out of consciousness, before the blackness opened and took him under . . .

The truth serum

Philadelphia, USA

Sodium Pentothal was developed in the United States during the middle of the nineteen thirties. It was originally used as a low dosage sedative, or sleep inducer.

Until another of its unique properties was discovered. This clear, liquidized drug was also an effective disinhibitor to the section of the cerebral cortex that stored memory and facilitated the release of information otherwise blocked or suppressed. In other words, Pentothal could help 'loosen' the mind and tongue, thus earning it the title of 'truth serum'.

In addition to this, the 'truth serum' produced an amnesic reaction, stimulating the long term memory while having no effect on the 'short term': this meant that subjects could recall 'buried' episodes and recall them, yet after the drug wore off, there would be no memory of the recollections.

Combined with regressive therapy, a form of freeing deep memory blocks through hypnosis, the 'truth serum' can produce dramatic results.

Rachel Saunders had arrived at the Trauma Care Center, a specially equipped room in the east wing of the Philadelphia Veterans Hospital, at seven o'clock that morning. She wore a cotton training suit and canvas tennis sneakers. No belt, no bra, nothing she could strangle herself with.

Stan Leibowitz was already there, waiting for her. Fresh and warm and reassuring.

There were two chairs, soft and heavily upholstered; they sat facing each other at the side of the room nearest the padded door, behind them the room was empty, except for the six-inch thick, cotton-covered squares of foamed rubber which covered every inch of floor and wall. Above, track lights lined the high ceiling, controlled by a dimmer switch, their initial brightness was intended to help remove the fear and uncertainty from the working area below.

Leibowitz talked to Rachel first, casual easy conversation, mundane, anything to relax her, to create the illusion that what was about to take place was not out of the ordinary.

Then he began work, injecting her with twenty milligrams of Sodium Pentothal from a twenty-three gauge syringe.

Three minutes later he began the induction phase of the hypnosis. Talking Rachel Saunders through the muscles of her body, from her temples to her toes, inviting her to release all tension. Deepening the hypnosis by timing the flow of his words to the rise and fall of her abdomen and chest, creating a cadence between his voice and her breath. Studying her movement, breaking his sentences at the peak of her inhalation, speaking as she exhaled, slowly, softly.

'You are floating ... In a warm sea ... A silent sea ... A healing sea ... The water is soothing, friendly, there is nothing but goodness in this water ... And you are part of this goodness, this feeling ... You are completely safe here ...' The psychiatrist's voice was barely above a whisper.

Her body was a shell, a hollow shell, floating on water. There was no weight to the shell, no separation between the water and her skin.

'I want you to leave your body in the sea. It will be fine there ... Nothing can happen to it, no harm, only healing ...

It is strong now, and it will be stronger when you return to it ... That's fine, Rachel, that's fine ... follow my voice, follow me outside ...'

The separation was beginning, as if a tiny portal had opened in the center of her forehead and a thin stream of consciousness was seeping out.

'We're going back to that place, that place in your memory, into that secret room ...'

Ten minutes from then, Rachel Saunders was inside that space in her mind that contained the horror of the Mantis, keeping it sealed away from her conscious thought. Most of the time.

She was walking, through a small office; there was stationery on the desk, 'Philadelphia Zoo' printed at the top. Past the desk, through a door, inside a corridor with gray metal pipes. Boilers and pipes, like a metal maze. An overhead light, wrapped in wire mesh, lighting a staircase leading down. Into a thick wet heat. She could see it, clear and defined.

'I'm no goin' down there, not goin' dow',' she began, her voice low and thick, the words garbled.

'It's all right, Rachel ... It's okay to go down there today. I'm with you,' Leibowitz answered.

'Josef?'

'Josef is with you, too,' the psychiatrist confirmed, 'breathe, in ... out ... in ... out ... it's easy.'

She was going down, as if she were sinking into warm, soft water. Water she could breathe. Surprisingly she did not struggle. She had struggled before, this time she was controlling her fear, breathing the wetness, keeping her eyes open, seeing.

'That's right, Rachel, control your breath, let your consciousness ride on your breath.'

Glass tanks, cages, animal eyes glowing in the dark. This was the area of the zoo in which the keepers kept the 'feed' animals, mice and rats. She knew that, figured it out, her mind working rationally. A rattlesnake in a windowed box, its tail crushed, its rattle broken, issuing a silent warning. More pipes, dripping with condensation. It was hot now, getting hotter.

She kept moving, floating forward, midway between a state of dream and memory.

'Where are you, Rachel? What do you see?'

'The end of a corridor, like a hallway ... A door; it's locked, the door is locked.'

'Locked?'

'Yes, I can't go in ...'

'You can't go in because the door is locked?'

'The door is locked.'

'Is that the reason you can't enter the room?' the psychiatrist repeated.

Rachel Saunders had begun to sweat, not the watery sweat of athletic exertion but the clinging film of fear. It was the first indication of abreaction, the uncontrollable release of emotion.

'Don't want to see what's inside,' she stammered, getting up from her chair.

Leibowitz stood at the same time, stepping aside, allowing her past, into the middle area of the padded room.

'What is inside that room, Rachel?' The psychiatrist's voice was demanding, not threatening.

Rachel Saunders began screaming. Taking deep, gulping breaths, and screaming.

Stan Leibowitz touched her shoulder as she sank to her knees.

'I am right here with you, Rachel ... You are not alone ...'

'Josef! Josef!'

'Josef is here.'

'I don't want him here, don't want him here. He doesn't know!'

'Doesn't know what?'

'Doesn't know who's inside the room.'

Stan Leibowitz backed off.

'He's going to be hurt!' she continued.

She was on her hands and knees, staring at the beige floor.

'I know who it is . . . Josef can't see him . . . He can't see!'

Then she straightened, clasping her hands together in front of her chest, as if she were praying, eyes open, looking at Stan Leibowitz.

'Oh no, oh no . . . I don't like this,' she whispered.

The door was open now; it had been opened from the inside. Light. Light coming from the space beyond the opening. Heat and mist, colored by the glow of light, enveloping her.

The psychiatrist placed his arm gently around her shoulder, sheltering her. He had used the regressive therapy four times with Rachel Saunders, four times since her trauma. Each time her reaction had been consistent, if somewhat less intense, than the previous session. This was different.

'Is he there, Rachel? Can you see him?' the psychiatrist asked. 'No need to get any closer . . . Just describe him to me.' This was new ground for him; he trod carefully.

She was in a hallway. Not at the zoo . . . This was somewhere else. This hallway had cloth walls, narrow and dark.

'Do you see him?'

Stan Leibowitz's voice entered her consciousness, guiding her. Asking her to face her fear.

Blood pulsed through her temples.

'Yes . . . Yes, I can see him.'

Standing in the partially opened door, vapor trailing from the room behind . . . the membrane between his body and the vapor undefined. As if his body were being created from the steamy vapor.

She exhaled, trying to maintain control. Seeing, even though she did not want to see.

'Willard Ng ... The Mantis ... You see him,' Leibowitz confirmed.

The figure was hardening, becoming separated from the vapor. Nose flaring and jaw jutting forward, mouth like a dark cruel slit below the spreading nostrils. No eyes. A forehead without eyes.

'No, it's not him. Not Willard Ng ... Willard Ng is gone ... The Mantis is dead.'

The psychiatrist felt a moment of euphoria. Rachel Saunders was through the tunnel. There was no monster, no Willard Ng. No Mantis. Dead. She had said he was dead ... *So why was she still shaking?*

Now the eyes became visible, as if they had always been there, hiding in the vapor. She knew those eyes. She had seen them before. The way they looked at her. Into her, through her. And the man's skin, *something wrong with his skin*.

And suddenly Rachel Saunders was fighting, punching, scratching; she caught Stan Leibowitz on the side of the face, her fingernails drawing blood.

'It's all right, Rachel ... It's all right ... It's over,' he said, wrapping his arm tight around her—

The way that Ken Sato had wrapped his arm around her in the hallway, restraining her. She gulped for breath, feeling her knees give way.

The psychiatrist coordinated his physical movement with hers, allowing her to settle onto the padded floor, to curl up, knees to her chest, hands covering her eyes. The Pentothal was wearing off and Rachel Saunders was crying softly.

'There is no need to remember any of this, Rachel, it will be gone from your mind, cleansed ...' Leibowitz began a variation on his usual posthypnotic suggestion when Rachel looked up. Eyes wide, staring at him.

'Oh no, I will remember this,' she said.

Rachel Saunders slept then, for twenty minutes.

'Ken Sato, Josef's cousin ... He's evil.' They were her first words when she came to ...

A visitor

Later, Josef wasn't sure how many minutes or hours had passed; he was awakened by footsteps against the bare floor of the meditation area.

His first thought was that Ken was home. Walking down the hall. Passing his own door and continuing in the direction of Josef's room. But that didn't make sense, it was the middle of the night.

Not Ken. Not Ken's footsteps, he realized as he sat up. In time to see the partition slide open.

A black silhouette filled the frame of the door. A man, staring in at him, eyes adjusting to the darkness. Then the man charged forward.

Tanaka reacted on reflex and adrenaline, rolling from the futon, finding his feet but not his balance; he threw a single punch that smacked ineffectively against his attacker's chest. Then he was encircled by massive arms, hoisting him like a rag doll, crushing inwards.

He exhaled, making room inside the grip, driving his right knee upwards. Down and up again, and again. The fourth shot caught the man's testicles.

His arms went slack, giving Josef space to drop to his hands and knees, rolling backward and to his feet.

They stood, facing each other.

The man was taller than Tanaka by half a foot and outweighed him by a hundred pounds. Plus he was quick, Josef could tell by the way he moved, edging forward, feinting with his hands and body. Pressuring. A *sumotori*; he moved like a *sumotori*.

My brother. You killed my brother, the thought centered Tanaka's mind.

The man took another step forward and Josef kicked. A high *mawashi geri*, using his instep, whipping his foot inward, pulling with an extra twist of his hips as he dug into the side of the thick neck. Dropping the man to his knees, eyes open and dazed.

And now I'm going to kill you, Tanaka vowed, stepping laterally, gripping the man's chin with his left hand while using his right to push against the side of his head. Moving it counterclockwise to prepare the muscles before the clockwise break. Vaguely aware of a pressure on his own right thigh, to the front, and to the rear.

Josef started the clockwise twist as the man began to rise, tightening his grasp on Tanaka's thigh, levering from beneath him. Destroying his technique as he heaved him backwards, into the solid wall of the room. Moving with him, gripping the waistband of Josef's undershorts, tearing them from his body as he threw him in the other direction.

Straight through the shoji partition. Following him, picking him up from the floor, pulling his naked body close to his own.

Do what I want with you now. Do what I want, he thought, holding Tanaka like a lover in the darkness, pressing himself inward against him.

Fuck you. I could fuck you. Like he fucks me. And you would be powerless to resist. Like I am powerless.

'From the Hyoo. This is from the Hyoo,' he whispered, lowering his head, pressing closer into Josef. Kissing him full on the lips, pushing his tongue inside his dry mouth. Deeper and deeper.

*

Then it came. The pain. Like a red searing fire, thick with heat, and loud in his head. He wanted to scream, needed to scream, to release the agony. But the pain would not let go.

Tanaka was wrenching, side to side, as hard as he could, teeth clamped on the fat tongue. Feeling the hardness die inside the man's trousers. Then he reached up, digging his thumb into the giant's right eye. The huge head jerked backward, and both tongue and eye came free at once.

Tanaka tripped over the futon as he fell.

All around him was noise, loud and furious, like the bellowing of a beast. Fighting for its last breath of life.

He rolled sideways, away from the sound. Then the fury caught him, blood and spit flying from its mouth, landing hard and crushing his lungs. Fingers digging into his throat, finding his windpipe, all technique and dignity discarded, replaced by the will to survive.

Tanaka raised his hands, wrapping his arms over the top of his assailant's, digging his own fingers inward. Wedging the man's windpipe between his two thumbs, pressing. Gripping the way he was being gripped.

They remained like that for seconds, one trying to outlast the other.

Our Father who art in heaven. The prayer began in Josef's head. That same tired prayer, unable to help him.

Hallowed be thy name. Not his voice, it was his brother's voice, whispering his prayer. His fingers were coming loose, like a rock climber on a perilous ledge, a chasm below ... *Hold on, hold on, hold on—*

A last, desperate effort, all his strength; he felt the windpipe begin to give, to break. Heard the man choke. Knew he had him, was killing him. Killing his brother's executioner. Killing him.

He pulled his right hand back and drove his hardened fingertips inward, just once, a short sharp strike, finishing the break, closing the supply of air to the lungs. Watched the man reel backward. Choking on his own blood.

Then a whirr of sound, like wind, whistling.

Again the wind. Louder. Louder. A bright light. A bolt of lightning. Then nothing.

'Josef? Talk to me, Josef . . . Talk to me.' Japanese. Someone was speaking Japanese.

He tried to answer but the fingers were still in his throat. He reached up. Felt his trachea, the swelling that had already begun. Dug in with his own fingers, cradled the displaced thyroid cartilage, moved it forward. *Better, that's better. I'm all right.*

'All right.' His voice repeated his thought, sounding gruff, foreign to him.

'Don't move, Josef-san, stay still.'

It was Ken Sato who spoke. Soothing.

Josef saw the *katana* in Ken's hands, its blade gleaming, wiped of blood.

The whirr, the lightning. It began to come together. He looked down. The wrestler's corpse lay on the floor, the wound to its neck as clean and as neat as if it had been made with a surgeon's incision. Flesh, bone, and muscle. No head.

'Maybe some damage to your upper ribs, Josef-san. Your arm only bruised, not broken. Spine is okay. Maybe slightly out of alignment.' Ken was touching him, gently, carefully, his hands tracing the outline of Josef's lower vertebrae.

Tanaka tried to stand.

'Easy, Josef-san. Move easy,' Ken said, assisting him to the side of the futon.

Josef could see the head now, lying on its side against the low night table, lips swollen and clotted with blood, a single eye staring at the lacquered leg of the table, black hair thick and oiled.

Josef stared at the puffy lips, his mind clearing.

The Hyoo. This is from the Hyoo. The last words those lips had spoken. Before they had kissed him. Tanaka's stomach turned; he looked away. Sick, he was going to be sick. He heaved once, then again, spitting up bile. Ken sat down beside him, wrapping his arm around his shoulder.

'I think we should call the police, Josef-san.'

'Bill Fogarty. I want to call Bill first,' Tanaka said.

Ken looked reluctant.

'We must report this, Josef-san. There will be much trouble if we delay.'

'Of course, Ken, I know that, I know that,' Tanaka replied, forcing a reassuring smile. 'Just let me call Bill, then the police.'

Ken Sato shook his head, reaching for the phone.

'Ken. Please,' Josef insisted, moving to stop him, 'that's the man who killed Hironori.'

'Killed your brother?'

'Yes,' Josef answered.

At first Fogarty did not recognize the low, hoarse voice on the phone.

'I've been injured, Bill, my throat's swollen ... But we got the son of a bitch, Bill. We got him.'

The lieutenant didn't need to ask who. He'd felt it coming. It had just been a matter of when.

'I'll try to hold the police back till you get here. We can have first look at this guy ... Ken Sato's apartment. I'm at Ken's.'

Then Josef put the phone down and turned toward his cousin.

'Thank you, Ken,' he said.

To Josef, it no longer mattered that he had defeated the man; it was Ken who had finished him. Ken who had come to his aid. He owed him. *Giri.* A lot of *giri.*

The smell of death

Fogarty took the hotel elevator to the underground car park. If the two surveillance men were still in the lobby he didn't want them trailing him to the scene of the crime.

He walked up the exit ramp of the garage and out into the street. Hailed a cab, showing the driver a piece of paper with Ken Sato's address written on it, in Japanese.

At four o'clock in the morning Tokyo traffic was thin. He was outside Sato's building in half an hour.

Inside, the place smelled like death. It was a strange smell, one which the lieutenant had grown familiar with in the past twenty years.

When he was young, new to homicide, and the old boys, detectives in their last years before retirement, said a crime scene smelled like death – before they had seen a body or found a trace of violence – Fogarty thought they were dramatizing. Adding a macabre edge to their jobs.

He hadn't smelled anything, not for the first few months. Then, little by little, he began to pick it up. Like a dog on a scent, specific fragrances in the air.

At first it was the more pungent odors, like the ammonia of urine or the stale, rubbery stink of dried faeces. As his senses became more refined he could detect blood, a somber muted odor that wafted below the surface of the sharper, more caustic ones. And the smell of fear and struggle, that musky odor of adrenaline mixed with body sweat.

Now Bill Fogarty was a connoisseur. And, as Ken Sato

greeted him at the door, the lieutenant, unselfconsciously and with only a slight lift of his head, inhaled. Two short, quick inhalations through his connoisseur's nostrils. He smelled blood, fear and death.

Josef was examining the corpse when Sato led the lieutenant into the bedroom. No need to open the door, they were able to walk straight through the torn panel of the shoji wall.

Tanaka was holding the dead man's right hand in his own; thick, gnarled fingers, as thick as two of Tanaka's.

'This is him. Look at his hand, broken and re-set, dislocated metacarpal,' Tanaka said.

He saw Fogarty's eyes dart from the man's hand to his disembodied head: the mouth, the heavy jaw, the high broad forehead.

'Ken saved my life,' Tanaka said. It was easier that way. Easier than going in to the whole thing.

Fogarty looked from the head to the sheathed *katana* lying on the ruffled quilt of the futon, then at Ken Sato. He nodded his head.

'I will call the police now, Josef-san. Please.'

Josef nodded and went back to the body, Fogarty knelt beside him.

'Look at his other hand. It was hidden in the photograph,' Tanaka said.

Fogarty stared at the callused hand, covered in tiny, coiled ringlets of black hair. The fingers were beginning to set, bent like talons in the earliest phase of rigor mortis. The man's fingernails were manicured, cut and polished. All except the little finger; it ended in a smooth pink knob of scar tissue.

'*Yubitsume*,' Tanaka said.

Fogarty was about to ask what *yubitsume* meant. Tanaka beat him to it.

'Finger-cut, the top joint of this bastard's little finger has been amputated.'

Finger-cutting, Fogarty had heard about it from customs officials and airport policemen. During a period in the mid-eighties when they had tried to keep organized crime out of Atlantic City. A network that included money launderers from the Far East.

The Japanese gangsters had arrived with plastic fingers to conceal their missing digits.

'*Yubitsume.*' Fogarty repeated the word as he stared at the hand.

It involved the severing of the first or second joint of the little finger. Then the appendage was wrapped in fine cloth and handed ceremoniously to the respective ganglord. The purpose of the 'finger-cut' was to atone for the amputee's transgression. Cowardice, disobedience, revealing gang secrets; any crime that did not justify expulsion or death was punished by self-amputation.

Tanaka met the lieutenant's eyes.

'Yakuza,' Tanaka confirmed.

First the police took Josef to the general hospital in Azabu; he was X-rayed and examined, then informed that the sixth and seventh ribs on the left side of his body had been fractured but not broken. No setting or binding necessary, just pain killers and ice compresses.

His trachea was basically intact with minor damage to the anterior portion of the thyroid cartilage, forming his Adam's apple. He would be hoarse for a week or two.

Then he, Ken Sato and Bill Fogarty were driven to the Tokyo Police Headquarters and interrogated, at first individually and then as a group.

The interrogation took place in a small room with a blackened window against the wall facing the chairs. The two interrogators were in plain clothes and wore no identification; they were exceedingly thorough, in a way that seemed more military than constabulatory. Concerned with anything the deceased may have said rather than with the actual killing. Almost a debriefing. Everything was recorded on tape, both video and audio.

Tanaka kept the word '*Hyoo*' out of his answers. Instinct mixed with paranoia.

The entire series of interviews took eight hours and in that time, although made obvious by the positioning of their chairs and the periodic glances from the interrogator towards the blackened window, the person, or persons behind the glass remained hidden.

And then it was over. They were shown the door. No mention of legal proceedings or police follow-ups. They walked out into an overcast Tokyo afternoon.

'What was that all about?' Fogarty asked as they headed for a taxi rank.

'It was about them knowing a hell of a lot more than we do,' Josef answered.

It's over and we're going home. Back to the USA, Fogarty thought as they squeezed into the taxi. *That's what it's really about.*

Tanaka and Fogarty got off at the Park; Ken Sato said that he was already hours late for work and stayed with the cab.

'The guy cuts off a man's head, gets grilled by the police for eight hours, then straightens his tie and hustles down to the office. Is that Japanese efficiency or is your cousin just an exceptional human being?' Fogarty asked, watching Sato depart.

Without answering, Tanaka turned and walked toward the entrance of the hotel. Fogarty caught up with him and together they marched into the lobby and to the elevator.

'C'mon, Joey, I've seen police officers, guys who've been on the force for ten years, men who have seen it all. Then it comes down to shooting somebody, actually making a kill and it destroys them. Guilt, months in therapy. And those guys are using a gun, not a sword. They're not slicing a man's head clean from his shoulders.'

Tanaka waited for the elevator door to close. 'Bill. The man did it for me; he's the only friend we've got here, the only one who has gone right over the line.'

'And you don't think it's strange—'

'That he wasn't a quivering ball of nerves, whining and shaking?' Tanaka's voice was taking on an edge.

'Yeah . . .Exactly.'

'You still don't understand us ... Nowhere near. You don't understand the difference between the public "face" and the inner man. Whatever Ken is going through, it's Ken's business, private and personal. He isn't going to add to my burden by unloading his emotions on me. He isn't even going to suggest that I leave his apartment. No matter how much danger I subject him to. You've got to start to realize that what you see here is not what you get.'

So should you, the lieutenant thought, keeping his mouth shut as the doors of the elevator opened. They got off, began walking to his room.

'Ken Sato has reminded me of something, Bill. He's reminded me of what being Japanese is about. Somewhere along the line I forgot.'

There was a quality to Tanaka's tone that Fogarty didn't recognize. Maybe it was the hoarseness of his voice but he didn't think so. There was something else, an attitude, a self-righteousness. And Fogarty never trusted the judgement of the self-righteous.

'So what are you going to do?' the lieutenant asked, sliding the coded entry card into the lock.

'Wait for you to pack—'

He's sending me home. I don't understand what 'being Japanese is about' so he's sending me home. Fogarty was livid at the thought.

'And then we'll change hotels. I'm coming in with you ...

Distance myself from my family. It's too dangerous,' Tanaka added.

Fogarty felt a strange gratitude mixed with anger. At least he wasn't being dismissed. On the other hand, why the hell wouldn't Tanaka let go, quit? He had accomplished what he'd set out to do. The man who had murdered his brother was dead.

The lieutenant wanted to go home. And he wanted Tanaka to go with him, but he knew better than to suggest it. He knew that whatever was going on here wasn't over.

Rachel Saunders put the receiver down. She had tried Ken Sato's apartment and received no answer. No answer again at Bill Fogarty's hotel. She'd left a message there and gone on to call Grace Tanaka at the family home. Only to be told by a house servant, in very broken English, that Mrs Tanaka was away, in a place that sounded like Botono. Rachel left her telephone number and hung up.

By then her intuition had been dulled by rational thought. Perhaps it was just as well she hadn't made it through to Josef or Bill. The idea of announcing that Ken Sato was 'dangerous' seemed a bit farfetched, particularly if she confessed to her method of deduction.

Yet the feeling remained with her; she couldn't shake it.

A solitary hunter

The Leopard lay alone in the bath. The water was tepid and his markings barely visible. He had been there a long time, thinking about love, loss and enlightenment.

His lover's name had been Hoshi Satoru. He had come from Aomori, the only son of a local fisherman.

It had taken a great deal of persuasion and a few yen to convince his father that the boy's future lay in Tokyo, as a player in Japan's national sport.

At first Hoshi had hated the big city, unused to its pace and pressure. He had wanted to go home, to forget about the business of wrestling.

The Leopard had taken him half way, permitting him to leave the stable and live for a time with him. A quiet period in which the boy could contemplate the direction of his life. It was during this period, when Hoshi Satoru had been most vulnerable, most open to suggestion, that the Leopard had taken him as his lover. Subtly, gently at first, sharing a bed, a single caress, no more than that. Self-control was the essence of the Leopard's seduction.

Until the day in the bath house, after the heat and steam had effected the transformation. The first time the Leopard had truly revealed himself.

He would never forget the boy's face as he approached him, rising from the water, walking slowly up the stone steps of the bathing pool.

Satoru's face was a study in fear, mixed with such

reverence, as if he were witnessing a miracle, the unveiling of something secret and sacred.

The Leopard had taken him then, as an animal takes another animal, without reserve. After that, the boy had been his; he had been marked as property.

When Satoru returned to the *beya* he was different, more driven, needing to win, to conquer. Needing to dominate others as he, himself, had been dominated. As if each opponent, each victory, returned him a step at a time to self-possession.

His ferocity earned him the fighting name '*Kuma*', the bear, and his *oyakata* believed he would make it into the *makanouchi*, or top division, within twelve years.

These great hopes were ended by a broken hand in the fourth tournament of his third year. Thrusting out with *tsukiotoshi*, he had connected awkwardly with his opponent's sternum, forcing his fingers backward, breaking the bones in his palm. The hand had been manipulated on the spot, an attempt to keep him in the *basho*. It was rebroken a week later and secured by a plaster cast. Only to be broken a third time while trying to strengthen it against the *teppo*.

By then, there was no returning to the life of a fisherman. He had become used to being a minor celebrity, to having people stare as he strolled the crowded streets of the Ginza. Of having mothers thrust their children into his arms, believing that a child held by a *sumotori* would grow to be healthy and strong.

Used to dreaming of the silk robes of the high-ranking *seketori*, of the apprentice who would walk beside him, carrying his umbrella.

Used to the Leopard's embrace.

He had cried like a baby in his lover's arms the day his topknot was cut. And his career as a *rikishi* was officially over.

Then came professional wrestling, Western style, staged and gaudy.

He maintained the outward appearance of a *sumotori*; he had learned to prepare the *chanko-nabe*, or tournament stew. Kept his calorific intake up, worked with weights, learned the movements of Western wrestling. But there was no real pay-off, no release. There could be no victory in a charade.

During this time of inner confusion the Leopard had not deserted him. Instead he offered consolation and guidance. And love, the only physical love that Satoru had ever known.

Until finally, the Leopard showed him the true way. As a mother teaches its cub the method of the kill. Allowed him to work beside him in the purification. Granted him the power of death.

And now it was over.

Satoru, his eternal child, had been sacrificed on the altar of enlightenment, leaving his creator to grieve. All things which are possessed will be cast asunder. That was the rule. Vengeance. That was also the rule. Not now, not here, but soon. Very soon.

The Leopard was weeping when he stepped from the water.

Now he was truly solitary, a solitary hunter.

The New Orleans

The Japanese have two types of hotels that are particular to their tight, almost claustrophobic living conditions.

The first is the 'capsule hotel', in which the sleeping accommodations are literally 'capsules', plastic boxes in which a guest can touch the ceiling and all four walls without actually moving from the center of his plastic box. These are intended for the traveling businessman but are often frequented by single men with apartments nearby, who rent a 'capsule' in order to enjoy the human contact and conversation available in the hotel lounge.

The other type of hotel is the 'love hotel', primarily set up for husbands and wives to escape the cramped atmosphere of the family apartment and share some uninterrupted love-making.

The New Orleans was a 'love hotel' in the heart of Shinjuku. It did very little tourist trade, with the exception of the prostitutes who brought their Western clients in for a quick *daite* (fuck) and featured a cowboy bar and grill with karaoke music – backing tracks of well-known American hits – mainly country and western. Many a slanted-eyed Johnny Cash had wailed a drunken 'Folsom City Blues' at the New Orleans.

It was the kind of place where a man could register without a passport and with any name that he chose. No questions asked.

It would take a few days for anyone to find an Irish cop and a half-caste Japanese at the New Orleans. And a few days was all Josef Tanaka figured they had.

Not even Ken Sato was privy to their new and colorful residence. Not a matter of mistrust, instead a matter of family safety.

The fact that Sato had been made aware of Hironori's assassination and of the threats to Mikio Tanaka had an unsettling effect on the lieutenant.

It was, he admitted, an inevitable consequence of the day's events, but one he could have done without.

The three of them met that night at a quiet restaurant in the Roppongi area, south of Shinjuku.

They removed their shoes at the door and sat on tatami mats. Fogarty kept an eye out for surveillance as he struggled with his chopsticks; Josef matched cousin Ken slurp for slurp.

There was no mention of what had happened hours earlier at Sato's apartment and it was driving the lieutenant crazy. He needed to exorcise it, the murder, the interrogation. All he was getting was a run down on family life at the Tanakas': mother away, father exhausted.

At least, for his benefit, Ken and Josef were speaking English. He tried to listen between the lines, to think Japanese. Concluded that Mikio Tanaka was unaware of recent events. For one reason or another the police were not keeping Josef's father abreast of their investigation. Everything was on a 'need to know' basis.

Then Ken launched into a description of his work on the docks. How, in the past fifteen years, he had progressed from negotiating simple shipping contracts to overseeing the takeover of several rival companies. He kept bringing up the name of a town called Shimanoseki. Looking at Josef as if the name had particular significance.

Fogarty had to control himself. He wanted to talk about the deceased *sumotori*, about the police, the interrogation.

Who was behind the blackened window?

He stared at Ken Sato. Found it impossible to believe that the guy had decapitated another man less than twenty-four hours ago. And here he was, talking about business, about shipping transistor radios from Shimanoseki to Pusan, Korea. And Josef attentive to his every word.

The lieutenant lost concentration on his chopsticks and accidently rammed one into his throat. It had the same effect as a finger, causing him to gag, spitting a deep fried slice of eggplant onto the table. A couple of nearby guests at the restaurant turned around. *Next thing, one of these midgets will think I'm dying and try the Heimlich maneuver*, Fogarty thought, smiling to reassure the concerned faces that he was fine.

'Okay, Fogarty-san, okay?' Ken asked, briefly studying the eggplant.

Then, not waiting for an answer, Sato returned to transistor radios.

Fogarty felt his face flush. He was humiliated, and he was getting angry. Enough was enough. He was ready to call an end to the evening when Sato's voice dropped to a hush and the circular pattern of conversation reached its centerpoint.

'It is your father's only concession to the Yakuza, Josef-san. The shipment of electronic equipment into Pusan. Against the Korean trade embargo.'

Josef nodded as if he understood.

'Over a ton of methamphetamine comes over from Pusan every ten months and we have nothing to do with it. We are clean, Josef-san, clean.'

Josef spoke a few words of Japanese, Ken answered and Fogarty listened. Things were linking together in his mind. The Imperial Gymnasium, most certainly run by the Yakuza, and now an involvement between the Japanese and Korean gangs and Tanaka Industries. Organized crime muscling in on big business. It was the same old story.

'Maybe we should pay another visit to the Imperial,' the lieutenant suggested when the conversation between Josef and Ken lulled.

'No good, Bill. Won't get us anything but trouble. The police will be waiting for us and chances are the "coach" has been sent on an extended holiday,' Tanaka answered.

Then Ken launched into a fresh flow of Japanese, excluding Fogarty. By the time Sato stopped Tanaka was nodding and saying, '*Hai. Hai.*' Fogarty knew it meant 'yes'. Then Tanaka turned to the lieutenant.

'Ken is going to use his connections at the dock. See if he can set us up with one of the main *oyabuns.*'

Last time Ken set us up, you almost got killed, Fogarty thought. So hard he was sure both men read his mind.

'*Oyabun*?' He covered by questioning the word.

'The Yakuza is run on the *oyabun–kobun* system,' Tanaka answered. 'Meaning father role–child role. An *oyabun* is the father, providing advice, protection and help in all matters, the *kobun* is the child; he provides complete loyalty and service.'

Fogarty nodded, thinking of Marlon Brando as the Godfather. He looked again at Ken Sato. He had the eyes of a hit man. Cold, like a snake. *Why the fuck do I have it in for this guy?* he asked himself.

'Perhaps Josef and I should meet with *oyabun* alone,' Sato said, answering the lieutenant's private question.

Because somewhere in his uptight, narrow mind he doesn't rate me. Doesn't figure me for much, Fogarty told himself, before turning to Sato.

'Ken-san.' He began with his own rendition of the Japanese 'love them on the outside, loathe them on the inside' smile. 'Josef and I have worked together before. We are both trained in these matters. It would be a mistake to work separately now.'

Ken seemed prepared for the lieutenant's resistance. He

smiled, nodded his head and acquiesced.

'I will arrange the meeting.'

Fogarty had a brief flash of Ken Sato, Shinto robes and sacred tea, rubbing shoulders with the Japanese equivalent of John Gotti. Doing business with him. It was tough to imagine. Then Ken Sato did something that really stretched the lieutenant's imagination. He gave him a gift. A box the size of a telephone book, hard, probably made of wood, wrapped in dark red paper and bound with twine.

'For your comfort, Fogarty-san,' Ken said as the lieutenant accepted the present.

Fogarty was at a loss for words. Found himself fumbling with the knotted twine.

'Maybe better to save my present for your hotel room,' Sato added, pouring the thick green tea.

Fogarty and Tanaka had adjoining suites at the New Orleans. The lieutenant's was called 'The Riverboat Room' and Tanaka's 'The Creole'. The decor was somewhere between a Southern Baptist church and a speakeasy. Stained-glass windows and ceiling-mounted fans.

Fogarty sat down on the edge of his four-poster bed.

A few days, that's what Josef had predicted. *I hope he's right*, Fogarty thought as the out-of-tune karaoke singer began lavishing his vocal on top of the music.

Then he got down to business, untying the last knot in the twine and tearing the heavy red paper from the wooden box.

'Jesus Christ,' he said as he lifted the lid. The .38 Smith and Wesson five-shot revolver, complete with quick draw shoulder holster, and twenty rounds of ammunition lay like a sleeping princess in its velvet-lined container.

Fogarty lifted the weapon, cradled it in his shooting hand. Squeezed, raising it upward, aligning his palm with the knurls of the combat grip.

'Josef!' he called. 'Josef, I want you to see something.'

Tanaka opened the door separating their rooms. Stood staring at the .38.

He had removed his shirt; it was the first time that Fogarty had seen the bruises covering his torso. Like great ugly spills of red and purple, swollen and inflamed. Suddenly the gun felt heavier in his hand, more solid, like it had a purpose.

'A gift from your cousin,' Fogarty explained, extending the weapon, butt first.

Tanaka walked forward, taking it from his hand. Examined it. 'This could cost Ken a couple of years in jail. Firearms are strictly banned here . . . He must trust you, Bill.'

Fogarty felt small, very small. As if Tanaka was reminding him of every negative feeling he had projected toward Ken Sato. Maybe none of it was justified, maybe it was all just one big cultural gap.

'Yeah, he's putting himself out for us, Joey, that's for sure,' Fogarty admitted.

'He's family,' Tanaka replied, then handed back the .38, turned and walked to his own room, closing the door behind him.

Fogarty stared after him. They were growing apart, he and Tanaka. Maybe it was Japan, maybe the pressure, but they were becoming strangers again.

Philadelphia, USA

Rachel could hear the telephone ringing as she unlocked her door. Six rings and her service would pick it up.

She grabbed it on the fifth, thinking it might be Josef.

'Hello?'

'Hello, Rachel?'

She thought she recognized Grace Tanaka's voice; but it sounded too close.

'Grace?'

'Yes . . . It's me.'

'You sound like you're right next door.'

'I'm in Boston, at my sister's place.'

Rachel picked up the anxiety in the husky voice.

'What's going on?' she asked.

'They thought it was safer if I got out of Japan—'

'Josef?' Rachel could feel her mouth go dry.

'He's fine, working with his American friend. I had no idea, Rachel … No idea … Josef's brother was murdered.' Grace Tanaka was just managing to control her voice.

'I know, Grace, I know. I need to talk to you, face to face.'

'I could come to Philadelphia.'

'How soon?'

Shabu, Part II

Their meeting with *oyabun* Tak Ofudo could not have been more convenient. Seven blocks from the New Orleans, on the outskirts of Shinjuku. Literally a walk for Tanaka and the lieutenant.

Ofudo was big time. Not only did he control all of the action in Shinjuku; he also ran most of the Japanese night clubs in the Ginza and handled the lion's share of distribution on imports from Pusan.

Ken Sato had come through again.

Fogarty buttoned the middle button on his jacket as they rounded the last corner and started counting street numbers, searching for Ofudo's office.

The slimline, quick-draw holster nestled nicely, an even eight inches beneath the lieutenant's right armpit. The five shot 'snubby' completed him. Before, he had felt like a city banker without a tie, only half-dressed. Now he was a cop.

'Are you telling me we're going to find a ganglord's office, right here, on a main street?' he asked.

'And a brass plaque with the title of his organization and their family crest on it,' Josef answered. 'The Yakuza is a recognized part of Japanese life.'

Two minutes later they found the plaque, on an imposing building which occupied the entire corner of a main intersection.

Printed on it in bold relief, 'YAMADA-GUMI, SHIN-JUKU', and something that looked, to Fogarty, like a five-pointed star with rounded edges.

'A cherry blossom,' Tanaka said, examining the pattern. 'Symbol of impermanence.'

Fogarty was immediately reminded of Mikio Tanaka's Chinese roses. The Japanese obviously had a thing about impermanence.

'Here today, gone tomorrow,' he said. It sounded more glib than he meant it to.

'It was a common Samurai crest,' Tanaka continued, ignoring Fogarty's remark and making him feel foolish. 'Reminded them of their own mortality.'

The lieutenant nodded reverently as Tanaka pushed the entry buzzer.

A quick fire exchange in Japanese took place and the door was opened. Two black-suited men with crew cuts and hatchet eyes glared out from the shadowed entrance hall. Each wore a gold lapel pin, depicting the same cherry blossom as was displayed on the door.

A moment later Tanaka and Fogarty were inside, being frisked and the lieutenant's weapon confiscated.

'You'll get it back later,' Tanaka assured him.

Thick Chinese carpets covered the vast floor space of Tak Ofudo's office, and leather-upholstered sofas sat in front and to the side of his wraparound desk. A fine, intricately cut Venetian chandelier hung from the twenty-foot ceiling and a life-sized bronze statue of a Samurai warrior, in full battle armor, guarded the drinks cabinet at the far end of the room.

The intended feel was wealth. Dark polished wood and old gold were the prevalent colors. The air conditioners hummed quietly and a thin trickle of smoke rose from the ganglord's cigar.

'Tanaka-san, Tanaka-san.' Ofudo greeted Josef as if he were an old friend. When he got up from his desk, there was little difference between his standing and seated height.

'Ofudo-san, we are honored that you have taken time

from your schedule to see us,' Tanaka replied, bowing as the ganglord approached.

'May I present my friend Bill Fogarty.'

Fogarty bowed and Ofudo offered his hand. It felt like a child's hand, small and very soft.

'Please sit down,' Ofudo continued, his voice as smooth as his hands and his English with little trace of accent.

'May I offer you refreshments? Tea, coffee, Coca-Cola? I am going to have Coca-Cola,' Ofudo continued.

Tanaka glanced at Fogarty and Fogarty nodded.

'Yes, Coca-Cola would be fine, Ofudo-san,' Tanaka answered.

Ofudo issued the order and the larger of his two body-guards walked briskly from the room.

'My men do not speak English, so we may have complete freedom of our words.'

'Thank you,' Tanaka answered.

'It is a family matter, that is all Sato-san has told me ... I have the utmost respect and regard for your family, Tanaka-san, so it will be my honor to assist you.'

Fogarty sat quietly, listening to Josef recant the events of the past two weeks. Amazed at how open Tanaka was with the *oyabun*, more open than he had been with the police or even Ken Sato.

Fogarty listened and watched, fascinated by the gang-lord's hands; tiny fingers, twitching nervously as Josef described the rogue *sumotori*.

'And what makes you think I can help?' Ofudo asked.

'Because the top joint of the man's little finger had been amputated,' Tanaka answered.

'*Yubitsume?*'

'It seemed to be.'

Ofudo shook his head; he appeared puzzled.

'We do not operate in such a manner, Tanaka-san. And certainly if there was a problem between my organization and your father I would be aware of it. We are a large group but our communication is very good, even amongst the Korean sectors. And even if an enforcer did exist, a man such as you describe, operating within my territory, I would be aware of that also.'

Tanaka believed the first part of Ofudo's statement, not the last, the bit about the enforcer. Something in the small man's eyes, a flicker of recognition, even fear had registered.

Tanaka needed a way in, something that would get the *oyabun* talking, really talking.

He continued, altering the emphasis of his story, stressing his obligation to his family; his need to protect them from further harm. Playing to the *oyabun*'s fatherly nature.

The small man was nodding his head, saying 'yes', over and over again. He well understood loyalty and duty.

When Josef spoke of his mother, of how Mikio Tanaka had sheltered her from the threat against their family, at the expense of his own health, both physical and mental, the *oyabun*'s face was a mask of pain and suffering.

Christ, the guy's going to cry, Fogarty thought.

At that moment, Ofudo's bodyguard reappeared, carrying a tray.

The *oyabun* looked up, the sadness draining from his features. He motioned for the man to place the tray in front of him.

It contained three tall tumblers, three white linen napkins, a crystal container holding ice cubes, a silver serving spoon, and three opened bottles of Coca-Cola.

Tanaka observed the subtle communication between the ganglord and his chief bodyguard. A mere flicker of the big man's eyes, indicating that the bottle in the center was intended for Ofudo. That would be the beverage that the man had tested for poison.

'Please, gentlemen, please,' the *oyubun* said, reaching

across to grip the center bottle, pulling it forward, away from the other two.

'Ice, Fogarty-san?' Ofudo asked.

'Thank you,' he answered. The ganglord nodded and the bodyguard dropped three cubes in Fogarty's glass.

Then Josef noticed something else, something about the bodyguard's right hand, the hand that held the serving spoon. There was a bruise, circular and relatively fresh, dead center between the man's thumb and index finger, no more than an eighth of an inch in diameter. The kind of thing that would easily go unnoticed, unless a doctor saw it.

Josef raised his head, trying to catch a glimpse of the man's eyes, but the bodyguard had turned away.

After that the meeting went quickly. And as Fogarty listened it became clear that Josef was, in fact, trading with the *oyabun*. Making it clear that he would use his inherited position within his father's empire to ensure a harmonious relationship with the *Yamada-Gumi*. In exchange for the *oyabun*'s protection. It was the kind of bartering that Fogarty never expected from Josef Tanaka. But probably the only line of credit that remained open.

The meeting was near a close when Tanaka said the single word that changed everything.

'*Hyoo*, do you know of a man or a group known as *Hyoo*?' He purposely spoke in Japanese and pronounced the word loud and clear. Stealing a glance at the bodyguard.

Fogarty followed Tanaka's eyes and saw the man straighten, his eyes widen. As if he had been smacked in the face.

The ganglord remained calm, but when he spoke his tone had iced.

'I am unaware of any faction or individual using that name ... I believe we have gone as far as we can with this meeting, Tanaka-san,' he said, standing. 'Please convey my condolences to your father and my kindest regards to your cousin, Sato-san. My man will show you to the door.'

Tanaka glanced at the bodyguard as he and the lieutenant crossed the room. Walking purposely close to him, meeting eyes so dark that it was difficult to make out their dilated pupils.

He waited until they were near the entrance door, far away from Ofudo's office. Then Tanaka turned to face him, smiling, extending his hand as if in gratitude.

'*Domo arigato*,' Tanaka said.

The man appeared confused for a moment, then tentatively extended his own hand.

Tanaka took it, looked down, then gently rubbed his thumb across the fresh bruising.

'Does your *oyabun* know that you are injecting his profits? That the man he trusts with his life is using his *shabu*?' Tanaka spoke softly in Japanese.

The bodyguard pulled his hand away and stepped back, his face flushed with rage.

Tanaka held his ground and Fogarty stared, unsure of what was happening.

Another moment and the bodyguard seemed to become frightened, looking up and down the hallway, making certain that no one had witnessed their exchange.

'Maybe we should talk privately,' Tanaka continued.

'Please, not here,' the bodyguard whispered.

'Give me a phone number,' Tanaka ordered.

The man repeated his number twice.

'Nine o'clock tonight,' Tanaka said as they left the building.

Fogarty adjusted his jacket, compensating for his reinstalled .38 as he and Tanaka walked, fast, covering an entire city block before the lieutenant broke their silence.

'What the hell was going on in there – between you and

the old man's heavy? What the fuck did you say, in Japanese?'

'The guy's injecting drugs,' Tanaka answered.

'What?' Fogarty said.

'Methamphetamine . . . His eyes, he had pupils like bullseyes. And his hand was bruised, between his index finger and his thumb.'

'His hand?'

'It's fast, he doesn't need to drop his pants or roll up his sleeves. Fast and neat, and unless he's in a real hurry there won't be any discoloration. Probably shot up while he was getting the cokes . . . I noticed it when he dished out the ice.'

Fogarty exhaled. Feeling, as usual, one step behind in the game.

'That could get him in trouble,' he said.

'Could get him killed,' Tanaka confirmed, 'and it could get us some information. You got a pen?'

Fogarty pulled a ballpoint out of his inside pocket and watched Tanaka write a phone number on the underside of his wrist. He wondered whose number it was. He didn't want to ask. He was asking too many questions. Like a rookie cop. Things he should have known, would have known if he had been on his own turf. Here, he didn't know anything.

Josef made the call at nine o'clock that evening. From the phone in his hotel room.

The bodyguard insisted on being called back, in fifteen minutes, and gave the number of a pay telephone with a Ginza area code.

A quarter of an hour later, Josef was talking to a reluctant informer.

Yes, he knew of the Leopard. The man was rumored to be an assassin. At one time associated with the *Yamada-Gumi*; the bodyguard had heard nothing of him for several years.

'What is his name?' Josef asked.

'I have heard him referred to as the Leopard, nothing more.'

'Have you ever seen him?' Josef pushed.

'Only once.'

Josef felt a flush of exhilaration. 'Describe him to me.'

'Tall, thin but very strong, and quick, his movements are quick—'

'His face, describe his face. Is he Japanese, Korean?'

'I could not be sure.'

'Why?'

'Because of his markings,' the bodyguard replied.

'Markings?'

'He is tattooed.'

'His face?'

'Completely covered, head to toe, marked like a cat. A Leopard.'

'But you say the man is an assassin?' Josef asked. 'Surely, he would have no way of concealment, could never walk the streets unnoticed.'

'The tattoo is visible only when the skin is flushed.'

'I don't understand,' Tanaka said.

'The type of work is done with special pigment, invisible beneath the normal color of flesh.'

'Is that possible?'

'Not with the electric needle. It is an old technique,' the bodyguard replied. He was beginning to sound nervous.

Tanaka thought fast. He couldn't go back to the *oyabun*. He would get nothing more from him. He needed something to go on, something more.

'Is there anyone else in the *Yamada-Gumi* with such a tattoo?'

'I have heard some of the men talk of it, but never seen another,' the bodyguard answered.

Find the man who did the tattoo. The thought struck and held.

'Who in Japan would be capable of such work?'

The bodyguard thought before he answered. He knew of two masters, one had done his own bodysuit. He withheld their names, he had given enough.

'Only a few of the old masters remain. All in Tokyo, perhaps it is one of them,' he replied. His voice sounded strained and Josef knew their conversation was at an end.

'I will not call upon you again,' Tanaka said, then hung up.

The bodyguard placed the receiver in its cradle and turned. There was a man standing near him, a tall, thin man in a dark suit.

The man was looking at him, smiling.

He wondered if the man was homosexual, trying to pick him up. It was not uncommon in the Ginza.

The bodyguard squared his shoulders and glared. Allowing his anger for being caught out in the act of passing secrets to an outsider flow outward from his eyes. As if it would melt the stranger with its heat.

Filthy fucking faggot, he thought, nodding his head in a quick, dismissive gesture.

Then he turned and walked away. Taking strong, challenging strides.

Three city blocks later he had completely forgotten the incident. Then the feeling caught him. A strange, fleeting feeling, as if someone were watching him, following.

He remembered the stranger, the thin man. He turned quickly, searching for him amidst the throngs of people. Saw nothing but tourists and businessmen, out for a night on the town.

The shabu, *the* shabu *is making me nervous, paranoid . . . I need to calm down, get a drink*, he decided.

The Pink Lady was one of the few non-member clubs in the heart of the Ginza.

Alcoholic beverages were expensive, the equivalent of twenty United States dollars for a glass of house wine, and service provided by young Japanese women dressed like *geishas*, but without the formal training.

The decor was gaudy, pink carpets and curtains, Western-style tables and chairs, with a few Las Vegas slot machines thrown in for 'atmosphere'.

The bodyguard sat at the long wooden bar, looked around at the mixture of Koreans, Americans, and the few Japanese who didn't know better and wondered what the hell he was doing at the Pink Lady.

Seven glasses of house red and five whiskeys later he figured it out – getting drunk, almost paralytic.

He asked for his bill, grumbled about the price, dropped five ten-thousand-yen notes on the counter and wobbled to the street. Looked round once but the alcohol had effectively drowned his paranoia.

He was a bit unsteady by the time he'd entered the Hagashi-Ginza, on the outskirts of the main district. The sidewalks had begun to narrow, the shops were smaller, less affluent, and the street lighting sparse. He thought of hailing a cab but there was nothing in sight.

His apartment was a mile from the Hagashi-Ginza, south, toward the international fairgrounds. One mile, a long way to walk with a bladder that felt ready to explode.

Ten excruciating minutes passed before he found an alley. Long, dark and deserted.

The *tanto*, or dagger, is to the *katana*, or long sword, what the pistol is to the rifle. A lethal weapon intended for use at relatively close range.

The Leopard's *tanto* was a museum piece. An original from the fifteenth century; forged during the Takeda period, a time in which the Samurai had risen from their ranks as military servants to rule over Japan.

Five hundred years ago the blade had been a strip of raw iron, heated on the forge, amidst ritual prayer and the invocation of the gods. Until the glowing orange metal could be pounded flat and folded inward upon itself. Over and over again, until the weaker elements were distilled and the iron became steel. Sharpened and baked in wet clay until its edge was white hot, then plunged into iced water, sealing its power for eternity. Capable of splitting a hair or being punched through stone without breaking.

The Leopard gripped the hilt of the *tanto* with his right hand, its eight-inch blade cutting edge upwards along the line of his forearm.

It was too late to prevent the bodyguard from talking. He knew that, understood that a minimal amount of damage had been done. However, it was not too late for punishment. For like his steel blade, he demanded refinement, insisted on the distillation of impurity.

He spotted the bodyguard as he crept even with the entrance to the alley. Fat and drunk, head down, hunched against the door, pissing.

He continued forward, tight to the wall, his dark suit a perfect camouflage to the overcast sky, the padded sound of his rubber soles muffled by the spill of urine against the pavement.

He didn't begin his charge until the bodyguard looked up. By then he was less than ten yards from him. Picking up momentum as he moved, his blade restrained like a sheathed claw.

The bodyguard fumbled with his cock, trying to tuck it in. Pissing all over his pants in the process. Raising his arms to ward off the attack.

The first incision of the *tanto* along the lateral side of both forearms, was so clean and quick that he sensed rather than felt his injury. Like a weightlessness in his clenched fists. He tried a knee but couldn't lift his leg, either leg. The same numbness that immobilized his arms was spreading downward. There was a wetness, thick and warm. Blood. Running from the slashes across the muscles at the front of his thighs. He was being cut, over and over again, his attacker's right arm moving like a scythe, across then back, across then back.

The jacket of his suit was shredded, as was his shirt beneath and the flesh of his abdomen. One final motion left a trail of blood along the base of his throat.

He could feel his flesh sting and tingle. He was helpless. Tears came to his eyes.

'What did you tell the half-caste?' The voice was effeminate, its lightness like a lewd, intimidating instrument.

'Talk to me,' the voice demanded, 'the *Hyoo*. What did you tell him about the *Hyoo*?'

The bodyguard felt his oppressor's weight, warm against his own body, controlling him, forcing him backward into the closed door. He felt weak, light-headed. How many times had he been cut? Ten, twenty? He had to get help. No time to stall or to lie.

'That the man is an assassin. That I had seen him once. In the bath house. That he was tattooed ... Like a cat, a jungle cat. Nothing more, I said nothing more. I know nothing more.' The outpour of breath caused blood to leak from his neck.

The Leopard smiled. He knew the bodyguard was telling the truth. Still, that did not excuse his lack of discipline. A bodyguard? This tub of lard was not fit to be a soldier. He did not have the breeding, the pedigree. A butcher perhaps, but never a soldier.

'And you thought we were not aware of your weakness ... For the *shabu* and needle? That we were not watching, waiting for the time that your habit would compromise your duty?' The thin voice continued.

The bodyguard trembled.

'You are a very sloppy man. A very undisciplined man.'

It was not the words that sent terror coursing through him; it was the deadness of the man's voice. As if he were accuser, judge and executioner.

'We have no place for men like you,' the Leopard stated. Then he turned away from the bodyguard, sliding his right arm upward as he moved.

The bodyguard felt nothing but relief. Deep and consuming. He wanted to fall to his knees and offer thanks to the man who had just spared his life. Instead, he stood silent, watching.

It was not until he tried to lift his left arm, to wipe the sweat and blood from his brow, that he truly understood.

His arm remained stationary, paralyzed. He looked down. Blood was gushing from his armpit.

Thirty feet from him, almost to the main street, the man had turned; he was looking back.

The bodyguard tried to call out, to beg him to return, as if, perhaps, he were unaware of the fatal damage that had been inflicted. No sound came from his mouth. His eyes remained open as he slumped down, his back sliding along the wall, until he was in a seated position, his legs crumpled beneath him, his vision beginning to blur.

The standing man was no more than a silhouette now, a dark silhouette with frayed, shining edges, glowing in the spill of light from the overhead lamp.

It was then that the bodyguard remembered the bath house, the tall man stepping naked from the steam, droplets of heated water forming a hazy aura around him. He had been scared then, just for a moment; he had denied his fear, putting it down to the strange markings on the man's body. But there had been more. It was the man's presence that he felt, like a weight upon his heart. The same presence that he experienced now. The presence of the Leopard.

Two minutes later he died, with his eyes open and the image of the beast engraved on his mind.

The Leopard waited, finally satisfied that his final cut, along the brachial artery of the bodyguard's arm, had drained the last of the man's life. Then he turned, shaking the blood from the *tanto*'s gutters, before re-sheathing the weapon and walking silently into the night.

Guardian of hell, God of wrath

Fudo is a Japanese deity. He resembles a young, curly-haired warrior and is usually depicted as fanged and surrounded by flames. He is both the Guardian of Hell and the God of Wrath, brandishing a sword in his right hand, with which to smite wrongdoers, and a rope in his left, for the purpose of binding them to their fate. Although fearsome in appearance, Fudo serves the good, protecting the faithful and working for virtue.

He also makes a powerful tattoo for the back, complementing a full bodysuit with the indication that the man wearing his portrait is not only on the side of right but also capable of upholding it.

Horimada III had been working on this particular bodysuit for eighty hours, or a little over a full year in tattoo time. He was just finishing the detail, shading the surface of Fudo's bared chest, using a most difficult technique, known as *hane-bari*.

Hane-bari involves a jumping movement of the needles, inserting them at varied angles into the flesh, controlling their depth, then 'jumping' them quickly to their next position, to control the amount of ink used and its consequent shading. It is not particularly painful. However, it is very exacting and Horimada III was squatting above his client, squinting, holding tight to his concentration when the bell of his shop's front door rang.

Horimada could not remember if he had locked the door or not, he often did when doing this type of work. He hoped that he had and that whoever was out there would give up and go away. He could not afford an interruption, not now.

Vaguely he heard the handle being tried and the bell ring again. Then footsteps, one pair light, one heavy and uneven. *A man with a limp*, he thought, jumping the needles a final time and withdrawing them.

He placed his *hari*, the wooden handle containing the needles, on top of his work bench, then wiped his client's bleeding flesh with a fresh cloth before he stood up.

The man had come all the way from Pusan for this appointment and Horimada was truly shamed by the interruption.

'I am sorry but I must attend to whoever is in the front office. I will be brief,' he apologized.

His client made a noise, midway between a grunt and a groan, the type of sound someone being massaged might utter in deep relaxation.

'Stay still, allow the ink to settle,' Horimada said, fearing the man would sit up and inadvertently scratch at one of his fresh wounds. 'I will dismiss them and return,' the tattooist added, pushing aside his curtained partition to enter his outer office.

A gaijin and a half-caste, Horimada thought as he scanned Fogarty and Tanaka. Neither seemed to fit the appearance of a future client, one was Western and too old and the other too elegant, obviously upper class.

As impatient as Horimada III was to return to his work, he was still a master and a gentleman. He bowed as he met Tanaka's eyes, welcoming both men to his shop, explaining that he was in the middle of an appointment and that, perhaps, they could return on another day.

Tanaka apologized for their unannounced arrival and promised to be quick, just an enquiry.

Their conversation was in Japanese and Fogarty listened, as if he understood, waiting for his cue.

He and Josef had worked out a plan, right after they had received Horimada's name and address from the Japanese Tattoo Association. Only three old masters remain in Tokyo, none with apprentices.

When Tanaka asked the Association's secretary about an 'invisible' tattoo, the old man had laughed. 'People speak of such work, but I have never seen any evidence of it.'

Now Tanaka was gesturing with his hands, tracing the outline of the invisible tattoo across his neck and face, speaking fast. And Horimada III was *not* laughing.

Then Tanaka used the word '*Hyoo*' and the tattooist went pale, turning once to look behind him at the curtain before holding up his hand in a signal for silence.

He was about to deny any knowledge of the Leopard, to insist that his two unexpected visitors leave his premises. Just as the lieutenant produced his police identification card and bronze shield.

'Police.' Fogarty said the word loud and clear, allowing his jacket to fall open, revealing the .38.

'The lieutenant,' Tanaka said in Japanese, 'is with the unit of international investigations.'

Horimada III stood motionless.

Certainly he knew the man that the half-caste was describing; he had entered his thoughts each time the door of his shop opened unexpectedly. He remembered him as if it were yesterday, his stink, his threats. He also remembered the letter of introduction from Tak Ofudo.

'Talk to me.' Tanaka spoke in Japanese, breaking through the tattooist's inertia.

Horimada cleared his throat. He was thinking of the man in the back room, within earshot of everything that was being said. The man was an employee of the Shinjuku *oyabun*.

'Please,' he whispered, looking round toward the back of the shop. Then he walked stiffly out from behind his desk and toward the front door, indicating that the two men should follow him.

'Please,' he repeated, 'I am working on a client. This is not good for my business. Not now, not now.'

He got to the door and opened it.

Fogarty and Tanaka walked to him and stopped.

'Tomorrow, you return tomorrow. First thing. Eight o'clock. I don't want trouble. No trouble, do you understand?'

'Give me the *Hyoo*'s name,' Tanaka insisted.

'No name, I never learned his proper name. I knew him only as Leopard,' Horimada answered, all but pushing Tanaka onto the sidewalk.

Tanaka stalled.

'I am speaking the truth,' the tattooist said.

'What did he look like?' Tanaka asked.

Horimada glanced over his shoulder. He could see the outline of his client against the silk; the man was seated. *Listening*?

Tanaka followed Horimada's eyes.

'My client is one of the *oyabun*'s soldiers. It is not good if I am heard talking to the police,' the tattooist explained.

Tanaka nodded as if he understood but kept the pressure on. 'His face, describe the *Hyoo*'s face.'

Horimada was desperate. Anything to get the policemen out of his shop.

'A picture. Tomorrow I will have a picture. I will draw it for you ... A good picture, I draw well; it is essential to my profession. Then you go, no trouble. Okay?'

'You be here,' Tanaka warned.

'I promise,' Horimada replied. He meant it.

Alka Seltzer

Tanaka phoned Rachel from the New Orleans.

A woman answered on the third ring. Too fast for the message service, too low a voice for Rachel.

'Hello?'

'Is this 215–568–3548?' Tanaka asked, thinking he had misdialed.

'Yes it is . . . Josef?'

'Yes.'

'I prayed it was you . . . Don't you recognize your mother's voice?'

'Mother? What the hell—'

'Your father thought the safest place for me was back here. I flew to Boston, then called Rachel.'

'I still don't understand,' Josef said.

'I know what happened, Josef. I know what happened to your brother.'

'I'm sorry . . . Sorry you had to find out,' he answered.

'It's better that I know the truth,' her voice caught, choked. 'Josef,' Grace Tanaka continued, 'if anything happens to you . . . It will kill me, and your father, and Rachel.'

'Nothing's going to happen to me.'

'You don't know that, Josef, you don't know that. You don't know what you're dealing with. You don't know . . .'

He picked something up in her voice, something left unsaid.

'And you do?'

Silence.

'You know what's going on here, Mother?'

'I've been talking to Rachel.'

'Rachel?'

'Josef, it's somebody close to our family, it's got to be . . . Somebody very close.'

'I still don't follow you,' he replied.

Grace hesitated; she knew she couldn't leave it unfinished. She could hear him waiting.

'I've known your cousin Ken for years, but I've never really known him—'

'What! What are you saying? What the hell are you saying?'

'Rachel was there, in that apartment.'

'Yes. And she had one of her psychotic reactions in Ken's apartment . . . Is Rachel suggesting that Ken—'

'Please, Josef, just listen to me.'

'No, Mother . . . You listen to me. I trust my cousin with my life. I won't hear anything against him, particularly when I don't believe that Rachel's judgement was exactly clear at the time.' He stopped, tightening the reins on his anger, remembering the night his cousin had defended him. Tried to save his life. He owed Ken Sato, *ninjo* and *giri*.

'All right, Josef, all right . . . Please, we've been so worried about you.'

'I appreciate that, Mother. But what I'm doing over here is what I'm good at. The fact that it's family makes it personal, but it doesn't change it. Bill Fogarty and I have been through this before . . . Worse . . . You and Rachel will just have to trust me.'

'Okay, Josef, okay . . . Please, don't get angry with Rachel over this; it wasn't her idea to mention any of it. Believe me,' Grace Tanaka retreated.

'She's not there?'

'No, she's with her . . .' Grace didn't want to say

psychiatrist; it seemed a further invalidation. '. . . doctor.'

'Tell her I love her, that I'm fine and I'll call her later . . . And I love you too, Mom . . . Bye.'

'Take care, Josef,' Grace whispered and hung up. She already knew she'd made a mistake. Even talking about Rachel and Ken Sato. It was not her business to speak to anyone about the things Rachel had told her, about the rape, the Pentothal treatment, the 'spontaneous insight'. That's what Rachel's psychiatrist had called her vision of Ken Sato.

It had been convincing when Rachel had gone through it with her; she wasn't so sure now.

Tanaka put the phone down and sat staring at the wall. He hadn't even known his mother was in the United States, his father had certainly not consulted him.

That knowledge worried Josef. Things were changing, escalating, the stakes getting higher. He needed to see Mikio Tanaka, to talk to him, to attempt some kind of agreement as to how to proceed.

Against his better judgement Bill Fogarty had eaten raw tuna belly on vinegared rice for lunch, and now, as he lay on his bed, the turmoil in his gut matched the turmoil in his head.

Next to him, on the table, a white tab of Alka Seltzer fizzed promisingly in a glass of water. He waited a few seconds, reached over and grabbed the glass, gulping the bubbling drink and swallowing the tablet before it had completely dissolved.

Then he stretched out on his back, covered his eyes with the hard, flat pillow and began to order his thoughts, sequencing the events of the last days.

First there was the ex-*sumotori*. He was definitely Hiro Tanaka's killer. And now he was lying on a slab in the police morgue, in two pieces. Fogarty had no doubt that Tokyo

Homicide, through fingerprints and dental records, had already come up with a computer file on him, maybe even established his ties with the man known as the Leopard.

'Leopard ... The Leopard.' Fogarty whispered the word, trying to envisage a man covered head to toe with the markings of a wild cat. It was difficult. *Tomorrow we'll have an artist's drawing of him. Hand that to the Tokyo police, along with the information linking him to Ofudo, and let them get on with it. That's the only thing left to do,* he decided, *now, if Josef will just listen to reason, we can get out of here and go home.*

Home. Christ, I miss it. I didn't think it was possible.

Philadelphia was going to seem like a small town. And he was going to feel like a cop again, 'plugged in', on top of things. He was sick of waiting for Tanaka to act as his interpreter, of being insecure about his own social graces, of continually being one step behind.

Josef sat opposite his father at the long dinner table; the house was quiet and they were alone in the room.

Mikio studied his son's face before he spoke. 'Do you think that it is over for me, Josef?'

Josef remained silent, uncertain as to the meaning of his father's words.

'Do you believe you have achieved a victory?'

'Victory?' Josef repeated.

'I know what happened in Ken's apartment, the wrestler,' Mikio continued. 'You have broken an arrow, Josef, you have not touched the bow.'

Ken Sato? Did Ken Sato tell him? Josef wondered.

'The police have placed two men at my office, a surveillance team on this house ... They have sent homicide officers to speak with me; about you, Josef, you and the American. Both of you are playing with fire.'

'What kind of fire?'

Mikio Tanaka shook his head.

'Yakuza?' Josef asked.

'The police don't think so, not directly. More likely one of the ultra nationalist groups.'

'The Zen Ai Kaigi?' Josef referred to the All Japan Council of Patriotic Organizations. Right-wing, predominantly fascist, and completely legal, the group had been extracting 'contributions' from major corporations for thirty years.

'They're not certain.'

'How about the wrestler, have they traced him?'

'He was a low grade enforcer—'

'So it is Yakuza?'

Mikio Tanaka shook his head. 'He was expelled six years ago, after an unprovoked attack on a politician, at a Socialist party rally. That was it. No record of the man for the past six years.'

Josef thought of the Leopard, of the information he had gleaned from Ofudo's bodyguard. *Did Mikio Tanaka know anything about the Leopard?*

'And that's as much as the police have told you?' Josef asked.

'I know that I'm not alone in this persecution,' Mikio answered.

Josef raised his head, met his father's eyes.

'There are at least five other industrialists who have suffered a family tragedy.'

'And what is the connection between you?'

'Overseas holdings, expansion into the West, mixed marriages, and,' Mikio hesitated, 'sons of mixed marriages.'

'My brother was not a product of your mixed marriage; he was Samurai,' Josef stated.

'Perhaps that is why they took him. Perhaps I did not deserve a Samurai son.'

'I don't understand.'

'They want Japan for the Japanese.'

Josef cocked his head and searched his father's eyes.

'We have become dissolutioned as a nation, a watered-down mixture of cultures,' Mikio continued, studying his son, believing he saw resistance where there was only resignation.

'It is true, Josef, it is true . . . Our wealth has been invested in Hollywood film studios and golf courses. Plastic surgeons straighten our eyes and Western blue jeans replace traditional dress.'

He stopped, hesitated, then, 'You are what we have become, Josef. Homogenized.'

'And you believe that?'

'It is a fact. We are without true power, have a third rate army . . . Most of our money lies on foreign shores.' His father sounded defeated. It made Josef sick inside, speechless.

'I am also the new Japan,' the old man said, 'with my Western wife, Western furniture, and Western son . . . And my Western investments.'

'Perhaps we are the future,' Josef said.

Mikio shook his head. 'There is no future in dissolution.' His voice was heavy with resolve.

'So what do you intend to do?' Josef asked.

'I intend to pull my money out of America, change the nature of my investments—'

'Bow to intimidation?'

Mikio Tanaka's face hardened. 'How long do you think I want to live with my wife eight thousand miles away from me, and, even then, I am not certain of her safety? And you, Josef, they will come after you.'

'And what happens if your acts of sacrifice don't appease these people? What happens if your Western wife is still unacceptable? Or your half-caste son? How far will you bend, Father?'

Mikio sat silent.

'I thought you were a warrior,' Josef added.

'No longer. I am old, and tired. When they took Hironori, they took my heart. There is no fight left in me.'

Josef stood up from the table. Saddened but not angry.

'I want you and the American to go home, back to your life. You have no business here, no life. You jeopardize me and the safety of your mother,' Mikio Tanaka concluded.

'Soon, Father, I promise,' Josef whispered.

Then he reached out and touched the top of his father's head, resting his fingertips in the crown of dyed black hair.

'You were born Samurai. There is no nobility in surrender. No respect. Don't give in to these people, Father, I beg you.'

A promise fulfilled

Horimada III had closed and locked his shop at ten o'clock, turning off all the lights except the single lamp above his drawing board.

It was now past midnight and he had drawn nothing. Not that the man's memory had escaped him; the cruel face would be imprinted forever.

It was fear that prevented him from transferring it to paper.

I could close up for a week, go to Nagasaki, visit friends. Maybe the police will find him by then; it will be over and I will not be involved, he reasoned.

Finally he laid down his charcoal and walked from the desk. Through the silk divide and into the front of his shop.

He stared through the window, out into the street. A few people wandered past; their laughter sounded frivolous and far away.

What have I done? he asked himself. *Nothing more than practice my profession. I am not a criminal. I have no obligation to comply with their request. To hell with the police. Let them come at eight o'clock and find an empty shop.*

He glanced quickly at his front door, making sure the 'closed' sign was facing the street, then turned, intending to shut off his drawing light before leaving.

Something distracted him, more a fleeting perception than a direct observation. Something wrong, out of place.

He turned and looked again. His eyes went straight to the fist-sized opening in the glass, directly below the handle of the door.

Tanaka saw it as they approached, the circular hole below the brass knob. The kind of perfect circle that a glass cutter makes.

He ran the last few yards, Fogarty behind him, the .38 causing the shoulder holster to bounce slightly as he moved.

The door was ajar and a single light glowed from behind the partition.

Horimada III was slumped over his drawing board, his arms stretched forward, encircling the paper, his head resting in the center of the uncompleted sketch. The tattooist wasn't breathing and there was a pool of blood at his feet.

Tanaka looked at Fogarty and the lieutenant read the confusion on his face.

'All right, Josef,' he said, taking control, 'I'm going to lift the guy's head, then you take the drawing off the board. After that, we're gone. Like we were never here,' Fogarty continued, taking a handkerchief from his pocket, slipping it like a cradle beneath Horimada's forehead and lifting, one hand either side.

The heavy head lifted up from the paper and something fell from its open mouth. Two objects, cylindrical in shape, pink with blood, and about one and a half inches in length. Dropped directly onto the blank paper. The doctor recognized them before the policeman.

'Bill, the man's been castrated.'

'Christ,' Fogarty grunted, dropping the head.

'Paper's blank anyway, nothing here for us but trouble,' the lieutenant added, turning away from Horimada's corpse.

They made it to the front door in time with the two police cars that skidded to a halt outside.

'Did you see another way out of here?' Fogarty's voice was controlled but sharp.

'There's a couple doors in the back, I don't know where they go,' Tanaka answered.

Fogarty followed Tanaka's retreat but it was too late.

Two armed policemen entered through the front while a third car pulled up in the alley behind the shop.

'Please, Mr Tanaka, place your hands above your head.'

Josef recognized the voice before he turned to face Chief Inspector Norikazu Ohtsuka.

'And you, Lieutenant,' Ohtsuka continued, scowling when he saw the holstered gun beneath the American's jacket.

'This man is dead, sir.' A uniformed policeman's voice cut in from behind them.

'He's been—' the man's voice stammered, 'mutilated.'

Ken Sato arrived at the municipal police building at eleven o'clock; he took the elevator to the top floor.

Below him, in the interrogation rooms that the criminal investigation units used, Bill Fogarty and Josef Tanaka were finding out a few of the reasons for Japan's record low crime rate.

Their interviews had been thorough and non-stop, taped and videoed. Every attempt being made to link the tattooist's murder with the self-defense slaying of the wrestler in Sato's apartment.

And Chief Inspector Ohtsuka was coming up dry. Police-men were the toughest to break; they were too familiar with interrogation procedures. *Besides that*, Ohtsuka thought as he stared quietly into the American's eyes, *the forensics report put the time of death a good seven hours before either Tanaka or the American arrived at the premises*. Mikio Tanaka had vouched for his son's whereabouts between ten and one o'clock while the desk clerk at the New Orleans swore that the American had not left his hotel room all night.

Ohtsuka had never really believed that Tanaka or Fogarty had murdered the tattooist; he was certain, however, that they were withholding information. The kind of information that separated him from the sanctimonious Miyuki Hashimoto and his private Bureau of National Investigations.

The chief inspector was furious when the call came from upstairs. His suspects were to be escorted to Hashimoto's office and turned over to the national police.

Ohtsuka delivered the prisoners himself, along with the relevant paperwork, and was abruptly thanked and dismissed. He barely got a look inside the plush offices, just enough to recognize Ken Sato. As Ohtsuka turned he heard him speak.

'Josef-san, are you all right—' and then the office door clicked shut.

Something about Ken Sato's voice; he had heard the voice before, two, maybe three hours ago.

Superintendent General Miyuki Hashimoto was forty-eight years old. He weighed one hundred and forty-seven pounds and stood five feet eight inches tall, his suits custom tailored to display his forty-four inch chest and twenty-nine inch waist. His coarse hair was jet black and cropped tight to his head, a strand or two of gray around his temples. His eyes matched his hair, dark, with flecks of silver where the overhead office lights hit them. He was the second most powerful man in the national police department.

He stood permanently at attention, as if he were being reviewed in a military parade. He kept glancing at Ken Sato as he spoke, as if Sato were the reviewing officer. Fogarty wondered what the connection was between the two men.

'We are not placing you under arrest,' Hashimoto stated.

Fogarty felt his shoulders relax and saw Josef look quizzically at his cousin.

'We are, however, going to send you back to the United States.'

Fogarty tried hard not to display his pleasure.

'The deportation papers are already being processed,' the superintendent added.

'I have a Japanese passport,' Tanaka said.

'Yes, but you are domiciled in Philadelphia,' Hashimoto answered. 'Would you prefer to be held on suspicion of murder?'

'On what grounds are we being deported?' Fogarty asked.

'Where would you like me to start, Mr Fogarty?' The superintendent's voice hardened. 'Obstruction of justice, interfering in a national police investigation. Costing tax-payers funds, just to keep you under observation.'

A knock on the door interrupted his flow.

Hashimoto answered it.

A medium-sized, blue-suited man handed the super-intendent a cloth-bound parcel.

Fogarty stared at the man's face. It was a fifty-fifty blend of pretty and cruel. The type of face that sticks in your mind: dark, curly hair and a full, almost effeminate mouth, wide cheekbones and small, deep-set eyes. Eyes that seemed to stare, continually.

The man held Fogarty's gaze as if he were challenging the lieutenant to recognize him. Smiling, a sly, cocky sort of smile. Finally Hashimoto dismissed him.

It was as he was leaving, caught in the shadow of the closing door that Fogarty remembered. He tried to imagine the same pretty face lit by the headlights of a car. On an unsolicited trip to Disneyland. He couldn't be certain.

When he turned again Hashimoto was unwrapping the brown-papered parcel. Unveiling the .38.

'Give me a goddam break,' Fogarty groaned, anticipating what was coming next.

'Firearms, Mr Fogarty, are banned in our country. The penalty for their possession is severe,' Hashimoto began.

Fogarty caught Ken Sato's eyes and held them. *You gave me the fucking piece, asshole*, he thought.

'We have put a trace on this weapon,' the superintendent continued. 'Thankfully, for you, Mr Fogarty, it is clean ... Did you smuggle it through our customs?'

Fogarty looked again at Sato. He could do a lot of damage now and cousin Ken knew it.

Sato stayed cool.

'I bought it here, in the Ginza. Black market. I couldn't tell you exactly where or from who. I thought I needed it for my self-protection,' Fogarty explained. 'I am a police officer,' he added with intended arrogance.

Hashimoto cleared his throat. 'You are not a police officer in Japan,' he answered sharply, 'possession of a firearm is a felony and warrants a prison term.'

Then, relaxing his tone, 'Look, gentlemen, we are in the middle of an important investigation. It involves not only your family, Tanaka-san, but several of our country's most important industrial families. I am doing what I can to keep your father apprised of developments and I assure you, he is being fully protected. You, and Lieutenant Fogarty, however, are obstructing justice. We have grounds to put you under arrest, but we have no intention of doing this. What I am going to do is have two of my officers accompany you to your hotel, where you may gather your belongings ... Your passports will be returned once you are inside the aircraft.'

Fogarty looked from Tanaka to Ken Sato, then at Miyuki Hashimoto. The whole thing was really beginning to stink.

Hashimoto's next words answered at least one of his questions.

'If Sato-san were not such a close friend of my father-in-law, Gichin Yamashito, our former chief of police, things would be a great deal more difficult. Now, please, count your blessings and have a safe trip to the United States.'

Hashimoto walked to his desk, pressed a button on the console of his phone and spoke in Japanese. Then he looked up at Josef.

'I ask you to trust me, Tanaka-san. I will keep you informed.' Then he handed Josef his card and private number. He bowed to each of them.

A minute later two plain-clothed officers arrived in the office.

Fogarty could not believe his luck.

'Pretty Boy' was one of their 'custodians'. He was still smiling as he walked behind Fogarty toward the elevator.

Norikazu Ohtsuka watched from his office window as the five men walked from the municipal building. He kept his eyes on Ken Sato, remembering his voice. High and distinct.

He was certain it was the same voice that had tipped him off to the tattooist's murder.

Ken Sato went with them to the New Orleans.

Fogarty had expected some acknowledgement from cousin Ken regarding the incident with the .38. Certainly his fabrication about buying the weapon in the Ginza warranted a little *giri*. He got nothing.

Sato was preoccupied with Josef's departure.

He seemed genuinely upset, continually reassuring Josef that he would stay on top of Miyuki Hashimoto. They spoke in Japanese now, Josef, Ken, and the two policemen. Fogarty moved between them like a robot, completely disconnected.

Josef requested a call to his father. Pretty Boy said they had three hours before the flight and all calls could be made from the departure lounge at the airport.

Fogarty kept eyeing the blue-suited policeman, trying

hard to recall the face that stared at him from the front seat of the limousine; he needed to be certain. A couple of insinuating smiles later his 'certainty level' hit ninety percent.

Ken Sato's goodbye to Tanaka was resplendent with bowing, hugs and emotion.

The lieutenant received a handshake. Ken's palm reminded him of sushi.

Then came the ride to the airport. An hour and a quarter of stony silence, Tanaka sitting ramrod straight on the passenger side of the front seat, Pretty Boy at the wheel.

Narita Airport was teeming with people. Fogarty and Tanaka were escorted to a private room, generally reserved for captive drug traffickers en route to the municipal building.

Tanaka made his telephone call and Fogarty requested a toilet.

Pretty Boy accompanied him to a small, private men's room.

Fogarty unzipped his trousers and pressed inward against the cold porcelain sides of the urinal. He kept glancing over at Pretty Boy, searching the features of his face, wondering if he could be mistaken.

Pretty Boy stepped closer and barked at him to hurry up. He was fidgeting with something in his pocket.

Fogarty turned back, breathed in and tried to relax. He hated taking a piss with somebody watching. He considered giving up, holding on until the airplane. Then it became a personal challenge. *Hell if I'm going to let this little shit freeze me out.*

He turned round once, intending to tell the cop to back off, give him some space. He saw it then, right there in the muscular hand. The polished stick.

Pretty Boy smiled and said something in Japanese. A word choked by a quick mocking laugh. He dropped the stick into his pocket and walked to the mirror. Studying his reflection as he ran his fingers through his hair.

Fogarty urinated, then zipped his trousers up slowly. Turning toward Pretty Boy he extended his hands, indicating his desire to wash them.

The Japanese frowned, grunted and moved over, giving Fogarty space at the sink. He continued to reshape his pomaded hair as Fogarty turned on the water. Both taps, opened full.

The plumbing hiccupped once then came on with a loud rush. Fogarty stepped back, as if to avoid the splash, spun quickly and caught Pretty Boy with the edge of his shoulder, ramming him hard into the metal towel dispenser. He used his body-weight to pin him while gripping firmly, holding both the smaller man's arms to his sides, prohibiting an attempt at the stick.

Fogarty used his knee. Once, twice, three times, driving it nice and sharp, up between the spread legs, forcing Pretty Boy's body to jump at the end of each impact. His screams were lost in the roar of gushing water.

When the Japanese felt suitably limp, the lieutenant dragged him by the hair, his knees skidding across the tiled floor toward the urinal.

'I saved it for you! See. No flush!' Fogarty growled, forcing the Japanese head first into the bowl. Then he flushed. The water poured down, soaking both his coiffeured hair and the collar of his suit. Finally Fogarty released him, watching the man struggle to his feet, heaving for air.

'Better hurry, we don't want to miss the flight,' Fogarty said, smiling as he walked from the lavatory. He felt almost giddy as he headed back towards the holding room. Turning once to laugh as Pretty Boy threw open the door and lurched into the hallway.

Tanaka and the other guard looked up with surprise when Fogarty entered alone. The lieutenant said nothing, simply walked to one of the plastic-covered chairs in the corner of the room and sat down.

A minute later Pretty Boy appeared, soaking wet and furious. He went straight for Fogarty, shouting oaths and waving his arms. Stopped by his partner who wrapped him in a bear hug from behind, forcing him to another plastic-covered chair in the opposite corner of the room. From there, the disgraced Japanese policeman sat and glowered at Fogarty for the remaining hour. Twice the lieutenant winked at him, then used his right hand in simulated masturbation, the old high school gesture that meant 'jerk off'.

Some things transcend the spoken word and the little man's reaction gave Fogarty proof that he had truly communicated. It was the high point of his afternoon.

They sat in the back of the aircraft, in the smoking section, stuffed between an American Barbie doll and a chain-smoking Buddha.

She had a Walkman and her own set of Dolly Parton tapes and the Buddha came complete with a carton of Camels.

Fogarty wanted to talk, about the police involvement, the beating he took en route to Disneyland and the mysterious Ken Sato.

Tanaka was non-communicative.

'My father said to tell you goodbye ... That he'd think of you when the Chinese roses bloomed next year.' That was all he said before closing his eyes, lowering his head and shutting the lieutenant out.

Fogarty leaned back, inhaled air that you could weigh by the pound, and picked up the spill of 'Delta Dawn' from the headset next door.

It was going to be a long, long flight.

III   Reckoning

Red mist

The building was located in the center of Tokyo, four blocks south of the Imperial Palace. It was a large building with high vaulted ceilings and wide open rooms. An elevated stage occupied its main room, fixed wooden benches sitting like pews in front of it. To the rear were storage rooms, filled with long swords and traditional armor, directly beneath them a subterranean dojo, with a polished pine floor, striking posts and body bags. Adjoining the dojo was a shooting range with fully automated targets.

At one time the building had been a kabuki theatre, now it was known, by a small circle, as 'the Fortress'; its steel reinforced doors protected by men who regarded themselves as modern Samurai. Dressed in black *hakama*, each as familiar with the steel blade of the *katana* as with the polymer frame of the Glock semi-automatic hand gun filling the holster above his right kidney.

Tonight the Guardians were particularly alert. There was a meeting of the Red Mist. A gathering of the clan. Warriors dedicated to the restoration of the Japanese Empire, the purification of their race and the re-armament of their country.

More radical than any of the four hundred sanctioned units of the legally recognized Zen Ai Kaigi, more committed than the Yakuza; their existence alone was a secret shrouded in blood and death.

*

Tak Ofudo was one of the first of the two hundred members to arrive. Alone, without the protection of his bodyguards, the ganglord walked quickly from his car, along a paved walkway that had been swept and scrubbed, to the dimly lit doors of the Fortress.

He was one of five Yakuza chiefs with affiliation to the Red Mist. Often, this secret inner circle of the Yakuza had used the power of their more public organization to fulfill the political aims of their elite society.

Miyuki Hashimoto arrived five minutes later, removing his shoes in the anteroom beyond the entrance, replacing them with slippers, before entering the main room.

It was a strange and incongruous sight: ganglords and policemen, politicians, military officers and Shinto priests, greeting each other as brothers, bowing low and subserviently, acknowledging homage to a higher goal.

The meeting was set for eight o'clock. Twenty minutes before the hour all members were present and accounted for, the wooden pews full and voices hushed.

The Leopard sat in silence, steam rising from the floor-level jets which circumvented his stone lair.

Above him, Lucite-wrapped photo portraits of his prey stared down like trophies on a hunter's wall. There were seven of them. All were male and most young, early twenties to mid-thirties. Some were captured by the camera in mid-scream, others had been stunned silent, staring straight, terror freezing their eyes.

Steam settled on the plastic casing, dripping like tears across their faces.

These faces gave him power, the fear they projected, the energy they dispelled in death.

Each was marred by imperfection, some obvious, some not so: blue eyes, light hair, they were the obvious ones, the product of interbreeding, insipid and weak of blood. With others it was more an expression, a certain way in which the facial features had set, molded by greed and avarice, the product of too much wealth, Western food, Western clothing, Western religion ... One, Hironori Tanaka, had been a cripple. Spoiled and made feeble by his affliction, his ability to wage combat broken with his body. A Samurai who had been bested in battle by a half-caste. Punished as much for that as for the sins of his father.

They had all been punished for the sins of their fathers.

Their weakness and imperfection gave the Leopard purpose. It was his duty to cull the flock.

He stood up and walked over the slatted boards to the center of the room; beneath his feet the condensed water ran through shallow gutters and down iron-grilled drains.

The sound of the trickling water ignited memories: melting snow and mountain rain. To a time in his life when there was great confusion, when ideology had given way to reality and heroes had become frail and human.

During this time he had journeyed across the sea, away from Japan, searching for insight and a new perspective.

Into China, through Tibet and toward the sacred land of Dolpho, a region unknown to most Westerners and untainted by modern culture.

His journey became a pilgrimage.

Employing Sherpa guides, climbing higher and higher into the Himalayas, through the Kang Pass and onwards to Crystal Mountain, waiting like a white pyramid against the blue sky.

He had found freedom on that peak, fourteen thousand feet above the plains of mankind. Space to think, to feel, to grow in tune with his heart.

And, one morning, something happened, something deep and mystical.

*

The temperature was four degrees below zero and he had just awakened. Ordinarily he would have remained in his sleeping bag, waiting for the Sherpas to cook breakfast and brew tea.

This morning was different.

Something was calling to him. No, not 'calling', more 'touching' his mind, heightening his senses, pulling him toward the cusp of inner vision.

Compelling him to crawl from his insulated bag and unzip the flap of his tent, to venture out into the stark white cold of daybreak.

At first he stood silent, bracing himself. Then he walked from their campsight, across the snow-covered rocks. Fifty, one hundred yards, turning once to make sure he wasn't lost.

That's when he saw the animal, perched on the ledge of a precipice. Close to him. Close enough to kill him.

Pale frosty eyes and a coat of misty gray, black rosettes clouding the depth of its thick fur. So rare that its very existence was shrouded in mystery and myth. The Snow Leopard. Alone. Solitary.

'His' Leopard was six feet long and perhaps one hundred and twenty pounds.

He must have walked right by the creature, passing within feet of its enormous claws and small, short-faced head. Like a mirage, blending perfectly with the rock and snow.

At first he was terrified; knowing that the creature preyed on blue sheep and yak, animals more than three times its own bodyweight. A man would be easy game.

His terror ended quickly; his training had taught him to accept death. And death at the claws of such magnificence could only be an honor.

Then he met the Leopard's eyes. They sparkled with the new sun.

And he knew. It had been the creature that had called to

him, waking him from his sleep, drawing him from his tent, his security.

The Snow Leopard was his spirit, his soul.

He took a step forward, toward the beast.

The rising sun crept from behind the mountain's snow-covered peak, momentarily blinding him.

When he could see again, the Leopard was gone.

Initially, he struggled against his 'need' for the tattoo. His religion, Shinto, forbade the degradation of the flesh. But this was not degradation, he argued with himself, this was not an ornament or decoration; this was the installation of 'spirit'. And wasn't the precept of Shinto based on animism and the worship of natural phenomena? The tattoo was his homage.

The tattooing began the following spring, in Tokyo. When the transformation of the Red Brigade into the Red Mist had become difficult, during a period in which his pragmatism was questioned, his leadership challenged.

A time when he needed the Leopard close to him, needed his clear eyes and sharp claws.

At first he intended the markings to cover only his shoulders and arms, to mid-bicep.

Then the work began and he grew addicted to the pain, as if the *hari*, with its hot needles and pounding rhythm were the Leopard's mouth, its teeth and tongue, caressing and devouring. Trading his skin for fire. Purifying him.

The invisibility of the ink had, initially, been a mistake; the pigment required to create the silver-gray markings had not contrasted properly with the exceptional tone of his own flesh. Disappearing as the work healed. Visible only during heat and sweat.

Then the significance of the 'invisibility' dawned on him. It would allow him to create an entity as secretive as the Leopard itself. Enable him to continue with the ink and the pain, until he had achieved ninety percent coverage of his body. A mirage that he could control.

A revelation, impermanent, like a vision.

Like the Snow Leopard itself.

He was ready now. Whole, centered. He walked from the steam room. Showered and dried. Dressed and marched toward the stage.

At five minutes before the hour, the curtain lifted. Two *o-daiko*, or great drums, each five hundred pounds in weight, with stretched cow-hide heads three feet across, were raised on wooden platforms to either side of the stage.

Two musicians were required to play each of the twin-headed drums. One to beat out the rhythm, while the other, positioned against the opposing head, improvised freely.

The four men walked on quietly, clad only in white loin clothes, their hair restrained by toweled head bands. Their drum sticks resembled thick war clubs as they took their places, crouching down in front of the massive *zelkova* wood drums.

They attacked the skins with a fury that was as much martial as musical. Slamming the sticks into the hide with all their strength. As if trying to break through physically to the man playing opposite them. At first the noise sounded like a disjointed thunder. Each beating his own rhythm, without inhibition.

Then, as the veins began to outline their sinew, sweat causing their bodies to glisten, the sound became cohesive. Improvisation and steady rhythm combining to establish unity. Swallowing its listeners, powerful yet tranquil, like a giant heartbeat. The audience held like a baby to its mother's bosom.

The sound built and expanded, until there was only the pulse, all commanding.

Each member of the Red Mist felt it, individually and as one. Their souls touched by a shared destiny.

Staring straight ahead, as the lights dimmed, leaving only a single spot, aimed at the center of the stage.

The war costume had belonged to an infantry commander in the fourteenth century. The jacket and leggings were cut from heavy cotton, layered with red, embroidered silk, and the chest shield and loin protector were composed of lacquered wooden plates, connected by intricately woven silk cords; the wood had been polished to a golden glow.

He wore a *jingasa*, a shallow bowl-shaped helmet and carried a sheathed *katana*, slung to his left side, while the shorter sword, the *wakazashi*, was pushed through the sash above it.

He moved effortlessly, as if he were being carried on the crest of the beating drums.

They were standing, waiting, fists clenched and raised above their heads.

The drums quieted.

The spotlight shifted, beam rising to highlight the portrait that looked down from the gallery above the podium.

It was a portrait of the Emperor of Japan.

'Allegiance to duty.' Ken Sato's voice cut the still air. Amplified by four wall-mounted speakers.

The unified voice of the two hundred repeated his vow.

'Discipline in conduct.' There was a tremor in his tone, adding clarity and strength.

'Humility.'

The word was repeated as emotions soared.

'To die in the service of our lord.'

There were tears in many eyes now. The true spirit of their race rekindled.

'Hail the Emperor of Japan.'

Two hundred voices, more a chorus than an echo.

Then the drums built and crescendoed a final time. Followed by perfect silence.

Ken Sato's speech was rehearsed, timed and meticulously prepared.

He was pleased to report that their treasury was full with 'contributions', that three of the major industrial families of the 'empire' had seen their way and made atonements for past transgressions; the remaining two were currently being guided towards enlightenment.

Sato went on to speak of the relevance to the Empire of the breakdown of the Soviet Union, of the availability of the defunct republic's nuclear warheads and of the inevitability of Japan emerging as the world's premier super power.

His speech was a mixture of hard fact, flowery metaphor and stirring patriotism.

Had Sato been standing on a soap box on a street corner, he would have been written off as a mad man spouting some eclectic, confused ideology. The single fact that gave power to his words was his audience. A gathering of some of the most influential men in Japan, united in their commitment. Men who could make things happen.

Many were older than Sato by a decade; some, including Tak Ofudo, were twenty years his senior.

It did not matter. Sato had proved himself, both as a man of thought and a man of action. He was the new Japan.

At seventeen years old, he had been one of the original members of Yukio Mishima's Red Brigade. He had taken part in the storming of the Defense League's National Armory.

By twenty he had seen beyond his mentor's romanticized views on Imperialism and had begun to rebuild from the remnants of Red Brigade, discarding those weaklings who had joined Mishima in making a laughing stock of the

Brigade's ideology: an ideology based on truth, Japan was being irrevocably eroded by Western materialism.

Sato founded the Red Mist in 1976, when he was twenty-four years old and fresh from a degree in corporate law.

He had studied Sun Tzu's *The Art of War* and Musashi's *Book of Five Rings*, studied them until he understood the precepts of combat, both with a sword, on the battlefield or in the dojo, and with starch-collared executives in the boardroom. He had practiced both.

He had memorized Lao Tsu's *Tao Te Ching*; he understood the art of ruling men. By love and by fear. Knew the difference between *bushi no nasake*, the tenderness of the warrior, and *bushi damashi*, the fierce spirit, battling in the face of death.

Keinosuke Sato was loved and respected.

The Leopard was feared and respected.

He finished his speech in a furor, urging the men to their feet, again to salute the Emperor of Japan.

Then, while they were standing, Sato signaled the drummers to play. The spotlight intensified, bringing not only light, but intense heat, to the center stage. Beaming down on the lone Samurai.

Ken Sato drew his *katana*, raising the blade above his head, reflecting the glare of the huge spot. Whipping it downwards and across, like a bolt of lightning, the whine of steel adding another dimension to the heartbeat drums, his war-cry punctuating their rhythm. Over and over again he cut and parried, striking and focusing on his imagined target without pause or deceleration. Cutting to the front, then spinning to cut behind. Whirling and dipping with absolute control.

Until the intense overhead beam, combined with his physical exertion, flushed the last of the moisture from Ken

Sato's body, producing the transformation.

He resheathed his *katana* and turned to his audience.

The Leopard.

Back in the USA

Japan Airlines flight 006 arrived in New York at twelve noon, twenty-five minutes late.

Tanaka and Fogarty cleared customs and grabbed a connecting bus to the United terminal. They had a few hours to kill before the short flight to Philadelphia.

Tanaka remained quiet and estranged as they sat having sandwiches and coffee. Fogarty was overjoyed to be home; he considered his friend's feelings and tried not to show it.

'Longest sixteen days of my life,' he finally ventured. Anything to break the silence.

Tanaka looked at him. Said nothing.

'Rachel's going to be glad to see you,' Fogarty added.

Tanaka nodded, his mouth set and his eyes vague.

Fogarty started to get angry. Enough was enough.

'Listen, kid,' he began, realizing that he hadn't called Tanaka 'kid' since they'd been away. He was already feeling stronger, on his own turf, 'We did as much as we could over there. With the stuff we handed them it's only a matter of painting by numbers. This thing'll be history in two weeks.'

Tanaka pushed himself from the table, stood up and walked away.

Fogarty almost threw his coffee cup after him. 'What the hell's the matter with you?' he muttered, watching his friend disappear amongst the crowd of people.

A little over two hours later they met again. In the departure lounge.

Tanaka walked up to the lieutenant. Fogarty's anger

dissolved when he looked into Tanaka's eyes. *He's hurting, really hurting*. The lieutenant read the pain.

'Bill, I've got to go back. Finish it,' Tanaka whispered.

'Yeah, sure you do, Son, sure you do,' Fogarty said, putting an arm aound Tanaka's shoulder, 'but first you've got to get rested, reorganized. See Rachel, put things right. You've got to clear your head, then you can finish it.'

It's finished now, I hope to God you never go back, the lieutenant thought, easing Josef toward the boarding gate.

They took a cab from the Philadelphia airport. Straight into the city, dropping Josef off at Rittenhouse Square before delivering the lieutenant to his condominium on the outskirts of town.

Tanaka hadn't spoken to Rachel in two days, and then the conversation had been strained, both of them skirting the issue raised by his mother. He wasn't sure how he would react when the subject came up face to face.

At least Grace Tanaka would be gone. Back to Boston. It wasn't that Josef didn't want to see her, but not just now, not until he had reconciled his position with Rachel.

The first thing he saw when he entered the tiny reception hall were the engineer boots, the ones he wore when he rode the Harley. They were sitting inside the coat closet, scuffed and dirty, in the exact position that he had left them.

He stood and stared at them, tempted, for a moment, to take the elevator back down to the underground garage and check on the bike.

It's all right, I left it under a tarpaulin. Tomorrow, I'll check on it in the morning, he decided, closing the door. He walked into the main room.

There was a fresh stack of magazines on the coffee table – *Esquire, Philadelphia, Modern Health* and a couple of medical trade journals – there was also a hint of dust on the mahogany table top, highlighted by a streak of late summer sun, creeping by the curtain of the window to the porch.

Behind the table, two cushions of the muted red wrap-round sofa were crushed as if someone had been recently sitting on them. And a saucer and cup in the kitchen, lying in the bowl of the sink, unwashed.

And the bed. One side unmade, sheet and duvet tossed aside, the other undisturbed.

Aside from this slight evidence of life, the place felt empty, hollow, as if he had happened upon the lair of some solitary creature. The loneliness saddened him, the sloppiness annoyed.

Tanaka straightened the place up before he unpacked. Order was important to him, more important than it had ever been in his life.

He called Rachel's office. The secretary recognized his voice and Rachel was on before he had even asked for her.

'Josef, you're home ... Thank God you're safe. I've missed you so much ... Give me half an hour to finish this appointment, then I'm on my way.'

Thirty-three minutes later he heard the key in the lock.

He picked up the delicate scent of the Chanel as he walked from the bedroom.

'Josef?' Her voice sounded tentative, almost shy.

It was as if he were seeing Rachel Saunders for the first time. The blonde hair, soft, no longer gelled back, the wide blue eyes and full mouth, made tantalizingly imperfect by a nose that was just a shade too broad and slightly flat.

She was wearing a navy blue Jean Muir suit and black, low-heeled shoes. Her legs were good enough not to need stockings, firm and well shaped.

He stood staring at her. Uncomfortable in her presence. Like they had never met and he was just here, an intruder in her apartment. With no business and nothing to say.

'Josef, are you all right?' Rachel's voice filled the void.

She walked to him, wanting to wrap her arms around him. Stopping short, reaching out with her hand, touching him first on the shoulder. Rising on her toes to kiss his lips. A cautious kiss.

'It's good to have you home,' she whispered.

He tried to meet her eyes and couldn't. Instead he took her gently in both arms and held her. Pulled her close.

She sensed his anxiety; it ran like a taut cord through his body.

'Sit down, Josef. Are you hungry? Do you want a cup of coffee? I'm going to have a cup of coffee.' She talked as she drew away from him.

'How long did my mother stay with you?'

She looked at him, understanding the real question behind his words. 'Three days,' she answered.

'You really upset her, didn't you?' His voice was edgier than he meant it to be.

'Josef, we talked, that's all. She was worried to death and I was too, and we talked . . . I trust your mother, Josef.'

'How long is she going to be in Boston?'

'Until your father tells her it's safe to go back to Japan.'

'I can't believe you said that about my cousin,' Josef continued; he didn't want to get into it like this but he was too tired to control himself.

'Josef, I told your mother something that happened in therapy, something very personal . . . I shouldn't have said anything, but it had just happened and I needed someone to talk too . . . It was a mistake talking to her like that . . . I'm sorry and she's sorry.'

He stood looking at her, her face was relaxed and for the first time since he'd known her, Rachel Saunders looked old to him, tired and worn out. He had a flush of guilt. *I've done that to her, taken her youth, her vitality. And now I'm about to hammer her some more.* He felt tears rush to his eyes.

'Come here, Rachel, come here,' he whispered, holding out his arms.

He mouthed the silent words 'I'm sorry' as they held each other.

They made love the following morning. And then it was Rachel who instigated it, pressing close to him, her hips warm against his groin.

His body responded.

She groaned as he entered her, moving slowly at first, building as they found their shared rhythm.

He looked down, into her face.

It had been such a long time and she was beautiful in the quiet light of morning, beautiful like she had been before all this started; her eyes were closed and her lips were wet, slightly open.

She sensed him, opened her eyes and smiled.

> *We smile*
> *even at death*
> *this happy morning.*

Ken Sato's haiku drifted from somewhere.

He lowered his head and kissed her, blocking the words from his thoughts.

Fogarty woke up and stared up at a white ceiling, listening to the continual drone of rolling rubber against cement, thinning to a hiss as the flow of traffic moved east, away from his window.

For the time it took his eyes to focus on the spider's web of criss-crossing cracks in the textured paint he thought he was still in Tokyo, at the New Orleans. It was a distressing thought.

Then, recognizing his own ceiling, he remembered that he

had vowed to have it scraped and repainted and knew he was home.

He closed his eyes again, lay back against the hard mattress and started to reassemble the pieces of his journey. It was not a comfortable task. He wondered how Josef was handling it.

Two hours later Bill Fogarty was entering the Roundhouse, en route to his office on the first floor. A few faces turned as he walked past.

'Welcome back, Lieutenant, everything all right?' Millie, his secretary, looked up as he crossed the sea of desks and ringing phones. 'Lieutenant, I wasn't expecting you for a few more—'

'I missed you, Millie,' he said, cutting her off, walking past.

Then he was inside his office and shuffling through the casework that had accumulated on his desk. Three missing persons and two homicides, the latter both gang-related and in the 'crack zone' of the north central section of the city.

His eyes caught on the faxed photo of one of the missing persons. It had been sent from the sheriff's office in Perkasie, a small town about forty miles north of Philadelphia.

Jane Rush was the name below the black and white facsimile. She was listed as a runaway.

Jane had a long, plain face with huge doleful eyes. Her hair was cropped close, like a boy's. She looked about twelve years old.

He ran down the page to the DOB line: 12/25/81 ... His estimate hadn't been far off. He pressed the button on his intercom. 'What's the story on this runaway? Jane Rush?'

Millie poked her head around his door a few seconds later.

'Case closed, Bill. She was found riding with a motorcycle club in Allentown. Screwed, tattooed and on the game.'

'Christ,' Fogarty muttered, looking again at the child's face.

'She's home now. Living with her mother and back in the eighth grade.'

Then Millie entered his office, readjusted her glasses and stared at the lieutenant. 'You don't look too well.'

'I feel fine,' Fogarty replied.

Millie nodded and kept her mouth shut. She'd worked with Bill Fogarty for ten years. She knew when to pry and when not to. 'Would you like coffee?'

'That's exactly what I need,' he answered, looking again at the reports on his desk. *A quart of caffeine and a homicide investigation*, he thought. Anything to relieve the feeling of impotence that had been clinging to him since Japan.

He and Josef had left a real mess back there. No matter how many times he told himself that the Japanese police would clean it up, his instincts told him differently. The little cop with the palm-sized night stick had been the giveaway. The police, or factions of the police, were somehow involved in the overall picture. Whose side they were on wasn't clear, but someone was dirty. And then there was Ken Sato.

Millie arrived with the coffee, black and instant. The aroma brought him home.

He focused on the first of the two crack homicides. A thirteen-year-old shot dead in broad daylight, on Diamond Street . . . He'd start there.

I'm turning Japanese,
I really think so

It was during the second week of his return that Rachel really noticed the change. At first it had seemed an obsession with order and cleanliness, then it was the motorcycle.

She'd driven home from her office and noticed the bike gone from its slip in the garage.

It was a lovely evening, the air fresh and crisp; she assumed he had gone for a ride. Happy, in fact, that he had. Grateful for any sign that he was easing back into his former life; lately he seemed to spend as much time talking long distance to Japan, usually to his cousin Ken, as he did talking to her.

When she walked into the apartment and found him sitting on the floor, legs folded beneath him, hips on his heels, meditating, she panicked.

'Somebody's taken your bike!' she blurted.

He looked up as if he had been shaken from a deep sleep.

'I sold it,' he said. His voice was flat.

'What?'

'I sold the motorcycle,' he repeated.

'But you just got it!'

He stood up and faced her. There was a look in his eyes that she had never seen before. As if he were appraising her, gauging her reaction.

'I don't want to ride an American motorcycle,' the hint of challenge in his tone.

275

'That's fine with me,' she answered, then softened, 'it's just that I know how much you loved it.'

He stood silent and shrugged his shoulders. Stepping aside to let her walk past him and into the bedroom.

'People change, Rachel, people change.'

She heard him say it from behind the closed door.

When she came out again, her office clothes replaced by a cotton training suit bottom and a loose T-shirt, he was kneeling on the floor, folding his karate gi.

'Are you going to the dojo?' she asked.

'I think it's time I get back to it, don't you?' Again a slight edge to his voice.

'Yes, probably do you good.'

He looked up.

'What time would you like dinner?' She kept it sweet. He'd been under enormous strain and she wasn't going to add to it.

'Eight, eight thirty.'

'What do you feel like eating?'

'Maybe some chicken—'

'Okay.'

'And *soba*.'

'*Soba*?' Rachel repeated the word.

'Noodles, made from buckwheat flour. I brought them back this afternoon, they're in the kitchen.'

Rachel smiled. It was unlike Josef to go food shopping.

'Do you remember how to cook them?' he asked. 'I believe Ken showed you.'

'That's right,' she answered, trying to keep the distaste out of her tone.

She walked into the kitchen. The *soba* was there, in a plastic bag with a lot of Japanese writing on it. Another bag lay beside the noodles. She looked inside and saw half a dozen sets of chopsticks. She was tempted to comment on the chopsticks, but thought better of it.

Maybe time I learned how to use them, she reasoned.

'See you later,' Josef called. Then the door clicked shut and he was gone.

Tanaka rode the bus west to 45th Street. It was crowded and he got the last remaining seat, near the front, next to a gray-haired woman with a streaming cold.

She coughed and sneezed, catching the spill in a filthy red handkerchief which she raised only after the first burst had already left her nostrils.

The woman's lack of consideration made him furious. In Tokyo she would have worn a face mask. Here, she seemed to take it as her privilege to infect others. Josef turned his head away, staring down at the litter-strewn floor of the bus.

He recalled his phone conversation with Ken Sato from earlier in the day. His cousin had been in touch with his friends at police headquarters.

'Some kind of conspiracy, a right-wing group, intent on bringing Japan's wealth back to Japan. Rearmament.'

Ken's information confirmed what his father had already told him.

'I feel useless,' Josef had replied.

Ken hesitated before he spoke again

'There may be something you can do ... Talk to your father. Advise him that perhaps this is not a good time to be investing in California.'

Josef was stunned by Ken's suggestion. As far as he knew, Mikio Tanaka had intended to pull out of his foreign investments.

Ken Sato picked up his cousin's silence. 'Just for the time being. Until the police can resolve the case.'

'I thought my father was pulling out of California.'

'He has resumed negotiations.'

Josef flashed on his last meeting with Mikio Tanaka. He had urged him to fight on. Maybe that was exactly what he was doing. He felt a surge of pride. Sato's voice sliced through his feelings.

'It is hard to return from heavy ground, Josef.'

'What are you saying, Ken?'

'Sun Tzu, *The Art of War*. When you enter deeply into others' land, past their cities and towns, it is called heavy ground ... It is very difficult to return from heavy ground.'

Josef remained silent, thinking.

'Perhaps it is best if Tanaka Industries is not so entrenched that it cannot withdraw quickly ... Do you follow me, Josef?'

'I'm not sure.'

'For the sake of safety, my cousin ... The time is not right to take new ground. The same applies to you.'

What did he mean by that? Was he speaking of the fact that Josef had chosen a life in the United States? Was he referring to Rachel?

'I think of you often, Josef ... Where do you belong, here or there?'

Ken's words had begun to hurt Josef's mind. Throwing doubt after doubt upon him.

'Please, Ken, look after my father,' he said. It was all he could manage.

Ken Sato waited a long moment.

'Of course I will, Josef ... I love you, cousin. Goodbye.'

Josef got off the bus a block east of 45th Street and walked toward the dojo.

The streets were a mixture of college students and blue-collar workers. Blacks, Whites and the occasional Chinese.

He approached a particularly pretty young woman, maybe eighteen or twenty. She was carrying a shopping bag and glanced up as she walked toward him. Her complexion was coffee-colored and her hair was thick, long and dark. From a distance of ten feet she appeared black and very good-looking. It was only as the gap between them closed that Josef noticed the slant of her eyes and the distinct mix of African and Oriental features. Full lips and wide high cheekbones, a small pert nose. In her case, the mixture worked. She smiled as they passed.

He smiled back and lowered his head. He felt a sort of shame. As if he had inadvertently stared at a disfigurement, disguised by the beauty of youth but none-the-less an irreversible imperfection.

He recognized it because he shared it. Knew its deep confusion and secret pain.

He turned and watched her walk away from him, strong full hips filling out the washed and faded denim of her jeans.

She moved with a streetwise confidence. Perhaps she was unaware of it, perhaps here it was okay. To be impure. Here in the mixed working-class fringes of an American city. But try Africa, or China, or Japan.

Where do you belong, Josef? The voice of cousin Ken dogged his footsteps as he crossed at the lights and walked up 45th.

The dojo was on the right-hand side, cut off from the street by a row of parking meters and a wide cracked sidewalk.

Tanaka pushed open the glass-fronted door and walked inside. Stopping behind the guard rail that separated the shoe-clad spectators from the polished, ice rink-sized floor.

There were fifteen people, warming up: five black men and one black woman, six white men and two white women and one Japanese boy whom Tanaka had never seen before. The others he recognized; he had either taught or trained with them during his years at the Philadelphia dojo.

'Mr Ta–na–ka!'

The greeting came from behind him. He knew who it was before he turned.

'Where have you been?' The friendly voice continued.

Jeff White carried a plastic cup of coffee in one hand and

his nylon training bag in the other.

He was twenty-nine and had been the East Coast free style fighting champion for three consecutive years. He was also an excellent pool player and he and Josef had spent several nights shooting pool, drinking beer and talking about the six months that White had spent training in Japan.

'I went home,' Tanaka answered.

'Tokyo?'

Josef nodded his head. 'Family business,' he confirmed.

'You're not leaving us, are you?' White asked.

The question caught Josef unexpectedly. He hesitated before he answered. 'Not for a while.'

'You training?' White continued, smiling.

Suddenly Josef didn't feel like training. 'No. I just stopped by to say hello. I'll probably start again next week . . . Is *sensei* Azato here?'

White shook his head. '*Sensei*'s in Barbados. Opening a new dojo. He loves it there, I think it's the women.'

Tanaka laughed.

'I promised I'd teach the first class, so I'd better get to it,' the tall black man continued, edging past Tanaka and down the stairs to the locker room.

'Good to see you back,' he added.

'Thanks,' Josef said, watching him disappear.

When White came out the door adjoining the dojo, he was wearing an immaculately cleaned gi and a square knotted black belt. By now, there were about thirty students on the floor and they snapped to attention.

Josef watched as Jeff White walked to the center of the dojo, beneath the wall-mounted portrait of a tiny, white-bearded Oriental schoolteacher. The teacher's name was Gichin Funakoshi and he was the founder of Japanese *Shotokan* style karate.

White knelt down gracefully; the class kneeling in front of him.

A bearded red-haired man, who Tanaka knew to be a Jewish dentist named Bornstein, called the group to order and barked the Japanese words for 'bow to the teacher'.

Josef remained as the class completed its warming up exercises and continued into the basic punching drills.

The Japanese boy was obviously the least experienced of the group and as the lines moved up and down the floor, responding to White's Japanese commands, punching in combinations of twos and threes, the boy kept glancing to his left in an attempt to follow the instructions.

He doesn't understand Japanese, Tanaka realized.

Then the total irony of what he was watching sunk in. There were hundreds of dojos like this across the United States, hundreds more throughout Europe. All started by Japanese, traveling like missionaries, preaching their doctrines and teaching their disciplines.

A hundred years ago, these disciplines would have been confined to specific *ryu*, or schools, and their techniques not taught outside the walls of the *ryu*. Now they were watered down and spread like big business, recruiting students and students who would become teachers. Selling their culture, trading Japan for the Yankee dollar.

He looked again at the single Japanese on the floor, the student having most trouble following instruction. He felt ashamed for the boy, wanted there and then to step out, grab him by the collar and lecture him on his heritage.

Instead he turned away from the guard rail, allowing his feelings towards the boy to cascade inward upon himself. He had begun to hate what he had become.

Tokyo, Japan

Ken Sato knelt in *seiza* at the base of his Shinto shrine. He cradled the sheathed *katana* in his hands, then, carefully, slid the blade from its case.

Candlelight flickered in the reflection from the polished steel.

The weapon had been forged in the sixteenth century, one of the last created by the master, Tsunemitsu.

The blade, itself, was three feet long and the blood gutters, running evenly along either side, were cut with exacting symmetry.

On the small, circular *tsuba*, or guard, below the hilt, six crows, circling in flight were carved into the metal. Their intent, to remind the swordsman of the strategy of combat: to surround the enemy, moving in circles, prohibiting escape or retreat, before the final attack.

Sato studied each detail of the sword. Contemplating both its beauty and its practicality. Balance, that is what the weapon represented. A perfect balance.

He resheathed the *katana* then closed his eyes, drawing breath slowly, entering the outer perimeters of meditation. Circling gently before traveling inwards toward emptiness.

Away from him, down the narrow corridor of his apartment, behind the shoji walls and inside the room in which he slept, a suitcase lay open and empty upon his futon. Beside it, the glow of a lamp revealed an airline ticket to the United States.

Rachel Saunders had spoken to Grace Tanaka three times since Josef's return. About Josef.

The older woman had noticed it too, the change in him, the indecision in his voice, the depressed quality of his tone.

She had invited them both to Boston.

'My sister would love to meet you; she hardly knows Josef ... God, I've been over "there" so long she hardly knows me, last time I was in Boston she was married to a stock broker ...' She was about to make some quip about her sister's third marriage but she cut herself off mid-sentence. She could feel Rachel's nerves, right through the telephone.

They had tentatively scheduled the visit for the weekend after next; Rachel would need to clear it with Josef but she knew he wanted to see his mother and the change would do them good.

Diamond Street

As far as Bill Fogarty was concerned Sugar Boy Grandistone could take his Uzi, smoke his crack, and march down Diamond Street blasting every two bit dealer and homeboy ganglord right back to Jamaica or Bogata or wherever the hell they came from.

He hated north central Philadelphia, the same way he hated every Sugar Boy and Water-melon King or however they were titling themselves this week.

Parts of the area were officially declared combat zones and killing another human being was as acceptable as spending the week's welfare check on a few rocks of crack.

The life expectancy in some of the 'hotter' zones was eighteen years. The victim of Sugar Boy's twenty rounds of semi-automatic fire was thirteen.

Fogarty was riding with Eugene Davis from narcotics. Behind them, another unmarked van carrying four black police officers followed like mourners to a funeral.

Nobody liked going to this part of town, particularly to make an arrest. But sometimes, when the pressure from City Hall was on, usually before an election, 'We'll Clean Up the Crack Zones' became a hollow battle cry.

Sugar Boy Grandistone was not hard to find. At nineteen years old he had a list of priors as long as the Cadillac stretch that carried him to his regular stops along the square patch of territory between Broad and Diamond.

Without the authorization of Sugar Boy, no one sold drugs within this four-mile area.

Usually one of his minions would step out from behind the tint-windowed door and handle negotiations, but if the buy was a big one or a show of power was necessary, Sugar Boy himself would appear. Dispensing crack or bullets, depending on the circumstance.

The thirteen-year-old alleged 'victim' had been hustling some local product when the white limo pulled to the curb. The kid had either been too stupid or too stoned to run. His twenty-six-year-old mother, who had been supervising the transaction from a tenement window, had witnessed the murder. Grief-stricken and strung out she'd gone to the neighborhood minister who, in turn, had gone to the press.

'Kill this fucking thing before it gets any uglier,' Mayor Winston Bright had ordered. After all it was an election year and he was black. They were 'his people'.

Sugar Boy was standing in the middle of the sidewalk, fifteen feet from his limo. Conversing with an equally young and well-dressed entrepreneur. The other man, almost certainly an important customer, was gesturing with his hands and stamping his right foot into the pavement to emphasize whatever it was he was talking about.

Even from half a block back Fogarty could see the piece outlined under the chest of Sugar Boy's custom-tailored suit.

'He's definitely armed,' the lieutenant commented to Davis.

'How the hell are we going to keep out of a gun fight?' Davis asked.

'We're going to do it just like we planned it,' Fogarty answered.

He checked his rear view. The team from stakeout was right behind him. Everybody, except Fogarty, was kitted out in Kelvar. Expensive vests, but they did save lives. Fogarty was philosophical; he reckoned he'd get shot in the face anyway, so why wear the extra weight?

'Come on, man, they're just a bunch of kids,' he said, pulling off slowly as the light turned green. *Kids that would sooner stand in broad daylight and die in a hail of gunfire than lose face and run. Kids that are probably carrying more money in their pockets than we make in a year.* He knew it and so did every man with him. There was no point in saying another thing. Nothing left to do but to do it.

Davis released the safety catch on the shotgun as Fogarty floored the police issue Chrysler and swerved in front of the white Cadillac, pinning it to the curb.

The narc car slammed in behind the limo, blocking escape to the rear.

Then it all turned into slow motion, like a black and white film clip, grainy and a bit distorted, but real. Very real.

The steel-reinforced passenger door of the Chrysler opened as Eugene Davis slid to his knees, using the door as cover, aiming his nine millimeter through the open window, directly at Sugar Boy.

The stakeout team was out, guns drawn, and surrounding the stretch while Fogarty crouched behind the front wheel of the Chrysler.

'Hands on your head, down on your knees, you're under arrest. Do it now!' Fogarty's voice sounded like a Doberman's bark.

The doors of the Cadillac were open and the driver and his two passengers were climbing out.

'Right hand on the car first, then your left.' He could hear the narc captain's voice like background music.

'On your knees, Grandistone, you are under arrest!' Fogarty repeated, stepping out from cover. He motioned toward the sidewalk with his .38.

Sugar Boy's customer was already down and quaking. He

looked like a disciple at his master's feet. His bodyguards and chauffeur, who didn't appear old enough to own a driving license, were positioned against the white Cadillac.

It was all down to Sugar Boy. And he was smiling, wide and happy.

'Hands on your head, down – on – your – knees,' Fogarty commanded, walking towards the six-foot-six teenager.

'How much you want to go away, man?' Sugar Boy asked, pronouncing 'man' as 'mon', and plainly annoyed at the interruption. 'All of you . . . How much?'

Fogarty figured Grandistone's bravado was for the benefit of his entourage. He kept moving, slowly and cautiously.

'This is crazy, man. I pay you, you leave me alone,' Sugar Boy continued. His eyeballs were glazed and hard.

He's high as a fucking kite, Fogarty realized.

'You want my car? New Cadillac, man. Keys inside . . . Bet you never owned no Cadillac. Take the car an' go back where ya' come from.'

Fogarty was ten feet away from Sugar Boy, steadying his nerves like a runaway horse. He held his .38 with his right hand, arm straight, aimed into the center of Grandistone's body while he lifted the cuffs from his pocket with his left.

'You go ahead, kneel down and we'll discuss it,' the lieutenant answered.

'You're wasting my time, man . . . I ain't going to prison. You know I ain't going to prison,' Sugar Boy said. Then, almost casually, he removed his right hand from the top of his razored skull and slid it down toward the inside of his jacket.

Fogarty crouched and fired. Hitting him low, two inches below the naval, dropping Sugar Boy where he stood.

It was a good shot; the 32 grain bullet broke Grandistone's pelvis, anchoring him to the sidewalk. Grandistone screamed and Fogarty rushed forward, raising his gun again, lining up for a follow through.

'Get off me, man!' Sugar Boy's voice was high and screeching.

Fogarty saw the black object in Grandistone's hand a moment before he pulled the trigger a second time. The bullet caught the padded shoulder of the teenager's silk suit and spun him sideways.

Grandistone's mobile phone skidded across the pavement.

'Calling my lawyer, man ... I was calling my lawyer.' The black youth whined from behind a wall of pain. He was still on on his knees.

'Got no right to shoot me, man. No right. Ain't packin' no piece ... Just a phone man, just a telephone. I'm a businessman, man, I ain't no hoodlum. Witnesses, I got witnesses!'

Sugar Boy Grandistone was still conscious and vowing justice when the back-up and ambulance arrived.

'The boy's never gonna walk again,' the medic whispered to Fogarty as they stretchered the drug dealer through the opened doors.

A couple of Dexies

A cab driver discovered the body at a bus stop. It was seven o'clock in the morning. At first he thought the young woman was drunk, slumped against a bench, beneath the streetlight.

He'd pulled to the curb and called from his car.

'Can I give you a lift? On the house?'

No answer.

When he got out and walked over, talking to her as he approached, he noticed she wasn't breathing.

He radioed in and got an ambulance.

The ambulance driver was tired; he'd finished his own shift at midnight, then received word that the next scheduled driver was sick. He took the second shift. When he got the body to the city morgue it was eight o'clock and he'd been working twenty hours straight.

Two doctors signed for the corpse. One was middle aged, wore spectacles and a short red goatee, the other was young, handsome, maybe half Oriental.

The ambulance driver took his chance with the younger, hipper-looking guy. 'You got anything to keep me going another couple of hours?'

Tanaka stared into the red-rimmed eyes.

'A couple of dexies, anything?'

Tanaka shook his head.

'C'mon, give me a break. This is my second day driving.'

'There's a coffee machine down the hall. Here's fifty cents?' Tanaka offered, digging into his pocket.

'Look, I'm under stress. I've had three shootings, two corpses, an OD—'

Tanaka was running out of patience.

'Plus a city cop who lost it down on Broad and Diamond ... Turned a nineteen-year-old kid into a paraplegic.'

Josef looked hard at the man. *Hadn't Bill said something to him about two crack homicides?*

'What's his name?'

'Don't know.'

'What did he look like?' Josef persisted.

'All those fuckers look the same to me ... Silk suits and felt hats—'

'The cop, I'm talking about the cop.'

'They all look the same too, except this one was white. Don't see many white cops in the north.'

Tanaka felt it right in the center of his stomach. Like a kick.

'Josef. We're ready.' Bob Moyer's voice interrupted them.

Tanaka looked once more into the tired eyes. 'I'm sorry. I can't help you. It's against the law.' He hardly got the words out, then he turned and followed Bob Moyer through the swing doors and into the operating room.

Mary Waters arrived half an hour later.

Her daughter, Virginia, had been missing since eight o'clock yesterday morning. She was a high school junior and had not reported to class. Nor had she returned to the house after school hours.

Ms Waters was a single parent and the corpse fitted the description of her only child.

Josef stood behind the small woman as Bob Moyer lifted the sheet from the dead girl's head.

'Is this your daughter?' The medical examiner's tone was soft yet firm and, for a moment, Tanaka's mind focused on the pale face on the wooden block.

'Virginia ...' Mary Waters' voice was a pained cry.

Tanaka supported her as her knees buckled, then led her from the room.

The autopsy was thorough and it was not until Moyer dissected the aorta – the main vessel carrying blood from the heart to the body – that the cause of Virginia Waters' death became known.

'Frothy blood in the chambers, there has been a quantity of air in the bloodstream . . . Embolism. Broke the rhythm of her heart. Got to find out how the air entered the bloodstream. This is going to be a long one . . . You all right, Josef? You seem somewhere else.'

'I'm fine, Bob. Please, go ahead.'

Moyer proceeded slowly, beginning with the stomach and working upward to the neck region. Examining each organ before and after he incised it from the body.

Finally exposing the interior vena cava, leading directly into the right side of the heart. The vein was purple and distended. The pathologist opened it with a vertical cut and and dark, foamy blood spurted.

'Air, she's full of air . . . I've got an idea.' Moyer moved back down the body and inserted his hand into the abdominal incision and under the pelvic organs, lifting them free from the body.

Josef watched as Moyer used his scalpel to cut the womb, from its top to the cervix, splitting it cleanly in two with his hands.

'What have we got here?'

Josef stared at the lump of tissue on the side of the womb, partly detached.

'Come on, Josef,' Moyer urged.

Josef concentrated on the pink tissue. Picking out the tiny head and the beginning of arms and legs.

'A fetus, Bob, seven, maybe eight weeks old.'

'Any second-year med student is going to know that.

What's the cause of death?' Moyer insisted.

Tanaka's mind was bouncing between Virginia Waters' corpse and 'the city cop who lost it on Diamond'.

'The blood indicates an embolism,' he answered.

'Induced by?'

Josef remained silent.

Moyer removed the fetus and placed it in a small bottle containing preserving fluid.

'An abortion?' Josef ventured.

'Looks that way. Forced introduction of liquid into the uterus. Probably soapy water from a syringe. If it's not completely full the air goes in behind the water. Gets between the placenta and the wall of the womb and, from there, into the vein network. Right on to the heart. Doesn't take long, a few minutes at most.'

'How the hell did she get to the bench?' Josef asked.

'That's one for Bill to figure out,' Moyer answered.

Josef almost said something then, about the tired driver and the incident on Diamond Street. He held his tongue. He didn't want to add strength to his fears by defining them.

'Let's take a look at the brain. That'll confirm it,' Moyer said, taking a clean scalpel from his tray.

An hour later Tanaka was scrubbed and dressed. He stopped at the front desk and placed a call to Fogarty at the Roundhouse.

Millie answered the phone. 'He's been sent home, Josef.' Her voice sounded strained.

'Was it the Diamond Street shooting?' Tanaka asked.

'It's gone right to Internal Affairs ... I swear they've got it in for him.'

'What exactly happened?' Josef asked.

'You'd better call him. I can't really discuss it. Not here,' Millie answered.

Josef rang Bill's number and got the answering machine.

He was in the process of leaving a message when Fogarty's voice cut through.

'It's a lot of shit is what it is.'

Josef could tell by the slur that Fogarty had been drinking.

'Load of fucking horseshit. Kid was cracked out. How the hell did I know it was a phone and not a weapon?'

'Bill, I'm coming over. Sit tight.'

Fogarty answered the door with a glass in his hand. There was a bottle of Glenfiddich on the mahogany table. Three quarters empty.

Half his face was covered by a stubble of beard, the other half, the scarred side, didn't grow hair.

'Good evening.'

'It's still morning, Bill,' Tanaka answered, stepping into the apartment.

'How'd you find out about it? Papers?'

'I haven't seen the papers. I got it straight from Millie.'

'She shouldn't be talk—'

'She said you were at home. No details.'

'Come on, sit down,' Fogarty said, offering Tanaka one of the four chairs that surrounded the dining table.

Then the lieutenant walked to his drinks cabinet and took out another glass.

'Forget it, Bill, I'm working,' Tanaka said, frowning at the Glenfiddich.

'On what?' His voice was gruff. He put the empty glass on the table, in front of Josef.

'A DOA. Female, sixteen years old. Air embolism, caused by a failed abortion.'

'Where?' the lieutenant asked, one hand on the litre-sized bottle.

'Cab driver found her on a bench, at a bus stop on Walnut. Two blocks from where she lived.'

'How the hell did she get there?'

'Bob Moyer thought you might be able to find out.'

Fogarty thought he detected an implication in Tanaka's voice. As if he had meant to add, 'but now that you've fucked up you're useless to us'. He stared at him a moment, letting the infraction pass. Then he poured himself another drink. 'Any news from Japan?' he asked.

'Bill, I didn't come to talk about Japan.'

Now Fogarty was sure; Josef was talking down to him. 'That makes a change,' he answered.

Tanaka bristled.

'Here, have a drink, you look like you've got a rod up your ass,' Fogarty said, pouring.

'And you look like a Vine Street wino,' Tanaka answered, pushing the glass away.

'Right,' Fogarty said. He lifted Tanaka's glass and downed the whiskey.

'Bill, what the hell have you done?'

Fogarty stared at him again.

'A nineteen-year-old kid,' Tanaka said solemnly.

Fogarty's lips tightened.

'He's never going to walk again, is that true?' Tanaka continued. Anything to get Fogarty to stop drinking and start talking. It was important he talked, for his own sake. Even if it was simply to get his story in shape for the investigation.

Fogarty kept staring and began to nod.

'Was it a bad call, Bill?' Tanaka pushed.

Fogarty lowered his eyes. *Was it a bad call?* He'd asked himself that question over and over for the past eighteen hours. A lot of Japan had been in that call, a lot of the impotence he had experienced there. Inability to perform as a policeman, humiliation. *Was it a bad call?*

'Probably,' he replied.

'Let's go over it, Bill, I want to know what happened.'

Fogarty looked up again. He'd been over it downtown, ten or twenty times. Tomorrow he'd been ordered to 'go over it' with a police psychiatrist. He didn't want to go over it now.

'Why?' He was starting to get angry. The same kind of anger he'd had in Japan. As if there were something he needed to do but couldn't. Something he needed to control but was unable. All Tanaka was doing was making him more anxious, uncomfortable.

'Because I want to know what happened,' Tanaka repeated.

'I don't want to go into it.'

Tanaka felt awkward, like he was with a stranger, prying into things that did not concern him. Maybe he should just get up and leave, give the man his space. Then he thought of Japan, of the lieutenant's unsolicited arrival. No question of prying there, Fogarty had bulldozed in, both guns blazing.

'I've got a right to know,' Tanaka insisted.

'Why?'

Fogarty took another swallow.

Tanaka reached across the table and placed his hand on Fogarty's, preventing him from lifting the glass again.

'Because maybe I can help you. Maybe you're going to need testimony to the kind of strain you've been under.'

'Your testimony?' Fogarty scowled, pulling his hand clear and lifting the glass.

'I was with you in Japan,' Tanaka said.

'You arrogant little prick,' Fogarty replied. He stood up from the table.

Tanaka rose with him.

'Are you questioning my judgement?' Fogarty continued, weaving around the table. He was drunk and he knew it; he also knew that, deep down, he was physically frightened of Josef Tanaka. Like an animal is instinctively frightened of another animal. He had seen what Tanaka could do with his hands and feet. That feeling added to his impotence, building into a fury. He could turn it inward upon himself or he could rail against his own fear. The whiskey gave him courage.

'Are you coming into my house to question me?' His voice was getting louder and he was moving forward, toward Tanaka.

Josef took a step backward. 'Bill, look at yourself ... You're exhausted, you're drunk—'

'You aren't a fucking policeman, you aren't putting it on the line every day ... You're a fucking doctor! What the hell do you know about my job?'

'Bill, I'm your friend,' Tanaka replied, but now there was a sharpness in his tone.

'Your friend, huh? Well, you treated your friend like a dickhead when he came to help you out.'

Tanaka had stopped backing up and Fogarty was eye to eye with him.

'What the hell are you talking about?'

'I'm talking about Japan. About you and cousin Ken. About me hanging around like a spare prick at a wedding while you two super dicks worked it out ... Then fucked it up.'

'Nobody asked you to come to Japan, Bill.'

'And nobody asked you to come to this apartment,' Fogarty countered.

Tanaka turned to leave then turned back again.

'You'd better straighten up. You look like shit and you smell like shit.'

Fogarty lunged forward, Tanaka side-stepped and the lieutenant buckled against the mahogany table. He grabbed the bottle and spun around.

Tanaka stood, staring, shaking his head.

'Christ, Bill, you're pathetic.'

Fogarty raised the bottle like a club.

Tanaka raised his hands, more reflex than self-defense.

'Don't try that Japanese shit with me . . . I'll put a bullet—'

'Listen to yourself, Bill, listen to yourself.' Somehow the phrase 'Japanese shit' offended Tanaka more than the threat of a bullet.

'Get the fuck out of here,' Fogarty growled.

Tanaka nodded and walked for the door.

'Question my judgement . . . What gives you the right to question my judgement?' the lieutenant ranted.

Tanaka opened the door and started for the elevator.

'It's the girl's mother, you stupid fucking asshole. It'll be the mother . . .'

Tanaka could still hear him as the elevator door closed. He wasn't even sure what he was talking about.

Not until he arrived at the police medical building on the University campus.

Bob Moyer was already there, putting the finishing touches on the autopsy report. 'It's all over, Josef, case closed,' Moyer said, looking up from his desk.

Josef stopped.

'Mary Waters confessed. Her kid got pregnant and she tried to abort her. When it all went wrong, she panicked . . . Had her boyfriend carry the girl to the bus stop, trying to make it look like it happened somewhere else . . .'

Josef nodded, thinking of Bill Fogarty.

'Catholic family,' Moyer continued, 'she couldn't live with the guilt. One mortal sin too many. You know it never entered my mind . . . That it could have been the mother.'

Josef sighed, shaking his head, then walked quickly to his office.

Turning Japanese, Part II

It was Thursday and Rachel Saunders left her office early. She deserved a break and she was taking it. Tonight a quiet dinner at home, tomorrow a flight to Boston. She was looking forward to seeing Grace, and she thought the sight of his mother, safe and well, would give Josef some peace of mind.

Yesterday had been a trial. Nine hours in surgery. She had promised Stan Leibowitz that she wouldn't go back to work yet but this had been an emergency. And she'd come through, like a champ.

Her patient was a female factory worker, employed by one of the huge wallpaper manufacturers along the industrial section of Cottman Avenue. Both hands severed at the wrist when the guillotine she operated slipped and dropped.

Rachel Saunders had led the team of surgeons that reattached the tiny nerves, blood vessels and tendons. It required two hundred and ten micro stitches.

The woman's hands would never be normal again but they would be functional.

'You'll have no feeling at first, but, in time, you will be able to pick things up and feel what you are holding,' she had assured the woman that morning.

'Dear God, you are a saint, bless you, God bless you,' the woman cried, looking at her hands below the wrap of gauze and bandage.

And now the 'saint' was going to take a little time for herself.

She was stronger now. Even the minor symptoms, the mild anxiety attacks, had ceased since the last regression. She felt free of the 'creature'. It was a strange feeling, clear and fluid, as if her mind had broken the last of its shackles.

It was six thirty when Rachel walked through the door of their apartment, put down her briefcase and headed for the kitchen.

An hour later she had completed preparation on her first ever tempura. Mushrooms, shrimp, pickled vegetables, onions and eggplant, all deep fried in a light *koromono* batter. She boiled the rice and placed each of the foods in its appropriate dish, then set the plates on the heated serving tray.

After that it was into the bedroom, out of her working clothes, into the shower and into the new kimono. She studied herself in the full-length mirror.

The silk of the kimono was black and without decoration. She had chosen it because it was simple and in striking contrast to her blonde hair. The other garments in the Japanese shop had been either red or green, and decorated with embroidered flowers and dragons. They seemed gim- micky and cheap when compared to the black.

She straightened her hair and darkened her eyelashes. She was just touching the blush-colored lipstick to her lips when she heard the key in the lock.

She felt a wave of self-consciousness, or maybe it was vulnerability. She considered taking off the kimono, hiding it in the closet.

What the hell was she doing anyway, playing Japanese?

'Rachel!' He was calling from the hallway.

She opened the bedroom door and entered the living room, studying his eyes for a reaction.

He seemed somehow bewildered.

'Well?' She covered his silence.

'Where did you get that?'

She stopped smiling. 'Do you like it?' Confidence drained from her voice.

'Black kimonos are for funerals,' Josef answered. He hadn't meant it to sound as hard as it did.

'Well, I thought I might wear this one to dinner,' she answered.

Josef stood silent and looked at her. It was like a sick joke playing over and over in his mind, a thousand variations on the same theme. Western furniture in shoji rooms, Japanese children who spoke only English, Samurai with wives from Boston and half-caste sons who lived in Philadelphia. And now the half-caste's future wife dressing up for a Buddhist funeral and calling it dinner at home.

He needed to talk about Bill Fogarty, of whether he'd been right or wrong. He needed to straighten things out in his mind. And all the time life kept getting more and more confused. Another time, he'd do it another time.

'Fine, let's have dinner then,' he said.

Rachel forced a smile and retreated to the kitchen.

She felt vulnerable enough without feeling like a fool. Still, she knew he'd been through hell in Japan, that he was worried for the sake of his family and that he was consumed with guilt for leaving.

Give him time, she told herself. *Put his feelings first and give him time.*

Dinner was eaten in near silence, with the exception of the *soba*. Josef slurped the slender noodles.

Rachel looked at him once, mid-slurp, and received her single compliment of the evening.

'Perfect, cooked just right, soft but not too soft.' Then he sucked the last of the *soba* into his mouth and forced a smile.

They went into the bedroom at ten o'clock.

'Reestablish a strong physical relationship.' That's what Stan Liebowitz had advised.

Josef took his clothes off in the bathroom, looked at his face in the mirror. Then he did something that he had not done since he was a child, attending private school, just growing into an awareness that he was not quite like the others.

He lifted his hands to his eyes, and with his thumbs, raised them on either side. He looked Japanese, complete and pure.

He stared at himself this way then removed his hands and continued looking at his face.

The straight eyes stared back at him. It was as if he had just spent his life savings on a work of art, brought it home, hung it up and discovered a tear in the canvas. Something that could not be mended. A flaw which utterly destroyed the value of the piece.

He took a hot shower and tried to wash the feeling away. When he came out and toweled dry, he put on a white terrycloth bathrobe and walked into the bedroom.

Rachel was sitting in the wicker rocking chair beside the bed.

She stood up as he entered the room. 'I'll never wear it again,' she said softly, removing the kimono.

She was naked beneath.

He studied her as she walked to the wardrobe and placed the silk robe on the shelf. Then, closing the door and turning, she came toward him.

Summer was over and she had stopped waxing her 'bikini line', leaving a line of gold silky hair growing in a fine trail upwards from the crown of her pubis. Above, her abdomen was tight and he could see the hint of muscle lying beneath the faintly tanned flesh. She had lost weight. It accentuated the length of her rib cage and the small rounded breasts with their disproportionately large nipples.

She had been a bit self-conscious about her breasts when

they first slept together. 'Silicone, I'm going in for silicone,' she'd vowed. But there was really nothing wrong with them. In fact, the thick pink nipples had always been a source of eroticism for Tanaka. An imperfection in symmetry that really aroused him. An intimate secret.

He opened his robe as she came closer, going up on her toes to kiss him, taking his hard penis in her hand and placing it between her legs.

He let his robe fall, bending slightly at the knees to allow himself firmly into the groove between her thighs. Cupping the warm flesh of her buttocks, pulling her to him, lifting her from the floor.

He broke from the kiss and she groaned as he slid back and forth, still not inside her. Then he opened his eyes, intending to guide her to the edge of the bed, to bend her backwards and enter her.

He caught a glimpse in the full-length wardrobe mirror. The two of them, entwined. Rachel's blonde hair, his skin dark against hers.

She settled on the side of the mattress, bending backwards, wrapping her legs up and around him.

'Yeah, come on, fuck me,' she whispered. It was the first time she had felt purely sexual since the trauma of her abduction.

Something compelled Josef to look again in the mirror. Perhaps her words were the catalyst, or the feeling of a third party, someone watching them, judging.

The Japanese man and his American whore. It was Ken Sato's voice that spoke in his mind, condemning him.

Rachel reached between his legs and found that he was no longer hard. He was pulling away from her.

Where do you belong, Josef, here or there? Again Sato's voice, the question repeated. Questioning the hypocrisy of his relationship.

'I can't. I just can't do it,' he said.

And suddenly it was as if they were two strangers. And Rachel Saunders was embarrassed, embarrassed and somehow ashamed.

She let him go and rolled away, using the sheets to cover her nakedness as he picked up his robe and wrapped it around his body.

'I can't take you to Boston.' His voice was apologetic but firm.

Japan Airlines' jumbo jet landed at San Francisco International Airport at three fifty-five in the afternoon.

Ken Sato was traveling first class.

Because his 'ceremonial' sword was classified a potential offensive weapon, it had been necessary for him to hand it to the captain of the plane for safe keeping.

The Japanese pilot returned the cloth-wrapped *katana* as Sato prepared to disembark.

'Have a nice day,' the man said, handing the weapon over.

'*Domo arigato*,' Sato thanked him in Japanese.

'Have a nice day'. The phrase sickened Sato. Sickened him because it was an American cliché, falling from Japanese lips.

He picked up his single suitcase from the carousel and headed for customs.

'That's a real beautiful sword,' the official commented, drawing the blade a few inches clear of the scabbard.

'Please, don't touch the metal,' Sato said, trying hard to keep his voice friendly.

The official looked up.

'The oil from your fingers stays on the steel. It will cause it to corrode,' Sato explained patiently.

'Oh, I see,' the thin Hispanic replied, resheathing the

blade and handing the sword back to Sato. 'And where is this exhibition?'

'At the Japan Center,' Sato replied. 'There will be costumes and armor as well as weapons,' he added.

'Well, have a good one,' the man said, smiling. Then he indicated that Ken could proceed to the exit.

Sato thanked him and smiled back, noting that the official made no entry in his computer regarding the sword.

He checked into a suite at the San Francisco Marriot, waiting for the porter to leave before taking the mattress from his bed and throwing it to the floor. He couldn't sleep on springs. Then he unpacked, hung up his clothes and went for a walk.

Straight to the notorious area of Market Street and Castro.

A decade ago, when he had first come to San Francisco, the Castro district had been carnivalesque, gay men parading arm in arm, wearing outrageous clothes and openly displaying their life style and affections.

AIDS had changed everything. Now there was a taint, a caution in the atmosphere. The entire community had been punished.

And Ken Sato approved of the punishment. He hated the theatrical mincing of homosexual men. Loathed its implied weakness.

There was nothing feminine about Ken Sato's homosexuality. If anything, it was a form of super masculinity, male dominating male. He had taken several before the kill. Forced them to submit. There was power in the act of penetration, sheer power.

He strolled north on Castro, toward Eighteenth Street, walking past several of the old bath houses, closed down and boarded over, illegal since the spread of the killer virus.

From Castro he grabbed a cab to Fisherman's Wharf. There

was a traditional Japanese restaurant on the west side of the pier, close to Marina Green. He ate dinner there, then returned to the Marriot. Spent the rest of the weekend walking the city, seeing the sights and relaxing. The weather was warm but not as humid as Tokyo, the sidewalks nowhere near as crowded and he enjoyed the accessibility of the Americans. To a point.

On Monday he met with the lawyers from Rand Inc and worked through a series of import contracts for the sale of ten million dollars worth of disk drives, manufactured by Tanaka Industries and housed in Rand's plastic consoles, stamped 'Made In The USA'.

On Tuesday he put the finishing touches to the contracts. Everyone was happy. Particularly Ken Sato; he knew the components would be obsolete in nine months and Rand would have to renegotiate for the upgraded parts.

He concluded his business at two o'clock in the afternoon, went back to his hotel and booked a ten o'clock flight to Los Angeles.

Turning Japanese, Part III

Josef went to Boston on his own, staying for one night in his aunt's house in Cambridge.

He needed to see his mother, to assure her that she was doing the right thing, staying away from Japan until the police had resolved the case. It was easier now, now that it was out in the open. They could talk about it, Hironori, the murder. They both cried. Wept without shame, and those tears, shared with his mother, cleansed him. Made him feel honest again.

Honest enough to tell her that he was leaving Rachel.

'Why?' she asked him, 'why?'

He had no answer.

The next morning, after a sleepless night, he still had no answer. It was just something that he had to do.

'You're going to hurt her; you are going to hurt her very, very much,' Grace Tanaka said as he was leaving.

It took him nearly a week to find another apartment.

One of the worst weeks of his life. There had been anger and tears, sorrow and the strange levity of letting go. All mixed together.

Rachel found reasons to work late every night; he slept on the sofa.

When they did see each other she was either crying or angry, or both. He was numb.

'Why are you doing this?' she asked him. The same question his mother had asked.

'I need to be alone.' His answer was inadequate and he knew it.

She just stared at him, shaking her head.

Bob Moyer was giving a lecture at the university. Something to inspire pre-med students to consider a career with the Department of Health.

He had forgotten his slides so Josef took them over.

That's where he saw the ad. Tacked to the bulletin board in the students' union. 'House to share. Ground floor, private entrance.'

He rented it by phone, sight unseen. Had a messenger bike take his references and a certified check for the security deposit, plus a month's rent, straight down to Spring Garden Street, near the Art Museum.

Then he slipped back to the apartment, in the middle of the afternoon and collected his bags. He felt like a thief.

Three suitcases and his training bag. That was it. There had never been that much of him at the apartment. It was Rachel's place. Always had been.

He shut the door, pushed his key through the letter box and dragged his belongings to the elevator.

The cab ride to Spring Garden Street was the loneliest, most hollow ride he had ever taken. As if he had sentenced himself to life imprisonment, solitary confinement ... And this was the trip to the penitentiary. Lack of self-knowledge had been his crime, Rachel his victim, and Bill, and himself.

'Is losing you the price of getting well?' That was the last thing Rachel had said to him; he couldn't get it out of his mind.

*

The place on Spring Garden Street was old and beat. Peeling paint and threadbare wall-to-wall carpets, plus that terrible smell of mildew and rotting wood.

He slept on a mattress on the floor for the first two nights, until the weekend.

Then he worked like a mad man, scraping and painting, tearing out carpets, sanding and polishing, scrubbing sinks and toilets.

He took a sick day on Monday and went shopping. Straight to the Japanese Center at New Market. He bought a futon, several low laquered tables and fifteen tatamis.

In Japan, room size was measured by the number of tatamis it took to fill the space. The straw mats were usually three feet by six feet and three inches thick.

His main room at Spring Garden Street was eighteen feet long and twelve feet wide, a nine-tatami room, enormous by Japanese standards.

He used the other six mats to cover the floors of his bedroom and the guest room.

On Monday evening he went to the lumber yard and bought a four-by-four piece of timber, instructing the workman at the yard to bevel the upper four feet of the wood until the top was about half an inch thick. He lugged it home in a cab.

Because he was on the ground floor he had sole access to a small garden, more precisely an eight-by-four patch of weeds.

'I don't give a damn what you do with it,' Louise, his new landlady, said when he mentioned using it as an exercise yard.

First he weeded the garden, then he dug the hole: three feet deep and wide enough at the bottom to wedge in a few bricks.

He fitted the board into the hole, tight against the bricks at the bottom, and filled the dirt in around it, packing it hard, giving no more than six inches of play to the top.

Finally he took a piece of specially cut foam rubber, two inches thick, a foot long and cut to match the width of the board. He positioned the center of the pad even with his solar plexus, fixing it to the wood with a straw rope, wrapping it round and round, until it formed a solid unit, the width of the rope running in hard ridges up along the pad.

He stepped back and looked at the *makiwara*, remembering when he and Hiro had built their first punching board in the back garden of the family house. *Twenty-two years ago* he thought, counting back the time.

'Got to hit it a thousand times each hand,' Hiro had told him. 'One year, every day, and you'll be a master.'

They had each hit it fifty times and their knuckles were like raw meat. Hiro had managed another ten strikes before he gave in. 'We'll build up to it,' he decreed. That had been fine with Josef. Hiro knew about those things.

Tanaka lowered his body into a front stance and slammed his fist into the center of the straw-wrapped pad. The *makiwara* gave on impact then snapped back into position, like a vertical diving board. He hit it again and again, switching from right to left stance.

At one point he heard the landlady's window open, felt someone watching him. He did not turn or look up, just kept punching until the feeling of being observed dissolved.

He focused his mind into the physical action of rooting his feet, rotating his hips and driving his fist in a clean linear attack. It was a physical meditation, a catharsis.

He continued for an hour, until the sweat flowed from his body and his knuckles had begun to bleed.

It was dark when he walked back into his apartment and ran a cold bath. He sponged first, before he got in, then sat in the water and tried to empty his mind.

Too much confusion, voices urging him in different

directions. And Rachel. Too painful to think of what he had done to Rachel. He wanted nothing more than to go to her now, to say it was all a mistake. Another mistake. To thank her for what she had given him in the past two years: love, a friend, a home. To beg forgiveness. But he could not, because the man that had accepted her gifts was not the man he needed to be. That was his confusion.

He felt hollow again when he lay down on the futon and pulled the duvet around him. The street sounds beyond his walls were unfamiliar, trucks and motorcycles, car horns. He wondered if Rachel were asleep. What she was thinking? How long before her love would fester and become hate? It would be easier if she hated him.

And Bill Fogarty. He'd come all the way to Japan because he thought Josef needed him. Walked right into the middle of Josef's bad trip. Over his head, out of his depth. Then returned to a mess of his own.

Tanaka rolled from his back to his side, curled his knees upward into his body. The simple shift in position caused him to think again of Rachel; he had often gone to sleep like this, her hips resting on his thighs, tucked into him as if they fitted together, her warmth soothing him.

'Oh God, what have I done?' He said it to the darkness of the room.

He sat up. Beside him, on the low bedside table, he could make out the silhouette of the telephone. He wanted to call her, tell her he had been wrong. That he was coming back, that everything would be the same as it had been. That he loved her, God did he love her.

Then he'd call Bill. Apologize for barging in on him half-cocked, unaware of the details of what had happened on Diamond Street. Apologize for Japan, for inadvertently drawing him into a battle zone.

Rachel and Bill, the two most important people in his life, his American life.

Then there was Japan. And Japan was the problem. Unresolved.

The thought rekindled the image of his father. 'They took my heart. There is no fight left in me.' Mikio Tanaka's words.

Josef had urged him to carry on, never to give in. But where was his son now, his ally? Eight thousand miles away, fucked up and confused.

He had an obligation to cleanse his mind, to put himself in order. Then he could be a proper support, make correct decisions.

He got off the futon and knelt on the tatami, hips on heels, in *seiza*.

'Our Father who art in heaven—' The prayer started and stalled in his mind. It was not his prayer. It had been given to him by the teachers at his Christian school, when he was too young to know who or what he was.

He didn't need prayer; he needed space to think. To find himself.

Josef, why are you doing this? Rachel's voice inside his head.

The question repeated, demanding an answer.

He sat and waited. Hours passed.

Heavy ground. In so far you can't withdraw. Fully committed ... Where do you belong, here or there? Ken Sato's words. Providing the catalyst.

Because I cannot commit myself to you, Rachel. Cannot give you something that is only half formed. You are my 'heavy ground', emotionally and physically. You represent a boundary that I am unsure of crossing. There have always been two selves to me, the American and the Japanese. Split. Unable to come to terms. And the longer I am with you, the stronger the American self becomes ... I had begun to forget Japan, what is there and what I had left behind. It was good to forget, comfortable, but it was also a negation ... My brother's death drew me back, not only to the country but to feelings I had buried. A spark was rekindled. As if I arrived with only one eye open and was forced, by the situation, to use both eyes. To enlarge my perspective. And now I see things from both selves simultaneously, all the time, and there seems no way to integrate this vision. And this causes me to question my identity, my responsibility to myself, my family, and to you . . . Perhaps I am too Japanese ever to find peace of mind in this country, to overcome the feeling of running away . . . And now, particularly, I must question my presence here. When my family is so vulnerable and my father struggling for his own survival. That is why I have withdrawn from you, from our situation . . . I am no good for you now, no good for myself, for anyone.

Tuesday came and Josef Tanaka did not show up at the medical building. It was the first time in two years that he had been absent without excuse.

Bob Moyer was not angry, he was concerned. Josef had seemed like a zombie since his return from Japan. Moyer had intended to sit him down and talk it through but the right time had never come.

For the past week, Tanaka had been unapproachable, detached and uninterested in his work. Moyer was patient, understanding; he put it down to personal problems, deciding to leave it alone. To let life take its course. But now he had to do something.

He tried the phone number that Josef had given him. It was engaged. Two hours and five attempts later the line was still busy. *Probably taken it off the hook*, Moyer surmised. Then a strange thought crossed his mind. He told himself it was impossible but it kept coming back.

Suicide . . . With the amount of strain the guy's been under, Christ, anybody's liable to think of it.

Bob Moyer jumped in his car and took a ride through the

gray morning, all the way to Spring Garden Street.

Tanaka's residence looked grotty from the outside. One of the old brownstones built after the Second World War. Sitting in the middle of a block full of similar residences, most in better condition.

Moyer walked the broken concrete of the entrance path to the door of the ground floor apartment. Looking around, he had another tinge of real anxiety. All the blinds were drawn. No sound at all coming from inside, no radio, no television, just a stony silence.

He rang the entrance buzzer. Nothing. Maybe the buzzer didn't work. He knocked, harder and harder. Tried the door and found it locked, then began to bang on the green-painted wood with the back of his fist.

'Josef, Josef!' He could hear the panic in his own voice.

He stopped banging and stepped back, lowering his shoulder for the charge. Then he heard the footsteps: quiet, cat-like steps from behind the door.

Listened to the click of the lock turn and saw the door open.

'Bob.' That was all Tanaka said. Standing there barefoot in his black divided skirt and thick cotton jacket. His hair was pomaded and swept back, tied in a small tight knot. Like some monk at the door of a monastery.

Bob Moyer didn't know whether to laugh or cry.

'Josef,' he answered, 'you didn't come in for work and I was—'

'Please, come inside.'

Moyer entered the main room of the apartment, stepping onto the small entrance mat which protected the tatami.

He saw Josef's street shoes lined up against the wall and took the hint. Removed his own and walked forward. There were no chairs in the room, simply a bank of cushions and a long, low, lacquered table. Tanaka walked ahead and sat down on one of the cushions.

Moyer sat beside him.

'Tea, Bob, may I get you tea?'

'No thanks, Josef,' Moyer answered. Waiting for Josef to drop the charade and apologize for not coming into work. At least to offer an explanation.

Josef was silent and Moyer began to feel uneasy.

'Josef, what the hell's going on?' he said finally.

Josef looked at the small man with his trimmed goatee and neatly parted hair. Looked right into the small eyes behind the wire rims of the prescription glasses. Saw a man trying to figure him out.

'I can't come in for a while, Bob. I'm going through some personal changes.'

Moyer laughed, a tight, nervous laugh.

Josef laughed. An identical laugh to Moyer's.

Then both men were silent again, staring at each other.

'Your personal changes are going to cost you a job,' Moyer said.

Josef didn't react.

'I can cover for you for a few more days, but after that—' Moyer stopped talking and shook his head.

'I don't want you to cover for me.' There was a finality in Tanaka's tone.

'You're making a mistake, Josef, you've got a talent for what you do, an instinct. Don't throw it away.' He looked hard at Josef then around the sparse room, changing tack, 'You've been right to the wall in the last month, Christ, anybody would have lost it—'

'Are you saying that this is losing it?'

Moyer met Tanaka's eyes. He'd gone too far to retreat, besides he had meant what he said, even if the words had slipped out.

Moyer shrugged his shoulders. Looked around the room again and back at Josef.

'Come on, Josef, this is pretty extreme.'

'Maybe I'm finding it, Bob,' Tanaka said.

Finding what? Moyer wondered. He was trying to be reasonable, but his patience was wearing thin.

'I can get you another week, Josef,' he said. His legs were beginning to hurt.

Josef watched as Moyer stood up, rubbing his knees.

He wanted to speak, to open up, to apologize, to ask for advice, even pardon. He couldn't do it. His emotions had frozen inside him.

'What the hell's the matter with you?' Moyer reached out as he spoke.

Josef turned from the hand, watching it fall clear of his shoulder. He didn't want to be touched. As if human contact would break the freeze; he'd splinter and fall apart. He had to keep everything tight right now. Until he figured it out, until he could come clean.

He lowered his eyes and walked past Bob Moyer, stopping at the door.

'Right, that's it then,' Moyer said, interpreting Tanaka's movement as indication that he should leave. He walked behind him, slid into his shoes, bending over to lace them up. 'Anything I can do for you, let me know.'

Tanaka met his eyes and shook his head. He couldn't even say 'thanks', couldn't get the word free of his throat.

'A week, Josef, I'll get you a week,' Moyer said, a touch of frost on his words.

Tanaka watched him walk down the broken path and climb into his BMW. The engine turned over; revved once and idled. He saw a glint of reflection from Moyer's glasses as the medical examiner glanced one last time toward Tanaka's door.

Then the BMW pulled out from the curb and drove away, turned a corner and vanished.

Tanaka closed and locked his door. Walked back into his apartment, through the small kitchen and out into the garden.

He settled into a front stance and pounded his fist into the *makiwara*. Over and over again.

Spaghetti

Bill Fogarty walked into the Roundhouse and took the elevator to the third floor.

The five men waited for him in the small conference room in the Police Commissioner's Office, two investigators, two suits from Internal Affairs, and Dan McMullon. Fogarty had expected a captain to preside over the departmental hearing. The Commissioner was a real surprise.

'Dan, I'm honored,' the lieutenant quipped as he walked into the room.

Dan McMullon's face gave it away before anyone else had said a word. He was smiling. The kind of smug, 'I'm about to do you a big favor' kind of smile that Fogarty had seen a few times since McMullon had stepped over the lieutenant's body en route to his position as Police Commissioner.

Fogarty was exhausted; he didn't really give a damn what happened, as long as it was quick.

Josef Tanaka had put it very succinctly ten days ago. 'You're pathetic, Bill, Christ you're pathetic.' That's what he had said and that's how Fogarty felt. Dragging his limping, booze-riddled body in front of five men, sitting in judgement, most of them a good ten years younger and not one with a quarter of his time on the streets.

He was a tired, old dog. Maybe, mercifully, they'd take away his gun and his badge and put him out of his misery.

No such luck.

Three of the assisting officers had come forward on his behalf. They had sworn that he had acted correctly, issuing three warnings before firing on Sugar Boy Grandistone. Then they had gone to work on Grandistone, extracting his confession to the murder of the thirteen-year-old boy. On top of which, someone had produced a nine millimeter Glock allegedly found on the drug dealer.

Fogarty was in the clear. Almost.

Dan McMullon kept his smile in place, returning Fogarty to active duty before he adjourned the hearing.

'You've got some good friends in the department, Bill.' His tone implied his belief in the lieutenant's guilt. 'Of course, there's still the chance that the kid will press a civil suit . . . That wouldn't look good for any of us.'

Fogarty studied the fat Irish face, all broken blood vessels and hanging jowls.

He was too weak to fight; he nodded and walked away.

Tentative faces greeted him on the first floor. Millie seemed on the verge of tears. Everyone was waiting, wanting to know what happened upstairs.

'I think I'm going to make it,' he said.

There were a couple of hand claps, a relieved 'yeah', and then Millie was rushing toward him holding a cup of coffee as if it were a magnum of champagne.

The chair at his desk felt like home and the strong black coffee peeled the final layers of sludge from his brain.

Fogarty thought of Josef Tanaka. He hadn't seen or spoken to him in over a week. Not since Josef had visited him at the Presidential. That was the first thing he intended to put right. He picked up his phone and dialed Bob Moyer's office. Recognized the medical examiner's raspy voice immediately.

'I'm back on the streets.'

'That's great, Bill, really great,' Moyer answered. A little too much effort in his tone.

'The boys down here backed me up pretty good,' Fogarty continued.

'They did the right thing, Bill, you're the best they've got,' Moyer said sincerely. There was still something hiding behind his words.

'Let me have a quick word with Josef, will you, Bob?'

Moyer went quiet.

'Bob?'

Fogarty could hear the doctor clear his throat. 'I haven't seen Josef in a few days,' Moyer said.

'What's the matter?'

'He's taking some time off, straightening out his head . . . Whatever went on in Japan really confused him.'

'I don't follow you.'

Moyer hesitated again. 'He's doing this whole Japanese routine, robes, tied-back hair . . . But serious,' he explained.

Fogarty swallowed the last of his coffee.

'I don't know how long I can cover for him . . . I've got him out on "compassionate" but it's wearing pretty thin,' Moyer went on.

'I'll go around and see him,' Fogarty said, putting down his cup, 'must be putting Rachel through it . . . I'd say she's had enough.'

'Josef's not living with Rachel any more,' Moyer replied.

The words hit him hard, like hearing the news that someone close had died unexpectedly, a member of the family.

'He's taken this thing pretty far, Bill . . . I've been around to where he's living. It was like talking to a stranger.'

'Where is he, Bob? You got a number?' Fogarty asked. He kept thinking of Rachel. *Christ, she doesn't deserve all this.*

There was no answer on the number that Moyer gave him for

Spring Garden Street so he phoned Rachel Saunders at her office.

She broke from her appointment and took his call.

'I'm more worried for him than I am hurt, Bill. And I'm hurt badly ... Stan Leibowitz has been helping me through it, I guess poor old Stan got more than he bargained for when he got me. He has some theories about why Josef is behaving this way but they don't change anything ... And, Bill, I need something to change ... I want him back, like he was before.' She barely controlled the tremor in her voice. Fogarty could hear it. He knew she was going to break down if he kept her talking.

'Why don't I come over and see you, after work?' he suggested.

Rachel didn't answer.

'Look if it's not convenient, I understand, believe me—'

'No, no, that's fine, that's fine. I'd love to see you, do me good,' she said.

He could hear the shift of emotion in her voice.

'After seven, I'll cook you dinner ... You like tempura?' She was trying to lighten it up.

'Make it spaghetti and I'll do my best to be there by eight.'

'Okay,' she answered, hesitating as her tone shifted downward, hardening, 'why the hell is he doing this, Bill?'

In Tokyo, had he seen it coming? Hadn't he felt it then, as if Tanaka were pulling away from him?

'We'll talk about it tonight,' he promised, 'see you later.'

He tried Tanaka once more. Nothing. He felt like going over there, getting into it with him, straightening him out before he saw Rachel. Handing her relationship back to her. With his compliments. The way he always felt when someone needed caring for, as long as it wasn't himself. He wasn't too good at that.

Millie interrupted his thoughts, handing him a fat manila

folder marked 'Grandistone, JM'.

'You're going to need these before the arraignment,' she said, glancing at his empty coffee cup.

Fogarty nodded his head; she took the cup and walked from the room. By the time she returned with the refill he was poring over the contents of the folder. Case reports and pictures.

Ugly pictures, of a young black boy named John Martine Grandistone, aka Sugar Boy, sprawled on a dirty pavement with a bullet through his spine. No matter what the kid had done, how much crack he'd sold and how many lives he'd ruined; he still looked like a victim. He was a victim. Of the streets. Fogarty knew that. He also knew that his decision to shoot had been valid. He'd been over it a thousand times, drunk and sober. He'd done right.

He sipped the fresh coffee, sat up in his chair, spread the files in front of him, and concentrated on being a policeman.

Three hours later, at half past twelve, he picked up his phone and dialed again.

Josef Tanaka listened to the ring. Loud and insistent, breaking his concentration. He wondered who it was, counting the people who had his number. Rachel, Bob Moyer, his mother, maybe Bill had it by now. He couldn't talk to any of them, not the way he needed to. He didn't trust himself, or what he might say.

He stared at the telephone until it stopped, then lowered his head and continued the breathing exercises. There were two distinct voices in his mind, both his own. One spoke to him in English, the other in Japanese.

The Japanese voice urged him to pack his belongings and return to Tokyo, reminding him of his duty to his family. Telling him that his life in Philadelphia had been a lie, an escape.

The other voice spoke of friendship and love. Told him to

take his three suitcases and a cab-ride back to Rittenhouse Square.

The voices agreed on only one thing; this time, wherever he landed, it had to be for keeps. No more head trips. His head trips were destroying everyone.

He listened to both voices. Sometimes they argued, sometimes one would stop entirely, allowing the other to dominate, to dictate the course of his future. It was easier when that happened, when everything was decided. Then, just when he thought he had the answer, a whisper from the other side would shadow his decision with doubt and the whole process would begin again.

And somewhere the knowledge that beyond the voices was the state of *mushin*, no-mindedness, an emptiness untainted by intellect and emotion. Inside that emptiness he would find the path of truth. Then he would need the courage to follow it.

He exhaled and settled back in his seated posture. His calves had gone numb. Four hours in *seiza* and three days without food were taking their toll.

Once, many years ago, he had performed the same discipline. He had been sixteen years old and it was during his first karate summer camp: five days in the mountains, four devoted to basic training and the last given entirely to the spiritual side of the discipline, fasting and meditation. Before the camp he had fantasized about sitting beneath waterfalls, tempering his body and mind, emerging as a *sohei*, a mixture of warrior and priest.

The reality was different. The water was freezing cold and the pressure on his head felt like a sledgehammer. He couldn't find a rhythm to his respiration or take his mind from the spasms of his empty stomach. When he adjusted his position against the hard rocks he was either shouted at or struck with a bamboo pole.

At first he had been furious with the senior students who were overseeing his torment. Powerless against them he had turned his anger inward, despising himself for getting into the situation to begin with, until the anger dissipated and left him with a deep sorrow. Inside the sorrow were memories of his life, locked in frozen moments, waiting to be revisited and reviewed.

Incidents in which he had let himself down, walked away when he should have fought, surrendered when he should have persevered. Moments which linked and interlocked, joining to form a one-way bridge to the present. And the present was hard and cold and punishing.

He saw the circle of his life, the endless repetition, negativity compounding negativity. It was then that he stopped believing in chance and fate; there was only opportunity. Discipline could break the circle, transform a negative pattern to a positive outcome. He could change and grow.

He breathed in his pain and accepted his situation. And in that instant of acceptance the images stopped, the internal dialogue ceased and he entered a state of peace. The first true inner peace he had ever known. As if a free and silent void existed where his doubts had been.

The sound of water falling, like a hollow roar, brought him back from no-mindedness. That was twenty years ago.

Now, as he breathed in, then out, consciously slowing the beat of his heart to mirror his controlled respiration; he felt the beginning of that void, descending like a soft cloak, smothering the flames of thought and desire. Time dissolved.

Two hours later the telephone rang.

This time he answered, his body responding automatically to its signal, a reflex. The touch of his fingers against the cool plastic felt hard and alien. No thought of who the caller might be.

The line crackled.

'Josef-san, Josef-san?'

Ken Sato's voice rose from the swirls of forming consciousness, pulling Josef back from the void, reconnecting him, bringing him home.

'Where are you, Ken?' Josef asked, the words forming naturally in Japanese.

'Los Angeles, California. I finish my business today ... Then, Josef-san, I wish to come and visit with you.' Sato also spoke in his native tongue.

'Yes. Please come, Ken,' Josef answered.

'You can arrange a hotel for me?'

'No hotel, Ken-san ... You must stay with me,' Josef answered, hesitating, 'I need to talk to you, Ken-san, very much.'

'Yes, cousin, I know, I know,' Sato answered.

Josef felt the reassurance of his cousin's words and tone, as if, finally, fate would be resolved.

'My plane arrives at ten forty in the evening,' Sato continued.

'I will be at the terminal to meet you,' Josef promised.

The loneliness of the bereaved hung over Rachel Saunders' apartment like a veil, casting the hint of shadow across its bright colored furniture and pale blue walls.

Fogarty kissed her on the cheek at the door, then sipped from a glass of Frascati while Rachel finished preparing their dinner.

'It's my own sauce, Bill, my mother taught me how to do it ... Hope you don't mind garlic,' she called from the small kitchen.

'Go ahead, there's no romance in my life anyway,' he answered, angry with himself for the insensitivity of his remark even before the boom of his voice had died in the room.

'Another ten minutes,' she said.

Maybe she didn't notice, he thought, knowing deep down that she had and was just excusing him.

He swallowed a large mouthful of wine and picked up a newspaper from the glass-covered coffee table. Anything to keep himself quiet. It was the late edition of the *Inquirer* and had a front page spill about the end of the recession.

Politics and economics had never held great interest for the lieutenant; his city wage was automatically adjusted to inflation and he still drove the same Buick Le Mans that he'd bought when he made Lieutenant, fifteen years ago. He was about to turn to the sports page and see if George Foreman had finally retired or if, at age forty-five, the number one contender was going to get another crack at the title, one more time. Old George gave Fogarty hope.

Instead, something at the bottom of the front page caught his eye.

MASHIRO HEIR FOUND MURDERED
IN WEST HOLLYWOOD

The headline caused Fogarty to straighten his back against the sofa.

He went on to read that David Mashiro, son of Gloria Reynolds and Hidetaka Mashiro – owner of Mashiro Leisure Industries Inc, including the Primus Film Distribution Co and Sunningdale Golf Courses in Santa Barbara, California – had been found dead in a parking lot adjacent to Sunset Boulevard in West Hollywood. The nineteen-year-old student had been decapitated. No clues or suspects were indicated in the Associated Press report.

Fogarty read the short piece twice, making a mental note of the date and place then put the paper down. All through dinner his mind kept returning to the 'Mashiro Heir' article.

Remembering the Tokyo theory about a conspiracy.

It was only Rachel's voice, talking about Josef, that brought him back to the here and now.

By the second cup of coffee, one thing had been resolved. No matter how much it hurt, and by the dark, hollow circles beneath her eyes, Fogarty had a fair idea of what Rachel's nights had been like, she was giving Josef his space.

'He's having a form of personality breakdown,' she said, repeating what Stan Leibowitz had told her, 'triggered by guilt. Somewhere inside, he believes *he* killed his brother . . . That psychological trauma compounded by going back to Japan, being forced to reimmerse himself in their culture. He doesn't know who he is and he can't really function till he finds out.'

Stan Leibowitz had advised Rachel to stay clear. For Josef's sake and for her own. 'Allow him the space to redefine himself, to work through his confusion. He's going to need to regain a perspective . . . Have faith in the reality of your relationship, in the fact that you have a deep and sincere love.'

Then the psychiatric jargon faded from her conversation and Rachel sat staring at Fogarty. Her eyes went wet and her voice quivered. 'Do you know how many times I've driven over there? Gotten to within a block or two of where he's living? Turned around . . . Afraid of what I'd find. Afraid he'd reject me. What's he doing to himself, Bill?' Rachel asked, suddenly desperate.

Fogarty absorbed her despair and shook his head slowly.

Suddenly the effect of Stan Leibowitz's counseling became apparent. The psychiatrist had created an intellectual boundary for Rachel Saunders. Had effectively placed a restraining order on her emotions. And it was already getting shaky.

The lieutenant had done some couch time himself, after the road accident. It had helped him bury the dead. To a point. This was different, Josef Tanaka was alive. And Bill Fogarty knew that he had better grab hold of him, and soon. Before Rachel tried.

He got up to leave at a quarter to eleven, shook Rachel's hand at the door, kissed her on the cheek, hugged her, told her not to worry. Did everything but sign a written guarantee that he would rescue the situation. Not that she had asked him to, that was never necessary with Fogarty, his own guilt trip dictated his behaviour.

Rachel stood in the hallway, watching him walk to the elevator, press the 'down' button. Listened to the sound of the lift rising on its steel cables, the door sliding open.

'Good night, Bill, thanks for coming,' she said. Then he was gone and she was alone.

She went back inside her apartment, locked and bolted the door. Began to cry, controlled her tears then stared down at the newspaper on the glass-topped table; her eyes drawn to the article at the bottom of the front page. The 'Mashiro' article. The same article that Bill Fogarty had been reading. She knew he had read it, as if his attention had given it life, made it stand out from the rest of the page.

She picked the newspaper up, began to read. By the third paragraph she was hyperventilating. *Losing it, I'm losing it.* The thought flashed like a warning light in her head. Then the images started – the winding staircase, the room at the end of the hall, the steam, the vapor. The man. Something in his hand, something long and shining.

She screamed, and the sheer explosion of air from her body seemed to regulate her, pull her back from the abyss; she dropped the paper, sat down, regaining a level of control.

'I want this to stop. Please God, if there is a god, you will make this stop ... I can not live with this. Please make it stop,' she whispered.

Perhaps it was in answer to her prayer, perhaps just the act of speaking caused her to regain control of her breathing, but the images ceased.

She took the newspaper and threw it in the garbage bin in the hallway, then checked and rechecked the lock and bolt on her door before going to her bedroom.

There she pulled the rug back at the foot of her bed, knelt down and unlocked a small metal box, sunken beneath the floorboards.

Inside was a loaded forty-five caliber Colt, a 'compact' officer's model automatic. Josef had insisted she have it; he had taken her to the police practice range five times. Until he was satisfied she could handle the weapon, shoot it straight. Her sure surgeon's hands made her a natural.

She hadn't even looked at the gun in six months. Now she placed it under her pillow.

No more ... I've had enough ... No more, Rachel Saunders promised herself as she drifted off to sleep.

Bill Fogarty headed for West River Drive. Got as far as the Art Museum and turned round. It was only a few blocks to Spring Garden Street.

The house was dark and quiet and the door to the garden apartment was locked.

Fogarty kept knocking.

Finally the upstairs window opened and Louise appeared. She wore rollers in her hair and her tone of voice matched the disgruntled expression on her face.

'He's not there!' she shouted.

'Do you know when he'll be back?' Fogarty asked.

'No. He left half an hour ago. In a cab. I don't know when he'll be back ... Now how 'bout givin' me a break and quit bangin' on the door.'

'I'm sorry.'

'Fine. Good night!'

The window slammed shut.

Fogarty stood a few moments then returned to his car. Sat a few more moments, looking at the run-down house, thinking of Rachel's question, *what's he doing to himself?*

'I don't fucking know,' he answered, then started his engine and continued his journey home.

Connection,
American style

Fogarty got to the Roundhouse at seven thirty the next morning.

He intended to spend some time reviewing the case notes on the Grandistone arrest before the arraignment on the twenty-fourth. Something else, sitting directly on top of his message pile, caught his eye.

The name Norikazu Ohtsuka and two telephone numbers, one for Tokyo Police Headquarters and one private.

Ohtsuka, Ohtsuka, which one was he? Fogarty tried to fit a face to the name.

His mind went back to Tokyo, to the dead tattooist and the short bull of a policeman who had confiscated the illegal .38.

Chief Inspector Ohtsuka, that was his name. Hell, he seemed as much in the dark about the case as me or Tanaka. And definitely pissed off when he was forced to surrender us to Ken Sato's buddy upstairs.

Fogarty picked up the phone and punched in the first set of numbers. Slammed it back down and dug through his top drawer for the piece of paper with Sato's telephone number on it. Used the same country and area code and dialed again.

Chief Inspector Norikazu Ohtsuka was still at his desk. First he made certain there was no one within earshot, then he spoke low and quickly.

'Your friend, Lieutenant,' Ohtsuka hesitated, catching

335

himself on the verge of using Josef's family name, 'may be in danger.'

'Are you talking about—' Fogarty began.

'No names,' Ohtsuka cut in.

Fogarty sat upright.

'I have reason to believe that a particular member of his family is involved in a plot against him.' Ohtsuka continued, looking up at his ceiling as he spoke.

Superintendent General Miyuki Hashimoto's office was directly above him. Two weeks ago Ohtsuka had followed Hashimoto to a meeting at the old kabuki theatre. Watched him, joined by a group of other 'faces', clamoring around Keinosuke Sato as if he were the Emperor himself.

'I'm listening,' Fogarty answered. 'Go on.'

'The man is in the United States now—'

'Where?' Fogarty urged. Something was beginning to gel.

'He departed from Narita Airport eight days ago, a Japan Airlines flight to San Francisco.'

Last night's newspaper article about the Mashiro heir flooded Fogarty's mind, along with images of the decapitated corpse of the wrestler in Sato's apartment.

'Alone. Is he traveling alone?' Fogarty asked.

'Yes.'

'He's coming for Josef.' Fogarty said it out loud.

The phone clicked and the connection was broken.

Ohtsuka sat staring at the telephone. 'No names,' he had told the American, 'no names'. He could not be one hundred percent certain that his line was not monitored or how deep the conspiracy went within the police force.

He glanced again at the ceiling then once at his closed door. No need to speak with the American again anyway. He'd fulfilled his duty, issued the warning.

Fogarty replaced the receiver.

'I've known it all the time, I've fucking known it all the time.' He was still repeating the message to himself as he walked from his office. He waited a few seconds for the elevator then ran for the fire stairs, down to the parking lot.

He drove fast, running lights, cutting in and out, obsessed with getting to Josef.

It wasn't until he skidded to a halt in front of the old brownstone that he calmed down. Something about the delapidated house, the quiet street, as if nothing truly out of the ordinary could take place there.

He began to feel a shade foolish. *Jumping the gun again. Should get a call in to the Los Angeles police department, see what they'll give me on the Mashiro case. Sato flew to San Francisco, not LA. Ohtsuka's information is all circumstantial. I'm linking coincidence to coincidence.*

He slipped from the car and walked to Tanaka's front door. Listened a moment, then knocked. Gentle footsteps from inside, someone walking toward the door, either barefoot or in slippers.

Fogarty straightened up, adjusting his Liberty-print tie. The last time he'd seen Josef, Fogarty had been drunk and unkempt. This time he'd be back on form.

The door opened and Bill Fogarty was lost for words.

Josef stood facing him, Ken Sato at his side. Both men were barefoot and dressed in *uwagi* and *hakama*; Josef's hair pulled so tight to his head that the features of his face resembled a mask.

There was a refined elegance to both Josef and Ken Sato, a coherence.

'Bill?' Josef's voice was soft and somehow condescending. As if Bill Fogarty were the last person he expected at his door.

Fogarty glanced quickly at Ken Sato and remembered why he had come. Still he said nothing.

'Would you like to come inside?' Tanaka stepped back as

he spoke, allowing the fragrance of sandalwood incense to drift out from the room.

Ken Sato bowed and hissed, '*Hai*, Fogarty-san,' as the big Irishman stepped onto the tatami.

'Hello, Ken,' the lieutenant replied, bending to remove his shoes.

Josef guided him to the cushions in the corner of the room and the three men sat down.

'Tea, Fogarty-san?' Sato asked.

Fogarty noted that Sato seemed in charge of the house. Recalling the 'tea ceremony' in Tokyo, he declined.

He had come to talk to Josef, to get through to him, to discuss the warning from Ohtsuka in Japan. Now it was impossible. In fact it seemed impossible to say anything at all. Words came to mind but they all lost relevance by the time he came to speak them. So he sat, mute.

Neither man did anything to ease his discomfort. Minutes passed and Fogarty began to get impatient. It was as if he'd entered the bedroom of two lovers, interrupting their deep communion, and now they were waiting patiently for him to get the message and leave.

'Look, Josef, do you think we could talk?' His gruff voice was in complete disharmony with the aesthetic surrounds. He didn't give a shit, he was tired of the charade.

'Please, Bill, talk,' Josef answered. Again the condescending tolerance.

'With respect, Ken, I didn't know you were coming to Philadelphia . . . I really need to speak to Josef privately.'

Tanaka looked as though he'd been slapped in the face, his eyes narrowed, and his lips tightened. He was about to protest when Ken Sato stood and walked from the room.

Fogarty struggled to begin; Josef felt like a stranger.

'Are you all right, son?'

Tanaka looked at him and held his eyes. 'I'm going to be. I just need some time. How 'bout you, the court case?'

'I'm basically off the hook, just need to go through the motions.'

They were both talking around it, the reason that Fogarty had come.

'Anything on your family, the investigation?'

'Bits and pieces, nothing conclusive. My father is bearing up, going ahead with his business in California.'

Fogarty sensed an opening. 'Is that what brings Ken to the United States?'

Tanaka straightened and for an instant he looked prickly, defensive. Then he breathed in, exhaled and relaxed.

'Yes, Ken had some company business in San Francisco. Coming here, to visit me, is personal,' he replied.

'Did he happen to stop in Los Angeles?' The lieutenant tried to keep the policeman out of his voice.

Tanaka caught the glint in Fogarty's eyes; he turned toward the kitchen. 'Ken?'

The kitchen tap stopped running and Sato reappeared. It was the last thing that Fogarty wanted.

'*Hai*, Josef?'

'Bill wants to know if you were in Los Angeles?'

Fogarty pasted on a false smile and looked at Cousin Ken.

'Yes, Fogarty-san, I was in West Hollywood. Four Seasons Hotel, beautiful,' Sato answered. Then he hit Fogarty with a grin that turned the lieutenant's stomach to lead. 'Contracts on the cable network,' Sato explained, turning to Josef.

'I said that my father was pushing ahead,' Josef added, looking at Fogarty.

'Why do you ask me this question?' Sato continued.

Fogarty had thought ahead.

'Because Josef had mentioned that his father was not bowing to pressure against him. I was wondering if he was taking his negotiations forward.'

Sato's grin faded, leaving his lips in a thin straight line. There had never been a smile in his dead eyes.

It was at that moment that the Leopard made his decision. Understood precisely what he had to do.

'Fogarty-san, while I am here, visiting Josef, I would like us all to take sake together. I think it is important that we speak. You are close to Josef-san, like family, and I feel nothing must be hidden from you.'

The words were fine, but Sato's tone of voice made Fogarty feel like he was being challenged to a duel at sunrise. It was a matter of honor. He had to say yes.

'Certainly, Ken, it would be my pleasure.'

'Give me the day to rest and to be with Josef. Then, tonight, we drink much sake. *Hai*, Fogarty-san?'

'*Hai*, Ken-san, *hai*,' Fogarty answered. He wondered if Josef made any decisions these days or if he was totally subservient to Cousin Ken.

'By the way, Josef, Rachel wanted me to send you her best wishes.' Fogarty couldn't resist the shot.

'How is she, Bill?'

It was the first that Tanaka had sounded real to Fogarty since he had arrived. At least the answer was spontaneous and didn't have the pre-programmed feel of a victim of brainwashing. The relief of hearing his old friend's voice had a settling effect on the lieutenant.

'I think you owe her a call,' Fogarty answered.

Tanaka lowered his eyes and nodded his head.

Ken Sato cleared his throat loudly and stared at Josef until they linked eyes.

Then, standing, Sato addressed Fogarty.

'Sake, much sake. Eight o'clock okay?'

Fogarty nodded, took his cue and stood up. He felt like kicking Josef in the ass, asking him what the hell was the matter with him, but he had more important things to settle. He stared hard at Ken, letting his eyes linger a moment on his hands, then his face, trying to spot anything unusual in the texture of the man's skin. There was nothing.

'I look forward to it, Ken,' Fogarty said, bowing.

Tanaka stood and Fogarty saw the pain etched into his features; at least there was hope behind the mask.

'See you tonight, Josef,' he said.

He didn't bother to tie his shoes, just slipped them on and walked from the house.

'He came to test your resolve. You must be strong, no weakness, no going back. You are Japanese.'

Fogarty heard Sato's voice as the door closed behind him. He could not understand the Japanese but the tone was scolding.

As clean as a Beverly Hills surgeon

As soon as Bill Fogarty got back to the Roundhouse he placed a call to the Los Angeles Police Department. Gave his ORI number, then hung up and waited for the identification code to be verified.

Five minutes later he called again, identified himself and was transferred to a deep smooth voice.

'This is Zimbalist, West Hollywood.'

'And this is Lieutenant William Fogarty in Philadelphia.' He didn't quite match the LA man for resonance.

'Yeah. What can I do for you, Lieutenant?' Laid back and disinterested.

'You've got a case out there, a homicide; the victim's name was given as David Mashiro.'

'Yes, that's true, Lieutenant.'

'Is the case still open?'

Fogarty could sense the other man begin to come alive on the other end of the line.

'It is, Lieutenant, now how can I help you?'

'I'd like some details.'

Zimbalist cleared his throat, 'I don't really have the authority—'

'Then who does?' Fogarty broke in.

'Could you tell me why you want this information?'

'Have you got a lead on the perp?'

'Why are you asking me these questions, Lieutenant? Have you got something out there?'

343

'No,' Fogarty answered. He knew it wasn't good enough.

'What I've got is, maybe, a correlated crime in Tokyo, Japan,' he added.

'Tokyo?' Zimbalist gasped.

'It's a long shot,' Fogarty conceded. But not nearly as long as he was making it sound.

'Right, here's what I can tell you,' Zimbalist drawled, 'we've got a couple of possibles. One drug related, the other ritual.'

'What do you mean, ritual?'

'Maybe some kind of S and M.'

'Explain,' Fogarty asked.

'I shouldn't really be doing this, Lieutenant.'

'Okay, let me help you,' Fogarty said. 'Was the wound made with a long-bladed weapon, almost a surgical edge, like a giant scalpel?'

'Which wound?' Zimbalist asked, but there was a softening in his tone.

'I read that the victim was decapitated.'

'The boy was sectioned, Lieutenant. Cut straight down the middle and divided . . . As clean as a Beverly Hills surgeon.'

'And you've got no suspects?' Fogarty leaned in a bit.

Zimbalist hemmed and hawed then finally said, 'Nothing solid.'

Fogarty remained silent, thinking.

'We don't believe it was drug related,' Zimbalist continued, 'the kid was clean as far as we can tell. Besides, wrong part of town for a gang killing . . . Maybe homosexual, West Hollywood is loaded with gays and we have the occasional "gay bashing".'

'And was David Mashiro homosexual?'

'Not according to his girlfriend.'

'So that leaves you with zip.'

Zimbalist didn't answer; he countered. 'What's this Tokyo thing about?' His voice implied Fogarty's debt.

'It's about Japanese killing Japanese, big business, extortion.'

'Organized crime?'

'If you're talking about the Japanese Mafia, I don't think so. This is organized, but not Yakuza.' Fogarty was desperate to get off now.

'How do you fit in, Lieutenant?'

'As a tourist in Tokyo who listens to the American cable news network.'

'Listen, I've been straight with you, now don't roll me a line of bullshit.' An edge inside the smoothness.

Fogarty owed the LA guy and he knew it. He gave him Chief Inspector Norikazu Ohtsuka's office number and wished him luck, knowing that if Tokyo suspected a link the case would go right to Interpol.

Then he remembered the expression on Ohtsuka's face when he was forced to surrender his prisoners to Sato's buddy, Hashimoto. Fogarty changed his mind. *Ohtsuka will probably hold on to the information and pick up Ken's trail when he gets back to Tokyo. Try to make the pinch on his own.*

Either way, the lieutenant figured himself to be a giant step ahead in the game.

Rachel Saunders was next on Fogarty's list. The last thing he wanted was a spontaneous house call from the estranged fiancée. Not with Ken Sato in the kitchen.

Her secretary said the doctor was in the middle of a consultation so Fogarty left his name and promised to call later.

After that his phone started ringing and didn't stop. Threats against the witnesses in the Grandistone murder case. Grandistone claiming his confession was coerced, switching lawyers, denying ownership of a firearm. Suing the city. Stuff that should have had the lieutenant climbing walls. He pushed it all to the back of his mind.

Right now he needed a plan, a strategy. A campaign of war.

Ken Sato would have one, that was for certain. And the battle was scheduled for tonight. Fogarty intended to make sure of it.

Josef Tanaka had made his decision.

He was returning to Japan.

First he would see Rachel, sit down with her and talk, empty his heart. He expected it to be the most difficult conversation of his life.

He did love her, sincerely and deeply. He owed her the years they had been together, her friendship and support, her love. And he could never repay them. He had seen what Japan had done to Bill Fogarty, watched the man's mind stretched to breaking point. He knew what a life there had done to his own mother, understood the loneliness of her soul, the taint of never truly belonging. He would not even offer Rachel the choice. He understood what she'd be getting into; she had no idea. It would be unfair.

He and Rachel Saunders were finished. He loved her enough to leave her behind.

After his personal life was resolved he would go to Bob Moyer and resign. Perhaps Moyer would save him the breath. By now, he was probably, and understandably fired.

Then Bill Fogarty. He'd take care of Bill tonight. Of all of them, somehow he knew that Bill would understand best.

Ken Sato walked from the kitchen.

He had improvised; he was carrying a tray containing the old iron kettle that had been in the apartment when Josef took up his tenancy, along with a porcelain bowl, a strainer, two clean dish towels and a wooden spoon. He had carried the tea with him, from Japan.

He smiled at Josef and nodded. 'Tea ceremony,' he whispered.

Tanaka laughed softly, for the first time in weeks.

Sato placed the tray in front of his cousin and left the room again.

When he returned he was carrying his *katana*.

Sato positioned the sword on a cushion to his left side, concentrating on the tea, straining it before pouring from the kettle into the porcelain bowl. As crude as his implements were, Ken Sato's dexterity gave both grace and significance to the ceremony.

He waited, inhaling the aroma, then offered the bowl to Josef.

Josef drank slowly, silently thanking Ken Sato for reminding him of what he was. Ken had been his ally in Japan and his strength here, in Philadelphia.

When Josef was finished he wiped the lip of the bowl with one of the white towels and handed the empty vessel to Sato.

Ken bowed his head, filled the bowl with tea and drank.

By the time he had finished both host and 'principal guest' were in perfect tune.

It was then that Ken Sato lifted his *katana*.

The sword was magnificent, each detail of its polished wood scabbard and flat braided hilt held Tanaka's eyes.

Ken looked up and held Josef's gaze for a moment, then, silently, he withdrew the sword from its scabbard.

He held it, edge inward toward his own face and blade parallel to the floor. The light of the candle that sat on the table beside them played gently on the rolled steel. Ken tilted the blade slightly and Josef could see his own reflection in the metal.

'This is purity,' Sato whispered.

Josef stared into his own eyes – his Western eyes – and

felt the tinge of irony in his cousin's words.

'In the beginning, one thousand years ago, the blades were copied from Chinese swords. There was no proper tempering, simply reproduction. The secret of Japanese purity had not been discovered and the metal was weak and unreliable,' Sato continued, moving the *katana* slightly as he spoke, his voice gentle and in perfect rhythm to the subtle movement of his hands.

'In one village, the swordsmith, watching his *daimyo* and his *daimyo*'s army return beaten from battle, their weapons bent and shattered, was unable to meet his master's eyes. Instead, he retreated to the mountains, praying to the Shinto gods to reveal to him the secret of forging a perfect weapon. He fasted and prayed, exposing his naked body to the autumn rain, the snow of winter and the heat of summer. Until, through the hardening of his own flesh and spirit, he came to know the means of tempering which leads to purity.

'Do you understand what I am saying, Josef?'

Sato's question broke the flow of his words.

Josef looked up. *Was there the hint of menace in Ken's tone?*

His cousin didn't wait for an answer.

'The swordsmith became enlightened. Learned to take raw iron and refine it. To fire it and pound it, to fold it and shape it, to fuse the best elements of the iron into a strip of steel. The finest steel in the world. To create a blade with an edge so sharp that it will cut a falling raindrop into even halves. Pure steel, Josef, pure.' Sato hesitated.

Josef met Sato's eyes; they were alive with something that Josef had never seen before. A fire, almost a hatred.

'Japan must become like the blade of this *katana*, Josef . . . The elements of weakness must be pounded from her body, until she is once again pure. Then her strength will be unequaled.'

Sato's words rang clearly in Josef's mind, coupling with

the reflection of his Western eyes in the white steel.

His discomfort was crippling. As if he were about to be exposed in a terrible lie. Every doubt about himself – who he was, where he belonged – returned in a single rush.

Ken drew the blade slowly in front of Josef, across the line of his throat. Holding it there, steady, before lifting it up, even with its scabbard, studying Josef's face as he cupped his left hand over the opening of the *saya* and drew the back of his blade through the pinching grip of his thumb and index finger. Until he had reached the razored tip, then he reversed his motion and fluidly slid the sword back into its *saya*.

The snap of steel against wood served to seal Josef's doubts.

'I love you, cousin,' Sato said, laying a soothing hand on Tanaka's shoulder.

And all the time, Ken Sato was thinking of Hoshi Satoru, his companion and lover. And the night he stood, watching from the shadows, as Tanaka beat the man to death. Mutilated him, ruined his beauty forever ... Forcing Ken Sato to destroy Satoru like a savaged dog. *Oh, dear cousin, how I have waited for my vengeance.* And now the time was near.

'I love you,' Sato repeated, reveling in the confusion he saw in Josef Tanaka's eyes.

The education of a bodybuilder

Fogarty got through to Rachel at half past five; he thanked her for dinner and asked, almost casually, what her plans were for the evening.

Rachel hesitated.

She would have liked to see him; she didn't want to be alone in her own apartment. Didn't want 'those' feelings back again, but she knew she couldn't lean on him, on anybody. Not even Stan Leibowitz; this time it was down to her.

'Why? Are you going to start dating me, Bill?' She finally managed a joke.

Fogarty flushed with embarrassment.

'The spaghetti was that good, huh?' she added.

'Magnifico!' He managed to keep it light.

Rachel cleared her throat and spoke seriously, 'I've got a reconstruction at seven o'clock, I'll probably still be in post-op at ten.'

'How do you feel?' Fogarty asked.

She hesitated again. *Scared shitless* was the answer.

'Better for having talked to you. You're a good friend, Bill,' she said. 'You still haven't seen him, have you?'

'No, not yet,' he lied, 'I thought maybe tonight—'

'You wanted me to come with you?'

Her question gave him the out he needed. 'I'd thought of

it, but it's probably better that I see him alone, first time . . .
I'll call you in the morning.'

'I'll be waiting for your call,' Rachel answered.

'Bye bye, Rachel.'

Bob Moyer looked up from his desk as Fogarty walked into
his office.

The doctor's glasses were balanced unsteadily on the end
of his nose. 'How you doin', Bill?'

Fogarty forced a smile and nodded.

'You're going to be all right with that thing on Diamond?'
It was more a statement than a question. Word had obviously
travelled.

'Yeah, it's gonna work out,' Fogarty answered, taking a
good look at Moyer. He recognized the symptoms. Whenever Moyer was under pressure he tugged at his goatee.
Today it was twisted into a red spike.

Abruptly, the doctor changed the subject. 'I've given him
the benefit of every doubt, Bill, it's not that I don't
sympathize for his loss, and the thing with Rachel, but it's
getting near the end,' he said.

'Then do what you've got to do, Bob,' Fogarty replied.

'What I should do is get rid of him.' Moyer said it like he
was admitting to a crime.

Fogarty nodded his head.

'Look, Bill, I don't want to, I mean, Christ I believe in the
guy, I picked him over a dozen applicants for this job. You
know how I feel about him . . . It makes me sick, plus I look
like an idiot,' Moyer continued, standing from his desk.

'You're no idiot, Bob.'

Moyer stood silent.

'Give it another forty-eight hours, can you do that?' the
lieutenant asked.

Moyer went for his goatee but settled for adjusting his
glasses.

'Just about.'

'And can you help me with something now? It's urgent.'

'Sure.'

'I want you to tell me how to make my skin flush without working up a sweat.'

'What?'

'Something I could take to make my skin turn red,' Fogarty repeated.

'Why the hell—'

'Is there something that'll do it?' The tone of Fogarty's voice snapped Moyer to attention. He thought for a moment.

'Niacin will do it.'

'How does it work?'

'Expands the blood vessels, enhances the circulation ... Side effects include a tingling of the skin and a pronounced reddening.'

'Is it an injectable?' Fogarty asked.

'Oral. Little white tablets.'

'Hard to get?'

'Hell no, it's a vitamin, B3 ... Bodybuilders take it all the time, they get a better pump in the muscles, more blood.'

'And it'll turn a person red?'

'Depends on how much you ingest. A hundred milligrams would make you look like a beet,' Moyer answered.

'How long does it take?'

'Five, ten minutes, depending on how much food's in your belly. Lasts about half an hour.'

Fogarty nodded.

'What the hell's it for?' Moyer finally asked.

'Just curious ... Can you get me some?'

'You can get it yourself, Bill, right around the corner. It's non-prescription.'

'Could I dissolve it in alcohol?'

'Why not?' Moyer answered.

'Thanks, Bob,' Fogarty said, turning and starting for the door.

Moyer gripped the end of his goatee between his thumb and index finger, sharpening the spike as he watched the policeman exit.

Fogarty was driving west along the river, holding the bottle in his right hand.

'Five bucks for thirty fifty-milligram tablets,' he marveled. He felt like he had just purchased a nuclear missile. He glanced again at the small brown bottle.

Thirty minutes, Bob said the whole thing only lasted thirty minutes, he thought, popping the lid, lifting the bottle and letting two tablets fall onto his tongue. *A good idea to familiarize myself with the stuff.*

He drove on, counting the minutes on his wristwatch. It was six o'clock.

At six thirty he was pulling into his car space at the Presidential. Nothing had happened.

He called Moyer from his apartment. 'This shit doesn't work,' he began.

'What—?'

'I took a hundred mills forty minutes ago and I'm still pale.'

Moyer thought a moment. 'Read me the label.'

'Hold on,' Fogarty said, lifting the bottle.

'Is it niacin or niacinamide?' Moyer asked.

'Niacinamide, 50 milligrams,' the lieutenant answered.

'There's your problem.'

Fogarty stayed silent.

'They're both B3 but only niacin gives you the capillary dilation ... You got the wrong stuff,' Moyer said matter-of-factly.

'Shit!'

'Are you entering a bodybuilding competition?' the doctor asked.

'Yeah, and at my age I need every advantage I can get . . . Thanks, Bob.'

He put down the phone and checked his watch. He had an hour before his date with Ken Sato.

The strange thing was he wasn't feeling any nerves. It wasn't like making an arrest, the knotted stomach, the dry mouth. This was something different, something inevitable. He was actually elated as he shaved before stepping into the shower.

He dressed in his best suit, a light wool plaid from Brooks Brothers, picked out a blue and white silk tie and chose a pair of tanned cordovans.

It wasn't until he laced up the shoes that reality smacked him. He'd selected the cordovans because of their rubber soles. He could move in them. Away from Ken Sato's blade.

He sat down on the side of the bed and heaved in a couple of good, deep breaths. The kind he used to steady himself. Christ he had it now, the stomach, the mouth, the sweaty palms. All of it and all at once. He began to shake, like a chill but without the feeling of cold.

Might not be him, might be nothing, just my imagination, he told himself. Then he realized that the frightened part of him had been telling the other part, the intuitive part, that 'it might not be him' all along.

Because if Ken Sato was the Leopard, Bill Fogarty was going to have to deal with it. His calm, elated self may have chosen his flash tie but intuition picked out the rubber soles.

I don't even have to show up, he told himself. By then he was already moving toward his gun safe.

He picked out a twenty-two caliber Beretta. 'A ladies' gun', by description, but also the preferred assassination weapon of the Israeli Mossad *Sayaret* teams. Lethal when directed through the eye and into the brain.

Loaded it with nine shorts and strapped it to the side of his right shin, inside a custom-made half-holster that was secured by two elastic bands resembling an old-fashioned men's garter. The loose bottoms of his trousers hung over the weapon concealing it.

He decided not to use his customary shoulder rig for his 'snubby', a short-barreled Smith and Wesson M649 Bodyguard. Not if he was sitting on a cushion with his jacket open. No, he would carry the hammerless weapon in his right pocket. He could even fire it from the pocket if he had to.

The snubby held five rounds of .38 *Thunderzap*. He slipped another five rounds into his pants' pocket. If it came down to it, he expected a lot from Ken Sato.

Finally he locked the safe, and walked to the door.

Twenty-five minutes before eight, he stopped in the late-night pharmacy in the Presidential's shopping precinct. This time he got niacin. Broke the seal on the bottle and poured half of the tiny tablets into the left side pocket of his jacket, the other half into the right front pocket of his trousers.

He had a harness on his nerves by the time he started the engine of the Le Mans; he'd done this so many times with so many variations.

At first, when he was new to homicide, he used to think about dying, contemplate the feeling of life ebbing from his body, from a gunshot wound, or a knife.

Used to lie awake at night, staring into the darkness, trying to imagine what it would be like. Then he would roll over in his bed and reach out for Sarah, touch her lightly with his fingertips, establishing a contact. And the warmth of her body would enter him like a fine electricity, flowing through his hands, up his arms, until he was encircled with it, protected by it.

Then he could sleep.

It had been different after the accident. Thrown from the

car he had wrecked, sprawled helpless on the hot asphalt of a New Jersey highway, watching through the windshield. Watching his wife and child being incinerated in the wreck.

He'd wanted to die after that. But not by his own hand; he'd wanted someone to kill him, like he had killed Sarah and Ann. Wanted it for a long time.

Endangered the lives of fellow officers, lost two promotions and very nearly his job. Until he got help. The same kind of help that Rachel Saunders was getting now.

After that his fear of death began to dissolve, break up piece by piece and drift away.

Until he was left with only the sorrow of his life.

Fogarty turned off the expressway at Spring Garden Street and drove slowly toward Tanaka's house. Parked directly in front and got out of his car.

The weather was finally changing and there was the first nip of autumn in the air. A fine mist.

He could still see the stars and the full moon, but it was the kind of weather that caused his knee to ache. Forcing him to make an effort to walk without the limp.

He breathed in, scanning up towards the house as if he expected an ambush. Nothing.

He got to the door and knocked, heard the shuffle of padded feet from inside. Waited.

Another little taste
of Japan

Ken Sato answered the door, smiling and bowing. As if he were the closest friend the lieutenant had ever had.

Fogarty noticed that Ken's costume was more formal than the one he had worn earlier. Long sleeves and finer material; he also wore *tabi*, white cloth socks, divided between the first and second toe.

'Welcome, Fogarty-san, come in. Please come in,' Sato beamed, stepping back to allow him to enter.

'Josef is in the kitchen, cooking ... *Makizushi*,' Ken said as Fogarty bent to remove his shoes, glancing at the rubber soles as he placed the shoes aside. A lot of good they were going to do him lying in the corner of the room. He was already beginning to feel foolish.

'*Makizushi?*'

'Fish and rice, rolled by hand,' Sato explained, 'maybe safer to go out ... What you think of Big Mac?'

At first Fogarty fell for the mock seriousness of Sato's tone; he stood lost for words.

Then Ken Sato did something that Fogarty had never seen him do before. He giggled, light and effeminate. Totally disarming.

Fogarty relaxed, just a degree but enough to allow his protective paranoia to shift down a gear.

'Come on, Fogarty-san, sit down, sit down,' Sato urged,

patting Fogarty lightly on the back as he guided him toward the cushions.

'Your leg okay, no problem?' Ken asked, watching the lieutenant position himself on the floor.

Fogarty followed Sato's eyes, right to the hump in his trousers, where the Beretta nestled along the line of his calf.

Christ, he's seen it, the thought no sooner registered than Sato said, 'Limp seems better, almost gone.'

Maybe he hasn't seen it, Fogarty reconsidered, shifting position, smoothing his pants over the bulge, forcing himself to relax.

'It's the weather, Ken, no humidity. Easier on the joints.'

Sato nodded his agreement, 'Same with me, Fogarty-san, my elbow is always most painful in the wet season.' He rubbed the joint. 'You call it "tennis elbow", but I believe mine began when trying to learn the art of the sword. Bad form in the beginning.'

Fogarty went for the opening. 'Do you still practice?'

Ken looked at him and smiled. 'Every morning, Fogarty-san,' he answered.

'Even when you travel?' Fogarty was doing his best to sound innocent.

'Yes, even when traveling.'

'You carry a sword with you?'

'It is not necessary to carry a *katana*. Many times I sit in one position and exercise my breath.'

'Breath?'

'If the breath is not correct, there is no *zanshin*. The art of the sword is like all military arts, without *zanshin* it is no more than a calisthenic, a physical exercise,' Sato continued, rubbing the spot above his elbow.

Fogarty nodded, thinking about the Mashiro homicide and wondering if Ken's elbow had recently seen a bit of overuse.

'*Zanshin?*' He repeated the word, turning it into a

question. He'd heard Josef use it, even had it explained to him. That didn't matter; he wanted Sato to open up, to somehow expose his intentions. *Get him talking about something close to him, then manipulate the conversation*, the old tried and trusted.

'*Zanshin* is a state of mental alertness, Fogarty-san,' Sato explained, 'created by controlled breathing. The breath dictates the condition of the mind. Like wind across water. If the breath is even, the mind is calm; it perceives danger instantly. Reaction is simultaneous with the perceived threat.' Sato finished his exposition by glancing in the direction of the Beretta.

Fogarty changed position again, straightening the fabric above the gun, suddenly aware of the itch that the elastic bands were causing. Smiling as he met Ken's eyes, becoming conscious of the mental chess game they were playing.

Sato reached out quickly and Fogarty barely controlled his urge to jump back, away from the hand that landed gently on his knee, above the gun.

'I respect you, Lieutenant Fogarty-san, I think you understand more than you concede . . . Humility is a valuable asset to a man at war,' Sato said, squeezing the lieutenant's knee reassuringly before withdrawing his hand.

Fogarty smiled again. 'Ken, I am not a man at war, just a friend who's come to dinner.' His words sounded insincere and his smile froze awkwardly, as if his lips were waiting for his mind to tell them where to go next. He breathed in and laughed lightly as he exhaled.

Sato mirrored the lieutenant's laugh. 'Laughter helps us regain an equilibrium. You notice, Fogarty-san?'

Fogarty laughed again. Feeling naked in front of Ken Sato.

Then there was silence. The kind that seemed more a test than a peace. As if one of them should say something but neither would give in. At least that's how it felt to Fogarty.

Josef came in from the kitchen, carrying a plate of steaming food. 'Bill, thank you for coming,' Tanaka said it as if it were the preamble to a more serious announcement. Positioning the plate between the two men Tanaka returned to the kitchen for the bowls.

'Bring me a fork, will you, Josef!' Fogarty called after him.

The *makizushi*, raw fish and soft rice, did nothing to elevate Fogarty's appreciation for Japanese cuisine. Nor did the noise of the cold noodles, dipped in a soy-flavored soup being slurped in joint harmony by the twin Samurai.

'I'm going back to Japan, Bill,' Tanaka said as the last of the noodles slid down the lieutenant's throat.

Fogarty looked up. Tanaka's hair was still pulled tight to his head, but his features did not appear as strained now. There was a quiet resolve to his full mouth and the storm had settled in his eyes.

Fogarty nodded his head.

'I'm going to see Rachel in the morning—'

'You think she'll go with you?' The lieutenant hadn't meant to sound presumptuous but his tone gave him away. He felt at once furious with Josef and protective toward Rachel.

'Of course not, Bill.' Tanaka's voice was instantly forgiving, 'I would never ask her. Besides—'

'Japan is for the Japanese,' Ken Sato finished his sentence.

Tanaka allowed Ken's words to hang in the air a moment. 'Then I'll go and square it with Bob,' he continued.

Fogarty stared at Josef; he wanted to ask him why. Why he had to mess it all up: his life, Rachel's, even Fogarty's. Like splitting up a family . . . Why? The question hung in his eyes.

Josef studied his eyes, nearly gray in the candle light, containing such sadness, such deep loss. Then he looked at the ugly scars, the thick waxen skin, dividing his friend's face in half.

The flickering light, the slowness of movement, the unspoken words between them; it reminded Josef of something.

Once, when he was a child, his father had taken him to the Noh theatre, where the actors cover their faces with special masks to signify the role they are playing. They move slowly and perform to quiet, purposely monotonous background music, intent on luring their audience into the dream realm of their performance.

There was an actor there that night. He was one of the two main characters in a play about a father who must watch his only son go off to war. To enter a campaign in which the young man's death is inevitable.

This particular actor was playing the part of the father and had worn a mask depicting such sorrow that by the time the play had ended, and the slow and stylized movements of the cast come to a halt, Josef could do nothing but stare at the old man's face and weep.

He had understood something that night, even as a child, about love and loss. That they were the bittersweet consequences of life itself. Inevitable with time.

And here they were again, in the face of his friend, behind the mask of scars.

He wanted to speak but he was held in a place beyond words.

'Josef-san has rediscovered himself,' Ken Sato said softly, 'we should celebrate for him. This is not a time for mourning.'

Fogarty turned toward Sato and believed he saw the hint of cruelty in his smile.

'Maybe it's time for the sake,' the lieutenant remarked.

Josef cleared the plates and returned with a bottle labelled *Kinpaku-Ozeki* and three shot-sized porcelain cups.

'Fifteen and one half percent alcohol,' Sato said, pouring. Then, raising his cup, 'To Josef's future.'

'*Banzai*,' Fogarty said flatly.

The rice-based wine was ten degrees above room temperature and about as appealing to Fogarty's palate as the *makizushi*. It tasted like neat vodka, with a hint of mildew.

Ken Sato poured often but was at least three drinks behind by the half way point on the bottle. And Fogarty was clearly feeling the alcohol.

Josef remained somber, occasionally glancing at the lieutenant as if he were about to speak but saying nothing.

Then Ken Sato started to sing. A low, throaty lament that reminded Fogarty of 'Old Man River' sung in Japanese. Heart, soul, and a rolling rhythm.

Ken stared at Josef as he sang. Until Tanaka joined in.

'Japanese tradition. A Samurai song of farewell,' Sato explained as Tanaka kept the tune together.

Sato rejoined his cousin for the chorus.

Fogarty nodded and knocked back another shot of sake. His contribution to the floor show. If he hadn't been mildly drunk the singing would have been too much to handle. It was the strange intimacy of the two men wailing that made him feel self-conscious.

He kept his eyes trained down, studying the muscular veined hands of Ken Sato, trying to decipher anything irregular in the pigment of his skin. Conjuring patterns and wondering if such a thing as an invisible tattoo was even possible.

The song died, its residue of emotion leaving tears in Tanaka's eyes.

Ken cleared his throat, uttered something in Japanese that sounded like an incantation and stood up. 'I must go and make pee,' he said, then walked from the room.

Fogarty listened to the rustle of Sato's *hakama* then the padded shuffle of his feet on the linoleum floor as he walked through the kitchen and toward the bathroom. Finally the sound of a door closing.

'Josef, do you think I could have a glass of water? I'm a little bit dry,' Fogarty asked.

Josef looked up; he was crying, unashamedly. He nodded his head, rose up from his folded-legged posture and followed Ken Sato into the kitchen.

Fogarty concentrated, waiting for the sound of the refrigerator door. It coincided with the flushing of a toilet from the back room of the apartment.

The lieutenant reached into the side pocket of his suit and came up with a handful of the white tablets.

He reached across to Ken Sato's cup. Was about to drop them in when he remembered Japan, the *oyabun*. Just like Ken to be wary of poison. He turned quickly, glanced at the door to the kitchen then dropped the five tabs of niacin into the bottle of sake. Shook it once and prayed that Moyer was right about alcohol not affecting the B3.

Josef returned with a tumbler of spring water. He placed it in front of Fogarty and sat down.

'Bill, I hope you understand what I'm doing. It's my duty; I'm his only son.'

'And this is your only life,' Fogarty answered.

'Bill, I'm Japanese—'

'That is not exactly true, Josef-san,' Ken Sato's voice caught them from the kitchen door.

Fogarty looked up, straight at the three-foot-long sword that Sato cradled in his hands.

'But if your heart is Japanese, then you must follow your heart,' Sato continued, walking forward.

He squatted down beside Fogarty and offered him the sword. 'You asked if I carry my *katana* with me. For practice. The answer is not always, but on this occasion I am . . .' he rested the sword in Fogarty's hands, 'complete.'

The lieutenant gripped the weapon loosely, his right hand around the hilt while his left wrapped around the wooden sheath. The wood was so finely polished that it had the texture of silk and Fogarty was surprised by the weight of the weapon; he had expected it to be heavier. Even in this position he was impressed with its balance; it just felt 'right' in his hands, like a first class rifle or handgun.

'If you would like to draw the blade, you are welcome to, Fogarty-san,' Sato said, 'my only request is that you do not touch the metal with your fingers . . . The oil from your body will stain the steel.'

Fogarty hesitated.

'Please, it is a fine weapon,' Sato insisted.

The blade came free of the scabbard easily, sliding upward as if on oiled bearings. There was hardly any friction between the silken wood and the tempered steel.

Fogarty placed the sheath on a cushion and held the silver studded hilt in both his hands.

There was something undeniably powerful in the perfect curve of the steel.

Ken Sato studied the lieutenant, gauging his reaction. 'Hold it up to the candle, Fogarty-san,' he instructed, 'allow the light to dance on the blade . . . That's right, follow the line of the steel with your eyes, see how it rolls and flows. Folded one thousand times, coated in clay, fired and plunged. Earth, flame and water.'

In the ancient teachings of *bugei*, or military arts, there is the school of *saiminjutsu*, a *ryu* that teaches the techniques by which an enemy can be hypnotized into defeat. By eye contact, by voice, by the subtle shifting of the body, or a mixture of these techniques, the enemy is lulled into a relaxed state of consciousness in which resistance is nullified.

Legend states that in feudal Japan, when survival itself was dependent upon the mastery of *bugei*, many heads were taken by those skilled in *saiminjutsu* – tranquil smiles still intact upon their disembodied faces.

Ken Sato began the technique as Fogarty and Tanaka studied the blade, using the *katana* to focus their concentration and his own voice to induce the hypnosis.

He spoke in gentle rhythms, subtle at first, hardly discernible from his regular pattern of speech, and all the while, guiding their eyes toward the waves of steel which became visible in the light of the flame, flowing and elegant.

'If you were to remove the cloth wrap from the hilt, Fogarty-san, and examine the steel which forms the "tang" of the blade, you would see that this *katana* has been tested and inscribed,' Sato continued, raising his tone to push at the outer perimeters of their consciousness, then lowering it to draw them in. Like weaving a web.

'The first inscription reads "Brought down cleanly – three men, 1592".'

Fogarty could see Ken Sato in the periphery of his vision. He was smiling, leaning forward, his hands folded and lifted in front of his body, as if he were praying.

'Criminals, laid one on top of the other, cleaved with a single stroke of the *katana* ... *Tameshi giri*, spirit cutting, a test of both man and blade.'

Fogarty didn't feel threatened by Ken's words, perhaps because he himself was holding the weapon – all the weapons – or, perhaps, it was simply Ken Sato's presence, the way he spoke, moving his hands slightly to orchestrate his words, shifting his body. Light and loose, he appeared thin and without muscle tone, almost ethereal. Creating a detachment from what was taking place.

Instead of fear or repulsion, Fogarty experienced a sense of awe and respect for the object in his hands. As if Sato's voice was giving him a direct link to the sword, bypassing his own circuitry of thought and emotion.

'Move your hands slightly, Fogarty-san, allow the light to play on the surface of the blade, that's correct,' Ken instructed.

Fogarty complied instantly. It was so much easier to go with the flow . . . Natural.

He could see the steel begin to move, as if the rolls of metal had become waves upon a silver sea.

He sensed the tension draining from his body and it was becoming difficult to think of Ken Sato as an enemy.

'The *katana* is an extension of life. It is the perfect weapon, Fogarty-san, the purest weapon, indestructible . . . Completely indestructible.' Sato continued, his tone barely above a whisper.

Fogarty was hardly aware of the weight of the *katana*; he was deeply relaxed.

'Observe the tip, narrow, and cut at an angle . . . How quickly it penetrates the human body.' The words were a preparation for death, an anaesthetic before surgery.

'And the grooves on the side of the blade, that's right, Fogarty-san, turn it slightly, see the blood gutters; they strengthen it for a strong cut. Imagine the enemy's blood. Running down the blade, channeled through the gutters . . . Many times this *katana* has tasted flesh. In its four hundred years much blood has flowed across its steel.' Sato's voice was now only a slight whisper.

To Fogarty, nothing seemed quite 'real', not even the sword. He was in a strangely comfortable state of mind. He wanted Sato to continue speaking, his words were massaging his mind, easing away his paranoia and anxiety.

'The finest blade is the blade that gives life . . . Perfect and pure, perfect and pure. . . . My *katana* will give life to all Japan.' Sato stopped speaking and looked first at the half-caste, then at the *bata kusai*, the 'butter stinker' – Westerners always bore the rancid odor of their fat-filled diets; both were like children, listening to a bedtime story.

Ken Sato could feel the electricity in the silent room, he was controlling their collective *ki*, that most subtle of energies – the animating force of all life. Centering it on the blade, molding it with his voice, raising and lowering the vibration of their thoughts according to his will. Lulling them into subconscious submission.

'More sake, Fogarty-san? And you, Josef?' Sato asked, his voice abruptly changing beat. And suddenly the spell was broken, by design not accident. For this was only a test of his *saiminjutsu*, to evaluate the susceptibility of his subjects. He was very pleased. The next phase would be physical, manipulated with the movements of his body.

Fogarty lowered the sword and Ken removed it from his hands, sliding the *katana* back into its *saya* with a single motion before laying it on the cushion to his left. Then he lifted his cup and offered it to the lieutenant.

'Please, Fogarty-san, share my spirit.'

Fogarty drank the remainder of the sake from Sato's cup. He went to refill it and Ken placed the palm of his hand across the opening.

'Thank you, but not now, Fogarty-san . . . Later.'

Then Sato stood up, lifting his *katana* and pushing it through the left side of his *obi*.

He walked slowly across the room, turning to face them from the far corner, squaring his body and gripping the tatami with the toes of his *tabi*.

He stared at a point on the wall, mid-way between Fogarty and Tanaka. Using the point to center himself, gaining a complete perspective of his environment and his prey.

Alarm bells were sounding from somewhere deep in Bill Fogarty's consciousness; he wanted to respond but it was like dragging himself up from a deep sleep. He wondered if it was the sake. Something had a hold on him. His brain felt like it was encased in wool.

Then Sato began to speak, in Japanese, addressing them simultaneously. To Fogarty it sounded like an impossibly long, single sentence, no pauses or breaks for breath. Just a beautiful flow of words. He had never thought of the Japanese language as beautiful before, but this was truly exquisite, vowels and syllables formed precisely, rising and falling like fine poetry. Sato's voice was as soft as before, but this time, there was a lilting sing-song pattern to his phrasing.

The poetry stopped.

'That is the *okudent*,' Tanaka whispered, 'part of the hidden teaching of Ken-san's school of the sword. A chant, to give life to the blade.'

Sato continued in Japanese, addressing Josef.

'*Hai*, Ken-san, *hai*,' Josef answered before turning to Fogarty.

When Tanaka spoke, he sounded breathless. 'My cousin honors us with this demonstration of his art.'

He's going to kill us, draw that sword and cut us to pieces, the thought was there, in Fogarty's mind, but the will to resist was missing.

He turned to Tanaka, searching for an ally, someone to verify his deep anxiety, to rouse him from his inertia. Josef met his eyes and answered his call with complete placidity. He smiled.

The smile drove a splinter of fear into Fogarty, the kind of fear that comes from being alone in the face of mortal danger.

Fear that should have demanded action, but it was coming from too far away. As if his consciousness had become divided, thought and action occupying separate hemispheres. No connection.

He looked back at Ken Sato.

Sato stood motionless, waiting.

Fogarty must have nodded his head at that point, even uttered an affirmative because Ken Sato drew his sword. It cleared its scabbard with the hiss of a snake.

And as soon as he moved, Fogarty was drawn back into the dance, compelled to watch.

Feet gripping the straw mats, hands wrapped round the hilt of the sword, every motion controlled and somehow delicate, spiraling toward him, arms extended, the draw of the sword leading to an overhead strike, flowing into a half turn which guided the *katana* horizontally, toward Fogarty's head.

The whine of the blade as the air parted above him.

It was the most fluid physical motion that the lieutenant had ever witnessed. He was drawn inside the motion, observing that, at times, Sato would use only his thumb and first finger to grip the hilt of his weapon, controlling the sword by balance and breath.

The breath. Fogarty could hear each breath. Some short and quick, matching precisely the movement of the blade, others long and suspended as the cut extended outward, giving a five-foot radius to the line of attack. It was a kind of magic. Intoxicating.

Ken Sato stepped forward, gliding toward Fogarty, this time the cut so much a part of the initial whipping action of the blade that Fogarty was aware only of the snap of metal against wood as Ken performed the *noto*, or resheathing, stepping back, away from his audience.

Bowing to them before standing motionless. There was not the slightest hint of sweat from his exertion.

Rachel Saunders returned to Rittenhouse Square at ten thirty. Exhausted. Not from surgery, but from the fear that during it she would relapse, endanger the life of her patient.

She couldn't go on like this, it wasn't working, nothing

was working. She would have to give up medicine, to continue was sheer irresponsibility.

She had failed, at everything, totally and utterly, and now she would receive her penance, a life alone, a life without love or purpose ... A life she did not want.

She locked the door of her apartment and walked to the bedroom, sitting down on the unmade bed, sliding her hand beneath the pillow, her fingers touching the cold grip of the Colt. She pulled the gun along the blue cotton sheets, lifting it, looking at it.

Hollow point bullets ... six rounds in the magazine, one in the chamber ... One was enough to obliterate everything.

It was her decision.

No god, no purgatory, no Catholic church to guide her. She laid the gun in her lap. Staring down at it.

She was completely alone and it was her decision.

The telephone rang. At first Rachel didn't hear it. Right next to her and she didn't hear it. Three times and she started to listen, to think. Four. Five. Another ring and the service would pick it up. *The hospital, an emergency, I can't do this, I'm being reckless, endangering life—*

She grabbed it on the sixth.

'Are you all right, Rachel, are you all right?'

It was Grace Tanaka's voice.

'Yes,' Rachel replied, mechanically.

'This is all such a mess, I'm so sorry, I've tried to talk sense to him ... If he loses you, Rachel, oh God, I don't want to think about it. He's throwing it all away. He loves you; you must believe that ... I've never known him like this, he's not himself.'

'It's okay, Grace, I'm not going anywhere.' Rachel lied some more.

'I've tried to talk to him ... Maybe Kenny can get through ... I know you don't like him but while he's there—'

'What? What did you say?'

'While his cousin is with him—'

'Where?'

'In Philadelphia. Ken Sato is staying with Josef there in Philadelphia.'

Rachel Saunders froze. Her stomach heaved in spasm and the images began to explode in her brain.

'Rachel? Rachel?' Grace Tanaka's voice sounded miles away, an echo from the abyss.

'Got to go now,' Rachel managed, pressing her finger down on the button of the phone's console. She let the receiver drop; it hit the floor with a dull thud. The dial tone buzzing in her head. She closed her eyes.

The man from 'the room' was right in front of her now; he was holding something long, shining ... Raising it slowly. She forced herself to look. It was a sword, a long-bladed sword. She raised her hands to her face, digging her palms into her eyes. Trying to block out her vision ... A new image. Graphic. The front page of a newspaper, the print small and black. *Mashiro Heir Found Murdered* ... Then Ken Sato's sword descended, cutting the paper in half. And he was there again. Like he had been in the hallway. His skin flushed and covered in the strange markings ...

'No ... I don't want this! No more! I want you to leave me alone!'

Rachel picked up the gun, placed her finger on the trigger.

'God help me,' she whispered. Knowing that God wouldn't help her. Because she didn't believe. In God ... In herself ... That was her sin.

She believed only in what stood before her. The demon in her mind.

'Now it is time for sake,' Sato whispered, removing the *katana* from his *obi* and sitting down as Fogarty poured.

'To Japan,' Sato said.

They lifted their cups.

Sato frowned after he swallowed and, for a moment, Fogarty wondered what could be wrong. Then he remembered the niacin.

It seemed such a long time ago that he had dropped the little pills into the wine. His action had, somehow, lost significance.

'Very sharp bite,' Sato said, looking into his cup, then at Josef. Aware of the exact amount of alcohol required to induce the transformation. Deeming it wise to remain within his limits. After all, the Westerner was armed.

Josef poured the sake.

'To purity,' Sato exclaimed. Throwing back his drink, swirling it in his mouth, then spitting it back into the cup.

'I have lost my taste for this wine,' he pronounced, scowling again.

Fogarty looked up and Sato met his eyes, shifting his stare to take in the policeman's horrible scars, inhaling his rancid odor. The stink of the West, fat and decadent.

Then, in another switch of moods, Sato relaxed, smiling bashfully as he turned from Fogarty to Tanaka. Studying the imperfection of his cousin's mongrel features. Again recalling the night that Tanaka had destroyed his lover. He had traveled half-way round the world for this execution.

'I love you, Josef,' he whispered.

This would be a great moment, vengeance mixed with cold pragmatism. Another warning to Mikio Tanaka and the rest of the infidels who would sell their heritage, trading swords for golf clubs and honor for celluloid. Both personal and historic, a new inscription on the tang of his blade.

Now it was time.

'Josef, I would like to offer our guest a demonstration of my control with the *katana* and your control as a *bugeisha*,' Sato said, lifting his sword as he stood up, remaining purposely close to Fogarty.

'True mastery of the sword can be demonstrated only by the performance of specific strikes and cuts, each with its varying degree of difficulty ... Permit me to execute the priest's robe cut,' he continued as Josef joined him on the tatami, a single body's length from the lieutenant.

Tanaka stood still, his feet spread a shoulder's width apart and his hands at his sides. He was completely relaxed.

'It is a downward cut, Fogarty-san, intended to part the rib cage and sever the heart,' Sato explained, drawing his sword in slow motion, raising it to a height even with his own shoulders then bringing the tip of the *katana* downward, following the vertical line of Josef's jacket before resheathing the weapon.

'Quite difficult because the blade must be drawn at the correct angle if the heart is to be penetrated.'

Fogarty sat and stared. His warning voice calling from far away, *Stop this. It's all fucked up. Wrong. Stop him now.* The thoughts trickling into consciousness, but without power or authority.

Then Ken Sato struck, this time with speed, such speed that Fogarty did not see the *katana* either leave or re-enter its scabbard. Simply the hissing sound followed by the smack of steel against wood.

'A clean cut,' Sato said, eyeing the razor-thin tear to the cotton jacket, above Tanaka's heart.

Sato turned his attention to Fogarty, studying his eyes, noting the slight dilation of his pupils, less than before.

Sato was still controlling him, but the policeman had begun to struggle within the confines of the *saiminjutsu*. There was a limit to all control.

The next cut would be the one.

He repositioned Josef, between himself and the lieutenant,

so that a horizontal slice through his cousin's body would also cleave the policeman's neck and sever his head.

He wanted to capture the expression on the butter-stinker's face at the exact moment that his friend's body was divided at the waist.

Often, these expressions of horror froze on the faces of his victims, setting like stone masks in the early phases of rigor mortis. The butter-stinker's face – scarred and ugly – would make a fine picture for his gallery.

'This is called the water wheel strike, named for its powerful, circular movement,' he explained and began to draw his sword in slow motion.

Fogarty felt the tingling begin in his feet, traveling up along his calves and thighs and into his groin.

At first he didn't make the link between the mild itching and the Vitamin B3.

Then it reached his face and he started to wake up.

'It comes across and through.' Sato's voice sounded far away, matching the slow, gentle sway of his body as he drew the sword in a wide arc toward Tanaka's mid-section, two inches below his navel.

Fogarty felt his skin flush. It was working, Bob Moyer's pills were working.

His mind was clicking into perspective, assembling his thoughts and purpose.

He peered at Ken Sato, the skin of his face, his neck, his hands. Searching for a sign. *Why wasn't the stuff affecting him? Had he taken enough?*

Then at the naked blade of Sato's *katana*. *How the hell did I let it get this far?* Fogarty's nerves and adrenaline cutting in simultaneously, pushing him to overload.

And all the time, Ken Sato's voice, like a distant rolling wave.

'The water wheel requires precise breath control and complete movement of the hips and waist to exact its full potential

... It is a fine cut for the *tameshi giri*, two bodies should be cleaved by a competent swordsman,' he explained, shaking the blade – symbolic of removing the enemy's blood from its surface – before guiding the tip between his index finger and thumb, returning the weapon to its *saya*.

Christ, he's telling me what he's going to do, Fogarty realized.

'Now I will perform the water wheel properly,' Ken Sato steadied his breath and focused his eyes on a spot between his intended targets, concentrating.

Fogarty shifted position, sliding his right hand down into the pocket of his jacket; the .38 felt cold and hard.

Josef Tanaka stood relaxed, waiting.

I've got to pull the trigger, got to do it, Fogarty commanded himself.

He hesitated, still searching for evidence, his own body alive with tiny currents of electricity as the niacin flooded his capillaries. Why the fuck was Sato not reacting?

'Control, Fogarty-san, control, right down to the beating of the heart and the flow of blood through the veins. Control, timing and judgement,' Sato whispered, the faintest hint of tension in his voice.

Judgement? Images of Sugar Boy Grandistone exploded in Fogarty's mind. *Christ, Jesus Christ, what happens if it's not him? If Ken Sato's not the Leopard?*

'Perhaps if you sit straighter, Fogarty-san, you will have a better vantage of the strike,' Sato suggested, gripping the tatami with his toes.

Fogarty squared his shoulders and straightened his neck, aiming the gun as he moved.

'Yes, Fogarty-san, that will be perfect.'

Then it began.

Fogarty sensed more than saw Sato's hand flashing toward the hilt.

It broke then, the pressure in his head, like a great dam

of water, impossible to contain.

'Goddamn it, no! No!' he shouted.

The blade had just begun its horizontal arc when Fogarty squeezed the trigger.

The first round exploded to the right of Sato's sternum, missing his heart, the shock of impact causing him to break the rhythm of his attack.

The second hit him lower, in the stomach; tearing a ragged hole in his jacket.

Then there was sound all around him, screaming and raging. Josef Tanaka's voice, 'You can't do that! Can't do that!' Loud and hollow, over and over.

Fogarty aimed again, an instant before Tanaka struck him, catching him in the wrist with the palm heel of his hand. Then Tanaka was right on top of him, snarling like a rabid animal, Fogarty struggling to throw him off.

'It's him, Josef, look at the motherfucker, look at your cousin!' The policeman just got the words out as Tanaka's fingers dug into his throat, 'The Leopard!'

Tanaka slackened his grip, confused, turning.

In time to see Sato lurch at him, his skin covered in the markings of the '*Hyoo*', blood gushing from his wounds and the blade raised above his head.

Josef moved fast, faster than thought, kicking from the floor, the heel of his foot connecting with Sato's gut, below the gaping bullet hole.

The thrust drove him backwards, caused him to stumble, giving Josef time to get to his feet. Staring. Forced to believe.

Tanaka shifted forward, slashing with the outer edge of his hand against his cousin's wrist. The *katana* dropped to the floor.

They were face to face.

'Get out of the fucking way. Give me a clear shot!' Fogarty's voice echoed from behind. Stopping Tanaka for the instant it took Ken Sato to speak.

'You were never anything, Josef, never anything but an embarrassment. To your family. Your country. Like your crippled half-brother. A boil. Ugly and putrid. Needing the lance.'

The Leopard was wounded, badly, his vision blurred and his ears singing. He was losing blood, growing weak. He could see them both, the half-caste close enough to taste and the butter-stinker on his knees, pointing his gun.

'Retreat', his animal instinct commanded.

His pride required the kill.

He shifted position, keeping the half-caste between himself and the policeman.

'Did you see the picture? Your half-brother's head? His brains running from his ears? Can you imagine his pain?'

The words poured like venom from the masked face with its jutting jaw and hollowed eyes.

'Move, fucking move!' Fogarty's voice pleaded.

'I have achieved orgasm looking at that picture,' the *Hyoo* hissed.

Tanaka attacked then, moving clockwise, driving forward, using the point of his elbow, intent on smashing it through that thin profane mouth.

Sato shifted and the elbow took out two of his teeth as it glanced off his jaw, then he countered with a right hand, fingers open, nails clawing downwards across Josef's left eye.

Tanaka swept the hand away, tried to lock the arm and got caught with a foot sweep; then the two of them were on the floor, Josef trying for a front choke while the Leopard bit at his hands and wrists.

Fogarty moved with them, rolled to his side, saw an opening and fired twice.

The first shot missed and his second passed straight through Sato's arm and into Josef's shoulder. Allowing Ken Sato to break free, twist to the side and grip the hilt of his *katana*.

Fogarty was squeezing off his final round when the edge of the blade whipped the gun from his hand, taking it with such force that it broke his wrist, the 'flinch' from his nervous system causing him to fly backward against the wall. He landed in a crouch, reached down and tried to get to the 22.

Ken Sato stopped three yards from him, weak from loss of blood, his right arm paralyzed and his vision failing.

He could make out the half-caste, like a blur, moving toward him from the side of the room; the policeman drawing another gun.

Retreat . . . retreat.

He held his sword in front of him, backing toward the door. Found the knob and turned as Fogarty's shot tore a patch of paint from the wall beside him. Then he was out, into the dark and mist, pulling the door closed behind him, turning to run.

His legs were strong; he could still run.

He heaved in a breath, his nostrils flaring. Stopped. He recognized her smell, faint and sweet. Remembered it. The way it had fouled his apartment in Tokyo . . . Hated it.

He looked down the paved walkway, saw a silhouette against the mist, standing in front of him, knees slightly bent, both arms extended.

Her smell . . . He knew her.

Heard the door opening behind.

Then the Leopard began his final charge.

He could hear his heart pound and his lungs laboring as his feet dug into the ground, pulling him forward. Toward the kill. Extending his steel claw, screeching his war cry. Screaming toward her.

Rachel Saunders watched him come, held him in the sights of the Colt, breathed out, squeezing the trigger as she exhaled. Beyond nerves, beyond fear ... In a vacuum, face to face with her demon.

He saw a silent flash of flame as the first bullet tore through the side of his neck. Then heard the explosion of the gun as the hollow point caused his flesh and muscle to disintegrate and splatter.

Momentum carried him forward.

She fired again, this time wide and to the left, missing.

She could see the point of his sword, like a diamond in the moonlight ... And his face, the skin of his face; the same face she had seen in the hallway, in Tokyo, etched with the same lines and patterns, like a mask of death ... Rushing toward her ... Ten yards, five yards.

She pulled the gun to the right and fired again. And again.

The fourth round tore the head from his body, leaving the remains of his spine like a short stalk, protruding from the hollow in the center of his shoulders.

The *katana* clattered to the ground as he collapsed three feet in front of her.

And the demon died in Rachel Saunders' mind, once and for all.

She had killed him.

After sitting alone in a bedroom on Rittenhouse Square, staring down the barrel of a gun.

Wanting to pull the trigger.

Frightened that if she did, her demon would be waiting on

the other side. That her weakness would cause him to cling to her soul, forever.

Face to face with her deepest fear, questioning her sanity; she had trusted herself, one last time. Trusted her instinct, her feelings.

And now it was over.

The police, alerted by a hysterical phone call from Louise LeLord, Tanaka's landlady, arrived three minutes later.

Within half an hour the crime scene was chalked, cordoned off and the body-bag unfurled.

The Leopard had vanished and it was Keinosuke Sato who was loaded into the plastic container, zipped up and taken to the morgue.

Fogarty, Tanaka and Rachel Saunders rode together, in the back of an ambulance, to the university hospital.

Tanaka was on a stretcher but he managed to hold Rachel's hand for the entire ride.

Both he and the lieutenant were taken straight to emergency while Rachel Saunders was interviewed by a police psychiatrist.

When asked if she would like to see her own doctor, Stan Leibowitz, she declined.

'But you have just shot and killed a man, Doctor Saunders,' the police psychiatrist insisted.

'I know what I have done. I know exactly what I have done,' Rachel said.

Twelve hours later, while examining Keinosuke Sato's *katana*, nine inscriptions were discovered on the tang, beneath the braided wrapping and silver ornaments: names and dates, the first given as 1592, the last as 1992.

A translator from the university interpreted the words. They were descriptions of the strikes used and the number required in each execution.

The developed film from Ken Sato's Nikon told the rest of the story: David Mashiro's disembodied head had made it to celluloid before his epitaph had been etched into the steel tang of Sato's *katana*.

There were still twenty-four blank frames on the roll of film. Reserved for the 'family reunion' at Spring Garden Street and, then, a trip to Boston.

Epilogue

An investigation by the Japanese National Police concluded that Keinosuke Sato and his accomplice, the former *sumo-tori*, Hoshi Satoru, had acted alone in the murders of at least seven people. That was the official stance.

The singular voice of protest against this conclusion came from Chief Inspector Norikazu Ohtsuka. He claimed that the crimes were part of a larger conspiracy.

Two days after he lodged his formal statement, Ohtsuka's body was found, slumped over the wheel of his parked car.

Verdict on death: unintentional drug overdose.

The news of the chief inspector's methamphetamine abuse by intravenous injection devastated his wife, family and members of his dojo. None of them had ever seen the physical fitness fanatic take so much as a cup of sake.

With Ohtsuka's death the case was closed.

Each of the four witnesses in *The City of Philadelphia* v. *Grandistone* murder case withdrew their testimony.

Consequently, Sugar Boy Grandistone was arraigned, tried and convicted on the lesser charge of trafficking in narcotics.

During the first term of his incarceration, Grandistone began a civil suit against Lieutenant William T. Fogarty and the City of Philadelphia. The lawsuit collapsed due to lack of any substantial evidence corroborating Grandistone's charges.

Bill Fogarty now holds the rank of Police Captain.

*

Josef Tanaka returned to his position as assistant to Chief Medical Examiner, Bob Moyer.

He and Rachel Saunders were married on Christmas Eve, in Christ's Church, Second Street, Philadelphia.

Bill Fogarty was best man and Mikio Tanaka joined his wife Grace at the ceremony.

The 'Red Mist' is currently in the process of reformation, under the leadership of Miyuki Hashimoto, Superintendent General of the Japanese National Police.

THE END